Amish
COOKING CLASS
BOOK 1

---·◦◦◦·---

THE SEEKERS

Amish
COOKING CLASS
BOOK 1

— ◦◦◦ —

THE SEEKERS

WANDA E BRUNSTETTER

BARBOUR
PUBLISHING

The Seekers © 2017 by Wanda E. Brunstetter

ISBN 978-1-63609-043-6

Adobe Digital Edition (.epub) 978-1-63609-235-5

Scripture quotations are taken from the King James Version of the Bible.

All German-Dutch words are taken from the *Revised Pennsylvania German Dictionary* found in Lancaster County, Pennsylvania.

This book is a work of fiction. Names, characters, places, and incidents are either products of the author's imagination or used fictitiously. Any similarity to actual people, organizations, and/or events is purely coincidental.

For more information about Wanda E. Brunstetter, please access the author's website at the following internet address: www.wandabrunstetter.com.

Cover Design: Buffy Cooper

Cover model photography: Richard Brunstetter III, RBIII Studios

Published by Barbour Publishing, Inc., 1810 Barbour Drive, Uhrichsville, OH 44683, www.barbourbooks.com

Our mission is to inspire the world with the life-changing message of the Bible.

Printed in the United States of America.

To my friend Mae Miller,
who has treated us many times to
some of her delicious Amish meals.

---

*But seek ye first the kingdom of God,
and his righteousness; and all these
things shall be added unto you.*
MATTHEW 6:33

Prologue

Walnut Creek, Ohio

A deep moan escaped Heidi Troyer's lips as she glanced at the clock on the far wall. Lyle was late for supper again, and she'd fixed his favorite meal—sweet-and-sour spareribs, pickled beets, Amish broccoli salad, and German-style green beans. For dessert she'd made an oatmeal pecan pie. But in all fairness, her husband had no way of knowing supper had been waiting for the last hour. This morning Lyle said he could possibly be late and had suggested a sandwich or bowl of soup for supper once he got home. Since the auction was only ten miles away in Mt. Hope, Heidi expected her husband would be home by now.

"That's what I get for assuming. Shouldn't have gotten carried away cooking a big meal." She sighed. What else was there for her to do this afternoon but cook? She'd washed clothes, hung them out to dry, cleaned the house, and pulled weeds in the garden. Boredom had set in until she'd decided to cook something—her favorite pastime. Heidi enjoyed spending time in the kitchen and often shared her baked goods with others in their community who had less time for cooking.

Woof! Heidi's Brittany spaniel rubbed against her leg, wagging his stubby little tail and interrupting her musings.

"I know. I know. You're desperate for attention."
Heidi filled her plate with food and took a seat at the
kitchen table. "Looks like it's just you and me again this
evening, Rusty."

The dog whined then grunted as he turned around
in a circle before lying down under the table. He gave
a long doggy sigh and rested his silky head on Heidi's
bare foot.

"Your life is pretty tough, isn't it, boy?" Reaching
down to rub his soft, feathery ears, Heidi felt grateful
to have Rusty with her. He was a good companion—
someone to talk to when her husband was away.

Heidi wiggled her toes and giggled when Rusty
started snoring. She rarely wore shoes in the house
unless she had company or was fighting the bitter
cold of winter. With spring less than a week away and
warmer weather making its appearance in Holmes
County, Heidi saw no reason to confine her feet in a
pair of shoes unless she went out.

Bowing her head, she closed her eyes and offered a
silent prayer before eating. *Heavenly Father, please keep
my husband safe as he travels home this evening. Help me
be more patient while I wait for him. Bless our family and
friends with good health. Thank You for the food set before
me. And thank You for getting us safely through the winter
months. Amen.*

As Heidi bit into a succulent sparerib, she thought
about the letter she'd received this morning from her
mother's sister, who lived in Shipshewana, Indiana. Aunt
Emma had been teaching quilting classes in her home
for the past several years, and every class brought a vari-
ety of interesting students. A few years ago, when she
and her husband, Lamar, spent the winter in Sarasota,
Florida, Aunt Emma opened her vacation home to six

local people wanting to learn how to quilt.

One line in her aunt's letter caught Heidi's attention. It read: *"I enjoy quilting, and because I like meeting new people, I'm thankful for the opportunity to share my ability with others."*

Heidi took a sip of water, letting a new thought take root in her brain. Having been married eight years, with no children to care for, she spent a good deal of her time rambling around the house, looking for things to do once all the basic chores were done each day. She was finally about caught up on things—even the decluttering in closets she'd put off doing until yesterday. She felt good about donating several items to the local Share and Care Thrift Store in nearby Berlin.

Heidi would soon plant a garden. She'd started growing tomatoes inside by the kitchen window from seed packets purchased at the local hardware store. She enjoyed keeping watch on their progress and tending the plants each day. Unfortunately, supervising the tomatoes' growth didn't take up much of her time.

She had been good at cooking since she learned as a child under her mother's tutelage. Whenever the days became boring or lonely, she brought out her kitchen utensils and whipped up a favorite old recipe or tried something new. Lyle sometimes teased her about trying to make him fat, even though he had nothing to worry about. His six-foot frame was lean and trim. It amazed Heidi how much he could eat and never gain weight.

She drummed her fingers along the edge of the table. *I wonder if I should consider teaching a cooking class. It would give me something meaningful to do and provide a little extra money.*

Heidi looked at the calendar hanging on the kitchen wall. If she made up several flyers and placed a few ads, perhaps enough people would sign up so she could begin her first class the second Saturday of April.

Heidi smiled as she forked a piece of broccoli into her mouth. *I can teach a total of six classes every other week from April through June and still keep up with the chores needing to be done around here.*

Grabbing a paper and pencil, she began sketching the layout of the flyer advertising her cooking class. Now Heidi could hardly wait until Lyle got home to get his approval on this new venture.

Chapter 1

Sugarcreek, Ohio

Loretta Donnelly's vision clouded as she sat on the front porch, watching her children play in the yard. Conner, with dark curly hair like his daddy's, was three. His sister, Abby, whose hair was medium brown like Loretta's, had recently turned five and would go to kindergarten in the fall.

"They are growing too fast and missing out on so much," Loretta murmured, pulling her long hair into a ponytail. She squeezed her eyes shut, struggling not to cry as she often did when she thought of Rick. He'd been gone nearly a year, but it felt like yesterday when she'd received the news of his death. Rick had been on a business trip. Loretta wished she had urged him to spend the night somewhere before heading home for the weekend. But having been gone for six days, Rick was anxious to get home. Loretta was excited for him to return, and so were the children. It was a shock when she'd received the horrifying news that an accident had occurred on the freeway. Rick had apparently fallen asleep at the wheel, causing his car to hit a guardrail and flip onto its side. Fortunately, no other vehicles were involved.

Loretta's eyes snapped open when her daughter

touched her arm. "Mommy, can I have a ponytail like yours?"

"Sure, sweetie, turn around." Loretta reached into her skirt pocket and found an extra hair band. Pulling Abby's shoulder-length hair back, she secured the ponytail with the band.

"Thanks, Mommy. We look alike now."

"You're welcome." Loretta bent down and gave Abby a hug.

After Abby joined her brother again, Loretta's thoughts turned to her financial situation. They'd been living on the money from Rick's life insurance policy, but it wouldn't last forever. Eventually, Loretta would need to look for a job, which meant finding a full-time babysitter.

Loretta's parents lived in Pittsburgh, Pennsylvania. Soon after Rick died, Mom and Dad suggested Loretta sell her house and move in with them. She appreciated their offer but didn't want to uproot the children. Loretta wanted to give Abby and Conner a simpler life, like they had here in Amish country, rather than exposing them to big-city living. Besides, it wouldn't be fair to move the children closer to one set of grandparents but farther from the other. Rick's parents lived in Colorado, and Loretta had no desire to move there. Residing in this simple home in this quiet town helped her feel closer to Rick. This was where she wanted to raise her children. Unless God told her otherwise, she planned to remain right here.

Loretta's attention turned to her children when she heard Conner's cry. She rose from her chair and hurried into the yard. "What's going on with you two?"

"He threw dirt at me." Abby wrinkled her nose. "Then he pulled my ponytail."

"Did you throw dirt back?"

Sniffling, Abby nodded.

Oh, great. Now they're both crying. "No more dirt throwing or hair pulling." She shook her finger at the children before taking hold of their hands. "Let's go inside now and get you cleaned up. After that, we'll have lunch."

Once Loretta made sure Conner and Abby were clean, she made peanut butter and jelly sandwiches. The two sat giggling about something on the cereal box still sitting on the table from breakfast. It was good to see how quickly they recovered from the argument they'd had outside. It was one of the benefits of kids their age—they could be mad one minute and happy the next.

While Abby and Conner ate their lunch, Loretta sat at the table, sipping a cup of tea, reading the latest edition of *The Budget* newspaper. After seeing what some of the local Amish scribes had written, she noticed an ad for cooking classes. The first class would begin next Saturday. Anything related to the Amish interested her, and it would be fun to learn how to make some traditional Amish dishes.

She took a sip of tea, letting the idea float around in her head. *I probably shouldn't spend the money right now, but if I can find someone to watch the children, I may sign up for those classes.*

Dover, Ohio

"How are things coming along with your wedding plans?" Charlene Higgins's friend Kathy Newman asked as they took seats inside Sammy Sue's Barbeque restaurant.

Placing both hands beneath her chin, Charlene groaned. "What wedding plans? Len and I haven't even set a date for the wedding, much less made any plans."

"I thought after he proposed last week you two would be working out the details for your future together." Kathy's pale eyebrows squeezed together.

Charlene drank some water before giving her response. "Len wants to wait until he's told his parents about our engagement before we set a wedding date."

Her friend leaned slightly forward. "When does he plan to tell them?"

"I—I don't know." Charlene fingered the fork lying on her napkin. "I'm worried his folks—especially Annette, won't approve of Len's choice for a wife."

"For goodness' sakes, why not?" Kathy lifted her gaze toward the ceiling. "They should be happy their son's fallen in love with someone who is not only beautiful but smart."

Slowly, Charlene pulled her fingers through the ends of her long hair. Ever since she was a girl she'd been complimented on her creamy complexion and shiny brown hair with golden highlights. When she'd reached her teenage years, her friends suggested she become a model. Charlene wasn't interested in pursuing that profession. After high school graduation, she'd gone to college and graduated with a Bachelor of Science in early education. For the last year she'd been teaching kindergarten at one of the elementary schools in Dover.

"Are you ladies ready to order?" their waitress asked, stepping up to the table.

"Most definitely. I'll have the pulled-pork flatbread." Kathy smacked her lips. "I love the caramelized onions and cheddar cheese on it."

Charlene looked over the menu a few more seconds then ordered the same thing. With so many choices, it was easier to go with a familiar sandwich rather than try something new.

"Now, getting back to Len needing to tell his folks about your engagement. . ." Kathy paused to pick up a slice of lemon and squeeze it into her water. "Why do you think he needs their approval? Is Len one of those guys who must check with his parents on everything?"

"I don't think so, but. . ." Charlene pointed at the window. "Look at that! Wish I'd brought my camera with me today."

"What are you pointing at? I don't see anything out of the ordinary."

"A flock of geese heading for the Tuscarawas River, but you missed them." Charlene continued to watch out the window. "Their wings were stretched out for a landing. Bet they made quite a splash." She slouched in her seat. "Wish I was over there on the bridge right now. I could at least get a picture of the geese on my cell phone."

"Too bad I missed it, but at least you got to see them come in for a landing." Kathy stretched her arms out like a bird. "I'm surprised you don't have your digital camera with you. You take it nearly everywhere."

"I was running late and didn't think to grab it before I went out the door. Wouldn't you know the one day I didn't have it was when I could have gotten a great shot?" Heaving a sigh, Charlene shrugged. "Oh well. I'm sure there will be other times I can photograph geese."

"Okay now, before the geese captured your train of thought, what were you going to say? Was it something about Len's parents?" her friend prompted.

"Yeah. Len's mother is quite domesticated. Her house is spotless, and she's an excellent cook." Charlene pursed her lips. "I, on the other hand, can barely boil water, which is why Len and I always go out to eat, rather than me cooking him a meal."

Kathy's forehead wrinkled as her mouth opened

slightly. "You'll never learn to cook if you don't practice."

"I am not going to use my fiancé as a guinea pig. He could end up with food poisoning."

"Don't you think you're being a bit overly dramatic?"

"Maybe, but the one time I had Len's parents to my condo for supper, I burned the roast, and the vegetables were overcooked." Charlene picked up her water glass and took another drink.

"Maybe you need a new timer for your stove."

"Or maybe I ought to take some cooking lessons."

Kathy smiled. "Hey, not a bad idea. In fact, I saw an ad in the paper the other day advertising cooking classes. If you're interested, I'll give you a call with the information as soon as I get home."

Charlene lifted her shoulders in a brief shrug. "I'll give it some thought, but unless the person teaching the classes is a miracle worker, I may be a lost cause."

"Don't be silly. You know what you need, my friend?"

"What?"

"A good dose of self-confidence."

Charlene didn't argue. Although she had little or no confidence when it came to cooking, she was plenty confident when it came to teaching her students. Of course, she couldn't feed her future husband properly by being a good teacher. *Maybe I will consider taking those cooking classes.*

Walnut Creek

Eli Miller had just started cleaning his barn when his neighbor Lyle Troyer showed up. They'd been friends a good many years.

"Hey, what's new with you?" Eli set his shovel aside.

"Not much. I have a box for you in my buggy though." Lyle grinned. "A gift from my *fraa*."

"You don't say. What kind of gift did Heidi send for me? It's not my birthday or any special occasion."

"Doesn't have to be. She made you one of her famous peanut butter *kichlin*."

Eli chuckled. "Your wife's cookies are good, but I didn't realize they were famous."

"Bet they will be after she starts teaching her cooking classes." Lyle thumped Eli's shoulder. "Heidi also asked me to find out if you'd like to come over for supper tonight."

"I'd be pleased to, but what's this about Heidi teaching cooking classes?"

Lyle leaned against the barn wall, folding his arms. "As I'm sure you know, she's a pretty fair cook."

"*Jah*, and so was my fraa, but she never taught anyone." Eli rubbed the side of his bearded face. As always, thinking about Mavis caused him to miss her. He could hardly believe she'd been gone a year already. If only she hadn't ridden her bike to visit a friend and stayed until the sun began to set, when there'd been less visibility. If Mavis had been using her horse and buggy that evening, she might still be alive.

Lyle bumped Eli's shoulder again. "Say, I have an idea. Why don't you sign up for Heidi's cooking classes?"

Eli's eyes widened as he touched his chest. "Me? You're kidding, right?"

"Nope. You've mention many times about how bad your cooking is. If you learn how to cook, you'd be eatin' a lot better meals than tuna sandwiches and hard-boiled eggs."

"Not sure I'd be comfortable taking classes. It'll probably be a bunch of women, and I'd feel as out of place as a child tryin' to guide a horse and buggy down the road." Eli walked over to the barn's entrance and gazed out across his property. Looking at everything, one would never know his wife was gone. The daffodils she'd planted a few years ago were bursting with yellow blossoms. The colorful hyacinths, in an array of pink, white, and purple, bloomed near the porch. Eli could almost visualize Mavis reaching down to take a whiff of their fragrance. She loved the smell of hyacinths, and in the spring she'd put a few in a vase on the kitchen table.

Several bird feeders swayed as soft breezes wafted through branches where they hung. Cardinals, gold-finches, and bluebirds ate in friendly comradery. An image of Mavis standing in front of the kitchen window came to mind, and Eli recalled her contented expression.

A few times she'd caught him watching her, and then they'd stood together and gazed at the birds gathering around the feeders. It seemed everywhere he looked these days a vision of Mavis materialized before his eyes. Eli hoped he could hold those precious moments in his mind forever. He never wanted to forget her sweet face.

Little things, such as feeding the birds, gave pleasant memories, but walking into the house was a different story. Gone were the days when he'd enter the kitchen and mouthwatering smells reached his nostrils. Eli remembered how his wife's pumpkin cinnamon rolls filled the whole house with their spicy aroma. Since Mavis knew they were his favorites, she made them quite often. Sometimes, even the fragrance of Mavis's hair would capture traces of what she had baked. When Eli greeted his wife after a long day's work, he wanted to hold her until the sun went down, filling his senses with the warmth of her body and scent of her hair.

Cherished flashbacks like these were bittersweet,

popping into his mind at unexpected moments. While agonizing to think about, they were also more precious than ever.

At least I have those treasured memories tucked away safely right here. Eli touched his chest, aware of his heart thumping beneath his hand.

"Hey, are you feeling okay?" Lyle nudged Eli's arm. "Did you hear what I said a few seconds ago?"

"What? Oh, uh. . .jah. I. . .I was thinkin' about something, is all." Eli's face warmed as he focused on his friend. "What were you saying?"

"Said you may be surprised who all shows up at Heidi's cooking classes." Lyle bent down to pluck a piece of straw off his trousers. "Heidi's aunt Emma hosts quilting classes in her home, and she's taught several men to quilt. Fact is, it's my understanding that they enjoyed it almost as much as the women did. According to Emma, some of the men became quite good at quilting."

"Is that a fact?" As he tugged his earlobe, Eli sucked in his lower lip. "*Danki* for the mention. I'll give it some thought."

Chapter 2

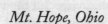

Mt. Hope, Ohio

Kendra Perkins turned toward the window, hoping the sunny sky would brighten her mood. She'd been staying with her friend Dorie Hampton for the past week—ever since Kendra's parents kicked her out of their house. She had only been allowed to take her clothes and personal items—nothing else. A year ago, Kendra would have never believed something like this would happen to her. It wasn't fair. What kind of parents could do such a thing? She shouldn't be punished for one little mistake.

Guess it's not a little mistake. Fingers clenched, Kendra swallowed hard. *What I did was wrong, but are Mom and Dad so self-righteous they can't admit to ever having made a mistake? Is there no forgiveness in their hearts toward their wayward daughter?*

Determined not to succumb to self-pity, Kendra turned her attention to the newspaper want ads on the kitchen table. She couldn't live in Dorie's tiny mobile home forever. She needed to find a job so she could support herself. She had to make a decision about the future of her unborn child before her October due date.

"Find anything yet?" Dorie asked, walking into the kitchen.

Kendra shook her head. "But then, I only began

looking a few minutes ago."

Dorie handed Kendra a glass of cranberry juice and took a seat at the table. "Maybe you should have stayed in college and continued working toward a career in nursing."

Kendra gave an undignified snort. "If Mom and Dad kicked me out of their house, they sure weren't going to keep paying my tuition." Her face contorted as she brought her fingers to her lips. "They think I'm a sinner, and they're ashamed of me for giving in to my desire and becoming intimate with Max. Since I'm the oldest daughter, I'm supposed to set a good example for my two younger sisters."

"Maybe they need more time to come to grips with this. After all, it's their grandchild you're carrying."

"Doesn't mean a thing. My dad's on the church board, and he made it clear that I've humiliated him." She sniffed deeply, shifting in her chair. "Guess he thinks the church wouldn't forgive me if they knew. So mum's the word, if you get my meaning. And Mom. . . Well, she can't think for herself these days. Even if she did want to help me, she'd go along with whatever Dad says."

Kendra wished she could forget what had happened, but how could she erase her pregnancy or her parents' rejection? She had considered not telling them about the baby, hoping her boyfriend, Max, would marry her. But things blew up in her face when she told him about the child and he'd asked her to get an abortion. Max was out of her life now. He'd found another girlfriend and joined the navy. With any luck, she'd never see him again.

Kendra wished she could have hidden her condition from her folks as long as possible, but with her small, 110-pound frame and five-foot-two height, it would be fruitless to try and cover up her pregnancy once she started to show. Consequently, she'd decided to tell her folks right away. She had hoped that, for once, Mom would stick up for her. *Guess I should have known better, 'cause she never has before—at least not on things where she'd have to go against Dad.*

Kendra wondered what excuse her parents had given to her younger sisters, Chris and Shelly, when she moved out. Had they told them the truth or made up some story, making it look like Kendra left of her own accord? No doubt, they'd kept it a secret, too embarrassed to tell her sisters the facts.

Swallowing against the bitter-tasting bile in her throat, Kendra left her seat and got a drink of water. She would never forget the look on Dad's face when she told him and Mom about her pregnancy. His eyes narrowed into tiny slits as his face turned bright red. Kendra feared he might explode. Instead, he turned his back on her, staring into the fireplace. Dad stood quietly several minutes, shoulders rising up and down as he breathed slowly in and out. Then, when she thought she could stand it no longer, he turned to face her. Speaking calmly, as though he was talking about the weather, Dad told Kendra he wanted her out of the house by the next day, and said she was not to say anything to her sisters about any of this. Without another word, he left the room and never looked back. Like a whipped pup with its tail between its legs, Mom followed meekly behind him. Kendra's own mother said nothing to her. Not a single word.

Scattering Kendra's thoughts, Dorie pulled the newspaper over and circled several ads. "I see a few openings for hotel housekeepers and waitresses."

"Okay, I'll check them out." Kendra gave an impatient snort. "Can't remember when I've ever felt so depressed. It feels like nothing in my life will ever be right again."

"Sure it will. It's gonna take time, but you'll see—eventually things will get better and work out." Dorie tapped the newspaper with her pen. "Hey, check this ad out. An Amish woman will be teaching cooking classes at her home in Walnut Creek."

Kendra squinted. "What's that got to do with me?"

"The classes are every other Saturday, beginning next week and going through June. You should go, Kendra. It'll give you something fun to do."

Kendra sat down with a huff. "I don't even have a job yet. How can I afford to take cooking classes? And what if I get a job and have to work on Saturdays?"

"You can worry about your work schedule once you find a job." Dorie gave Kendra's arm a gentle tap. "There's no problem with the classes; I'll pay for them. Even though your birthday isn't till December, let's call it an early present."

Berlin, Ohio

The muscles in Ron Hensley's neck twitched as he drove around town, looking for a parking space big enough for his motor home. He settled on the German Village parking lot, but his vehicle took up two parking spots. Ron noticed a few other free spaces and hoped no one would complain. His pounding headache and jitteriness indicated a need for coffee and something to eat.

Ron's funds were getting low, and he had to find a place to park his RV for a few days. It wasn't cheap to put fuel in the tank, so for now, road travel must be curtailed.

Sometimes Ron wondered why he'd chosen this way to live, but his rationale took over. This was the way it had to be. How many times had he told himself the outdated motor home was less expensive than owning a real home or finding an apartment to rent? It also gave Ron a chance to travel and meet new people, even if he did take advantage of their hospitality. His predicament could be frustrating though—especially when funds ran low and he couldn't afford to buy food, cigarettes, or beer. Ron figured at this point in his life things were as good as they were going to get. His motor home didn't have all the bells and whistles, like newer models, but it served his purpose, and that's what mattered.

Stepping inside the German Village market, Ron spotted a small café. He went in and ordered a cup of black coffee and a ham sandwich, then took a seat at one of the tables. As Ron watched the people in the market, many of them Amish, he thought about how trusting most Amish folks were. Not like most English people he'd met.

Last week Ron had parked his RV on an Amish man's property in Baltic. He'd eaten several good meals the man's wife had prepared, and they'd even given him money when he told them he was broke. The week before, Ron had camped in Sugarcreek a few days then moved on to Charm. This was his second time in the area. He'd been to Holmes County a year ago, but he didn't hang around too long.

Might stay longer this time if I find a good place to park my rig. Ron scratched his receding hairline. If he remembered correctly, Amish communities were abundant here, so it shouldn't be too difficult to find the right house.

Ron lingered awhile after he finished eating and drank a second cup of coffee. He slid his fingers over his short, slightly gray beard and smoothed his mustache. The sandwich and coffee sure hit the spot, and the trembling had stopped.

Ron belched then quickly looked around. Activity continued in the marketplace. No one seemed to have heard the rude sound. At least nobody looked his way.

Sure could go for a piece of pie. Ron noticed a young Amish man's plate on the table close by. Creamy chocolate spilled out between the crust of his pie, and a mountain of whipped cream swirled over the top. Ron's mouth watered, and he turned his head away so his stomach wouldn't win out. *Nope. I don't need any pie. Can't afford to spend the extra money on it either.*

Feeling more alert after two cups of coffee and ready to hit the road, Ron cleared his dishes from the table and headed out of the market. He was almost to the door when he spotted some flyers pinned to a bulletin board. One advertised an auction in Mt. Hope. Another told about a tour of an Amish home, which included a meal. A third flyer advertised some cooking classes in Walnut Creek. He pulled it off the board, because there were directions to the Amish home. Ron wasn't interested in cooking classes, not to mention he had no spare money to pay for them. But this might be a good place to park his motor home for a while. If the lady of the house cooked well enough to offer classes, she might offer him some free meals. In return, he could help around the place. Walnut Creek was less than ten miles away. *Think I'll head over there right now and check things out.*

Walnut Creek

On her way back from the mailbox, Heidi stopped at the phone shack to check for messages. She found one from her mother. Heidi listened as Mom told her how things were going at their home in Geauga County. The message ended with Mom saying she'd talked to her sister, Emma, the other day and had passed on the news about Heidi's plans to teach cooking classes.

Heidi smiled, sitting up straight on the stool. *Mom's obviously happy about this or she wouldn't be spreading the news. I'm happy too, but a bit* naerfich, *wondering how things will go.*

Heidi was about to step out of the phone shack when the telephone rang. She turned and picked up the receiver. "Hello."

"Heidi, is that you?"

"Jah. Is this Aunt Emma?"

A chuckle erupted on the other end of the line. "It certainly is. I heard from your *mamm* the other day. She said you were making plans to teach cooking classes."

"I am. The first class will begin next Saturday. To be honest, I'm a bit apprehensive, wondering how it will go."

"I understand. When I taught my first quilting class, I was so naerfich I could hardly eat breakfast the morning it started."

Heidi's stomach tightened. If Aunt Emma, an experienced quilter, had felt nervous, she could only imagine how she would feel next Saturday morning.

"Not to worry though," Aunt Emma quickly added. "Once all your students show up and you begin cooking, your nerves will settle, and your skills will kick in. Believe me, you'll simply relax and have a good time."

"I. . .I hope so." Heidi shifted the receiver to her other ear. "Cooking for Lyle, or even when we have company, is one thing, but teaching strangers to cook could prove to be a challenge."

"You'll do fine. I have every confidence in your ability to teach your students. Speaking of which, how many are signed up for your class?"

"Only one woman and our neighbor, Eli, so far, but I'm hoping I'll get more before next week."

"I'm sure God will send the people He wants you to teach." Aunt Emma's tone sounded so confident. "Ask for His guidance, and remember, I'll be praying for you."

"Danki. I feel better after talking to you."

"Do keep me posted, and should any of your students share a personal problem with you, don't hesitate to seek God's wisdom on their behalf."

Heidi gulped. She remembered hearing how Aunt Emma had mentored several of her quilting students. *Maybe those who come to my class won't have any problems they need to share. I hope that's the case, because I'm not sure I'm up to the task.*

"I sense by your silence you still have some doubts."

"I do have a few," Heidi admitted, "but it helps knowing you'll be praying for me."

"I'm sure others will pray as well."

Heidi opened the door and peered out when she heard the rumble of a vehicle outside. It surprised her to see an older model RV coming up the driveway. "Someone's here, Aunt Emma, so I'd better hang up. Danki for calling, and I'll keep you informed on how things go with my classes."

"All right, dear. I'll be anxious to hear. Now have a good day."

Heidi told her aunt goodbye, hung up the phone, and stepped outside in time to see the vehicle stop near the house. *I wonder who it is and what they want.*

Chapter 3

M ay I help you?" Heidi asked, walking up to the man who had gotten out of his motor home. She figured he might be lost and in need of directions.

He took a step toward her and extended his hand. "My name's Ron Hensley, and I'm havin' a problem with my rig. It hasn't been runnin' right today. I'm afraid if I keep pushing, the engine might blow."

"I'm sorry to hear it. Maybe you need a mechanic to look at your vehicle."

"Well, the thing is. . ." He paused, rubbing the back of his neck. "I don't have the money for repairs right now. What I need is a place to park my RV till I figure out the problem and fix it myself." He looked down at his worn-looking boots then back at Heidi. "I'm kind of in a bind. Would ya mind if I stayed here a few days?"

Taken aback by his unexpected question, Heidi glanced toward the road. *I wish Lyle was here so he could handle this situation.*

"I understand your hesitation." Ron shifted his weight. "I don't want to put you out, and I normally wouldn't ask, but I'm kinda desperate right now."

Heidi swallowed hard. *Please, Lord, help me do the right thing.*

No sooner had she silently prayed than Lyle's driver, Eric Barnes, pulled in. *Thank You, Lord.* She hurried down the driveway to speak with Lyle.

"You look upset. *Was is letz do?*" Lyle asked in Pennsylvania Dutch after he waved goodbye to Eric.

"I'm hoping nothing is wrong here, but I am a little concerned." Heidi gestured to Ron and told Lyle the man had asked if he could park his motor home on their property a few days while he worked on it.

Lyle's forehead creased as he rubbed the side of his bearded face and glanced toward the man standing beside his RV with his hands in his pockets. "What'd you tell him?"

"Nothing. I was hoping you would get here and could handle things." Heidi clasped her husband's arm. "He introduced himself as Ron Hensley. I'm thankful you came home when you did, because I wasn't sure how to respond."

Lyle patted her hand tenderly. "Don't worry; I'll take care of this. You can either go with me to talk to him or head into the house."

"I'll go inside." Glancing briefly at Mr. Hensley and his dented motor home, Heidi hurried inside. Pausing in front of the living room window, she watched her husband approach the man. *I wonder if Lyle will let Mr. Hensley stay here. Or will he ask him to find someplace else to work on his vehicle?*

Heidi felt sorry for Ron. He looked unkempt and dejected, like his paint-chipped motor home. The man's eyes didn't sparkle, and he seemed to have trouble making eye contact. He was obviously down on his luck and needed a place to stay, but she hoped it wouldn't be here. With her cooking classes starting soon, she didn't need the distraction. Besides, Lyle was in and out because of his auctioneering duties, and Heidi would feel uncomfortable having a stranger on the premises.

Moving to the kitchen, she took some leftover lentil soup from the refrigerator to heat for supper. After pouring it into a kettle, Heidi placed the soup on the propane-gas stove and turned on the burner. While it heated, she'd make a tossed green salad and set out the bread she had baked yesterday, along with fresh, creamy butter and a jar of local honey. It'd be more than enough for the two of them.

By the time the soup was thoroughly heated, Heidi had finished making the salad, so she set the table. *I wonder what's keeping Lyle. Seems like he's been talking to Ron a long time.*

She headed for the living room to look out the window, but saw no sign of Lyle, Ron, or his RV. *How strange. I wonder where they could be.*

Goose bumps erupted on her arms. *Could Ron have kidnapped my husband?* Heidi had read about the kidnapping of two teenage girls up in Canton a few months ago. Their parents were wealthy, and the girls had been held for ransom. Fortunately, the police found and rescued them, and they'd been returned to their parents, unharmed, while the kidnapper went to jail. Things didn't always turn out so well, however.

But why would anyone kidnap Lyle? she reasoned. *We're not rich.*

Heidi began pacing. *I need to calm down and stop allowing my imagination to run wild. If Mr. Hensley took Lyle, surely I would have heard the rumble of his vehicle, like I did when he drove into our yard. Of course, I was outside at the time.* She moved across the room. *I should quit fretting and go check for myself.*

Heidi was almost to the door when Lyle stepped in. Relief washed over her, and she rushed into his arms. "What's going on? Is everything okay? When I looked out the window and didn't see you or Mr. Hensley, I became concerned."

"We were on the back side of the barn, where he parked his RV so he'd be closer to the outhouse we no longer use."

Her eyes widened. "He's staying?"

"Jah. We talked awhile, and he seems like a decent enough person."

Heidi pursed her lips and, placing her hands on her hips, she stared up at him. "Ron's going to use the outhouse?"

"He probably won't use it himself, because there's a bathroom in his motor home. But the holding tank is getting pretty full, so I suggested he empty it in the outhouse." Lyle took off his straw hat and hung it on a wall peg. "I agreed to let Ron stay a few days, and told him he could get water from our garden hose."

Heidi fingered her apron band, wondering if she should express her opinion or remain quiet. She wouldn't usurp her husband's authority. Still, she had the right to express her opinion, since there were times she'd be here by herself. Sometimes, her husband could be too trusting.

Lyle lifted Heidi's chin with his thumb. "You're not pleased with my decision to let him stay, are you?"

"We don't know anything about Mr. Hensley."

"You're right, he's a stranger, but I don't believe he means us any harm." Lyle slipped his arm around Heidi's waist. "He's down on his luck. Maybe the Lord sent Ron to us for a reason. We need to show him God's love."

Heidi remained quiet. She would pray Ron got his

vehicle fixed soon and could be on his way to wherever he was going.

———⚬◦⚬———

Ron's stomach growled as he leaned against the pillow on his bunk and drew a deep breath. The sandwich from lunch had worn off, and all he could think about was the pie he wished he'd gotten for dessert. Once he had taken care of the RV and gotten himself settled, all he'd eaten for supper were a few crackers and cheese slices, which weren't nearly enough to fill his growling belly. The compact refrigerator in his tight kitchen area was practically empty.

Shoulda used what little money I had left to buy some food when I was at the market in Berlin today. Jaw clenching, he groaned. *Sure can't drive over there now, or anywhere else, for that matter. The Troyers would figure out I lied about my rig not running right. If there's another market close to their place, I'll walk over there tomorrow. I need to find a way to make some money too.*

Ron crumpled the cracker wrapping. *This old vehicle not only eats up gas, but I'll need to get more propane for the stove and water heater soon.*

Since he'd shot off his mouth and asked if he could stay here until he got his rig fixed, Ron would have to walk everywhere until he moved on. He'd have to pretend he was working on the rig, or it might look suspicious. *If I can find a ride into town, maybe I'll buy a new set of spark plugs when I get my retirement check at the end of April. Then, when I'm ready to move on, I can replace the old plugs and say my rig's running good again.*

Ron had to admit the Troyers seemed like nice people. Their farm wasn't elaborate, but at first glance he noticed it was well kept. It was especially nice to be parked at a place where he could stretch his legs and breathe in the country air. Open space was what he needed. It helped him feel less claustrophobic.

"Sure can't say the same about this tin can on wheels," Ron grumbled, looking around his tightly confined home. Even though his bunk wasn't as comfortable as a real bed, at least it was someplace to lay his head. From his position at the back of the rig, Ron saw all the way through to the driver's seat. The small kitchen area was directly behind the driver's seat, with a table and a bench that folded down from the wall. These could be made into an extra bed, but Ron never bothered, since he had the bunk area in the back. If he chose to, the passenger and driver seats could be swiveled around and used with the table when eating. Since Ron was always by himself, he didn't bother to do that either.

He grimaced. *Even if I wanted to, it would be impossible to entertain in this sardine can. I can barely move around in here myself.*

One nice feature in the motor home was a decent-sized closet. Ron kept a lot of his things there and in the storage box attached to the outside of the vehicle.

The small bathroom sufficed, with a shower, sink, and toilet. And here, in the area where he slept, a dresser had been built into the wall, with several drawers where he stored clothing.

Ron wadded the cracker wrapping and threw it toward the garbage bag by the side door. It missed by inches. *Great! Story of my life. No wonder the Amish couple agreed to let me stay here a few days. All they had to do was look at me and this junk heap I'm driving to figure out I'm hard up.*

Determined to put his problems out of his mind for the night, he closed his eyes and tried to sleep. Things might look better in the morning. After a good night's rest, maybe he'd have a clearer head and could decide what his next move should be.

Tap! Tap! Tap!

Ron's head jerked as his eyes snapped open. Unexpected noises always put him on alert. Once he figured out someone was knocking on the outside of his rig, he leaped up, nearly tripping over the garbage sack. He combed his fingers through his hair. *Get ahold of yourself.* Ron forced a smile and opened the side door. "Hey, what's up?"

Lyle blinked and took a step back. "If you haven't already eaten, I thought you might like some of Heidi's lentil soup. She made a big batch and we had plenty left over." He held out a lidded container. "It's still warm, if you'd like to eat it now. She also wrapped two slices of homemade bread for you."

The mention of soup caused Ron's stomach to rumble. "Yeah, I'd appreciate it." He took the soup gratefully, noticing a nice-looking dog sitting by Lyle's feet with its ears perked and head tilted to one side. It looked almost like the critter was trying to figure Ron out.

"By the way. . ." Lyle pointed to the animal. "This is Rusty. He's pretty friendly once he gets to know you."

"Okay. Umm. . .tell your wife thank you. Oh, and I'll bring the container back to your house in the morning. Will that be soon enough?"

Lyle nodded, and Rusty's tail wagged. "Have a good night, Ron."

"Same to you." Ron closed the door, grabbed a spoon, and took a seat at the table. Opening the lid, he dug into the soup, not bothering to get a bowl. From where he sat, the fridge was easy to reach. Fortunately, he still had a little butter left. Spreading some over the soft slices of bread, Ron couldn't wait to take a bite. "Lyle's wife is some cook. If I play my cards right, I might get to sample a lot more of her cooking."

Chapter 4

"Today's the big day, jah?"

Lyle's question startled Heidi. She hadn't realized he'd come in from doing his morning chores.

"Yes, it is a big day for me, and I'm a little naerfich," she admitted.

He walked over to the table where she'd been going over the list of things she wanted to cover during the first class. "There's no reason to be nervous. I'm confident you'll do fine." Lyle placed his hands on Heidi's shoulders, massaging them a few minutes before leaning down to kiss her cheek. "More than fine, in fact."

She smiled. Her husband had a positive attitude and always offered encouragement when she felt discouraged or had doubts about something. Was it any wonder she'd answered with a confident yes when he'd asked her to marry him? In addition to his pleasant personality, Lyle was a fine-looking man. He'd caught her eye the moment she'd first seen him at a young people's singing in Geauga County. Noticing his thick brown hair and dark brown eyes, Heidi had found it difficult to look away.

Lyle had been working at his uncle's farm in Middlefield the summer they'd met, and by the end of August, when he returned to his home in Holmes

County, Heidi was head over heels in love. Afterward, they'd kept in touch through letters and phone messages, and Lyle came back to her house several times to visit and get better acquainted. Heidi felt as though they were meant to be together and had no doubts about leaving Geauga County and moving to Holmes County to spend the rest of her life with Lyle.

Glancing at the clock, Heidi rose from her chair. "I'd better get breakfast started. Soon it'll be time for my students to arrive."

"Why don't you keep it simple this morning? You won't have as much kitchen cleanup to do." He opened a cupboard door and took out a clean mug. "In fact, coffee and toast would be enough for me."

"But I usually fix ham and eggs most Saturday mornings. Since you have an auction today, a big breakfast is a good way to start your day."

"I don't need it, Heidi." Lyle poured himself a cup of coffee. "But if you insist on fixing more, I'll settle for a bowl of cold cereal to go with the toast. If I get hungry later on, there'll be plenty to eat at the auction. In fact, if you'd like, I can bring something home for supper."

"Okay. We both have a busy day ahead of us, and it would be a treat if you brought something home. Danki for offering, Lyle."

"You're welcome. Life has many small pleasures, and getting a take-out meal now and then is one of them." The look Lyle gave her was no less than adoring. She watched her husband open the pantry door and take out a box of cereal. "Think I'll fix a bowl and take it out to Ron."

With her lighthearted mood twisting in a different direction, Heidi released an exasperated sigh. "I can't believe he's still parked behind our barn. Isn't he ever going to get his vehicle running well enough to leave?" Tugging on the narrow strings of her head covering, she frowned. "Ron originally asked if he could spend a few days, but he's been here a week already."

"He doesn't have money for the parts he needs." Lyle set the cereal on the table and took three bowls down from the cupboard. "Ron's done a few chores to help me outside this past week. The least we can do is offer him a few meals and a place to stay until—"

"Until what, Lyle?" Heidi crossed her arms. "If he has no money to fix his motor home, how is he going to earn any staying here? I'm beginning to wonder if Ron plans to stay on our property indefinitely. Doesn't he have a job or a family to call for the help he needs?"

"Ron's made no mention of family, but he did say the RV is his only home. He also said he has no job, only a small monthly retirement check."

"If he has no home, then how's he getting his mail?"

"A post office box, but he didn't say where."

Heidi touched the base of her neck, feeling warmth beneath her fingers. "How can we be sure he's telling the truth? Maybe he's a drifter who uses people to give him money and food."

"I haven't given him any money."

Heidi felt relief hearing that much at least. Still, she had to wonder how much longer it would be before Ron moved on.

"Are you okay with me giving him a bowl of cereal?" Lyle nudged her arm.

"Jah. While you're out there, though, would you please find out how much longer he's planning to stay?"

Lyle nodded. He went out the door a few minutes later, and Heidi got out the bread to make toast. As much as it bothered her to have Ron parked in their yard, she needed to be kind and put her Christianity into practice.

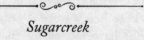

Sugarcreek

Loretta scurried around the kitchen, hurrying to get breakfast made for the children before her pastor's eighteen-year-old daughter, Sandy, came over to watch them while she attended the cooking class. She'd been worried about finding someone to watch Conner and Abby and felt grateful when Sandy offered.

Loretta poured Conner's favorite cereal into a bowl then took out the kind Abby liked best. After placing a hard-boiled egg and a piece of toast on a plate for herself, she joined the children at the table. "It's time to pray." She clasped both of their hands. "Dear Jesus, thank You for this food we are about to eat. And thank You for Sandy, who will be coming here soon to spend time with Abby and Conner. Help them be good and have a fun time while I'm at the cooking class today. Amen."

"Amen," Abby echoed.

Grinning, Conner bobbed his head. "Amen."

Loretta smiled. How thankful she felt for her two little ones. They'd become even more precious to her since Rick died. Closing her eyes, she added a brief silent prayer: *Help me be the kind of mother my children need, and show me how to guide them down a path of humility and simplicity.*

Mt. Hope

"Are you okay in there?"

Kendra groaned as she stared at her pale face in the

mirror. "I'll be okay, Dorie. Give me a few more minutes and I'll be out." Bile rising in her throat, she turned toward the toilet and vomited a second time. When her stomach emptied, she rinsed her mouth and wet a washcloth to wipe her cheeks. She'd hoped the morning sickness would have passed by now, but this past week it seemed even worse. In addition to her stomach doing flip-flops, some mornings she'd experienced dizzy spells or awakened with a pounding headache. Fortunately, nausea was the only symptom plaguing Kendra so far today.

"Wish I could eat something in the mornings without feeling sick to my stomach," she muttered, pushing her short auburn hair behind her ears. Since she'd become pregnant, most breakfast foods and some of her other favorite meals, like pizza, upset her stomach.

Many times when Kendra was growing up, her mother would make dippy eggs and toast for breakfast. For now, until the morning sickness passed, she'd switched from eating eggs or even pancakes, to having saltines and mint tea. Usually by lunchtime, Kendra was able to eat without getting sick.

Taking a deep breath, she left the bathroom and joined her friend in the kitchen. "Sure hope I can get myself together. I should be leaving for the cooking class soon, and if I keep feeling this way, I won't be able to go."

Dorie opened a cupboard door and took out a box of saltine crackers. "I'll fix you some tea while you nibble some of these."

"Thanks." Kendra massaged the bridge of her nose, hoping a headache wasn't forthcoming.

"It's good you don't have to drive far to get to the Amish lady's house." Dorie gave Kendra a cup of tea then finished eating her scrambled egg and bacon sandwich.

"Yeah, it's only about nine miles from here. If traffic is light, I should be there in ten minutes or so." Kendra had to take a few more deep breaths as she chewed; then she swallowed the cracker. She loved bacon, but this morning even the smell of it on Dorie's sandwich made her queasy. "Sure hope I don't get sick while I'm at the class. Think how embarrassing it would be. And what if the Amish lady's only bathroom facility is an outhouse?"

"Don't worry; I'm sure their house will have an inside bathroom." Dorie poured herself a glass of tomato juice. The site of the thick reddish-colored juice made Kendra's stomach turn, and she had to look away.

After Dorie drank her juice, she got up and took her dishes to the sink. "I don't think you have anything to worry about."

"I'm gonna take a few crackers with me too." Kendra opened a drawer and took out a sandwich bag. "What if the odor of whatever she teaches us to cook makes me feel nauseous?"

"You worry too much." Dorie stepped behind Kendra and massaged her shoulders. "I'll put some mint tea in a thermos, and you can take it along."

"Okay, thanks." Tea would be better than coffee. Kendra found even the smell of the dark brew to be objectionable. "Oh, I'm supposed to bring an apron with me to the class. Do you have one I can borrow?"

"Sure thing." Dorie opened a drawer and pulled out a lime-green apron. "Here you go."

"Thanks." It wasn't Kendra's favorite color, but at least the apron would cover her baggy shirt and jeans and hopefully keep them clean.

"Do you have any plans while I'm gone today?" Kendra asked.

"Thought I'd tidy up around here and maybe repot

my African violet." Dorie pointed to the flower sitting by the kitchen window.

While Dorie got out the thermos and brewed more tea, Kendra returned to the table. She reflected on how she and Dorie had been friends since high school. *If I'd only listened to her when she voiced concerns about Max, I wouldn't be in this predicament right now.*

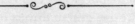

Walnut Creek

Ron was about to pour himself a second cup of coffee when a knock sounded on his side door. He'd been somewhat prepared for it, since Lyle usually came out to talk to him each morning and often brought something to eat.

Lyle smiled when Ron opened the door. "If you haven't eaten already, I brought a bowl of cereal for your breakfast."

"That's mighty nice of you." Ron took the bowl gratefully. The other day he'd walked to the market nearby and spent his last few dollars. Now, only a little food remained in his dinky refrigerator, so any food offered by the Troyers was appreciated.

"I'll be leaving for an auction soon," Lyle announced. "You're welcome to come along if you like."

Hesitating a moment, Ron shook his head. "I have no reason to go to an auction, but I'll chop some wood while you're gone if ya like."

"It would be helpful. Heidi and I are having friends over for a bonfire next week, so the wood will be put to good use." Lyle started to walk away but turned back to face Ron. "I was wondering how much longer till you're able to work on your rig."

Ron glanced up at the house then back at Lyle. "You want me to leave? Is that what you're sayin'?"

"No, it's not. I only asked because when you first came here you told us it would only be a few days." Squinting, Lyle shuffled his feet. "How much money do you need to buy the parts to fix your motor home?"

Ron shrugged. "Can't say for sure. My retirement check should arrive by the end of the month. Maybe then I can hire one of your drivers to take me to get the check as well as the parts I need."

"So you want to stay till then?"

"Yeah. If it's okay with you. Don't want to put you out or be an inconvenience to anyone though."

"No, it's fine." Lyle gave a quick nod.

"Thanks for your understanding." Ron quickly shut the door before Lyle had a chance to change his mind. He'd made the right decision choosing this Amish house to stop at. From what Ron could tell so far, the Troyers were easy marks.

Chapter 5

Dover

Charlene glanced in the hall mirror one last time, to be sure her hair looked okay. She had debated about wearing it down, but since she'd be taking cooking classes, it might be best to wear her hair in a ponytail so it didn't get in the way. Her stomach tightened, thinking about the classes she'd agreed to take. *What if the recipes she gives us are too difficult for me? What if I'm not teachable? I could end up making a fool of myself. Well, at least Len's mother won't be there to see me mess up.*

Charlene cringed, reflecting on the time she'd been invited by Len's parents to join them for Thanksgiving. When his mother, Annette, asked Charlene to bring a pumpkin pie, she'd considered buying a store-bought one. However, wanting to impress her future mother-in-law, Charlene made the pie from scratch. Big mistake. She'd ended up using too much evaporated milk and, to make matters worse, hadn't cooked the pie long enough, for the inside was runny. Fortunately, Len's mother had made an apple pie to serve. But things really fell apart when Annette asked Charlene to whip the whipping cream. Charlene was horrified when she started up the mixer and liquid splattered out of the bowl, some ending up on Annette's lovely blue dress. Was it any wonder the woman had never warmed up to her? No doubt she hoped her son would choose someone who was capable in the kitchen. Charlene wanted Len to be proud of her cooking abilities and hoped by taking the classes there might be a chance to prove herself to Len, as well as his mother.

"What do you think, Olive?" Charlene looked at her cat sitting on the couch, head bobbing as she silently watched her. She'd given the name to the feline because of the cat's pretty, olive green eyes that were a sharp contrast to her fluffy gray fur. "Am I crazy for going to these cooking classes?"

Olive meowed and curled into a ball, oblivious to her owner's nervousness.

"Guess not." Charlene shrugged her shoulders then picked up her purse. She was about to head out the door when she remembered she'd left her cell phone on the kitchen table. Besides having the phone for emergency purposes, she planned to GPS her way to Heidi Troyer's home. She'd been to Walnut Creek a few times and knew the back roads could be tricky. Charlene had never been good with directions, so without the GPS she'd probably end up driving around for hours and be late for the class or miss it altogether.

Charlene got in her car, set the GPS, and headed down the road toward Holmes County. After passing through Sugarcreek, it suddenly dawned on her that the apron she was supposed to bring remained on the back of a chair in her kitchen. *How did I miss seeing the apron when I went back to get my cell phone?*

Glancing at the clock on her car dash, Charlene figured she would have enough time to stop at Walnut Creek Cheese and pick up an apron from the kitchen supplies section.

A short time later, Charlene entered the store and

found a pretty lavender apron—her favorite color. She paid for it and hurried back to her car. As long as she didn't get lost, arriving on time shouldn't be a problem.

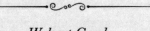

Walnut Creek

Eli left his house and headed for the barn to get his bike. Since the Troyers lived nearby, it was kind of pointless to hitch his horse to the buggy. Riding the bike would be quicker, and the fresh air and exercise would do him some good, even though it wasn't his favorite mode of transportation.

"What was I thinking, agreeing to do this?" Eli muttered. "Lyle must have caught me in a weak moment when I agreed to take his wife's cooking classes. I'll probably bumble my way through every lesson and end up looking like a fool."

He thought about the stale toast he'd had for breakfast and was reminded, once again, how badly he needed to learn how to cook. Hopefully a few other men would be in the class, or maybe Lyle would be there to offer moral support. The thought of taking a cooking class with a bunch of females made Eli's stomach tighten. Most women he knew were good cooks, so he wasn't sure why any Amish women in their community would need to take Heidi's class. One thing was for sure—he was not wearing an apron, even if it had been requested, although if he had a mind to, he could have taken one Mavis used to wear.

"Whelp, I may as well get this over with." Eli slapped his straw hat on his head, pushed his bike out of the barn, and climbed on. *Sure hope Heidi lets us eat whatever we cook today. I could use a decent meal for a change.*

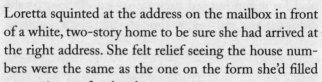

Loretta squinted at the address on the mailbox in front of a white, two-story home to be sure she had arrived at the right address. She felt relief seeing the house numbers were the same as the one on the form she'd filled out to sign up for the classes.

She pulled her car into the driveway in time to see an Amish man with brown hair and a matching beard get off his bike. Since he had a beard, it meant he was married, so she assumed he was Heidi's husband.

When Loretta got out of the vehicle, the man glanced her way and gave a quick nod; then he stepped onto the front porch and knocked on the door.

That's odd. Loretta stood beside her car, watching. If he was Heidi's husband, surely he wouldn't knock on his own door—unless it was locked, and he'd forgotten the key.

A few seconds later, the door opened, and the man went inside.

She glanced around the property. Although modest, the house, barn, and other outbuildings were neatly kept, and the yard looked well maintained. Noticing the fenced-in fields behind the place, she assumed the land also belonged to the Troyers. But an RV was parked near a freshly tilled garden. *I wonder why an Amish person would have a vehicle like that.*

Loretta looked quickly away when she saw a man peek out the motor home's side window. *Guess it's none of my business.* She turned and hurried toward the house. Remembering her apron and notebook were still in the car, she spun around to get them.

Except for the motor home, Loretta didn't see any other vehicles in the yard. She figured the others were either late, or perhaps she was the only one who'd signed up for the class. If that was the case, she'd receive more individualized attention and could learn to cook Amish-style meals quicker than if other students were there, asking questions.

Loretta grabbed her apron, and as she closed the car door, another vehicle pulled in. A few seconds later, a young woman, wearing her long hair up in a ponytail, got out of her car, holding her purse in one hand and a lavender apron in the other. She offered Loretta a pink-cheeked grin. "Are you here for Heidi Troyer's cooking class?"

"Yes, I am." Loretta smiled in return.

"Same here."

They stepped onto the porch together, and Loretta knocked on the door. When it opened, an Amish woman, who appeared to be in her late twenties, greeted them with a welcoming smile. "I'm Heidi Troyer; welcome to my class."

Loretta could hardly take her eyes off this beautiful young woman. Her shiny dark hair peeking out the front of her white, cone-shaped covering and her sparkling blue eyes set against a creamy complexion made her appear almost angelic. If not for her plain Amish clothes, she could have been a runway model. With her own medium brown hair and average-looking brown eyes, Loretta felt plain by comparison.

"Come in and take a seat." Heidi motioned to the living room, where the Amish man who had entered the house before them sat in the rocking chair. He gave a nod then looked down at his black boots. Loretta expected Heidi to introduce him, but instead, she moved over to the window and peered out. "Our last student hasn't arrived yet, but when she gets here, I'll ask everyone to introduce themselves, and then we'll move into the kitchen to begin our first lesson."

Loretta took a seat on the couch, and the young woman with the ponytail sat on the opposite end. It felt awkward sitting here without proper introductions.

Glancing at Heidi, who continued to look out the front window, Loretta guessed their teacher felt as anxious as she did right now.

Picking a piece of lint off her dark blue maxi dress, Loretta discreetly dropped it into her purse. She wasn't about to let it fall on the floor of this spotless room. While the living room had no decorative items or pictures on the walls, a few candles sat on the end tables. Two sets of mounted deer antlers hung on either side of the fireplace. A man's straw hat hung on one, so Loretta figured since the antlers were being put to good use, they would be allowed in the Amish home. A beautiful antique oil lamp sat on the mantel, and an oval braided throw rug lay on the floor under the coffee table in front of the couch.

The coziness of this room was so inviting, Loretta wished she could duplicate it in her own home. She'd never been one to display a lot of fancy doodads and didn't even own a TV. To some her decor might seem meager and plain, but it met her and the children's needs.

I'm too practical to spend money on things if they don't serve a specific purpose other than for decoration, she mused. *Sometimes I wish my parents had joined the Amish church, because I'd probably have fit right in.*

"She's here!"

Heidi's excited tone startled Loretta, and she nearly jumped off the couch. Apparently, only three women had signed up for the class, which meant, with so few here, they'd be able to move through the lesson quickly and hopefully learn a lot. Loretta could hardly wait to begin.

Curious as to what was going on outside, Ron peered out the side window of his motor home. According to the flyer he'd seen on the bulletin board in Berlin, this was the day Heidi's cooking class was supposed to begin. No more cars had arrived at the Troyers', so everyone who signed up was probably here.

Ron needed to get the garden hose in order to refill the motor home's fresh-water tank but had waited until he was sure no one else was in the yard. The last thing he wanted was to be pulled into a conversation with anyone right now—especially a bunch of strangers.

Ron stepped outside and headed for the outdoor spigot on the side of the house. It was a bit chilly for April, but he felt the sun's warmth on his face when he looked up.

As he walked by the vehicles parked in the driveway, Ron noticed two of them were smaller cars, and the other was a minivan. They all appeared to be older models. Near the vehicles, a bicycle leaned against a big tree. Ron remembered seeing an Amish man ride in on it.

He turned on the spigot and pulled the hose toward his RV. While the tank filled, a red-tailed hawk caught his attention. Gripping the nozzle, Ron watched the majestic bird sailing round and round in the expanse of the open blue skies. For a fleeting moment, he wished he were as free as the hawk as it caught a draft and went farther out of sight.

Ron's thoughts returned to the people who'd arrived, wondering why they'd chosen to take a cooking class. "Must be nice to have a purpose in life," he muttered under his breath.

He turned and watched the road. For a Saturday, hardly any traffic went by. Of course, on a back country road such as this, there weren't many cars—mostly horse and buggies.

It was nice having his motor home parked closer to the Troyers' house. Lyle had suggested it the other day, saying it would be easier for Ron to get fresh water from the garden hose. The view of the fields by the back of the barn was okay, but since his holding tank was now empty, there was no point staying parked near the outhouse. Here, closer to the house, was better. It gave Ron the advantage of seeing what was going on around the place, as well as the comings and goings at the house. It would also give him a chance to see if the Troyers followed a routine, so he'd know when they were gone.

"Oh, great!" Ron jumped back. He hadn't been paying attention, and water gushed out of the full tank, soaking his pant leg. Quickly, he turned off the hose and screwed the lid back on the water tank. Dragging the hose, he walked toward the house. Once there, he turned off the spigot and reopened the hose's spout. This way all the water would drain out as he rolled the garden hose back on the reel.

"Guess I need to change my trousers." Ron swept his hand over the wet spot. *Wonder if Heidi would mind if I hung my pants on her clothesline to dry? Then again, maybe I'd better not. I'll drape 'em over the passenger seat and they can air-dry that way.* Tapping his foot, he grunted. "What I really need is a cup of hot coffee."

Ron stepped into his motor home, grabbed the teakettle, and went to the sink to fill it. In his haste, he turned on the faucet full force. It sputtered loudly, and before he could react, water squirted out, spraying his face and the front of his shirt. "Super! I forgot the air needs to be forced out of the line before the water flows smoothly." Ron set the teakettle on the counter and turned the water pressure down until he heard the pump switch off.

"Now I need to change my shirt." Ron's knuckles whitened as he clenched his fingers. "I can tell this is gonna be a great day." What he wouldn't give for a real cup of fresh-brewed coffee right now. But all he had was some of the instant kind. *Maybe after I change my shirt and trousers I'll see if Heidi has some java to spare.*

Chapter 6

Loretta felt sorry for the Amish man sitting in the room with her and the other young lady. As he fiddled with his suspenders and stared at the floor, it became obvious the poor fellow felt out of place.

So as not to stare at the man or make him feel worse, she glanced quickly out the window. *What looks even more out of place is the beat-up motor home in the yard. I wonder who owns it and why it's parked here.*

From where she sat, Loretta had a good view of the yard. She'd watched intently as an older man came out of the motor home and stood near her minivan. She'd been curious when he came closer to the house. In fact, it appeared as if he had walked underneath the window near where she sat. A few minutes later, he pulled a hose toward the RV. While filling the tank, he looked first at the sky then toward the road. The man moved his mouth too, like he was talking to himself.

Loretta had to stifle a giggle when she saw water spurt out of the tank. The man didn't look too happy when he came toward the window again. She looked away so he wouldn't see her watching him then glanced toward the RV again as he went inside and shut the door.

Turning her attention back to those in the room, Loretta tried to think of something to say. She wanted to ask their names and why they'd signed up for the class but didn't want to appear nosy. Leaning back in her chair, she remained quiet.

Eli felt as out of place as a donkey showing up for church. It reminded him of the day he'd found Mavis hosting a quilting bee at their home. Fifteen women sat around a quilting frame in her sewing room, chattering like a bunch of noisy magpies. He'd tried to be polite and even managed a quick "hello" but then hurried from the room before anyone engaged him in conversation.

Eli had no trouble talking with a group of men, but when he had to talk to more than one woman at a time, he became tongue-tied. It was worse with women he'd never met before, like today. If not for his need to learn how to cook, Eli would have rushed out the door and pedaled home as fast as his legs could go.

He glanced around the room and noticed one of the women wearing a long blue dress with matching apron in her lap. She seemed to be staring at him. *Sure hope she doesn't say anything to me.* Eli wished a trapdoor would appear in the floor so he could crawl inside and disappear. Averting his gaze, he studied a worn spot in the knee of his trousers. *Probably should've worn a different pair. Didn't want to get too dressed up for a cooking class though. I'm likely to spill something and end up with food on my clothes.*

Eli reflected on the time he'd helped Mavis shuck corn and ended up with a mess all over his clean shirt. In a gentle tone she'd scolded him for wearing one of his nicer shirts to take part in a messy job. So this morning he'd put on clothes he thought were the most appropriate.

Heidi returned to the room a few minutes later,

accompanied by a young woman with short auburn hair and dark brown eyes. She then asked everyone to introduce themselves and tell what they hoped to learn during the cooking classes.

When nobody responded, Heidi motioned to the young woman with a ponytail. "Why don't you go first?"

"Oh, okay. My name is Charlene Higgins, and I signed up for these classes because. . ." She paused, blinking rapidly. "Well, to tell you the truth, my cooking is terrible. I've heard most Amish women are excellent cooks, so I signed up, hoping by the time I get married I'll be more comfortable around the kitchen and won't starve my poor husband."

Heidi smiled. "Thank you, Charlene. Now who would like to go next?"

Eli sat quietly, wishing he wouldn't have to say anything, but his turn would eventually come. He was on the verge of introducing himself when the woman with long brown hair spoke up.

"I'm Loretta Donnelly, and I'm interested in the Amish way of life, so I'm hoping to learn how to make some traditional Amish dishes."

Heidi nodded and motioned to the auburn-haired woman standing beside her, holding a lime-green apron and beige-colored tote in front of her stomach.

"My name's Kendra Perkins. I can make a few things fairly well, but my friend Dorie thought taking the cooking classes would be something fun for me to do."

"Thank you, ladies. That leaves you." Heidi motioned to Eli.

"Well, umm. . . My name is Eli Miller." His face heated as he gripped the arms of the rocking chair. "To be honest, I can't do much more than boil water, so I'm here to learn how to cook." He looked over at Heidi and grimaced. "That is, if you think I'm teachable."

"I believe anyone who has a desire to cook can learn, and if you can read, you should be able to follow a recipe. Why don't we all go into the kitchen now and begin our first lesson?" Heidi's sincere smile caused Eli to relax a bit.

After everyone washed their hands and put on their aprons, they took seats around Heidi's long kitchen table. Eli insisted he didn't need an apron, so Heidi didn't force the issue.

She handed each of them several pieces of paper and then stood at the head of the table. "For those of you unfamiliar with the basics of cooking, I've written down some necessary information, including how to measure the liquids, dry ingredients, grated cheese, dried fruit, eggs, butter, shortening, molasses, and syrup." Heidi paused to be sure everyone paid attention. She tried to make her voice clear enough and did her best to keep her composure. It wouldn't be good to let on to her students that she was a bundle of nerves. *I hope my decision to teach these classes wasn't a mistake.*

Heidi drew a quick breath as she collected her thoughts. "Let's see. . . . Oh yes, I've also included a list of the different types of flour, sugar, creams, cooking oils, and yeasts. In addition, I've written down how to reduce or increase a recipe, included a list of substitutions when you don't have an exact ingredient, as well as given directions for selecting the proper kitchen utensils, kettles, skillets, and baking pans." She looked at each of her students. "Before we proceed, does anyone have a question?"

Charlene's hand shot up.

"Yes?"

"Will we be expected to use all the ingredients you have listed during our every-other-week cooking classes?"

Heidi shook her head. "There's no way we can make enough dishes in our six weeks of being together to use everything listed on your papers. You will, however, need this list when you are cooking in your own kitchens." Since Charlene and Eli had already admitted they had limited cooking skills, it had been a good idea to put together the handout sheets.

Heidi was about to give everyone the ingredients and utensils they would need to make her favorite breakfast casserole when a knock sounded on the back door. She excused herself to answer it, hoping whoever it was wouldn't stay long, because they only had until one o'clock to finish the first lesson.

"Should I, or shouldn't I?" Ron contemplated out loud as he looked down to make sure the clean shirt he'd put on was buttoned.

A reasonable amount of time had passed since the young auburn-haired woman had gone into the Troyers' house, so now seemed as good a time as any to knock on Heidi's door.

Ron toyed with his mustache as he shook the few grains of instant coffee left in the jar. "Maybe she'd let me hang my clothes on her line to dry."

Stepping outside, he had walked briskly toward the house. *Come on now. What's the worst she could say?* He'd ask for a cup of coffee first, then bring up his need to wash clothes.

Holding his coffee mug while toying with his mustache, he had second thoughts about interrupting

Heidi's class. But it was too late to worry about it now; she'd already opened the door.

Heidi tipped her head. "Did you need something, Mr. Hensley?"

"Uh. . .yeah, and please call me Ron. Would you happen to have any fresh coffee made?"

"As a matter of fact, I do."

"Would ya mind filling my cup? I'm almost out of the instant kind, and it doesn't taste the same." He made a choking noise while shaking his head. "Nope. Nothin' beats a good cup of the real thing."

"No problem. If you'll follow me to the kitchen, I'll pour you a cup."

Ron hesitated, shuffling his feet a few times. "Well, uh, I saw you have company and don't want to interrupt. I can wait here on the porch."

"Not a problem. The people in my kitchen have come for a cooking class, but it'll only take me a minute to fill up that mug. Come on in, Mr. Hensley. My students won't mind."

Ron was well aware of Heidi's cooking classes, but he didn't let on. He wasn't about to tell Heidi he'd seen her ad on the board at the market in Berlin, and it had prompted him to show up here. He followed her into the kitchen and stopped short when he saw three women and an Amish man sitting at the table, looking at him with curious expressions.

Heidi's kitchen was spacious. A far cry from the tiny one in his motor home. It almost made him dizzy seeing all this space in one room. Ron had been cramped up in his RV so long, he'd forgotten what living in a house was like.

"Class, this is Ron Hensley." Heidi motioned to him. "He's here to—"

"Whew! This is good news." The Amish man pushed his chair away from the table and hurried across the room. "It's nice to know I'm not the only man attending Heidi's cooking class today. I was worried for a while there." The man shook Ron's hand vigorously. "My name's Eli Miller. It's nice to meet you."

"Oh, well, I. . ." Ron stopped talking, as an idea formed. *If I were to attend Heidi's class, it would give me an opportunity to be in her house and scope things out. Who knows what kind of treasures are scattered about that could bring a good price at the pawnshop in one of the bigger towns outside of Holmes County?*

Putting on his best smile, Ron looked over at Heidi. "Would you have room for another student? I can't pay you now for the classes, but I should have enough money in a few weeks, when I get my retirement check."

Heidi stared at him quizzically. "I didn't realize you were interested in learning how to cook Amish-style meals."

He bobbed his head enthusiastically. "It's always good to learn new things. Especially if it's a simple meal I can make easily in my RV."

The Amish man thumped Ron's back and pointed to an empty chair at the table. "I'm sure glad you're here. Why don't you sit down?"

Ron handed Heidi his empty mug and took a seat. *Sure hope this isn't a mistake.* He bit the inside of his cheek. *I'd better wait and ask about doing laundry some other time. I'll have to be careful what I do and say while I'm in this house so neither Heidi nor her husband catches on to my plan.*

Chapter 7

Thank goodness this class is only twice a month. Ron
fidgeted while everyone else sat quietly, waiting for
Heidi to get started. He felt like a rabbit wanting nothing
more than to bolt. Fact was, he'd rather be doing anything
other than sitting here with a bunch of strangers. Ron
had no desire to get acquainted with any of them either.
The fewer people who knew him, the better.

*Maybe I should have offered to do something for Lyle
out in the barn today.* As soon as possible, Ron planned
to have a talk with him about doing a few more things
around the place to help out. He didn't want to appear
as if he were taking advantage of their good nature. It
could arouse suspicion.

As Ron sat in his chair, he looked around the
kitchen, trying to take everything in. He'd already
noticed how spacious it was, but the room was also clean
and neat. Everything seemed to have a place. Raising
his eyebrows, Ron glanced at the floor. It was so clean
and shiny a person could probably put their plate down
there and eat off the floor. There was nothing unneces-
sary in this kitchen. Most things he saw had a purpose.

Something in particular caught Ron's attention—a
collection of oil lamps on top of the kitchen cabinets. They
looked old. He figured they might be worth some money.

Since Lyle was an auctioneer, he may have picked them up at one of the events he'd attended. Of course they could also be something one of their relatives had handed down.

An idea formed as Ron counted the lamps—ten altogether—a sizable collection. *I'll bet if two or three suddenly vanished, it would be awhile before they'd be missed. How often do Heidi or Lyle look up there to admire the lamps? I wonder what other treasures are in this old house.* Ron rubbed his chin, shifting in his seat. *Getting inside the barn to look around for treasures shouldn't be a problem, but if I can figure out a way to come into the house when nobody's at home, bet I could walk away with a lot of good stuff.*

Doubts clouded Heidi's mind about having Ron take part in her cooking classes. Did he plan to stay parked on their property from now until the end of June, when the classes would end? If he moved on, would he return every other week to finish the classes? She suspected he might be up to something but couldn't put her finger on it.

Lyle had no objections to Ron being here. Perhaps she shouldn't either. Besides, Eli seemed pleased to have another man in the class. Maybe for some reason Ron was meant to be here.

Pulling her thoughts back to the matter at hand, she took a baking dish from the refrigerator. "Today we'll be making what I call, 'Amish country breakfast,' and this is what it looks like after it's been put together. Since we won't have time for everyone to make their own dish today, we will take turns mixing the ingredients. Once everything is in the nine-by-thirteen pan, it will go into the refrigerator and stay there overnight." Heidi placed the baking dish she'd taken from the refrigerator on the table and removed the foil covering. "In the meantime, I will bake this dish, because I put it together last night and it's sufficiently chilled. When it's done, everyone will get a sample to eat, along with a bowl of cut-up fruit, which we'll be making next." She paused and gave each of them a recipe card. "I've written the directions for Amish country breakfast on each of your cards so you can make it in your own home whenever you like." Heidi didn't mention it, but she'd also included some scripture on the back of everyone's card. After praying about this, she felt led to do it. Today's quotation was from Psalm 46:10: *"Be still, and know that I am God."* Hopefully, one or more of her students would find it meaningful, as it had been to her since she'd become a Christian. Many days when she'd been bustling around the house or yard, Heidi paused to reflect on those words. Then she'd take a break and sit quietly to pray and thank God for all He'd done in her life.

"Who gets the breakfast casserole you'll be baking tomorrow?" Ron leaned forward, staring at the dish with hungry eyes.

"Two of my friends will be coming over Monday morning to help plant a few early vegetables in my garden, so I'll serve it to them."

Ron heaved a sigh and sat back in his chair.

Heidi's heart softened toward him a bit. "You and the others will get to eat the one I'll be baking today."

He grinned. "Okay."

"Now, before I put the casserole in the oven, we'll need to add the topping." Heidi gestured to the three cups of cornflakes she'd set out. "One-half cup of melted butter needs to be added to these." She took out the butter she'd measured before her students arrived, placed it in a small kettle, and set it on the stove. "When melting butter, it's important to keep the burner on low so it won't burn."

Everyone gathered around the stove as Heidi

demonstrated. Once the butter was melted, she brought it to the table and poured the liquid in with the cornflakes. Then she handed Loretta a wooden spoon and asked her to stir it until the cornflakes were thoroughly coated. Afterward, Heidi asked Kendra to pour the mixture over the top of the casserole.

"Now it's time to bake this delicious country casserole." Heidi put the foil over the dish again and pointed to the recipe cards she'd given each student. "You'll see the oven needs to be set at 375 degrees."

After Heidi put the casserole in the oven and set a timer for forty-five minutes, she got out another nine-by-thirteen pan. Then she gestured to the three-by-five index cards. "The first thing we'll need to do is grease the pan. I usually use coconut oil for this purpose, since it's one of the healthiest oils and works equally well as shortening for greasing."

She placed a jar of coconut oil on the table. "Who would like to do the honors?"

"Maybe I should," Charlene spoke up. "Since greasing a pan is easy, I shouldn't goof up." She went on to tell about the mistake she'd made at Thanksgiving with the pumpkin pie, and then the whipping cream fiasco at her future in-laws' house.

Poor Charlene. Heidi couldn't comprehend how the young woman could have so much trouble with what she, herself, saw as a simple task. Heidi had learned to mash potatoes at a young age and caught on quickly. She set the baking pan and coconut oil in front of Charlene then handed her a paper towel.

Charlene tilted her head, causing her ponytail to swish over her shoulder and rest against her chest. "How much oil should I use?"

"Take only enough to grease the bottom and sides of the pan," Heidi prompted.

All eyes were on Charlene as she dipped a piece of the paper towel into the creamy, solidified coconut oil. It wasn't enough to grease the whole pan, but before making any comments, Heidi waited to see how well Charlene did with the small amount she'd taken.

With lips held tightly together, Charlene squinted as she spread the oil on one side of the pan. "Looks like I may need more." She reached back into the jar and spread some more around, until the other three sides and bottom of the pan were greased.

"Good job." Heidi handed each student two slices of bread, keeping four of them for herself, to show them what to do. "We'll start by layering half of the bread, ham, and cheese, and then each of the layers will be repeated."

Heidi opened the refrigerator and took out the ham she'd cut into small enough pieces to cube, along with a one-pound brick of cheddar cheese. After giving everyone a knife and small cutting board, she asked them to cut their pieces of ham into small cubes. She watched as everyone did as she asked, and hid a grin when Ron popped a piece of ham into his mouth. *The poor man must be hungry.*

Next, Heidi demonstrated how to grate the cheese. Then she passed the brick of cheese around, along with the grater, and each person took a turn. With the exception of Eli scraping his knuckles, things went fairly well.

"Are you okay? If you need a bandage I have some with me." Loretta reached for her purse. "Between my two little ones, someone always has a boo-boo, so I make sure to keep bandages on hand."

"I'm fine." Eli held up his hand. "My knuckles aren't bleeding. It'll take me awhile to get the hang of using this thing though." He handed the grater to Ron. "Your turn."

Ron made quick work out of grating a pile of cheese, causing Heidi to wonder if he'd done it before.

"Now that we have the cheese shredded and the ham cut, you'll put them in the baking pan on top of the bread slices," she instructed.

"Which goes first. . .the meat or cheese?" Charlene questioned.

"Start with bread, then meat, followed by cheese. This way, the cheese melts down over the meat. Once the first set of ingredients is down, you'll place a second layer of bread, meat, and cheese."

Heidi watched her students take turns creating the layers. Little conversation transpired between them as they all seemed to be concentrating on the task at hand.

Next, she took six eggs from the refrigerator and gave one to each student, keeping one for herself. She also placed six bowls on the table, along with wire whisks for everyone. Then Heidi demonstrated how to beat the egg with the whisk and asked the others to follow her example.

It took Eli a few tries to get his egg beaten, but the others managed okay with theirs.

Heidi set a container of milk on the table and poured enough to make three cups, which she divided equally into six small bowls. "The next step is to pour the milk into your beaten egg mixture and stir until well blended."

Charlene groaned when some of the liquid in her bowl spilled out and onto the table. Her shoulders hunched as she looked up at Heidi with furrowed brows. "Oops. Sorry about that."

"It's okay. You didn't spill much." Heidi handed Charlene a clean sponge to wipe up the mess.

When Charlene rubbed the area, her sponge caught the bowl of egg-and-milk mixture, sending it spattering onto Heidi's clean floor. "Oh no!" Gasping, Charlene slapped her forehead. "Now look what I've done."

"Don't panic. It could have happened to any of us."

Heidi went to the utility room to get the mop.

When she returned, Charlene jumped up and took it from her. "Since I'm the one who made the mess, I'll clean it up." A blotch of red erupted on both of her cheeks.

"If ya give me a sponge I'll wipe off the table where some of the egg mixture landed," Eli offered.

Loretta took the bowl and whisk and then put them in the sink to wash, while Kendra dried the pieces.

This is not going as planned, Heidi thought with regret. But everyone seemed to be taking it in stride and helping to clean up the mess. Everyone but Ron. He stood with arms folded, gazing around the kitchen.

Heidi got another egg, along with more milk, and handed them to Charlene.

"Let me see if I can attempt this again." Charlene cracked the egg and gently whipped it with the whisk. Slowly, she poured in the milk. This time she did it perfectly, and blushed when everyone clapped. "Thank you. Thank you very much." Giggling, she stood and took a bow.

Maybe this incident wasn't such a bad thing. Heidi licked her lips with cautious hope. Everyone seemed to be more relaxed, and it was nice to see them working together and encouraging Charlene. Even Ron's attention seemed to have returned to the matter at hand.

Next, Heidi asked her students to pour the milk-and-egg mixture over the layered items in the baking dish. When finished, she covered the dish with a piece of foil and placed it in the refrigerator to set overnight.

"Does anyone have any questions?"

Kendra, whose face had grown pale all of a sudden, raised her hand. "Where's your bathroom? Think I'm gonna be sick."

Heidi pointed. "Down the hall, last door on the left."

Covering her mouth, Kendra dashed out of the room.

Chapter 8

Sure hope that little gal doesn't have the flu." Ron's face tightened as he plucked at his shirt collar. "The last thing any of us needs is to get sick because of her. If she wasn't feelin' good, she should've stayed home today."

"There's a virus going around at the school where I teach, but so far I've managed to escape it." Charlene crossed her fingers. "I hate taking sick leave. It confuses my young students when they have a substitute teacher."

"What grade do you teach?" Loretta asked. She felt it was time for a little conversation.

"Kindergarten at an elementary school in Dover. To some of the children I'm like a surrogate mother; they become dependent on me."

Loretta smiled. "My daughter will start kindergarten in the fall. She's excited about going to school."

"How many children do you have?" This question came from Heidi.

"I've been blessed with two—Conner, who's three, and Abby, who recently turned five. Do you have children, Heidi?"

Heidi's shoulders drooped a bit as she slowly shook her head. "The Lord has not seen fit to bless my husband and me with children, but we find plenty to do here to fill our days." She glanced toward the hall door.

"I'd better check on Kendra. Loretta, if the timer goes off, will you please take the baking dish out of the oven?"

"Certainly."

After Heidi left the room, Loretta's attention turned to Eli. Even though he smiled occasionally, she detected a sense of gloom in his brown eyes—the same look of sadness she felt whenever she thought about her deceased husband. It was hard to hide one's pain when it felt so raw. Loretta did her best to keep a cheerful attitude—especially around her children. When she was alone in her room at night, however, she let her guard down. During those times, Loretta gave into her grief and allowed the tears to flow. Weeping was part of the healing process, just as her acceptance of what could not be changed. When some people lost a loved one, they became bitter and angry at God, but Loretta's faith remained strong through it all. Instead of turning against God during her time of grief, she leaned heavily upon Him for strength and guidance.

The timer dinged. Since Heidi wasn't back yet, Loretta opened the oven door, took out the baking dish, and placed a pot holder under it on the counter. She inhaled deeply as the delicious aroma flooded her senses. Apparently, it had affected the others too for they all lifted their heads and sniffed the air.

"The casserole smells like somethin' my wife used to make." Eli looked longingly at the dish.

"Used to make? Doesn't she make it for you anymore?" Ron asked.

Eli lowered his gaze. "Mavis died a year ago. She was hit by a vehicle while riding her bicycle."

"I'm sorry for your loss." Charlene's quiet tone was sincere.

"Life ain't fair," Ron muttered. "In fact, if you ask

me, most of the time it stinks."

"I lost my husband a year ago too. It's been hard for me and the children, but I won't allow bitterness or despair to set in." Loretta returned to the table, and as she spoke, she looked at Ron. "Life isn't always fair, but we all have much to be thankful for, even if it's something little. So it's best to focus on the positive."

Kendra's legs trembled as she stood at the sink and rinsed her mouth with a paper cup she'd found on the vanity. She hated making a spectacle of herself and dreaded going back to the kitchen where she'd have to face those people. Did they suspect she was pregnant? How much longer could she keep it hidden? The tops Kendra liked to wear when she wasn't pregnant would soon be unable to hide the baby bump, revealing her condition.

Kendra thought about her parents and how they'd asked her not to tell anyone about her predicament. Of course, it wasn't for her sake they didn't want the word to get out. Dad's only concern seemed to be about how he would look to the people at church if they found out one of their board members had a daughter who'd really messed up. He was so self-righteous.

It doesn't matter what anyone thinks, she told herself. *Since I'm not attending church anymore, I don't have to face those people.* Kendra pulled her shoulders back. *I don't know the people who are here taking Heidi's class, and until today, they weren't acquainted with me. So it shouldn't matter whether I tell them or not. Some might look down their noses at me, but maybe a few won't think I'm a bad person. After all, everyone's made a few mistakes at some time in their life.*

Tap. Tap. Tap. "Are you all right, Kendra? Is there

anything I can do for you?"

"No, I'm okay. I'll be out in a few minutes." Kendra appreciated the Amish woman's concern, but she wasn't about to let Heidi come into the bathroom and see her looking like this.

After splashing cold water on her face and pushing damp hair behind her ears, Kendra drew a deep breath and opened the door. It surprised her to see Heidi standing in the hallway. She figured the teacher would have returned to the kitchen.

"Your face is awfully pale, and you appear to be shaken." Heidi gently touched Kendra's arm. "I'm concerned about you."

"No need to worry. I feel better since I emptied my stomach."

"Maybe it would be best if you went home and rested. I can send some of the breakfast casserole with you to eat when you're feeling better."

Kendra shook her head. "No, I'm okay. I'm sure I can make it through the rest of the class without getting sick again. In fact, my stomach is growling from smelling your casserole. Oh, and I also brought some mint tea and saltine crackers. They usually help settle my stomach."

Without a word of argument, Heidi slipped her arm around Kendra's waist and walked with her back to the kitchen. The comforting gesture brought tears to Kendra's eyes, and she blinked to keep them from falling onto her cheeks. Now was not the time to give in to her up-and-down emotions.

Still shaken and drained, Kendra took a seat at the table. "Sorry for the interruption. My stomach started doing flip-flops all of a sudden."

"Maybe you've come down with the flu," Ron

suggested. "It might be better if you went home so none of us gets exposed to it any more than we've already been."

"I've had the bug many times over the course of my twenty-two years, and it's not what's troubling me." Kendra's jaw clenched. "Believe me. What I have is not the flu."

"What do you have?" Charlene asked.

Kendra placed both hands on her stomach. "I'm expecting a baby, and for the last several weeks, I've been dealing with morning sickness."

Eli looked at Kendra, remembering his wife's pregnancies a few years back. Those started out as happy days, when all seemed perfect and right. The first time Mavis got pregnant, she had no morning sickness. The second time was quite the opposite. Almost from the start, when she suspected she was in a family way, nausea hit the poor thing every morning and sometimes lasted throughout the day. Mavis never complained about feeling sick. She'd put on a brave face and say, "This is the best kind of sickness. It means my pregnancy is normal."

She loved every minute of being pregnant—until the first miscarriage. What a disappointment for both of them. They'd thought the second pregnancy was going well, until the unexpected happened.

Eli flinched, remembering the day as if it had just occurred. Mavis had been doing laundry. She'd made several trips up and down the basement stairs and then trudging outside to the clothesline. Eli had been cultivating an area in the backyard for a new flower bed his wife wanted. Leaning on his shovel, he'd stopped to watch Mavis come out with another load of clothes to hang. Her smile seemed like a permanent part of her face as she hummed a pleasant tune. It made Eli smile too.

Since it was close to noon, Mavis suggested they have lunch on the porch. "You keep working on the flower bed, and I'll bring some sandwiches out." Whenever the weather cooperated, Eli and Mavis often took the opportunity to eat lunch on the porch. Sometimes they'd have a picnic under one of their lofty maple trees.

Eli had worked diligently, his appetite increasing, while he looked forward to taking a break with his wife. Time passed as he got the ground ready, and soon he began to wonder what was taking Mavis so long to make those sandwiches. Even now, chills ran up his spine as he thought about the soft whimpers he'd heard that day when he'd set the shovel down and gone into the house.

His heart thumped when he entered the kitchen and found his wife lying on the floor. He ran to Mavis, cradling her body, while she kept repeating, "It happened again, Eli. We've lost another *boppli*."

Eli forced his thoughts back to the present. *I hope Kendra's pregnancy goes well for her.*

Loretta glanced at Kendra's left hand but saw no sign of a wedding ring. *Perhaps she's an unwed mother-to-be. Of course, it's possible Kendra is married and either doesn't have a ring or isn't wearing it today. Either way, it is not my place to judge, and I certainly won't ask the poor girl about her marital status.*

"I can't speak from experience, but it's my understanding that morning sickness goes away after the first few months," Charlene interjected.

Loretta nodded. "She's right, but then everyone is different. I felt queasy all the way to my sixth month when I was expecting Abby. But with Conner I hardly had any morning sickness at all."

Kendra gave a brief shrug before placing her elbows on the table.

Loretta motioned to the baking dish on the counter. "The timer went off while you were out of the room, Heidi, so I removed the casserole from the oven."

Heidi smiled. "I appreciate it. By the time we get our fruit cut up, the breakfast casserole should be cool enough to eat."

"Then let's get to it!" Ron clapped his hands so loud Loretta nearly jumped out of her chair. "I'm starvin', and the smell of that country breakfast is about to drive me crazy."

By the time the casserole cooled sufficiently, Heidi's students had finished cutting the fruit. Loretta and Charlene had peeled a few apples and cut them into bite-size pieces. Kendra sliced bananas while Ron and Eli peeled some tangerines and separated them into sections. Heidi expected Ron to eat a piece, but to her surprise, he put them all in the bowl she'd provided.

Once vanilla yogurt had been mixed in, Heidi took the bowl to the dining room and set it on the table. Since they'd used the kitchen table for putting the meal together, it would be nice if they ate in the other room, where she'd previously set the table.

When Heidi returned to the kitchen for the casserole, she invited everyone to take seats at the dining room table.

"Is there anything I can do to help?" Loretta stepped up to Heidi.

"There's a pitcher of water in the refrigerator. You can take it to the dining room and pour some in everyone's glass."

Loretta did as Heidi asked then joined the others at the table.

"This is a simple yet tasty breakfast meal." Heidi gestured to the baking dish. "The best thing about it is it can be made the night before and then popped in the oven the following morning."

Ron smacked his lips noisily. "I can hardly wait to dig in."

"We Amish always offer a silent prayer before our meals," Heidi mentioned. "I hope each of you will thank God with me for the food we are about to eat."

Ron's brows drew inward. "I'm not much of a prayin' man, but out of respect for you, I'll bow my head."

Heidi understood some of her students might not be Christians, but she saw no reason not to pray like always. And since no one had offered an objection, she bowed her head and closed her eyes. *Heavenly Father, thank You for the opportunity to share with these people some of my Amish recipes. After the short time of being with Ron, Eli, Loretta, Charlene, and Kendra today, I have come to realize You may have led them all to my home for more than cooking lessons. As You did for my aunt Emma, please give me the wisdom I need to conduct the next five classes.*

Chapter 9

Sugarcreek

Loretta smiled as she watched her children playing in the yard. Soon after she'd returned from the cooking class, she'd come outside to till the soil in her garden and do some planting. Seeing Heidi's garden plot had given Loretta the incentive to get a few of her vegetables seeds started. Being in the house all winter made her long to be outside in the warm sunshine. Spring brought forth a healing strength, rejuvenating deep within her soul. God had a way of helping a person mourn their loss, and Loretta found nature and the welcoming of the new season part of that process.

While she planted a row of peas, Abby and Conner played happily nearby. They enjoyed being outside and were full of energy. Her children got along well, although at times Abby could be a bit bossy. For now, at least, her little brother went along with whatever she wanted to do. No doubt there would come a time when Conner would want to be in charge and become his own person.

Humming as she went down the first row, dropping peas into the freshly cultivated soil, Loretta thought about how things had gone during the class today. Heidi had been so kind. Even when things got a little out of hand, she'd been patient. Heidi explained things well too, always demonstrating before asking the students to do what she asked. *What a shame she has no children. I'll bet she'd make a good mother.*

Loretta glanced at her kids again. *I can't imagine my life without them.* She'd thought it so many times before, but it was the truth.

She could hardly wait to go back to Walnut Creek for another class in two weeks. The breakfast casserole they'd eaten before heading home turned out delicious and had been quite easy to prepare. Loretta planned to fix it for breakfast soon, and hoped the children would enjoy it too. She figured whatever they made at the next cooking class would also be a treat. Loretta also wondered if Heidi would give them another recipe card with scripture on the back, as she had today. It was a good idea, as everyone needed God's Word to guide and direct them through life. Loretta especially appreciated the reminder to be still and focus on God. As busy as she kept these days, she didn't feel complete until she opened her Bible and spent time alone with God.

Loretta's thoughts went to the people she'd met today. Despite coming from different walks of life, Heidi's students had one thing in common—they all wanted to learn how to make some traditional Amish dishes. Of course, for some it went beyond that. Charlene, Eli, and maybe even Ron needed to learn the basics of cooking. Loretta hoped that, as they took five more classes together, she would get to know the others more personally. After only one lesson, they felt like strangers to her. *Of course,* she mused, *they might not want to talk about their personal lives.*

Loretta wasn't sure how much of her life she'd be willing to share either. It was much easier to open up to people she knew well than discuss personal matters with strangers.

Spending time at Heidi's house had made Loretta feel a bit connected with the Amish way of life. This was another reason she looked forward to going again. She hoped to learn more simple ways to incorporate in her life, as well as the children's.

"Mommy, come quick! There's a snake over here!" Abby's shrill voice drove Loretta's thoughts aside.

Jamming the seed packet into her pocket, she hurried over to where her daughter stood pointing. While Loretta had no fondness for snakes, for the sake of her children, she was determined to put on a brave front. *Sure hope it's not a big one though.*

"Look, Mommy. . .it's right over there." Abby moved close to Loretta and stood clutching her hand as she continued to point a shaky finger.

Conner, who'd been playing with his truck in a pile of dirt several feet away, joined them. "I wanna see the snake!" Hopping on one foot and then the other, he spoke with the excitement of a three-year-old.

When Loretta spotted the creature, she sighed with relief. "That's not a snake, sweetie. It's a salamander. Come, take a look." Leaning down, she put her arms around both of the children and urged them forward. "See, it has little legs, and there's a red stripe down the middle of its back."

Eyes wide, the children bobbed their heads. Abby got brave and moved a little closer.

"Salamanders live in damp areas, such as under leaves and rocks," Loretta explained.

"Can I pet it, Mommy?" Conner's eyes widened.

"Oh, I don't think it would hold still for that. If we get too close the salamander will most likely scurry under a rock."

"Can we put the critter in something and bring it

in the house?" Abby squatted down and reached out to touch the tiny amphibian. "It's cute. We could name him Oscar. He could be our pet."

Although Loretta felt no connection to the salamander, she understood the way her daughter felt. When she was Abby's age and discovered the wonders of nature, she often brought things home. Now she'd have to tell her children the same thing her father told her when she was a girl. In fact, Loretta could still hear his words echoing in her ears. "As nice as it would be to take care of this salamander, he belongs here in his natural environment," she told the children.

Abby's lower lip protruded. A few minutes ago she'd been afraid of the creature, and now she wanted to make it a pet.

"Our yard is his home, and I'm sure you will see him again. When you do, be sure to sit quietly so you don't scare him."

Abby seemed satisfied with Loretta's explanation. Conner was content, appearing almost spellbound as he studied the salamander. Loretta stayed with the children, observing the creature until it finally crawled off.

Conner clapped his hands. "That was fun!" He turned and scampered back to the dirt pile and his toy truck.

Abby reached up and took Loretta's hand. "Can I help ya put seeds in the ground?"

"Of course you may." Loretta squeezed her daughter's fingers tenderly, then handed her the packet of seeds. It pleased her to see how the children found pleasure in simple things. She hoped, with her guidance and love of nature, Abby and Conner would grow up to appreciate everything God created.

Mt. Hope

"How'd things go at the cooking class?" Dorie asked when Kendra entered her friend's cramped living room. "Did you have a good time?"

"The Amish teacher's nice, and we made a tasty breakfast casserole, but I really messed up." Kendra flopped onto the couch with a groan.

"How so?" Dorie took a seat in the chair across from her.

"I got sick to my stomach and barely made it to the bathroom before I threw up." Kendra frowned deeply. "It was embarrassing, but that's not the worst of it."

"What do you mean?"

"I blurted out in front of everyone that I'm pregnant."

Dorie's eyes opened wide. "What made you tell them?"

Kendra shrugged. "Figured I may as well admit it so they didn't think I exposed them to the flu. Plus, after my parents' negative reaction to the pregnancy, guess I was hoping for a positive response from at least one of Heidi's students."

"What did they say?"

"Not much. The one lady—Loretta—mentioned how she'd felt during her pregnancy. No one even asked if I was married, or when the baby's due. If they had learned I'm not married, they might have been condemning like Mom and Dad were." Kendra massaged the back of her neck, hoping to release some of her tensions. "Sure hope when I go back in two weeks, I don't get sick again."

Dorie left her seat and stood behind the couch to take over massaging Kendra's neck. "If you do throw up again, at least no one will be concerned about getting the flu. Hope your teacher didn't have a smelly out-house." She coughed several times, as though gagging.

"I didn't see one, and they did have indoor plumbing. In fact, except for the lack of electric lights, Heidi's bathroom didn't look much different from yours or any other bathroom I've been in."

"Really? I figured the bathroom in an Amish home would look pretty plain."

"Well, I didn't see pictures on the wall there or in any other part of the house I was in. But some pretty towels hung in the bathroom, in addition to scented hand soap and hand lotion on the vanity."

"Interesting. So getting back to the people you met . . . Maybe they didn't know how to react when you told them you were expecting a baby. You don't have a ring on your finger, and my guess is they weren't going to pry with a bunch of nosy questions."

"Yeah, I guess." Kendra closed her eyes, letting Dorie's magic fingers relax her muscles. "Once I get better acquainted with everyone, I'm hoping I'll feel more comfortable. I'd especially like to know Heidi. She seems nice. Sure wish my mom was more like her." Kendra sighed and quickly changed the subject. "Thanks again for letting me use your car today."

"No problem. I wasn't going anywhere."

Kendra's cell phone rang. She pulled it out of her pocket and swept a hand across her forehead. "It's Shelly. I wonder what she wants."

"Why don't you answer and find out?"

"Most likely Mom told her the reason they kicked me out. She's probably calling to say how disappointed she is in her big sister and wishes I'd been a better example for her and Chris. As Dad likes to point out, 'they're still impressionable teenagers.'" Kendra shook her head. "I can't deal with it right now. Shelly can leave a message if she wants to."

Dorie took a seat on the couch beside Kendra. "This isn't the first time your sister has called. You should be honest with her." She clasped Kendra's chin, turning her head so she was looking directly at her. "Shelly's reaction might surprise you. How long will you keep avoiding her?"

"I'll return her call eventually, but not today." Kendra stood, arching her back. "I'm tired. Think I'll go take a nap." She grabbed her cell phone and hurried from the room. She appreciated her friend's concern but didn't like being told what to do.

Walnut Creek

"How'd things go with your first cooking class?" Lyle asked, entering the kitchen where Heidi sat at the table making a list of things she wanted to cover at the next class.

She looked up at him and sighed. "The cooking part went well enough with the students, but I think I may have underestimated my job as their teacher."

Lyle pulled out a chair and sat down. "What do you mean?"

"Two of the students, Eli and Charlene, can't cook at all, so I had to go over some of the basics before we started making the breakfast casserole."

"It's understandable. For some folks, cooking doesn't come easy like it does for you."

"I didn't have a problem with sharing some of the fundamentals, but I wasn't expecting a few of the people who came here to share their troubles." Heidi went on to tell Lyle about Kendra's pregnancy. "Then there's Eli, who obviously still misses Mavis, and right before she left today, Loretta mentioned being a widow."

"Do you want my opinion, Heidi?"

She nodded slowly.

Lyle placed his hand on her arm. "In addition to showing your students how to make some special Amish dishes, I believe you could end up helping them deal with whatever problems they have."

"I've been thinking the same thing, since that's how things turned out with Aunt Emma and some of her quilting students." She pulled in a breath and released it slowly. "I only hope I'm up to the task."

"If you ask God to help, He will give you the wisdom to say the right things and know when to say them."

Heidi patted Lyle's knee. "You're right of course." She appreciated her husband's insight and would try to take his advice.

"Something else interesting happened this morning, shortly after my students and I came to the kitchen."

"What was it?"

"Ron showed up and is now officially taking my class."

Lyle's mouth opened slightly. "I'm surprised he'd be interested in a cooking class, and even more surprised you agreed to teach him."

"Why wouldn't I?"

"Since you expressed concern about Ron parking his motor home in our yard, I wouldn't think you'd be open to him coming into our home and joining your other students."

"I couldn't very well say no—especially since Eli seemed to want Ron in the class."

Lyle leaned slightly forward. "How exactly did this all come about?"

Heidi explained how Ron had come to the door asking for coffee, and then Eli had assumed Ron was part of the class. "One thing led to another, and the next thing I knew, Ron was a new class member. It all happened so fast."

"But your classes will go through the end of June. Does Ron plan to stick around our place that long?"

Heidi lifted her hands, turning them upward. "I never got the chance to ask."

Lyle rose from his chair. "I'd better get this straightened out right now and see what he has to say about it. By the way, I brought sub sandwiches home for our supper. Got one for Ron too."

"Oh good. It will be nice not to have to cook tonight. We'll have the leftover coleslaw from the other day along with the sandwiches."

"Great." Lyle grinned.

Heidi watched as her husband went out the door. *I hope Ron doesn't take it wrong when Lyle questions him. I felt like I got to know Ron a little better during class, but I still feel uncomfortable around him. Sure hope he can be trusted and that I won't regret letting him take the class.*

Chapter 10

Ron opened his closet door and peered in. With the exception of his few items of clothes, nothing else occupied the space. Of course, he'd recently emptied it after visiting a pawnshop the week before he'd shown up at Heidi and Lyle's place. The closet was useful and could hold a good deal of things. He hoped within the next few weeks he'd have it filled again. First things first though. He needed to figure out a way to get inside the Troyers' when no one was home.

Ron considered flaking out on his bunk for a short nap, but before he could head in that direction, someone rapped on his side door. Yawning, he opened it and was surprised to see Lyle, holding a plastic sack. "Didn't know you were back from the auction." Ron stepped out and shut the door behind him. "Never heard a vehicle pull in."

"I asked my driver to drop me off out front by the mailbox so I could check for mail." Lyle shuffled his feet, kicking a small stone with the toe of his boot. "Is it all right if I come inside? There's something I want to talk to you about."

"No problem. I've been wantin' to talk to you too." It was a good time to let Lyle inside the RV. Aside from being a little messy, nothing looked out of the ordinary.

Lyle stepped inside, and Ron swung the driver and passenger seats around so they could sit comfortably. "Should I start, or do you want to go first?" he asked after they'd both taken seats.

"Guess I'll say what's on my mind." Lyle cleared his throat. "Heidi mentioned you took part in her cooking class today."

Ron gave a nod. "I enjoyed it too and hope I'll get the chance to be part of the next five classes."

Lyle gave his earlobe a tug. "I see. Well. . ."

"So I was wonderin' if you would mind if I kept my rig parked on your property a few more weeks."

Lyle worked his fingers through his thick, full beard, while looking steadily at Ron, as though sizing him up. Letting his hand fall in his lap, he spoke. "Did you come here thinking you would stay indefinitely?"

"Course not. I needed a place to park my motor home until I could get it running smoothly again." Ron shook his head. "Never expected to get involved in a cooking class, but now that I have, if it's okay with you, I'd like to see it through."

"If I'm hearing you right, you want to stay here through the end of June?"

"Yeah, but I'm willing to do some chores in exchange for letting me stay. Could we work something out?"

Lyle sat several seconds then slowly nodded. "I'll make a list of several things needing to be done and give it to you in the morning."

"Thanks for the opportunity." Ron held out his hand, as if to seal the deal. After shaking Lyle's hand, Ron thought of something else. "Say, I was wondering . . . . Do you think your wife would mind if I use her clothesline to dry some of my things?"

"That shouldn't be a problem. Do you have a way to wash your clothes?"

Ron scrubbed his hand down the side of his face. "Unless I'm close to a laundromat and have money to spare, I usually wash 'em there." He pointed to his small kitchen sink. "Wouldn't expect Heidi to wash my clothes. Nope, that'd be asking too much."

"Umm. . .we'll see how it goes." Lyle lifted the plastic bag he'd brought in with him. "Before I forget, I picked up some submarine sandwiches on my way home and got one for you. Hope you like turkey with cheddar cheese."

"Much obliged. Truth is, I can eat most anything, but I've always had a fondness for hoagies." Ron took the plastic bag. "At least that's what I've always called 'em."

Lyle remained in the chair a few more seconds then stood and moved toward the side door. "See you tomorrow, Ron. Have a good night."

"Yeah, same to you."

As soon as Lyle left, Ron took a seat at his table and dug into the sandwich. It would be too risky for him to get close to these people, even though they were kind and hospitable. He couldn't afford to let any sentimental emotions take over, or he might leave here with nothing but a few pleasant memories. While pleasant memories were nice, what Ron really needed was money.

Saturday evening, as Eli ate a bologna and cheese sandwich for supper, he reflected on his day. The cooking class had been interesting, and he'd felt relief when another man showed up. Being the only Amish person in the class, though, he didn't fit in with the rest of them. Of course Heidi was there, and even though she was Amish, she was also the teacher, not to mention an expert cook.

"Maybe I'll never be able to cook a halfway decent

meal," Eli muttered. "Might be eatin' sandwiches and hard-boiled eggs the rest of my life."

He thought about the three English women in Heidi's class. Two of them, Kendra and Charlene, wore makeup and dressed in what he saw as clothes made for a man. Loretta, however, wore a long skirt with a cotton blouse. From what he could tell, she had no makeup on her face either. If her hair had been pulled back in a bun, and she'd worn a Plain dress, she would have almost looked Amish.

Eli's musings scattered when he heard scratching on the door. "Okay, Lady, I hear ya." He rose from his chair, opened the back door, and let the black lab out.

Returning to the table to finish the rest of his sandwich, Eli's thoughts were redirected to Heidi's cooking class. *I wonder what her other students would've thought if I'd told 'em I make caskets for a living.*

Eli's profession, which he'd learned from his grandfather, wasn't something he normally talked about with English people. Everyone in his Amish community knew what he did for a living, but he had a hunch the women in class, and maybe even Ron, would think making caskets was a creepy kind of job. Well, it might be disturbing, but when someone died, their family needed to purchase a coffin, and his were made according to Amish custom. Nothing fancy, just a simple pine box. What Eli never expected was the one he'd worked on only a few weeks before his wife's death would end up having Mavis buried in it.

Eli drank the last bit of milk in his glass and took the dishes to the sink to wash. *Mavis never minded doing dishes.* He filled the sink with detergent and warm water then reached for a sponge. He didn't hate doing dishes, but it wasn't his favorite chore either. Of course he didn't enjoy doing any of the inside chores his wife used to do. *Mavis isn't coming back,* Eli reminded himself. *And unless God directs me otherwise, I'll never get married again. So I may as well do the inside chores without complaining.*

Canton, Ohio

Bridget Perkins had no more than entered the kitchen to begin making supper than her middle daughter, Shelly, stepped into the room. "I called Kendra again today, but I only got her voice mail." Tilting her head to one side, Shelly pursed her lips. "I don't understand why Kendra doesn't return my calls. Doesn't she realize I'm worried about her?"

Bridget moaned. "I don't believe your sister cares about anyone but herself."

Shelly pushed her shoulder-length auburn hair behind her ears. Her resemblance to Kendra was uncanny. If Shelly's hair were shorter, they could have almost passed as twins.

Leaning against the counter, Shelly folded her arms. "Something's going on, Mom, and I have a right to know what it is. Don't you agree? After all, I'm part of this family too and I'm not a kid. I'm eighteen years old."

"There's nothing going on you need to know about." Bridget reached for a potato to peel.

"It doesn't make sense for Kendra to move out and not tell us where she's living." Shelly moved closer to the sink. "Did you and she have a disagreement about her boyfriend? Is that the reason she moved out?"

"Your sister left this house because we asked her to. End of story."

Bridget turned at the sound of her husband's deep

voice. "Gary, I didn't realize you'd come home. You mentioned this morning you'd be working late this evening."

"I changed my mind." He looked at Shelly and narrowed his eyes. "You are not to have anything to do with your sister! No more phone calls or text messages. Do you understand?"

Shelly blinked. "How come? Has Kendra done something wrong?"

"She's pregnant." His voice lowered to a more reasonable pitch. "And you're not to tell anyone about this situation. Understand?"

Shelly's mouth formed an O. "What are we supposed to say when people at church ask where Kendra is?"

"We'll tell them the truth. She moved out, and we don't know where she is." His nostrils flared like a bull ready to charge. "I will not bring shame on our family because your sister couldn't keep her emotions in check. She messed up and needs to pay for her mistake."

Bridget pressed her lips tightly together. She didn't agree with the way Gary chose to shut Kendra out of their lives, but she wouldn't usurp his authority.

———◦◦◦———

Dover

It was five o'clock, and Charlene and her fiancé, Len, were on their way to dinner. When Len said he wanted to take Charlene someplace special, she'd suggested a four-star restaurant in Millersburg. Chinese food was one of Charlene's favorites, and she'd been to this place last year with her friend Kathy. It was about an hour's drive through some pretty country, plus it would give them more time to talk privately.

"You're beautiful." Len reached across the seat of his

Suburban and clasped her hand, bringing it to his lips. "You look great in that lavender dress."

"Thanks." Charlene squeezed his warm fingers. She'd taken extra care getting ready for her date with Len. *Could this be the time we'll set our wedding date?*

Charlene had been blessed with thick, shiny hair. Since it was long and hung past her shoulders, she could wear it in several styles. Tonight, she'd worn it down and had used a special brush to add body and soft, bouncy curls. She'd pulled one side up and secured it with a sparkly barrette. Charlene wore dangly, bronze-colored earrings with tiny jewels, blending well with her simple but stylish dress. She'd brought along a cute little shrug to ward off the chilly night air. The April days were getting warmer, but evenings could still be cold, reminding her it was only the beginning of spring.

"Len, your car still smells new inside." Charlene ran her hand over the smooth leather seat. "You keep it so nice, and it looks brand-new."

"Yeah, it's hard to believe I've had it almost a year already." Len patted the steering wheel. "I hope to have this baby a long time."

"How'd your day go?" Charlene asked.

"It went well. The clients I saw were impressed with the solar panels and ended up placing an order for their new home."

Len was a sales representative and worked for his father, who owned an energy company. Solar panels were becoming more popular, especially with the farming communities.

"I'm glad to hear it. You don't normally work on Saturdays." Charlene looked at her handsome fiancé, thinking, *How did I get so lucky to land a guy like him?* Len was incredibly good looking, with dark, wavy hair and dreamy chocolate-brown eyes. There was a certain ruggedness about him. At times she couldn't help thinking what a handsome cowboy he'd make.

"The people I met with today own a huge dairy farm and want to go totally solar," Len explained. "They have quite an operation going at their place, and today was the best time they could see me. So tonight we are celebrating my closing of a pretty big deal."

Charlene felt a bit disappointed but managed to keep her composure and remain in a happy frame of mind. This was something important for Len, and she was glad for him, but she had hoped he might be ready to set a wedding date. *Now that would be something to celebrate.*

"Sure hope you like the restaurant I chose." She reached across the seat and gave his arm an affectionate pat. "I've been there once with a friend, and what we had to eat was exceptionally good."

"I'm so hungry I don't know what I'll end up getting, but with Chinese food, we could order several dishes to share, and probably have leftovers to take home."

As they drove east on Route 39 toward Millersburg, Charlene stared out the window. The farmland and countryside were beautiful, as it had been in Walnut Creek when she'd gone to the cooking class earlier today. She had planned to tell Len all about it but changed her mind, wanting in the weeks ahead to surprise him instead.

"How was your day?" Len glanced Charlene's way.

"It went well. I've been thinking of a project I want to do for my kindergarten class before the school term lets out."

"What kind of project?"

"I'd like to take a group photo of our class and then take individual photos of each of my students." Charlene's excitement mounted, thinking about it.

"The pictures will be gifts for the children, as well as their parents. It will give them something to remember me by."

"Sounds like a nice idea." Len gestured to Charlene's camera bag. "I see you brought your camera along this evening."

"You know me—I try not to go too many places without it. I missed taking some photos of geese when Kathy and I went to lunch in Dover recently."

"Well, maybe you can take a picture of our food at the restaurant." Len chuckled.

"You're such a tease." Charlene giggled, then her eyes widened as they passed a field where a few horses grazed. "Len, quick, turn around. I saw a horse lying down, and I'm sure it's giving birth. If it is, I'd love to get a few pictures. Can we go back, please?"

"Okay, but we can't be too long, 'cause we don't want to eat a late meal. I'll pull in to this road up ahead, and then we'll turn around and go back to where you saw the horse." Traffic was light, and Len had no problem turning around. No one was behind them, and he drove slowly.

"There! It's right there!" Charlene pointed as she got out her camera and made sure the setting was correct.

Len maneuvered over to the lane they'd previously been in then pulled his vehicle onto the shoulder of the road and turned off the engine. They both got out and stood by the fence rails. Fortunately, the horse she'd seen lying down wasn't far from the fence, or Charlene might never have seen it.

What an amazing sight to watch this event occur. She and Len had gotten there in the nick of time. The owners of the horse, a middle-aged man and woman, must have known their mare was about to foal, for they arrived in a utility vehicle shortly afterward.

Out of respect, Charlene asked, "Is it okay if I take a few pictures?"

"Sure, go ahead." The lady smiled then turned around to help the man, who Charlene assumed was her husband.

The mare was a beautiful chestnut brown with a black mane and tail. Charlene was in awe.

"Can you believe we're seeing this?" Len poked Charlene's arm. He seemed as thrilled as she was.

She held her camera steady, snapping a sequence of pictures. Some feet appeared; then a nose; and soon after, the colt's head emerged. The man helped by pulling the shoulders and hips out, followed by the back legs. As Charlene took more photos then paused to watch the process, she was amazed at how efficient these people were in helping with the foal's delivery. While the woman wiped the small horse off and cleaned out its nostrils, the man commented that they needed to wait and make sure the foal was able to stand okay. All seemed normal when the mare turned around and started licking her baby.

Tears sprang to Charlene's eyes as she watched the foal try to stand on wobbly legs then stumble and fall. The colt was precious, and a replica of its mother, with a dark mane and tail and chestnut-colored body.

Shortly after, the woman walked over to the fence to join them. "My name's Kitty Albright, and that's my husband, Ward, over there. Is this the first time you've seen a foal being born?"

"Yes," Charlene murmured, almost reverently. "I couldn't believe it when we drove by, and I'm so glad I had my camera with me. Thanks for allowing me to take the pictures. I'll make sure you get some copies, if you like."

"Thanks anyway, but this is sort of 'old hat' to us." Kitty grinned. "I'm glad you got to witness what I like to call a miracle. Here on our farm we see plenty of miracles."

"I can imagine." Charlene took more photos when the colt managed to stand and started to nurse shortly thereafter.

"Guess we'd better get going," Len suggested, leaning close to Charlene.

"Oh, okay." She looked back one last time and noticed that behind this amazing scene, a beautiful sunset had formed. *I have to get this shot.* As she snapped one last picture of the adorable colt, a loud crash occurred.

"Oh no!" Holding his hands against his cheeks, Len groaned. "Someone just hit my car!"

Chapter 11

Walnut Creek

"My, my. . .where does the time go?" Heidi shook her head, staring at the calendar. It was Monday already, and not much time to spare before her friends arrived to help plant the garden. "I am so *narrisch*."

"Foolish about what?" Lyle stepped behind Heidi, resting his chin on her shoulder.

"During my cooking class on Saturday, I mentioned two of my friends would be coming over today to help with my garden." Heidi massaged her forehead. "Goodness, I've had so much on my mind lately, I almost forgot. I'd better take out the breakfast casserole and get it heated before Sharon and Ada arrive." She glanced at the clock. "Oh dear, I don't have much time."

He kissed the side of her neck. "Slow down and try to relax. Seems like you're always rushing about."

Heidi couldn't argue the point, but keeping busy helped keep her mind occupied, especially during times of self-doubt.

As she took the casserole dish from the refrigerator and placed it in the oven, Heidi reflected on how her inability to give Lyle a child had created self-doubts. The doctor had explained that some women with an ovulation problem like hers eventually became pregnant.

Heidi apparently wasn't one of those fortunate people. She'd suggested they adopt, but Lyle felt differently, and his answer never changed: *"If God wants us to have kinner, it will happen in His time."*

Heidi kept quiet and accepted her husband's decision. But it was hard seeing others enjoying their children. Ever since she was a young girl, Heidi had looked forward to becoming a mother someday.

Refusing to dwell on this, lest she fall prey to depression, Heidi took the coffeepot from the stove, filled Lyle's thermos, and handed it to him. "How long will you be gone today?"

"Besides running a few errands this morning, I need to be in Farmerstown at noon. The auction is supposed to be over by four, so I'll be home by suppertime." He gave her a hug. "Enjoy your visit with Sharon and Ada, but don't work too hard in the garden, okay? Looks like it'll be a warm day."

"I'll be fine." Heidi smiled. "Enjoying time with my two best friends is almost a guarantee, but I won't promise not to work hard. You know how I get when I'm busy with something."

Lyle tweaked the end of Heidi's nose, gave her a kiss, and headed out the door. "Don't fix a big meal tonight," he called over his shoulder. "How about sandwiches?"

"All right." Once more, she appreciated her husband's thoughtfulness.

Heidi leaned her forehead against the kitchen window and watched as Lyle patted Rusty's head before getting into his driver's van. The dog barked in protest and sat in the middle of the driveway, watching as the van drove toward the road.

Lord, please be with my husband today, she silently prayed. *Keep Lyle safe, and help things go well at the auction.*

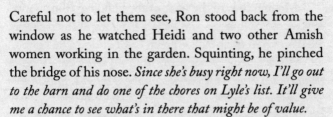

Careful not to let them see, Ron stood back from the window as he watched Heidi and two other Amish women working in the garden. Squinting, he pinched the bridge of his nose. *Since she's busy right now, I'll go out to the barn and do one of the chores on Lyle's list. It'll give me a chance to see what's in there that might be of value.*

Slapping his baseball cap on his head, Ron opened the door and stepped out of the RV.

Heidi looked up from her kneeling position and waved. He waved back and hurried toward the barn. The last thing he wanted was to engage in a conversation with three women chattering in a language he didn't understand as they planted seeds.

Wonder what they're saying. For all I know, they're talking about me.

When Ron entered the barn, he grabbed a shovel to muck out two empty stalls. Lyle had explained the other day that one of the horses pulled his buggy and the other belonged to Heidi. Both animals grazed in the pasture now, where Lyle had put them this morning before his driver arrived. Ron assumed that Lyle might be at an auction someplace in the area. Auctions fascinated him— especially how fast auctioneers could talk. If he didn't forget, he planned to ask Lyle how he'd gotten into such an interesting line of work. In any case, if it was like before, Lyle wouldn't arrive home for a good many hours.

After Ron finished cleaning the first stall, he took a break to look around the barn. Several old milk cans stood against one wall, but those were too big to fit in the closet where he kept his stash. He'd look for some smaller items he could hide in his RV, and hopefully Heidi or Lyle wouldn't notice some things were missing—at least not till he was long gone.

Moving toward the back of the building, Ron spotted several old canning jars on a shelf. Looking at them closely, he discovered their bluish-green color and several bubbles in the glass. *These should easily fit in my closet, but I'd better wait till the Troyers are in bed some night before I sneak in here and get them. Sure hope I won't get caught in the act.*

Ron reflected on a time, a few years back, when a feisty old farmer in Kentucky threatened to shoot him if he didn't put back the old milk cans he'd taken. With his rifle pointed right at Ron, the man ordered him off his land, saying if he saw him again, he'd shoot first and ask questions later.

"Coulda used a guy like him at my side when I was fightin' the war in Vietnam," Ron muttered.

"I appreciate you both coming to help me today," Heidi told her friends as they sat on the back porch, taking a break. "Now that I'm teaching cooking classes, I'll be spending more time in the kitchen planning menus and making a list of things I'll need to cover during the next five classes."

Sharon leaned forward, one hand on her knee. "We're happy to help with your garden."

Ada nodded. "Once things start growing, if you need help weeding, please let us know."

"What about your own gardens? I'm sure you'll be plenty busy with those."

"Our *kinner* will help." Sharon drank some of the iced tea Heidi had made earlier. "My two oldest will soon be out of school for the summer, so they'll keep busy helping me in the garden, among other things needing to be done."

The mention of children caused Heidi's body to tense. Thankfully, Ada changed the subject and asked how the first cooking class went.

"Quite well. Five students attended, and they all seemed interested in learning to make some traditional Amish dishes." Heidi chose not to mention anything about her students' personal lives. She'd only just met them and, from the little she'd learned, felt it best to keep quiet about any personal problems her students had rather than turn it into something akin to gossip.

"Who's watching your youngest kinner today?" Heidi asked Sharon.

"My mamm." Sharon's dimples deepened when she smiled. "She's always pleased whenever she's able to spend time with Timothy and Eva."

"My two little ones are with their *grossmudder* today," Ada put in.

Heidi's own parents came to mind, and she remembered Mom saying when she and Lyle got married, how she looked forward to having more grandchildren. Struggling not to give in to self-pity again, Heidi thought about her brothers, and how they'd been blessed with children. Lester and his wife, Vera, had two boys and two girls. Richard, the oldest, was married to Edith, and they were parents of three girls and four boys.

Heidi pulled her shoulders back. She would not give in to despair. "Whew!" She fanned her face. "It's like summer today, instead of early spring."

"You're right," Ada agreed. "I hope things don't start coming up in our gardens and then get zapped by an early morning frost that often happens during the first month of spring."

"I don't usually put things like tomato plants in the ground until all danger of frost is gone." Heidi gestured to her garden plot. "But it's fine to plant peas, radishes, and beets this early in the year."

They continued to visit until Sharon suggested they get back to work, since she only had a few hours left to help.

While her friends headed back to the garden, Heidi took their empty glasses inside and placed them in the sink. Glancing out the kitchen window, she spotted Ron tinkering with something under the hood of his motor home. It still concerned her that Lyle gave permission for Ron to remain on their property until the end of June. He'd even said it was okay for Ron to hang his clothes on Heidi's clothesline. It almost seemed as if he planned to remain there permanently.

Will Ron leave after the last cooking class or come up with an excuse to stay longer? Heidi hoped he didn't have that in mind, because she wasn't used to having a big old motor home sitting on their property. It looked so out of place on an Amish farm—more so than English clothes hanging on the line.

Dover

Charlene stood in the corner of the playground, keeping an eye on her kindergarten class as they enjoyed recess. *Oh, to be young and carefree again.* She flexed her tense shoulder muscles, thinking about all that happened Saturday night. Her date with Len had started so well. Up until they'd stopped to watch the foal come into the world, things had been nearly perfect. What excitement to see the mare give birth and capture it all on camera. The photos turned out amazing, including the one of the mare and nursing colt, with a beautiful sunset in the background. Too bad their evening ended on a negative note. Once Len's vehicle was hit, everything fell apart.

Charlene squirmed, remembering the horrible ordeal when the car crashed into Len's Suburban. Poor Len. The vehicle wasn't even a year old. The accident ruined their whole date. Because the car's bumper had gotten pushed into one of the back wheels, the Suburban had to be towed back to Dover, and their dinner plans were canceled.

Charlene apologized—it seemed like a hundred times—but her fiancé assured her, "It wasn't your fault."

The people who'd hit Len's car also apologized, saying they felt terrible about the unfortunate accident. The driver explained they were gawking at the colt and hadn't noticed Len's Suburban at first. By the time they did, it was too late.

After exchanging insurance information, Len called for help, and he and Charlene rode back to Dover with the tow-truck driver. Len and the driver talked the whole time, but Charlene tuned them out, fretting over what happened. Len squeezed her hand and said, "It's gonna be okay." But even with his assurance, she felt terrible. If they hadn't stopped to see the mare give birth, everything would have been fine.

Charlene breathed in and out slowly. *If Len found it his heart to forgive me, then I need to get past this guilt, because the accident really wasn't my fault.*

———————◦⚬◦———————

Sugarcreek

Loretta felt as if the chores would never end. By the time the children went down for their naps, she was exhausted and tempted to lie down too. But if she stopped now, the rest of her tasks would never get done, at least not today.

Hoping to increase her energy, she drank another cup of coffee then headed for the clothesline, making sure the back door was left open. With the storm door closed, no bugs could get in, but enough screen was exposed so Loretta could hear the children if they called out.

A sense of peace settled over her as she took the towels off the line, breathing deeply of their fresh-air aroma. Loretta owned a dryer, of course, but whenever she washed clothes and the weather was nice, she hung them outdoors. It wasn't merely to save money on electricity. She enjoyed the lingering scent—especially on the sheets and towels.

When the clothes were all off, Loretta picked up the basket and started for the house. The storm door held fast when Loretta tried to open it. *That's strange. I'm sure I didn't lock it from inside before I stepped out.*

Perplexed, she set the basket on the porch and yanked on the door handle once more. A piece of heavy furniture would have been easier to move. Despite not wanting to wake the children, she pounded on the door. If the only way she could get in was to rouse Abby and Conner, then they'd have to do with less sleep now and go to bed earlier tonight.

After knocking on the glass door several times with no response, and wiggling and jiggling the handle again, a sense of panic came over Loretta. She paused to pray. *Heavenly Father, please help me get this door open. My children are inside, and they need me.* The words from Psalm 46:10 Heidi had written on the back of the recipe card for the breakfast casserole came to mind: *"Be still, and know that I am God."*

Chapter 12

Loretta's heart pulsated as she pounded on the storm door, thunder sounding in the distance. *Lord, please get me inside.* If only one of the children would hear her.

"Abby! Conner!" She called their names repeatedly, continuing to beat her fists on the door. *Lord, I need Your help. Why aren't You answering my prayer?*

"Be still, and know that I am God."

She drew a deep breath, forcing herself to calm down.

After what seemed like hours, Conner showed up, rubbing his eyes.

"Honey, please open the door for Mommy." Loretta spoke softly, so as not to upset her son.

He tipped his head, looking at her curiously through the glass. "The door is open. Come in, Mommy."

She shook her head. "Only the big wooden door is open. The door with glass and screen in it won't open for me. Sweetie, pull down on the handle, please."

Conner jiggled it, but the door didn't budge.

More frustrated than ever, Loretta asked her son to go get his sister.

"Abby's sleepin'."

"I realize she's taking a nap, but you need to wake her up."

"What if she yells at me?"

"Tell your sister I asked you to wake her up and she needs to come open the door for me right away."

"Okay." Conner trotted off and returned a short time later with Abby at his side.

Loretta felt relief. "Abby, I can't get the door open. See if it will open from inside."

Abby pushed the handle down, but nothing happened.

"Try pulling the button above it straight up," Loretta instructed. "If it's locked, that should let us open the door."

Standing on tiptoes, Abby kept trying but to no avail.

Loretta saw no other choice but to remove the storm door from its hinges. First, she'd need to find the right tool in order to do the job.

"I'm going out to the garage to look for a tool," Loretta called to her daughter. "I want you and Conner to go to the living room and wait for me there."

"Okay."

Loretta hurried across the yard. Before she made it to the garage, her elderly neighbor, Sam Jones, showed up.

"Is everything all right, Mrs. Donnelly? With a storm approaching, I wanted to check." The wrinkles on his forehead deepened. "Heard you shouting and pounding. Wondered if you'd gotten locked out of the house or something."

"I did, in fact. I can't open the storm door from the outside, and the kids can't get it open from inside." Loretta gestured to the garage. "I came here to find the right tool to remove the door from its hinges."

He held up one hand. "Not to worry. I've been locked out of my house a time or two. I'll get the door off for you." Sam stepped inside the garage.

Loretta walked back to the porch. No need to tell her neighbor where the tools were. Sam used to come over to visit with Rick while he did things in the garage. The two became good friends. Sam was devastated when Rick died. He told Loretta once that he felt like he'd lost a son.

"Mommy! Mommy!" Abby yelled from the living room.

"What is it, sweetheart?" Loretta peered in through the glass door but couldn't see the children.

"I hear thunder," Abby whimpered, finally stepping up to the door. "Conner's scared too. He's on the couch, holdin' two pillows against his ears."

"Don't worry. I'll be with you both shortly. Sam is getting a tool from the garage to help me get inside."

Telling Abby about Sam seemed to calm her fears, for she went back to the living room. Loretta stayed by the door, relieved when she heard the children giggling. It sounded like Abby was reading her brother a story.

A few minutes later, Sam showed up, and in no time, he had the storm door off.

"Thank You, Lord," Loretta murmured. *What a blessing to have a good neighbor like Sam.*

Mt. Hope

Tired from a day of fruitless job hunting, Kendra went to bed early. Dorie was on a date with her boyfriend, Gene, so the house was quiet.

Kendra plumped up her pillow and crawled into bed, thankful her friend's mobile home included this small guest room. Sleeping on the couch held no appeal, but Kendra would have crashed there if Dorie had nothing else to offer.

Distant thunder rumbled, and a gentle rain fell from the storm that had passed through earlier. For her, the rain hitting the metal roof of the mobile home worked like a lullaby on a baby.

As Kendra closed her eyes, lulled by the soothing sound, the scripture verse Heidi had written on the back of the recipe card for the breakfast casserole came to mind. *"Be still, and know that I am God."* She thought about praying, the way she'd done since she was a young girl. But what was the use? God hadn't responded to the one thing she'd recently prayed about.

Kendra felt discouraged and wondered sometimes if God was real, or just a supernatural being someone had made up so they'd feel better when praying. Well, Kendra didn't need some Bible verse to make herself feel better. What she needed was a job and someone to tell her what to do about the baby. Should she keep the child and try to raise it alone? Would it be better to put the infant up for adoption? *Mom and Dad sure won't help me raise my baby, even if this innocent child will be their first grandchild.*

She rolled onto her side, trying to find a more comfortable position. *If I keep the baby, what kind of a life do I have to offer? What if I never find a suitable job? Even if I do secure employment somewhere, who'll watch the baby when I'm at work?*

The sensible thing would be to adopt it out, but Kendra couldn't do it unless she knew for certain the little one growing inside her would be raised in a good home with loving parents. Since God hadn't answered her prayers about this, maybe, if He did exist, He was mad at her too.

She clenched her fingers until her palms ached. *That creep, Max. If he'd asked me to marry him instead of getting involved with someone else and then running off to join the navy, this wouldn't be a problem right now. While Mom and Dad might have been angry about my promiscuousness, they may have eventually accepted things if I'd gotten married.*

Though the rain slowly stopped, faint flashes of lightning reflected on the wall, and occasional claps of thunder continued to rumble.

Kendra rolled onto her back again, staring at the ceiling. *What a pickle I've gotten myself into.* Her eyes and nose burned with unshed tears. *I need some answers, and soon.*

Walnut Creek

Heidi entered the bedroom to the sound of her husband's gentle snores. Thankfully, the storm had abated, or she'd be hearing that too. The battery-operated light on the nightstand glowed, and Lyle's Bible lay across his chest. He'd had a long day and gone to bed soon after they finished supper.

Gently, she lifted the Bible and carried it to her side of the bed. She'd meant to do her devotions this morning, but Ada and Sharon arrived earlier than expected, so she'd put her Bible reading on hold.

Taking a seat on the edge of the bed, Heidi opened the Bible to Psalm 127. Reading silently, her eyes came to rest on verse three. *"Children are an heritage of the Lord: and the fruit of the womb is his reward."* She'd read this passage many times, and it always put an ache in her heart.

Tears welled and her shoulders slumped as the

longing for a child took over yet again. *Help me, Lord, to be content and stop dwelling on what I cannot change.*

Heidi finished the psalm, set the Bible aside, and picked up the notepad on her nightstand. *I should concentrate on my next cooking class and decide what dish to teach my students how to make. Haystack might be a good choice. It's a healthy, traditional Amish meal to serve for lunch or supper. It's not difficult to make either.*

Heidi turned off the light. With one less thing on her mind, hopefully sleep would come easy. She was pleased her garden had gotten planted today before the rain fell. *Thank You, dear Lord, for all my blessings, and the rain we needed.*

It was close to midnight when Ron looked outside. The rain had stopped an hour ago, and now he'd have to dodge puddles. Regardless, a little water or mud wouldn't stop him from carrying out his plans. *No light coming from the Troyers' windows—that's good.* He grabbed a flashlight, stepped out of the motor home, and headed for the barn.

When Ron entered the building, the horses neighed and moved around restlessly in their stalls. "Hush, you two. There's nothin' to get excited about." Ron went to each horse and patted them on the nose, hoping to get them comfortable with his voice.

He'd need to work fast and hoped neither Lyle nor Heidi woke up because of sounds from the horses. If they caught him in the barn at this time of night, he'd have to come up with a legitimate excuse for being here.

Ron made his way to the back of the building, thankful the horses settled down. Shining his light up ahead, he spotted the canning jars he'd seen earlier today. Four of them sat side by side on a shelf, but Ron only took two. *Would they miss a third?* With no more thought, he reached for another jar. As Ron wrapped his fingers around the cool glass, something wiggled in his palm. In the nick of time, before dropping the jar, he caught it in his other hand, seeing a spider crawl out between his fingers. The eight-legged creature must have been on the back of the jar when he took it down from the shelf.

Seeing all the cobwebs, he should have known better. Ron put the third jar back, shook the spider to the floor, and stomped on it. No point pushing his luck. Since he'd be sticking around the Troyers' several more weeks, there'd be plenty of time to get more loot. A little here. . .a little there. . . Soon there'd be enough items to make a trip to the pawnshop in Dover or New Philadelphia. Of course, he'd go when Heidi and Lyle weren't home. They'd become suspicious if they saw him driving his rig when it hadn't been fixed.

"Bide your time," Ron whispered as he opened the door to his rig. Stepping inside, he kicked off his shoes and left them lying by the door. Tomorrow he'd knock the mud from the soles. His RV looked messy enough without getting dirt all over the floor. *Heidi and Lyle are so trusting, by the time they realize some of their treasures are missing, I'll be long gone.*

Chapter 13

"Are you ready to teach your second class this morning?" Lyle asked as he sat beside Heidi at the kitchen table.

She nodded. "We'll be making haystacks."

"Yum." He smacked his lips. "Might be good for supper tonight. Unless you have something else planned."

Heidi smiled, lightly brushing her hand against his. "I'd figured on serving it for supper since all the ingredients are here."

"Will there be enough?"

"Jah. I bought plenty of everything."

"I look forward to it. Oh, before I forget, I spoke with Ron after the auction." Lyle reached for his cup of coffee and took a drink. "He's eager to take part in your class today."

"I'm glad, and I hope the rest of my students feel the same way."

"How could they not?" Lyle set his cup down and clasped her hand. "They're learning from the best cook in all of Holmes County."

Heidi rolled her eyes at him. "I doubt I'm the best, and you might be a wee bit prejudiced."

"Maybe so, but you're an excellent cook. Why else did I choose you among all the other young women who wanted to marry me?" Chuckling, he winked at her.

She swatted his arm playfully. "You're such a big tease."

"True, and isn't it one of the reasons you love me so much? You enjoy a little teasing."

She gave his beard a gentle tug. "A little humor is good for everyone. Which is why I chose Proverbs 17:22 to write on the back of everyone's recipe card today. 'A merry heart doeth good like a medicine.' It's one of my favorite verses."

"God's Word is full of good advice." Lyle leaned closer to Heidi and kissed her cheek before pushing back his chair. "I'd better get going or I'll never get to Abe Miller's place to find out how much he'd charge for a new open buggy."

"Can we afford it right now?" Heidi questioned.

"I'm not sure. That's why I need to ask about the price. Afterward, I'll be heading to Charm to pick up a few things. Should be home by the time your class is over or possibly a bit later, depending on if I run into anyone I know and end up chatting a spell." Lyle grabbed his straw hat from the wall peg, lifted his hand in a quick wave, and headed out the door. "Hope you have a good class," he called over his shoulder.

"Danki. See you later, husband."

When the door clicked shut, Heidi left the table and put their empty cups in the sink. As she washed them along with the breakfast dishes, she watched out the window until Lyle's horse and buggy was out of sight. Already she felt lonely without him.

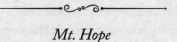

Mt. Hope

"How are you feeling this morning?" Dorie asked when

Kendra entered the kitchen.

"Not bad. I felt a little queasiness when I first woke up, but it's better now. With any luck, I'll make it through the day without throwing up." Kendra moved across the room to fix a cup of mint tea. "How was your date with Gene last night?"

"Good. Better than our last date when it rained, although we had fun bowling once we dried off after running from Gene's car through the parking lot. This time, we drove up to Canton, had dinner, and went to see a movie. Since I don't have to work Saturdays, it was nice going out on a Friday night rather than a Monday evening." Dorie took a box of cold cereal from the cupboard. "What'd you do all evening?"

"Not much. Went to bed early again. Had a hard time falling asleep though. Like almost every night here of late, too many thoughts swirled in my head."

"Were you rehashing the situation with your parents?"

"Yeah, but I can't stop fretting about what to do when the baby comes." Kendra gave a slight shake of her head. "Any way I look at my options, it's a no-win situation."

"What do you mean?"

"If I put the baby up for adoption, I'll always wonder where the child is and if he or she is well cared for." Rocking back and forth, Kendra placed both hands across her stomach. "How could I forget about a baby I carried for nine whole months? The child is already a part of me. It's not something easily forgotten."

"Like I've said before, no one's forcing you to put your baby up for adoption." Dorie put two bowls on the table and took a carton of milk from the refrigerator. "You could keep the child and raise it yourself. A lot of single mothers are doing that these days."

Kendra pulled the silverware drawer open and removed two spoons, placing them on the table. "When you say it like that, it sounds so right, but raising a child by myself would be a challenge—especially since I won't be getting any help from Mom and Dad." Frowning, she lifted one hand. "And how will I take care of the baby financially? I have no job yet, and what if I'm not able to find one?"

"I'm sure the right one's out there, Kendra. You have to keep looking. Don't give up."

"Easy for you to say. You have a good job. Besides, even if I worked at a fabulous place, I'd need to find someone to watch the baby after it's born." She sank into a chair as a heavy sigh escaped her lips. "Paying a babysitter could be expensive, not to mention all the things I'd need to buy for the baby. Sure wish I had lots of money in the bank."

"I'd offer to babysit, but my work hours might not be the same as yours." Dorie took the seat beside her. "Too bad your folks won't let you move back home. Maybe your mom would babysit, and you could go back to college and get your degree."

Kendra's jaw clenched as she lifted both hands in defeat. "Fat chance! It will never happen—not with Dad feeling the way he does and Mom with no apparent mind of her own. She goes along with whatever he says."

"Never say never. Sometimes people change their minds on issues they once held firm to."

"Not Dad. When he decides something, he doesn't budge. And as far as my education goes. . .well, let's just say, my dream of becoming a nurse is just that. . .a dream. It's never gonna happen." Kendra grabbed the cereal box and poured some into her bowl. For the moment, her stomach had settled. "Can't solve this problem right now, so for today at least, it'll be fun to learn how to make another Amish recipe."

"Do you know what she'll be teaching you today?"

"Not sure, but I'm anxious to find out."

Walnut Creek

"No, Lady, you cannot go with me today." Eli shook his finger at the shiny black lab. The persistent dog followed him to the end of the driveway, wagging her tail as she barked at him.

Since the weather was nice, Eli chose to walk to the Troyers' house. He and his dog often went for walks, so Lady probably figured she'd be welcome to come along.

"Guess I'd better put you in your pen, or you'll end up following me all the way there." Eli grabbed Lady's collar and led her to the chain-link pen. "Now be good, and no barkin' while I'm gone." He made sure the dog had plenty of water, gave her a quick pat, and closed the gate.

Woof! Woof! Woof!

Eli whirled around. "Quiet now! I'll be back in a few hours. Then you can run all over the yard and carry on all ya want."

Whimpering, the dog quieted and lay down, nose between her paws.

As Eli headed down the road in the direction of the Troyers', he puckered his lips and whistled a pleasant tune. Although he hadn't expected to like the class, he'd enjoyed helping make the breakfast casserole during the first cooking lesson. Heidi's patience and ability to explain things well made it easier for him to come back. He'd known the Troyers a good many years, and that made being there more comfortable too. The best part, though, was when Ron showed up. Eli felt less conspicuous no longer being the only man in the class.

Heidi had included some scripture on the back of the recipe card she'd sent home with him. Eli appreciated the reminder to be still and focus on God. Sometimes he got busy in his shop or around the yard and didn't take time to be one-on-one with his Lord.

Following the directions on the front of Heidi's recipe card, Eli had tried to duplicate the breakfast casserole in his own kitchen. It hadn't tasted too bad, but the texture wasn't quite the same, and most of it stuck to the baking dish. He'd managed to dig it out, though, and enjoyed eating the casserole for breakfast three days in a row. *Sure was better than cold cereal or a boiled egg,* he mused. *Next time, though, I'd better use more cooking oil to grease the baking dish. Think Mavis would be pleased I'm learning how to cook.*

Eli stopped walking for a moment, and glanced around. From the way things looked, today's weather was off to a good start. Spring was getting into full swing now, with flowering shrubs blooming and tree seeds whirling through the air. Despite the few cooler days they'd had this month, warmer temperatures were slowly winning out. Eli was glad the days were getting longer too. It was no longer dark when he quit work for the day and came inside to start supper. He looked forward to the longer days of summer, when he could get more done in the yard.

Overhead, Eli watched a pair of Canadian geese fly past, honking in their own conversational way. Some birds in the area had already nested, while others were in the stages of building a nest. The other day, Eli had noticed a pair of tree swallows taking up residence in a bluebird box he'd mounted on the fence. No wonder this time of year made him feel ambitious. As Mavis used to say, "Spring is a glorious season—especially after a long, cold winter."

Eli started walking again, and had only gone a short distance when a minivan pulled up beside him. He recognized the driver right away.

Loretta leaned toward the window on the passenger side and rolled it down. "Are you heading to Heidi's?"

He gave a nod.

"Would you like a ride?"

Eli felt tongue-tied and could barely make eye contact with her. *Sure hope I don't stutter.* "Umm. . .thanks." He opened the door and got in, keeping his gaze on the seat belt as he fumbled to get it hooked. The silly thing wouldn't connect, so with a huff, he gave up trying.

Loretta reached across the seat. "Here, let me help you. That seat belt buckle can be kind of stubborn at times." She clicked it together. "There you go."

His ears burned. *She must think I'm a dunce for failing to do something as simple as hooking a seat belt.* "Thanks," he mumbled, barely able to look at her.

When Loretta pulled onto the road, the silence grew unbearable, until Eli sneezed—not once, but eight times. He blew his nose and shyly muttered, "Sorry. Spring allergy season."

It seemed to break the ice a little when Loretta glanced at him and smiled. "How have you been these last two weeks?"

"Nothing to complain about. How are things with you?"

"Not too bad except for when I got locked out of my house a few days ago and my kids were still inside."

"What'd you do?"

"Sam came over and took the door off its hinges. In the nick of time too, before a storm came through."

"Yeah, it hit here too." Eli wondered who Sam was. *Maybe he's Loretta's boyfriend. Well, it's none of my business, and I'm sure not gonna ask.*

"I'm anxious to find out what we'll be making today. Did you enjoy the first class?" She seemed determined to carry on a conversation.

"Yep."

"Same here. I made the breakfast casserole last week, and my kinner loved it."

Eli jerked his head. "You know Pennsylvania Dutch?"

She laughed. "I don't speak it fluently, but I can say a few words."

"How'd you learn 'em?"

"Well, I . . ."

Seeing a cow had wandered into the middle of the road up ahead, Eli only had time to point and shout, "Look out!"

Chapter 14

O h my, that was too close!" Loretta's heart palpitated
after swerving to avoid hitting the cow. Thankfully,
no cars were coming in the other lane, where the animal
now stood, looking like it couldn't care less about what
had almost happened.

"Bet that critter belongs to the Troyers." Eli scanned
the area. "Don't see any other cows at least. I'll hop out
and see if my coaxing is any good. Go ahead up the
driveway so you're not sitting in the middle of the road.
I'll follow behind with the cow and guide her into their
yard." He opened the door and stepped out of the van.

Loretta wiped her sweaty palms against her long
skirt as she turned up the Troyers' driveway. She hoped
Eli could get the cow to do what he wanted. The thought
of him in the road sent chills up her spine. What if a car
came and didn't see him in time?

After looking in the rearview mirror, Loretta felt
relief seeing Eli and the cow meandering up the driveway behind her van. With little urging from Eli, the cow
seemed as if it knew where it belonged. She remained in
the van until he pushed the gate fully open and got the
animal inside, giving its rump a pat.

When Loretta got out of her vehicle, Eli stepped
up to her. "Sure hope this cow belongs to the Troyers.

Even if it doesn't, it'll remain here till our cooking class is over. Then I'll go looking till I find the owner."

"Based on how it acted, my guess is the cow belongs here." She looked directly at him, slowly shaking her head. "I'm glad you called out to me in time. I hate the thought of killing, or even injuring the cow. Not to mention damaging my van. Since it's my only vehicle, I can't be without it."

"All's well that ends well." Eli offered her a shy-looking grin. "Should we go on up to the house now?"

"Yes." Loretta glanced around the yard. So far hers was the only vehicle in the yard, other than Ron's motor home. "Looks like we're the first ones here."

Walking side by side, she and Eli stepped onto the porch. After a brief knock, the door opened, and Heidi greeted them. "It's good to see you. Please, come inside."

When they entered the house, Eli told Heidi about the cow on the road, and how he'd put it in the pasture. "I assumed it was your cow."

Heidi's lips compressed. "I bet it is. Soon after Lyle left this morning, I went outside to hang a few towels and noticed the gate to the pasture was open. I shut it, of course, but the cow probably made her escape before I came out."

"Could be." Eli bobbed his head. "I made sure the gate latched after I put her in."

"Danki for taking care of it. I have no idea how the gate got open, but I appreciate your help." Heidi motioned to the living room. "You're welcome to sit in there until the others arrive. I'll join you as soon as I finish what I'm doing in the kitchen."

Eli removed his straw hat and shuffled into the living room. Loretta followed. He took a seat in the rocking chair and got it moving, while she seated herself on the couch. Uncomfortable with the silence and needing to say something, she asked how long Eli had lived in Walnut Creek.

"I was born in Mt. Eaton, but when I turned six, my folks moved to Sugarcreek, which is where they still reside."

"What a coincidence. Sugarcreek is where my children and I live."

He stopped rocking. "You're lucky to have them. My wife and I wanted kinner, but she miscarried twice. To make matters worse, she got cancer and had to have her uterus surgically removed." Eyes closed, Eli massaged his forehead. "Our hope of having children ended of course."

"I'm sorry for your loss. It seems you and your wife went through a lot."

"We did, but our love proved strong, and we enjoyed every minute we had together." Opening his eyes, Eli lifted his hands and let them fall in his lap. "Life is hard, but God's been with me through it all. Wouldn't be where I am today without His help."

She nodded. "He's been with me as well. I couldn't have coped with my husband's death if not for the strength I continue to draw from the Lord, as well as Christian family and friends."

Heidi entered the room and was about to take a seat when a knock sounded on the front door. "Sounds like someone else has arrived." She went to answer it and returned with Ron at her side.

Eli let his head fall against the back of the chair and drew a deep breath through his nose. Loretta assumed he was glad Ron had come back for another class. Even for a sociable English man, which Eli was not, being among a bunch of women—in a cooking class, no less— would probably be difficult. From what Loretta could tell so far, Eli was a kind, gentle person, although a bit on the shy side.

He must miss his wife as much I do Rick. Loretta swallowed against the sudden lump forming in her throat. All this pitying got her nowhere. Determined, she directed her focus on something else.

Ron sauntered into the room and took a seat in the recliner.

"Nice to see you again." Smiling, Eli tipped his head.

"Same here." Ron pulled the lever back on the chair to put his feet up. It felt good to sit in a chair like this. He hadn't enjoyed such a comfort since he and Fran split up. After the divorce, it wasn't easy letting her keep the house and everything in it, but he'd seen no point in fighting for it. Since Matt and Gail were still in grade school at the time, Fran needed a home to raise them in.

Ron hadn't seen his ex-wife in a good many years and didn't even remember how old the kids were anymore. *Probably in their forties by now,* he figured. One of the reasons he'd split years ago and headed out on the road was so he wouldn't be stuck paying child support.

Things went well with him and Fran when they'd first gotten married, but a tour of duty ending after Vietnam soured their relationship. Ron had struggled with the trauma of the war ever since. Many nights he'd wake up screaming, with his body drenched in sweat. The heinous war had affected his personality. Ron's mood swings and harsh temper drove a wedge between him and Fran and caused their children to fear him. While he'd never abused them physically, his impatience and sharp tongue often left Matt and Gail in tears.

Ron's thoughts came to a halt when the grandfather

clock bonged on the hour, just as Kendra and Charlene showed up.

Heidi gestured to the two young women. "Looks like everyone is here, so why don't we all go to the kitchen and get started?"

Begrudgingly, Ron put the recliner in the upright position and followed the others. The only bright spot in being part of this class was that it gave him another chance to look around the place, plus an opportunity to eat one more decent meal.

When Charlene entered Heidi's kitchen, it surprised her to see so many items sitting on the table—lettuce, cheese, olives, tomatoes, onions, green pepper, celery, corn chips, and two cans of beans. "What are we making today?" she asked.

"It's called 'haystack,' and we Amish like to fix it for lunch or supper." Heidi went on to clarify how each of the items needed to be chopped or grated. "We'll also brown some ground beef and add mild-flavored salsa to it. The soup that will be poured over the top must be combined with milk and heated."

"What are we supposed to do with it all?" Kendra's eyes widened as she motioned to the table. "And why is the recipe for this meal called 'haystack'?"

"Once I explain the rest of the procedure, you'll understand. Now, after the vegetables are chopped, they'll be placed in separate bowls, along with rice, beans, ground beef, and cheese sauce. Afterward you can put whatever items you want on your plate, making a tall haystack." Heidi smiled. "Are there any questions?"

Charlene's hand went up. "Do the eggs need to be sliced or chopped?"

"Usually they're chopped, like the vegetables." Heidi moved toward the table. "So if everyone will put your aprons on, we'll get started. Excusing the men, if they'd rather not borrow an apron from me," she added.

Ron shook his head. "Don't need an apron."

"Me neither," Eli agreed. "Getting food on my clothes is nothing new for me."

Charlene winked when she looked over at Loretta and saw her smile. *Cutting up veggies and piling them on a plate should be easy. This is one meal I'm sure I can fix without messing up.*

While Kendra and Ron waited for their instructions from Heidi, he glanced around the kitchen.

"So, which car do you drive?" Kendra, normally quiet, struck up a conversation.

"Don't have a car. I'm staying here right now." Ron shoved his hands into his pockets. "You probably noticed the motor home parked over by the Troyers' garden."

She nodded.

"It's not only my mode of transportation, but I live in it too."

"It's nice of Heidi and her husband to let you park on their property. How long have you been friends with them?"

"Only a little while. Since my RV isn't running right, they gave me permission to park the rig here till I'm able to fix it." Ron preferred not to say much more. He hardly knew this girl, and after these classes were over, he'd never see her or any of the others again. Besides, there was something about Kendra that got on his nerves. He couldn't put his finger on it though.

"I've never seen the inside of a motor home, but I

always thought how neat it would be to travel around in one." Kendra pushed a strand of hair behind her ears. "From what I've seen in magazines, some of the newer models are like living in a house. Some have large rooms, flat-screen TVs, and a few models are even equipped with electric or propane fireplaces."

"Mine's not that glamorous." Ron puffed out his cheeks. "I'm lucky I could afford to buy this old clunker."

"Regardless, I'd love to see what the inside looks like," Kendra persisted. "Would ya mind showing it to me?"

This girl was too bold. No wonder she irritated him. What business did she have, asking to see where he lived? Ron didn't want anyone inside his traveling home, especially now, with the items he'd hidden in the closet. If Kendra was anything like his ex-wife, she'd want to snoop in all the cupboards and the closet as well. *I'll have to come up with some excuse not to let her into my rig.*

"The inside of my RV is no big deal." Ron kept his voice on an even keel. "In my opinion, there's nothing worth seeing in there. Besides, after class I'll be busy doing some things for Lyle."

"I'm glad to hear you're helping them around the farm." Kendra looked at him squarely. "It's the least you can do for these nice people letting you stay however long you're planning to be here."

Where does this sassy little gal get off making a comment like that to me? Ron was about to tell Kendra what he thought, when Heidi stepped between them and began explaining what they needed to do.

He gripped his wooden spoon so tightly he feared it might break. *Good thing Heidi spoke first, or I may have said something I'd later regret. Wish some people would mind their own business. I'll be glad when I have enough loot to move on down the road.*

Chapter 15

Heidi noticed how everyone sat forward, as though eager to learn something new today—even Ron, who rarely smiled. Kendra, normally quiet, had begun a conversation with him. Heidi wasn't sure if her students truly enjoyed the class or were simply enthusiastic to make haystack so they could eat the tasty meal. She too looked forward to eating haystack. It was one of her favorite meals.

While Heidi's students chopped their vegetables, she took two packages of ground beef from the refrigerator. "Any volunteers to brown the beef?"

"Not me. I'd most likely burn the meat. It happened the last time I tried to fry bacon." Eli stroked his throat and grimaced.

"You probably turned the burner too high." Heidi took out two frying pans and poured a little cooking oil in each. "Even if I use a nonstick pan I always put oil in the bottom for added flavor and to add a touch of moisture to the meat." She handed one package of beef to Kendra and the other to Ron. Since they'd been conversing, Heidi hoped pairing them would go well. "Why don't you start browning the meat? When it's partway cooked, Loretta and Charlene can take over. Eli, you may want to watch the procedure to see how it's done."

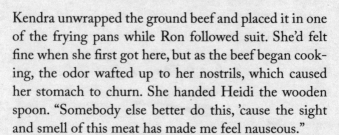

Kendra unwrapped the ground beef and placed it in one of the frying pans while Ron followed suit. She'd felt fine when she first got here, but as the beef began cooking, the odor wafted up to her nostrils, which caused her stomach to churn. She handed Heidi the wooden spoon. "Somebody else better do this, 'cause the sight and smell of this meat has made me feel nauseous."

Loretta stepped forward and took the spoon. "Maybe you ought to step outside for a breath of fresh air. The good country air always helped when morning sickness hit me."

"A cup of mint tea might settle things down. How about I fix it for you?" Heidi offered.

Moving toward the back door, Kendra nodded. "Thanks, Heidi. I'll drink it when I come back inside. I forgot to bring some with me today."

When Kendra stepped onto the porch, she stood at the railing and drew several deep breaths. Getting out of the kitchen and away from the strong meaty odor brought some relief. She'd come mighty close to getting sick and didn't want a repeat of the last class when she'd barely made it to the bathroom in time.

She gazed at the landscape, while recollections circled inside her head. *Before I got pregnant, the odor of meat cooking never bothered me at all. My belly wasn't sensitive to much of anything back then.* Kendra placed her hands firmly on her stomach, which had begun to pooch in the last two weeks. *Are you a boy or a girl? Well, what does it matter? I probably won't get the chance to be your mama.* Tears of frustration pricked the back of Kendra's eyes. *Sure hope I find a job soon.*

She'd scoured the newspaper want ads and made

numerous calls to hotels, bed-and-breakfasts, and rest-aurants in the area, but all the jobs she'd seen listed had already been filled. Kendra wasn't sure how she'd cope with her morning sickness even if someone offered her a job. Somehow, she would manage and make it work. Relying on Dorie indefinitely was not an option. It wasn't fair to expect it either. Dorie had her own expenses to worry about.

Kendra tipped her head back. Not a cloud to be seen. The birds in Heidi's yard twittered and tweeted as though they hadn't a care in the world.

"Wish I could say the same," Kendra muttered. It wasn't in her nature to feel so negative, but after finding out she was pregnant and then the breakup with Max, she'd become bitter and hopeless—even more so when Mom and Dad kicked her out. Obviously, she'd disap-pointed them, but did it mean they no longer loved her?

Kendra's sisters came to mind. She still hadn't responded to Shelly's messages. *What's the point? I won-der what Shelly and Chris would say if I told them I was forced to leave home and the reason for it.*

Kendra moved away from the railing and took a seat on the porch swing. The gentle swaying as she pushed her feet against the wooden porch floor helped her relax.

Sighing, she closed her eyes and tried to visualize who her baby might look like when he or she came into the world. Would it have auburn hair and brown eyes like hers, or end up with curly black hair and blue eyes like Max?

Kendra nearly jumped off the swing when the back door swung open and Heidi stepped out. "We're ready to layer the ingredients on our plates. Are you feeling up to joining us now?" She handed Kendra a cup of tea.

"Umm. . .yeah, I do feel better." She lifted the cup

and took a sip. "Thanks. This is good, and breathing the country air for a while helped my stomach settle."

Heidi smiled. "I'm glad. Hopefully the tea will help too."

Kendra stood and followed Heidi into the house. She felt hungry now and couldn't wait to try the haystack.

———◦◦◦◦———

"Charlene, are you crying?" Loretta felt concern when she noticed tears rolling down the young woman's cheeks.

Charlene shook her head. "It's those onions I chopped. They made my eyes water."

"Their strong odor has a tendency to do that sometimes." Heidi handed Charlene a tissue. "Now that everyone has finished chopping their vegetables, let's begin the layering process." She demonstrated on her own plate how to put the items down in the order given, to create their individual haystacks.

Once everyone piled the ingredients on, Heidi demonstrated how to pour the cheese sauce over the top. "Some of you may want to add your favorite salad dressing too." She pointed to the bottles of ranch, thousand island, and Italian dressings she'd set out.

Following behind Charlene and Kendra, Loretta filled her plate with all the goodies. The sight of everything piled up on her plate made Loretta's mouth water. It looked and smelled delicious.

After the men filled their plates, everyone followed Heidi to the dining room. When she bowed her head for silent prayer, Loretta and the others did the same. Once the prayer ended, they all dug in.

"How have you all been doing since our last class?" Heidi questioned.

"I've been looking for a job, but haven't had much luck." Kendra clicked her fingernails against the tabletop. "I'm willing to take almost anything, but I keep hearing there are no openings right now."

"Don't give up." Loretta wished she could do something for this girl. "Keep watching the newspaper or use a computer. The internet is a great search tool."

"I've done that already. Since my folks kicked me out of their house when they learned I was pregnant, I don't have a computer anymore. My friend Dorie, whom I'm living with now, has a laptop." Groaning, Kendra leaned her elbows on the table. "She's done so much for me already. I hate to ask if I can keep borrowing hers."

"So you're not married?" The question came from Ron.

Kendra shook her head. "If I was, I wouldn't be in such a mess and might not need a job at all."

"I'll keep my ears open, and if I hear about something, I'll let you know," Charlene spoke up.

"Jobs often become available here in our Amish community," Heidi added.

Loretta couldn't imagine what it must be like to be in Kendra's situation. It would be difficult enough to try and raise a child on her own, but to have been thrown out of her parents' house was beyond belief. What kind of a person would force their own child to leave? Kendra needed help, not condemnation.

Kendra lowered her gaze. "Okay, let's not talk about me anymore."

As if sensing Kendra's discomfort, Heidi turned to Loretta next. "How did your week go?"

"There were a few tense moments when I got locked out of the house." Forehead wrinkling, Loretta dropped her hands to her sides. "My children were inside, and I panicked because they couldn't get the door open, either."

"What did you do?" Charlene leaned forward.

"Fortunately, one of my neighbors heard me pounding on the door and came right over. Sam took the door off its hinges so I could get in before the storm hit."

"For the most part, things went well for me since the last time we were all together." Charlene's brows puckered. "Except for the date with my fiancé, which started out perfect, but ended horribly wrong."

"What do you mean?" Loretta asked.

"Len and I were on our way to Millersburg for dinner. Halfway there, we passed a field where a mare was giving birth to a foal. I asked Len to pull over, since I'd never seen the birth of a colt before. I'm glad I had my camera with me, but when we were ready to head back to Len's vehicle, everything fell apart." Charlene paused and took a breath.

"What happened?" This question came from Kendra.

"Someone hit his Suburban. He had to have it towed back to Dover, and we never made it out to dinner." Charlene wrinkled her nose. "I ended up fixing sandwiches after we took a taxi to my place, where Len called his dad to come get him."

"At least neither of you was in the car when it got hit. You could have been hurt." Heidi commented.

"Yes, we were thankful."

Heidi gestured to Eli. "How have you been?"

He shrugged his shoulders. "Same old, same old. Always busy in my shop."

"You have an interesting profession. Would you mind telling everyone what you do?"

Eli pulled at his shirt collar then rubbed the back of his neck. "Well, I. . .uh. . .make caskets, and also some wooden furniture." He cleared his throat a couple of times. "Most of us don't like to be reminded of death, but the truth is, out of five thousand people, five thousand will die, and most will need a coffin."

No one said a word, until Charlene started asking several questions about his profession. Eli seemed to relax and was willing to respond.

"Ron, do you have anything to share?" Heidi looked in his direction.

"Nope. I'll just listen to the rest of you yammer."

Loretta cringed. Did he have to be so rude? In an effort to put a positive note on things, she gestured to her plate. "This haystack is delicious, Heidi. My children might enjoy helping me make it, so I'm going to try this recipe at home sometime next week."

"It's good, but all that chopping of so many ingredients seems like a waste of time," Ron garbled around a mouthful of food. "Don't think I'll ever make it though." His chin jutted out. "It ain't worth all the effort."

Tension showed on Heidi's face as her lips compressed. She was obviously hurt by Ron's comment.

It was difficult, but Loretta refrained from saying anything about the man's negative attitude. If it wasn't worth the time to fix a nice meal, why was he taking the class?

She glanced at Eli, who'd been gobbling the food down like it was his last meal. "What about you, Eli? Will you try making haystack on your own?"

He lifted his broad shoulders in a brief shrug. "Maybe. Except for browning the beef, it wasn't too hard. Can't go wrong cuttin' up vegetables and opening a can of beans."

"Don't forget the rice we cooked on the stove after we browned the beef," Charlene interjected.

"True, but if I were to use the kind of rice that cooks

in a minute, I could probably manage." Eli took another bite and blotted his lips with a napkin.

Loretta smiled at Heidi. "Thanks for showing us how to make this healthy meal."

"You're welcome." Looking a little more subdued, Heidi handed them each a recipe card with the directions for making haystack. "Now you'll be able to try it at home. Oh, and please don't forget to look at the Bible verse I included on the back."

"I may make this for my future in-laws sometime." Charlene blotted her lips with a napkin. "My fiancé doesn't know I'm taking these classes. I want it to be a surprise."

"It's always fun to surprise someone," Kendra spoke up.

"Yeah, unless it's an unpleasant surprise. Some surprises, like my ex-wife kickin' me out of our house years ago—now that was anything but pleasant." Ron looked over at Kendra. "See, you're not the only one who was given the boot."

The room became quiet as all heads turned to look at Ron.

Loretta couldn't form a response. Since she knew none of the details, she thought it best to keep quiet.

Heidi, on the other hand, spoke quickly. "You're right, Ron. A surprise such as that would certainly be difficult to take."

"Are you and your wife back together?" Eli questioned.

"Nope. Been divorced a good many years." Ron forked more food into his mouth. It was obviously a topic he'd rather not talk about.

Ron listened as the others discussed various topics, but

he remained quiet. Discussing his messed-up life was something he wouldn't even consider. No one could fix his problems anyway, so no use talking about it. He'd already said too much. *Wish I had never mentioned my ex-wife. If I'd continued the discussion, someone would have probably asked if I have any children. Blabbing the whole story would have been a mistake. These people would most likely look down on me. Either that or feel sorry for the poor Vietnam vet.* He drew his fingers into his palms. *I don't need anyone's pity.*

"Did you have a good two weeks since we last saw you?" Eli nudged Ron's arm.

"Didn't do much. Tinkered around the RV's engine a bit and helped Lyle with a few chores," Ron mumbled. *I'm sure this fellow means well, but I don't feel like answering a bunch of questions. Guess this is what I get for taking Heidi's cooking class. Don't think Eli realizes I'm not the sociable type.*

"My fiancé likes to work on vehicles when he isn't busy at his job," Charlene interjected. "I could ask him to take a look at your motor home. Maybe he'd find the problem."

"I ordered a part, and thanks, but no thanks. I'll fix my rig once the part comes in."

Ron finished eating and set his fork down. He felt relief when Charlene pulled a photo out of her purse to show everyone. It took the focus off him. Ron had to admit, the picture of the colt and its mother looked interesting—especially with the beautiful sunset in the background.

"I saw a local photo contest advertised in the paper the other day," Kendra commented. "You oughta enter your picture. The ad mentioned it's being sponsored by a photography magazine."

"Maybe I will." Charlene's straight white teeth showed when she gave a wide smile. "Someone has to win, right?"

All heads nodded.

A few minutes later, Heidi's husband entered the room. "Sorry to interrupt." He paused near the table and grinned at Heidi. "I got home earlier than expected, but I didn't think I'd find you here in the dining room. I assumed your class would take place in the kitchen."

"It did, but we came out here to eat the meal." She gestured in the direction of the kitchen. "There's plenty left if you'd like to fix a plate and join us."

"Okay, I'll get some food in a minute." Lyle opened the china hutch door and removed a tall vase. Then he put something inside it and closed the door. From where Ron sat, it looked like money Lyle stuffed inside the dark blue vase.

What's that guy thinking, hidin' money in such an obvious place? And with all of us sitting here, watching, no less. Some folks are too trusting.

Chapter 16

Dover

Three days passed since Charlene attended Heidi's second cooking class, but she'd been too busy to try making haystack. With school winding down in a few weeks, there were so many extra things to do. She planned to have a special program for her kindergarten class the last day of school. The children would entertain their parents with songs they'd learned during the year, as well as acting out a story Charlene chose from one of the books she'd read to the children. She'd taken individual photos of her students the other day, and those would be given out during the program as well.

As soon as school is out at the end of May I'll get serious about practicing my cooking skills, Charlene told herself as she heated a few pieces of leftover pizza in the microwave for supper.

Olive, who lay on the throw rug near the sink, lifted her gray head as though sniffing the air. *Meow!*

Charlene clicked her tongue while shaking her head. "No pizza for you, my little feline." She pointed across the room to the cat's dish. "Your dinner's over there."

The timer went off, and after Charlene took the pizza out of the microwave, she poured herself a glass of iced tea and took a seat at the kitchen table. Savoring the tangy pepperoni, sausage, and mozzarella cheese, she took time to scan the local newspaper. Her eyebrows rose when her gaze came to rest on the newspaper article Kendra had mentioned during the last cooking class. AMISH COUNTRY PHOTO CONTEST.

Kendra was right. The contest was sponsored by a well-known photography magazine, one Charlene had paged through many times at the grocery store. As she read the details and learned what was required, the thought of entering the contest sparked an interest. The photos would be judged on different categories, such as nature, scenic, seasons, or animals—all taken in an Amish community. Unlike many photo contests, and to be respectful of the Amish, this one did not include a people category, since most Amish objected to having their picture taken.

The photo Charlene took of the foal and its mother depicted Amish country and qualified for three of the categories—scenic, nature, and animals.

Charlene stopped reading and pulled the envelope out of her purse, where she'd put the picture on Saturday. In her opinion, this photo was the best she'd ever taken. In fact, she might even enlarge and frame it.

It still surprised her that she'd managed to capture the sunset's glow illuminating both horses' coats. *I wonder if the judges will notice.*

As she read the rules further, Charlene became more determined to enter her picture. The photo's orientation was required to be in a portrait layout and not the landscape option. An address was listed where it should be mailed, or it could be submitted via a JPEG attachment to the website they listed. She'd already printed the picture from her printer to show everyone in Heidi's class, but it would be easier to submit online. As stated, she had to make sure her name was included, as well as where the picture was taken. The photo needed a title, not longer than six words. *Think I'll call it "Ending to a Perfect Day."*

The article also indicated the judges would pick a winner from each of the categories mentioned. The winners would receive a year's subscription to the sponsoring magazine. What made Charlene sit up and take notice was the last part of the rules. *"A Grand Prize will also be selected from all the photos received. The winning photo will appear on the cover of the magazine, and the photographer shall receive a two-year subscription to the publication."*

Charlene saw no reason this picture would not qualify. *I'm going to submit it and see what happens. How nice it would be to have a photo I took on the cover of a magazine.* Leaning back in her chair, she heaved a sigh. *Maybe it's wishful thinking.*

Mt. Hope

Kendra stared out the kitchen window as she sat at the table, eating supper alone. Dorie went out with her boyfriend again, leaving Kendra to fend for herself. "This is becoming a habit," Kendra muttered, picking at her salad. "But then, I can't expect my friend to stay home all the time just to keep me company."

Dorie had a life of her own before Kendra showed up, and she'd already been more than hospitable. She was Kendra's only friend who had responded to her frantic call the day Dad kicked her out of the house.

Kendra wondered if Dorie and Gene's relationship was getting serious. They'd been seeing a lot of each other lately. Dorie was lucky to have a boyfriend who, from what Kendra could tell, practically idolized her. Gene always seemed willing to do whatever Dorie wanted, and he was good about bringing her little gifts, not to mention complimenting Dorie on her looks.

The skin under Kendra's eyes tightened as her lips parted slightly. It wasn't right to envy her friend, but she couldn't help it. Dorie had a job, a boyfriend, and a place to call home. Her parents were still speaking to her too. Kendra had nothing but an unborn baby she had no idea what to do with, plus a lot of unpleasant memories from her relationship with Max. It hadn't always been that way. Things were good with them in the beginning, but everything went sour when Kendra got pregnant. Max turned on her like a badger going after its prey. He'd accused her of having been with someone else. Heaping coals on the fire, he'd eventually admitted having a relationship with another woman the whole time he'd been seeing Kendra.

I wonder if his new girlfriend is pregnant too. Bitterness welled in Kendra's soul, and she covered her face with her hands, trying to get the image out of her mind of Max pointing his finger and accusing her of having cheated on him.

Kendra pounded the table and gritted her teeth. "Yeah, right. How dare he accuse me, when he was the one cheating? I must have been blind not to have seen it."

Max had rejected Kendra and wanted nothing to do with their baby. He'd even suggested she get an abortion. Although Kendra had drifted from her Christian beliefs, she could never end her child's life. The baby deserved a chance to live and grow up in a healthy, stable environment.

Tears stung her eyes as she pressed her hand against her baby bump. *Short of a miracle, I can never offer you a good home or stable environment, little one. It would be you and me against the world, always needing a handout from a friend like Dorie.* She swallowed hard, nearly choking on the sob rising in her throat. *If things got really bad, we might end up on the street, begging for money.*

Kendra's head jerked when her cell phone rang. She'd barely managed to pay the phone bill for April, and if she didn't find a job soon, she'd have to cancel the service, which would mean no more calls or text messages.

She picked up the phone and looked at the caller ID. *Oh great, it's Shelly again. I may as well answer or she'll keep calling.*

Kendra swiped her thumb across the screen. "Hi, Shelly. What's up?"

"That's what I'm hoping you'll tell me. I've tried calling several times but you never answer or respond to my messages. Are you avoiding me, Kendra?"

"Not avoiding exactly." Kendra switched the phone to her other ear. "Just don't have anything to say."

"How about telling me why you left home without letting me know where you were going?" Kendra heard the irritation in her sister's voice.

"Did you ask Mom or Dad?"

"Yes, and they said they didn't know where you were."

"What else did they tell you?"

"Dad said you're pregnant. It is true, Kendra? He kicked you out?"

"Yeah, I'm expecting a baby, and Dad sent me packing when I told him."

Kendra half expected her sister to hang up, or at least make some negative comment.

A few seconds ticked by before Shelly spoke. "So where are you staying?" No caustic comments or accusations. Only a simple question.

"I'm in Mt. Hope, at my friend Dorie's."

"Well, you need to come home so we can help you. You can't take care of a baby alone."

Neck bent slightly forward, Kendra folded her arms over her stomach. "Didn't you hear what I said? I'm an embarrassment to our parents—especially Dad. He doesn't want me there anymore, and he made it clear that I should keep my mouth shut about the pregnancy. I'm sure he's worried someone at church will find out." She sucked in a breath. "And of course, that would be terrible. Someone might frown on a board member who couldn't keep his daughter from messing up."

"That's ridiculous. We're family, and family needs to stick together during good times and bad. I don't care about Dad's threats or what he's worried about either."

"What do you mean? What else did he say?"

"Dad told me not to contact you. No text messages or phone calls." Shelly laughed. "But you see where that got him. Even though he's our father, I don't agree with what he said, because it's just not right."

"You'd better do as he said, Shelly. Same goes for Chris. Don't make things worse for yourself."

"I don't care. He can't keep me from talking to my sister."

"It's a tough time for me, and it hurts to know Mom and Dad don't care about anyone but themselves." Kendra flexed her fingers. "Don't worry about me, sis. I'll manage somehow. Just keep your grades up in school and stay away from untrustworthy guys like Max. Oh, and make sure you don't do anything wrong, or you're likely to get kicked out of the house."

"Kendra, I. . ."

"Can't talk any longer. Dorie's car pulled in." Kendra

muttered a quick goodbye and clicked off the phone. In some ways she felt better for having talked with Shelly. In another way she felt like pond scum because, by succumbing to Max's charms, she'd let her whole family down.

Kendra cleared her dishes and had begun putting them in the sink when Dorie came in. Thankfully, Gene wasn't with her. The last thing Kendra needed right now was to watch those two hanging all over each other.

"Guess what?" Dorie's face broke into a wide smile. "Gene and I ate at Mrs. Yoder's Kitchen tonight, and I found out they are looking for a part-time dishwasher."

Kendra bit the inside of her cheek. "I need more than a part-time job. Besides, washing dishes isn't the kind of work I want to do."

"Beggars can't be choosy." Dorie draped her sweater over the back of a chair. "It could work into a full-time job, or maybe a waitressing position will open up." She moved closer to Kendra. "I'd apply for the job if I were you."

"Okay, I'll go to the restaurant tomorrow and put in my application. Since it's within walking distance, I won't need to borrow your car." Kendra gave a half-hearted shrug. "But then since you'll be working tomorrow, I wouldn't be able to borrow it anyway."

Dorie slipped her arm around Kendra's waist. "Try not to worry. Things will get better soon; you'll see."

"Yeah, right." Kendra turned away from the sink, pressing her hands to her temples. "Nothing ever works out for me."

Walnut Creek

Ron watched out the side window of his motor home as Heidi and Lyle got into their buggy and rode out of the yard. Earlier, Lyle had mentioned joining some of their friends for supper this evening and said they wouldn't be home for a few hours.

This is the perfect opportunity to sneak into their house. Ron rubbed his hands briskly together. *Providing the doors aren't locked, that is.*

He waited until the horse and buggy were out of sight then stepped out of his rig and glanced around. *Good thing they don't have close neighbors.*

When he got to the front porch and tried the door, he discovered it was locked. *Drat!*

Hoping the back door might be unlocked, Ron hurried around the side of the house. There, he spotted the Troyers' dog, lying on the porch with his nose between his paws.

Ron stepped cautiously onto the porch, but the dog didn't budge. *Stupid mutt. Some watchdog you are.* But then Rusty was used to him by now. Ron shook his head when the dog lifted his head, tail thumping against the wooden floor. "Go back to sleep, Rusty."

He turned the doorknob and felt relief when it opened. Upon entering the kitchen, Ron grabbed a few cookies from the plastic container he spotted on the counter. He ate one and stuffed two more in his shirt pocket. Then he made his way to the dining room, opened the hutch, and lifted out the vase he'd seen Lyle put money in on Saturday. Ron whistled when he saw the bills were still there. Placing the money on the table, he counted ten twenty-dollar bills.

Ron chewed on his lower lip. *How many should I take?* He knew better than to take all the money. A few missing bills may not raise any suspicion. Lyle might think he'd miscounted when he'd put the money in the vase. Ron put seven twenties back and kept three. Given the opportunity, he'd check the vase again in a few days and see if any additional money had been added. If so, he'd take a few more.

"Easy-peasy." Ron made his way back to the kitchen. He'd stayed at many places during his time on the road, but none quite as easy as this. By the time he left here at the end of June, he'd have quite a haul. People who left their doors open when they weren't home were just asking to be ripped off.

Ron looked up at the oil lamps above one of the cupboards. Since he was here, he might as well take a few of those too.

Chapter 17

Sugarcreek

Loretta stoked the logs in the fireplace and took a seat on the couch. While the afternoon had been warm, the evening grew chilly. She tried to relax, watching the flames rekindle as the wood popped and sparks disappeared up the chimney. Today seemed long, and it had been difficult getting the children settled in their beds. "It's my fault," she murmured. "I shouldn't have let them eat candy so close to bedtime."

Recently, Loretta had tried to practice better eating habits—for herself, as well as the children. But when they whined, she sometimes gave in to their requests for sugary treats, which made them hyper.

Since Rick's death, it had been difficult to keep from giving in to their whims. They needed their father, especially as they were growing up. A parent's "tough love" approach was never easy, but even more of a challenge for a single parent. Loretta reminded herself it was how a child learned—even if it meant refusing them something they enjoyed.

From where she sat in the living room, looking out the side window, Loretta enjoyed watching a few birds flitting around to find a roosting spot for the night. She glanced toward Sam's place and thought about his raspberry patch, which was slowly coming to life. He'd mentioned how he'd planted the bushes a number of years ago when his wife was still living, and each year the mass seemed to get thicker. The long stems leafed out, and tiny white flowers became visible. Loretta could almost taste the sweetness of the juicy red berries and how they melted in her mouth. Sam was good about sharing his bounty with her and other neighbors. This year it might be fun to make raspberry jam. *I wonder if Heidi makes jelly. Bet she does.*

When Loretta closed her eyes, a memory, which seemed like yesterday, popped into her head. It had been a quiet, warm summer evening. After she and Rick took turns reading a bedtime story and had watched their daughter fall asleep, they'd tiptoed out to the front porch for some alone time. They'd visited awhile, and when Loretta surprised Rick with the news he'd be a daddy again, he'd pulled her into his arms. "I'm so glad. Do I dare hope it's a boy this time?"

Loretta had smiled and gently pinched his cheek. "Whatever God chooses to give us will be a blessing."

Shortly after, Sam ventured over and joined them on the porch. He'd brought a bucket of raspberries he'd picked that afternoon.

"If you've got some ice cream, I've got the topping," Sam announced.

After Rick shared their good news with Sam, he suggested they make it a celebration. The three of them enjoyed vanilla bean ice cream, topped with Sam's luscious ripe berries. Sam had seemed as excited for them as they were with the blessing and promise of another child.

Loretta opened her eyes and picked up the cup of hot chocolate she'd fixed herself after tucking the children in bed. How many nights had she and Rick sat here, enjoying each other's company and the warmth of the fire? How lonely she felt without him.

Sighing, Loretta reached for comfort by lifting her Bible from the coffee table and opening it to her favorite passage—Psalm 23:1–3: " 'The Lord is my shepherd; I shall not want. He maketh me to lie down in green pastures: he leadeth me beside the still waters. He restoreth my soul: he leadeth me in the paths of righteousness for his name's sake.' " She closed her eyes. *Thank You, Lord, for leading and guiding me. Help me become a blessing to all those I meet. Give me wisdom in raising my children, and keep us safe throughout this night. Thank You for every blessing in my life. Amen.*

Sparks flared upward from the burning log in the fireplace, fizzling out as they rose higher. Her husband's life had vanished like the fire's sparks—here one second, gone the next. *Will my life ever feel complete again?* Loretta hoped so, for her sake as well as the children's. Difficult as it was to remember those days, Loretta wanted—no, needed—to keep the memories alive. When the children grew older, they'd no doubt have many questions about their father. There were so many good memories she could share with Abby and Conner.

Loretta lifted her cup and was about to take a drink when the telephone rang. She set the cup down and hurried to the kitchen to answer it. *Sure hope I remembered to turn the ringer off the extension upstairs so it doesn't wake Conner and Abby.*

As soon as Loretta entered the kitchen, she grabbed the receiver. "Hello."

"Hi Loretta, it's Becky from church."

"It's nice hearing from you. How have you been?"

"Super busy right now. I'm on the planning committee, and I wondered if you'd be able to help with our church yard sale, which is a week from this Saturday."

Loretta's face tightened, feeling a twinge of irritation. Becky hadn't even bothered to ask how she and the children were doing. Didn't she care?

"I'm sorry, Becky, but I won't be able to help with the yard sale. I have another commitment that day." Loretta looked at the calendar, where she'd circled the date of the next cooking class. *No point telling Becky what I'll be doing that Saturday. She'd probably think it wasn't as important as the church function.* She stared at the floor. *When did I become so cynical? Who am I to say what her response would have been?*

"It's fine. I understand," Becky replied sweetly. "I hope you have a nice evening, and I'll see you at church this Sunday."

"Okay. Bye, Becky." Loretta hung up and returned to the living room to finish her drink, which was now lukewarm. Looking upward, she prayed, *Lord, help me avoid being judgmental.*

Walnut Creek

"You're awfully quiet," Lyle commented as he and Heidi headed for home. "Didn't you have a good time at the Rabers' tonight?"

"Jah, I did. It was a pleasant evening, and I enjoyed holding their new boppli." She pulled her shawl tighter around her neck to ward off the chill permeating the buggy. It was hard to believe the weather had been so nice earlier today.

Lyle nodded. "He's a cute little guy."

"Holding him made me long for a child of our own even more." Heidi released a lingering sigh. She could

145

almost smell the baby lotion reaching her nostrils when she'd held the precious bundle an hour ago. "We're missing out on so much not having children of our own. If only God would give us a miracle."

Lyle let go of the reins with one hand and took hold of Heidi's hand. "We agreed to accept our situation as God's will."

"No, it's what you decided. This is easier for you than me." She inhaled sharply, hoping to hold back forthcoming tears. Every time the topic of her inability to conceive came up, an unseen barrier wedged between them. If only Lyle would change his mind about adoption. Tonight had been such a pleasant evening, and Heidi didn't want it to end on a sour note. Whenever she was around children, her longings sprang to the surface, even though she tried hard to keep them buried.

"Let's talk about something else." She squeezed his fingers. "You never did say what you found out about getting another open buggy."

His teeth clicked together. "Don't think it's gonna happen this year, Heidi. The price I was quoted is more than I care to spend right now."

"It's okay. Our old buggy is fine."

"Jah, it's probably good for another year or so."

"Say, when we get home, would you like a few of the molasses kichlin I made earlier today?"

"Normally I'd go right for 'em, but I ate too much supper tonight, so I'm still pretty full." He let go of her hand and thumped his stomach.

"You gobbled down your fair share of fried chicken, all right." Heidi chuckled. "I'll make sure to put several cookies in your lunch bucket tomorrow."

"Sounds good."

They rode in silence the rest of the way. While

being lulled by the buggy's gentle sway, Heidi almost fell asleep listening to the steady *clip-clop, clip-clop* of the horse's hooves against the pavement.

When Lyle pulled the horse up to the hitching rail, he handed the reins to her while he got out and secured the animal. Bobbins usually cooperated and remained at the rail, but Lyle never took chances. A few years ago, two small children in their community waited in their father's buggy. Before he got his horse secured, it backed up, turned, and bolted. The children were lucky their dad caught up with the buggy and was able to subdue the horse before it ran into the road. What turned out to be a frightening adventure for the little ones ended well. Unfortunately, that wasn't always the case. There had been many accidents due to horses bolting when they became spooked by something, or sometimes for no apparent reason at all.

Once certain Bobbins had been secured, Heidi got out of the buggy. While Lyle put the horse in the barn, she headed for the house, using a flashlight to guide the way.

Upon entering the kitchen, she turned on the gaslight over the table, which illuminated the room with a warm glow. Since her nerves were a bit frazzled, and she felt more awake now, Heidi turned on the stove to heat water in the teakettle. While getting a cup from the cupboard, she noticed several cookie crumbs on the counter. "Well, that *schtinker*," she murmured. "Looks like my husband sampled some of the molasses *kichlin* before we left home."

Grabbing a sponge from the kitchen sink, Heidi cleaned up the mess and put the crumbs in the garbage can. After the water heated, she fixed herself a cup of chamomile tea and took a seat at the table.

Several minutes later, Lyle came in. "How about a

cup of tea?" she asked.

"Sure, and I've changed my mind about the *kichlin.* Think I'll try a couple to go with the tea." With a playful grin, he winked at her.

Heidi lifted her gaze toward the ceiling. "From the looks of the *grimmel* I found on the counter a few minutes ago, I'd say you already had a taste of my cookies."

His forehead wrinkled. "No I didn't, Heidi. Never went near the cookie container."

Setting her cup down, she pursed her lips. "I suppose I could have dropped a few crumbs when I put the cookies away and just didn't notice."

"You know how it is. We all do things without realizing it." Lyle's eyes widened, and his voice lowered to a whisper. "Or maybe we have a *maus* in the house."

"Oh dear. Don't even suggest such a thing, especially since I'm conducting cooking classes here in the kitchen. I can only imagine my students' response if a mouse made an appearance during one of our classes."

Lyle tickled Heidi under her chin. "I was only teasing." He opened the plastic container and took out three cookies. After placing two on a napkin, he ate the third one. "Yum. Yum. I'm a *glicklich* man to be married to such a good cook."

"Danki." She smiled. "And I'm lucky to have a man who appreciates my efforts." Heidi truly was thankful for her husband. Once more, she vowed to quit feeling sorry for herself because they had no children and remember to count her blessings.

After tossing and turning several hours, Eli got out bed. *Think I'll head to the kitchen and get a drink of water.*

He'd only taken a few steps toward the door when

he tripped over a boot and bumped into his dresser. "Ouch!" Eli leaned over to rub his knee, and when his head came up, he clipped it on the top of the dresser. "Not fun."

Fumbling for his flashlight, he clicked it on and looked in the mirror above the dresser. The bump on the head didn't look too bad, but boy, his knee sure hurt.

Limping his way to the kitchen, Eli gritted his teeth. *If Mavis were here now she'd get me a glass of water, and put Arnica ointment on my knee. My wife always did pamper me.*

After turning on the gas lamp over the table, Eli stood at the sink, looking out the window while he filled his glass with cold water. The moon, reflecting on the pond at the edge of his property, caught his attention. Little ripples formed when a slight breeze occurred, turning the moon's image into diamond-like shapes, sparkling on the water's surface.

His stomach rumbled as he turned back around. There were no snacks in the refrigerator, and not a single cookie filled the cookie jar. What he wouldn't give for something sweet to munch on right now.

Sure hope Mom gives me more kichlin soon. He tilted the glass, gulping down the water. *Store-bought doesn't taste the same as homemade.*

Eli limped across the room and lowered himself into his favorite chair at the table. Staring into space, he reflected once again on the wonderful years he and Mavis shared, and some of the silly things they used to do. He laughed out loud, recalling the night neither of them could sleep. They had no dessert or snacks that evening, and both craved something sweet. After tossing and turning to no avail, Mavis came up with a crazy idea. "Let's make a batch of kichlin." Of course,

Eli didn't disagree. Later, as they sat at the kitchen table sharing milk and peanut butter cookies, he announced, "These are the best tasting cookies I've ever eaten. Think they taste better when they're right out of the oven."

Mavis smiled and poked his belly. "Now, don't get used to the idea. I'm not planning to get out of bed in the wee hours and bake cookies often."

Eli looked at his empty cookie jar as his mind snapped back to the present. *Think I'll drop by my folks' place later this week and see if Mom's made any cookies recently. If not, I'll stop at one of the bakeries on my way home. It's not good to have an empty cookie jar in the house.*

Chapter 18

Thursday afternoon, while Heidi was taking a pie from the oven, Lyle came into the kitchen. "What smells so good?" He breathed deeply. "Yum."

"I made a pie using some of the peaches I canned last year." Heidi noticed Lyle held the vase from the dining room hutch.

"Did you take any money from this?" His forehead creased as he lifted it up.

She shook her head. "Since the money we put in there is for things we're saving up for, I'd never take anything without checking with you first."

He tipped his head. "Hmm. . . Could have sworn I put $200 in here the other day, but now there's only $140. Maybe I had less than I thought." He scratched the side of his head. "Am I getting forgetful all of a sudden? I'm only thirty. Could old age be creeping in already?"

Heidi touched his arm. "Don't be silly. We all forget things."

"True, but I'm almost sure. . ." His voice trailed off as he leaned against the counter. "You don't suppose one of your students took it?"

She shook her head briskly. "I don't see how. We were all here in the dining room at the same time, so there was no chance anyone could have taken it without the others seeing."

"Guess you're right. Even so, I'd better put this in a less conspicuous place." Lyle opened the cupboard door where their dishes were kept and placed the vase on the top shelf next to some empty canning jars. Then he turned to face Heidi again. "If you haven't started supper yet, why don't we go out for a bite to eat?"

"Well. . ." She tapped her chin. "I'd planned to fix a meat loaf, but if I don't have to cook this evening, it'll keep the kitchen cooler. And when we get home, I can work on my lesson plan for the upcoming cooking class."

"Then it's settled." He pulled her into his arms for a sweet kiss. "Besides, you work hard around here and deserve a break from cooking once in a while."

"I got a break the other night, when we went to the Rabers' for supper, remember?"

The skin around Lyle's eyes crinkled when he smiled. "You're right, but we spent the whole evening visiting, which didn't give you any time to prepare for your next class, as you'd hoped to do then. Speaking of which, what dish will you be teaching them how to make this time?"

"I thought of sweet-and-sour meatballs at first but changed my mind. Think I'll teach them how to make German pizza instead."

His eyes gleamed as he wiggled his brows. "It's one of my favorites."

Giggling, Heidi gave his stomach a gentle poke. "You have a good many favorites, dear husband."

———⚬⚬⚬———

Sugarcreek

"It's good to see you, son." Mom gave Eli such a tight

squeeze it nearly took his breath away. For a woman of small stature, she had great power in her hugs.

"It's good to see you too." Eli sniffed the air. "Whatcha been bakin', Mom?"

She took a plastic container from the cupboard and opened it.

Eli's mouth watered. "Banana whoopie pies. You're a good mamm. You always remember those are one of my favorite cookies."

She chuckled and squeezed his arm tenderly. "Don't worry. I'll send plenty of them home with you."

"How about now? Do I get to eat one before I go?"

"Certainly, and you're welcome to stay for supper."

Eli shook his head. "As hard as it is to turn down the offer, I have a few errands to run in Berlin. Then I'm heading right home. There's work waiting for me in the shop."

Mom's forehead wrinkled. "Okay, but you have to promise to come over for a meal soon. I always fix more than your *daed* and I can eat." She put a whoopie pie on a plate and handed it to Eli. "Would you like some milk to go with it?"

"Sure, but I can get it."

"That's okay. Please take a seat at the table and let your old mamm wait on you. I don't get the chance to do it often."

Eli pulled out a chair and sat down. "One of these days I'm gonna invite you and Dad to my house for a meal."

She peered at him over the top of her glasses. "Oh? Have you found a woman friend? Are you courting again?"

His body stiffened. "Course not. No one could ever replace Mavis."

"Starting over with a new fraa would not mean you are replacing your first wife." She poured him a glass of milk and placed it on the table.

His mother meant well, but insinuating he find a new wife did not sit well with Eli. She ought to realize how much he'd loved Mavis and still did. Did Mom think he could forget what they'd once had and move on with his life as though Mavis never existed?

Eli took a breath and blew it out. The best thing to do was change the subject. "So where's Dad this afternoon? Figured he'd be off work by now."

"He went to the dentist's. They'll be seating his new crown, so it could be awhile before he gets home."

Eli glanced at the clock above the refrigerator. "Guess I won't get to see him then, 'cause as soon as I finish this treat I need to go."

Mom's lower lip protruded. "But Eli, you only got here a few minutes ago. We don't get to see you as often as we'd like. For that matter, we even hoped you might sell your place and move closer to us."

"I'm not sellin' my place." Eli's shoulders tensed. "It's been my home since Mavis and I got married, and it'll be my home till the day I die. I won't change my mind neither."

Mom winced. "Calm down, son. You don't need to be so testy. I meant no harm."

A sense of guilt came over Eli, and he quickly apologized. "Sorry, I'm a bit sensitive when it comes to the idea of leaving my home. Mavis was everything to me, and I miss her something awful. I could never leave the place that holds so many special memories."

Mom rested her hand on his shoulder. "I don't understand exactly how you feel because I haven't lost my mate, but a mother's heart hurts to see her child, grown or otherwise, brokenhearted." She paused, clearing her throat. "I won't bring up the topic again, but if you ever want to talk, I'm here for you, Eli."

"Danki." He bit into the whoopie pie. "This is *appeditlich*."

She took a seat beside him. "I'm not one to brag on my baking abilities, but I must agree—these cookies turned out delicious."

A short time later, as Eli headed down the road with his horse and buggy, he glanced at the container on the seat beside him. As much he liked Mom's banana whoopie pies, even over a period of a few days, he could not eat all twelve of them. *Mom means well though. She only wants the best for me, even with her insinuating I should get married again.*

He clicked his tongue and snapped the reins to get Blossom moving a little quicker. He'd brought Mavis's horse out today, thinking she needed a workout. Trouble was, the lazy animal wanted to poke along. Time was dwindling, and if he didn't get to Berlin soon, he'd have to take care of his errands quickly in order to get home at a reasonable time to finish some work.

To save precious minutes, Eli took a shortcut. As his rig crested a hill, he caught sight of a woman by her mailbox, near the edge of the road. "*Ach*, it's Loretta." Eli pulled back on the reins. Then he waved and called out to her.

With her mouth open slightly, she waved in response.

On impulse, he directed Blossom up Loretta's driveway, even though he was pressed for time. For the moment, it didn't seem to matter. "So, is this where you live?"

Smiling, she nodded. "What brings you out my way?"

"I was at my folks' place. I believe I mentioned they

live here in Sugarcreek. Funny thing is, I've been past this place many times but didn't know until today that you lived here."

"Most likely it's because our first meeting was at Heidi's cooking class. So even if you'd seen me, it would have meant nothing. You'd have probably thought I was just another English woman working out in her yard."

"Maybe so." Eli couldn't put a finger on it, but he felt relaxed talking to Loretta right now. Something about her mannerisms reminded him of Mavis. Her looks were different, of course, but Loretta's soft-spoken voice and quiet demeanor were similar to his wife's.

Remembering the container of cookies, he picked it up. "Do you or your children like whoopie pies?"

"What child doesn't like whoopie pies?" Loretta giggled. "Call me a kid, but I love 'em too."

"Well, good, 'cause my mother gave me several banana-flavored whoopies, and I'd like to share 'em with you."

"How nice." Deep dimples showed in Loretta's cheeks when she smiled. "I'll run up to the house and get another container so you can keep yours." Before heading up the driveway, she added, "I'd invite you in, but Abby and Conner are napping. They'd most likely wake up if they heard us talking. Then I'd never get them back to sleep."

"It's okay, I understand." Eli handed her the container. "I'm actually heading to Berlin to get a few things, and afterward I need to go right home. There's plenty of work waiting for me there."

"Okay, I won't be long. How many should I take?"

"Leave me two and you can have the rest."

"Are you sure? I don't want to cut you short."

"Not a problem." He thumped his stomach. "I don't need the extra pounds, and I'm most happy to share."

While Eli waited for Loretta to return, he glanced around her place. It looked like the house and garage sat on half an acre or so. The lawn appeared to have been recently mowed, and he noticed a weed-free garden on one side of the yard. Did Loretta take care of it herself, or might a friend or relative help out? Another home sat next door. Eli saw a man walking around a berry patch.

Mavis's horse grew restless and stomped her front hooves. "Settle down, Blossom. We'll be on our way soon."

Loretta returned a short time later and handed him the container. "The children will be happy when they wake up to such a nice snack. Please tell your mother thank you."

"I will."

"Oh, and feel free to stop by anytime you're in the area. I'd like you to meet my kinner."

Eli grinned. *There she goes again, using a Pennsylvania Dutch word.* "I'll take you up on the offer, 'cause I'd enjoy meeting them too." He gave a small wave. "See you at the cooking class a week from Saturday."

"Yes. I'm looking forward to it."

Eli paused long enough to watch Loretta wave at her neighbor then walk over to his yard. *I wonder if the man she's chatting with is the "Sam" she's mentioned a few times during class. He looks old enough to be Loretta's dad.*

Eli shrugged his shoulders and whistled a tune as he backed the horse and buggy onto the road. For some reason, after seeing Loretta, he felt carefree and was glad he'd given her some of Mom's whoopie pies. It felt good to do something nice for someone. *Paying it forward— that's what it's called.* Eli thought of the scripture on the back of the haystack recipe card he'd received from Heidi. This was what it meant to have a merry heart.

Mt. Hope

When Kendra left Mrs. Yoder's Kitchen and headed back to Dorie's, her spirits lifted a bit. She'd been hired to wash dishes. Even though it wasn't her first choice, at least some money would be coming in soon, which meant she could help her friend with expenses. Kendra felt grateful she'd be working afternoons and some evenings, because mornings were still the worst for her when it came to dealing with the nausea. The best part of all was that she wouldn't have to work Saturdays and miss any of the cooking classes. Tomorrow would be her first day on the job, and then she wouldn't work again until Monday. She'd have a day to get oriented to her duties, and then two days off.

Sure wish there was something fun to do this weekend. It's boring to sit around while Dorie goes out with Gene. When he comes to her house, it's even worse, 'cause I have to hide out in my bedroom to give them private time together.

Kendra stopped walking and bent to pick up an aluminum can someone had carelessly thrown on the sidewalk. *Some people have no respect. Littering to them is no big deal.* She tossed the can in the nearest trash container and continued on.

Kendra looked at her shadow, which, like her profile, revealed a small baby bump. Instinctively, she rubbed her hand over the swell on her stomach. Then she glanced up as she rounded the corner. Approaching Dorie's house, she came to a halt. "It can't be." Seeing a familiar car parked in the driveway, Kendra groaned. Her body tensed as her hand went from her stomach to her forehead. *Oh no, it's Dad. What does he want?*

Chapter 19

Kendra's legs trembled as she approached her father getting out of his car. Did she dare hope he had come to apologize and ask her to return home, or could there be something else on his mind?

"Hi, Dad. I. . .I'm surprised to see you here."

His eyes narrowed as he glared at her. "Don't know why. You should have expected me."

"Wh–what do you mean?" Her hands moved jerkily.

He took a step closer, nostrils flaring. "Don't play games. You know precisely what I mean. You disrespected me and turned a blind eye to what I asked you not to do."

"What was that?"

"You talked to Shelly about your pregnancy and blamed your mom and me for throwing you out."

"It's the truth, isn't it?"

"Don't get smart." A vein on the side of his head twitched. "To make things worse, Shelly blabbed the whole thing to Chris. Now they're both upset."

And I'm not? "Are they upset with me for getting pregnant or upset with you for kicking me out?" Kendra kept her chin high and her voice even, refusing to let her defenselessness show. She'd always knuckled under when dealing with her dad. But no matter how much energy it took, today Kendra would not let him intimidate her.

His voice rose a notch. "Watch your attitude, Kendra."

She shifted her weight. *He's avoiding my question.*

"I came here to warn you."

"Warn me about what?" Kendra's anger increased. It took every ounce of resistance to keep from shouting at him.

"Your sisters are impressionable, and they've always looked up to you." He loosened his collar. "I've forbidden them to contact you again, and I warned them that if they do, they'll also be kicked out of the house."

Her mouth dropped open. "You're kidding! It's not right to punish Shelly and Chris because you're angry at me." She'd never dreamed her dad could be so cruel or unreasonable. What had come over him to be treating his family like this?

"I'm not punishing them. I am protecting my youngest daughters. If you care anything about your sisters, then do as I say, and stay away from them." His thick brows squished together. "Do you hear me? No more interaction, including phone calls, text messages, email, or social media communication."

Before Kendra's response spewed from her lips, he got back in his car and drove away. She'd wanted to tell him to leave. This was her home, although temporary. Dad had no right to come here and berate her. *How could my own father, who I used to look up to, treat me like this?*

Shoulders sagging and eyes watering, she shuffled toward the mobile home. *So much for the verse from Proverbs 17:22 Heidi gave us. If Dad has anything to say about it, my heart will never be merry. Thank goodness Dorie isn't home yet, because I need to be alone right now so*

I can cave in and have a good cry.

Kendra had never deemed herself a weak person emotionally, but since she'd become pregnant, her emotions were all over the place.

She entered the mobile home and sank to the couch, letting her head fall forward into her hands. It was bad enough the future of her unborn baby grew more uncertain each day, but having no communication with or support from her family made it ten times worse.

"What I allowed to happen with Max was wrong, but must I pay for my sins the rest of my life?" Trembling, Kendra looked upward.

No response. Not that she expected any. Her throat constricted. *God's abandoned me, just like Mom and Dad.*

The front door opened, and Dorie stepped in. She stood next to the couch, looking down at Kendra through squinted eyes. "From the looks of your gloomy expression, I'm guessing you didn't get the dishwashing job."

"No, I got it, all right. I start work tomorrow."

"Then why the sad face?"

"My dad paid me a visit. He was waiting outside when I got home from the job interview."

"Uh–oh. What'd he say?"

"Chewed me out for talking to Shelly and confirming that Dad kicked me out. I guess the truth hurt." Kendra wiped the moisture from beneath her eyes. "He told me under no uncertain terms that I am to have nothing to do with my sisters."

Dorie sat on the couch beside Kendra. "You're not a child. He can't tell you what to do. Besides, you're not living under his roof anymore."

"No, but he can make life difficult for Shelly and Chris. If I try to contact my sisters, he vowed to kick them out too."

"How terrible." Dorie gave Kendra a hug. "I'm sorry you have to go through all this turmoil, and your sisters too. Your dad's being so unreasonable. Someday he'll regret how he's treated his family."

"I hope he does, but Dad's so stubborn I doubt he cares about anyone but himself. And he calls himself a Christian?" She sniffed. "If I do get to keep my baby, none of my family will get the privilege of knowing him."

"Or her." Dorie bumped Kendra's arm. "It could be a girl, you know."

Kendra forced a smile. "Thanks for letting me vent. I needed to get some stuff off my chest."

"No problem. That's what friends are for."

❦

Berlin

"Thanks for the ride," Ron told Lyle's driver as they left the post office in Berlin, where he'd picked up his government check. "If you'll swing by the bank in Walnut Creek before we head back to the Troyers', I'll cash my check and get you paid."

Eric nodded. "I'm curious. How long have you known the Troyers?"

"Met 'em early April."

"And you've been staying with them ever since?"

Ron rubbed the back of his neck. *What's with this guy and his inquisitions?* "I'm not stayin' with them. They've allowed me to park my rig on their property till I could get it running good again."

"And have you?"

"Not yet. Had to order a part, and it hasn't come in." He held up his check. "Until I got this, I had no money to pay for the part." Quickly changing the subject, Ron pointed to a line of cars up ahead. "Looks like traffic's stopped for some reason. Hope we won't be late getting to the bank."

Eric craned his head. "From what I can see, there's road work up ahead. Don't think it'll take long to get through it though. I see a flagman letting one lane go."

They waited alongside a huge field. Ron noticed the acreage had already been cultivated and how healthy looking the turned soil seemed to be. An Amish man with three plow horses skillfully maneuvered his team down the next row, along with what looked to be some sort of seeder attached. One big tree, almost completely leafed out, stood stoically in the open field.

"It's amazing what the Amish accomplish in our modern-day world, isn't it?" Eric looked in the same direction as Ron.

"I guess so." Ron shrugged. To him, plowing with horses seemed like too much labor. He also wondered why a tree as big as this one would be left in the middle of the field to work around. *It'd be easier to cut the thing down, wouldn't it?* He'd no sooner thought it than he noticed the Amish man stop and wave at someone coming from the back of the field, where the barn and farmhouse stood. It was a woman, and as she approached the big sprawling tree, he saw that she carried a picnic basket.

Ron didn't want to watch anymore, but he couldn't turn away. While this lady, who he assumed was the man's wife, smoothed a dark-colored tablecloth over the ground and took things out of the basket, the farmer steered his team of well-behaved horses around the back of the tree.

For a split second, Ron experienced a tinge of regret, observing a simple act between the Amish couple. *If only Fran and I. . .*

He leaned back and tried to relax, but sitting in this traffic got on his nerves. *When will we ever get going?*

⸻ ⚬⦳⚬ ⸻

Walnut Creek

It hadn't taken Eli long to get home after he'd run errands in Berlin. Work awaited him in the shop, but he no longer felt ambitious.

"Think I'll take a minute to relax before I delve into work." Eli talked as if someone was there with him. He'd done it often since Mavis passed away.

After making himself a cup of coffee and taking a whoopie pie from the container, he went outside to do a little porch sitting. Blowing on the cup of steaming brew, he stared out toward his pond. Mavis had wanted a pond so badly, and they'd been fortunate to come across this farm to buy. Eli felt his body relax as he bit into the sweet treat. Except for the rippling from a mallard duck swimming peacefully over the surface, the rest of the pond held a coating of film from pollen settling on the top.

Eli rubbed his hand over the armrest of his chair, observing the pollen there too. *Guess I should have wiped this off before I sat down.* An image of Mavis bustling around to wipe off the porch furniture came to mind. Another pleasant memory to reflect upon.

After taking off his boots and wearing only his socks, Eli tucked his feet under Lady, slumbering in front of him. As a frog croaked and several others joined in, a grunt escaped the dog's lips. Then Lady stretched her legs out to the side and made lapping noises as she settled in.

"You like the peace and quiet too, don't ya, girl?" Eli

rubbed his foot over her fur. This was the kind of quiet-ness he immersed himself in every chance he got. Almost every occasion brought memories of things he and Mavis had enjoyed. When spring arrived, once the chores were done, the porch always drew their attention. Many evenings they'd watched deer grazing on tender sprouts coming up in the meadow adjoining their back property.

Among the daisies, which recently started blooming, spotty clusters of mustard weed glowed yellow near the pond. Colorful butterflies, and even a few dragonflies, made their way through the warm spring air. One dragonfly was not so lucky when it ventured out over the pond. A fish jumped out at the exact moment, grabbing the tasty meal. As the fish splashed down under the water, the duck spread its wings and took flight. Quick as a flash, Lady jumped up, barking on the porch's edge while watching the duck fly away in protest.

As the mallard flew over the house, still quacking, Eli smiled and took the last swig of coffee. Reluctantly, he pushed himself out of the chair. "Guess I better get something done instead of sittin' here watching time go by." Looking back toward the woodshed, Eli noticed a black-and-white critter heading to a stack of wood he'd piled near the shed the other day. "Oh great. Hope that skunk doesn't decide to take up residence here. Sure don't need that."

———⟋ ⟍———

Sugarcreek

"Anyone want a banana whoopie pie?" Loretta asked when Conner and Abby woke up from their naps.

They both nodded with eager expressions. "Did ya bake 'em while we were sleepin'?" Abby questioned.

"No, a man I met at the cooking class brought them by awhile ago. His mother made the whoopie pies, and he wanted to share some with us."

"Is he a nice man?" Abby clambered into a chair.

Scrambling into his booster seat, Conner echoed, "Nice man?"

"Yes, he is." Loretta appreciated Eli's quiet, pleasant demeanor from the first time she'd met him. He'd seemed shy at first, but after visiting with him a few times, he'd become more relaxed and talkative. With the exception of Ron, everyone attending Heidi's classes seemed nice. Something about Ron bothered Loretta though.

Heidi and her husband are kinder than me. Loretta took a seat between her children. *Since Rick died, maybe I've become too paranoid, but I'd never let a stranger stay on my property a full day, much less the three months it will take to complete Heidi's cooking classes.*

"Mama, are ya gonna give us the cookies?"

Loretta blinked. "Of course, Conner. I'll also pour you a glass of milk."

A few minutes later, Loretta sat at the table with her children, eating the delicious whoopie pies. She looked forward to seeing Eli again. Someday soon, maybe the children would get to meet him.

Chapter 20

Walnut Creek

Eli leaned against the porch post, breathing in the morning's damp air. Fog was lifting, while shafts of sunlight patterned streaks through the misty break of day. Spiderwebs in various parts of his yard hung heavy with the morning dew. The temperature climbed as the sky's milky haze parted and a beautiful blue spread out in its place. "Looks as if a nice day is rolling in." Eli leaned down to pat his dog's head then stretched and leaned back, getting the kinks out of his sore muscles. His knee felt better this morning, but his back hurt some, due to bending over to work on a coffin he'd started making yesterday.

Glancing toward the woodpile stacked close to the house, he put his work gloves on and yawned. It would have been a good morning to stay in bed a bit longer, but Eli never cared much for sleeping in. For as long as he remembered, even as a young boy, he liked morning. *"A body misses a lot if they stay in bed too long,"* his dad always said. Mavis had been an early riser too. One more of the things she and Eli had in common.

Eli looked toward the sky again. *Better get this woodpile relocated before I head to the Troyers'.*

Turning his attention downward as he walked toward the firewood, Eli spotted more ruts in the grass. "I'm getting sick and tired of that irritating *bisskatz* makin' holes all over my yard. Probably diggin' for grubs." Eli stomped the divots back down, making them level with the lawn. Lady followed him, head down, sniffing the ground.

Eli had waited up last night, and the night before too, but never saw any sign of the skunk. He'd also set out a cage to trap the critter but ended up catching the neighbor's cat instead. "Guess the animal's only doing what skunks know how to do." Eli tried to make light of the situation, even though his yard had begun to look like swiss cheese.

I'll worry about finding the little schtinker later on. Eli filled the wheelbarrow and hauled the wood over to the shed, while Lady returned to the porch and flopped down. Despite the clumps in his yard, Eli's mood was cheery. Every day since the last cooking class he'd read Proverbs 17:22, reminding him of the importance of having a merry heart. Not even the skunk put a damper on his mood this morning. He looked forward to going to Heidi's again and wondered what plans she had for their class today. Eli was also eager to talk with Loretta and hear how she and her children enjoyed the whoopie pies he'd given her. *Think I'll walk to the Troyers' house again. Maybe Loretta will drive by and, like the last time, offer me a ride.* He smiled. Whistling through his lips, a merry tune followed.

Walking back for another stack of wood, Eli glanced toward his pond. The mallard duck was there again, only this time a female swam with him. Slowly they zigzagged through the water then went to the far end where a cluster of cattails grew. It wouldn't be the first time a pair of wild ducks nested on the pond's bank. Eli looked forward to seeing little ducklings that could hatch most any day.

After several more trips to get the firewood stacked, Eli figured one more load would finish the job. When he'd moved the last heap, Eli had noticed a hint of skunk odor on the bark of the wood. Now as he put each piece into the wheelbarrow, the sickening smell became stronger. "Bet this is where the skunk's been hiding."

He picked up the next log, and an all-too-familiar black-and-white critter sat looking at him. Jumping backward, Eli jerked his arms around. The skunk turned and lifted its tail. It all happened so fast. Waving his hand in front of his nose, he watched in defeat as the rascal darted out of the yard toward the fields behind his place. "Go ahead and run! That's where you belong, you smelly ole critter!"

Eli's dog slept on, as though nothing out of the ordinary had happened. Eli shook his head. *Good thing too. Lady would have gotten sprayed if she'd gone after the skunk.*

Luckily, the full brunt of the spray missed Eli. Only a little spritzed on his arm. Remembering how his mother used tomato juice on the family dog when it got sprayed by a skunk, Eli headed back to the house.

He'd bought a few tomatoes at the store in Berlin the other day, so he cut one in half and rubbed it on his arm. Too bad he'd rolled up his sleeves earlier while he was stacking the wood. Otherwise, his shirt might have gotten sprayed instead of his skin. Next, he gave his arm a good scrubbing with soap and water. Then, leaning close to his arm, he took a whiff. His sinuses were clogged due to spring allergies, but as far as he could tell, no smell lingered.

Eli glanced at the kitchen clock and grimaced. "Don't know where the morning went." Hurrying to his room for a clean shirt, he heard Lady barking outside. "Sure hope that ole skunk didn't return, but if I don't leave now, I'll be late for the cooking class."

Sugarcreek

The phone rang as Loretta gathered up her things and waited for the babysitter to arrive. She was tempted not to answer, since the last call she'd received was a person trying to sell her something she absolutely didn't need. However, when Loretta glanced at the caller ID and saw it was Sandy, she answered right away.

"Sorry to be calling at the last minute, but I woke up with a sore throat and don't want to expose your kids. I'd hoped I might feel better after sucking on some throat lozenges and gargling with salt water, but it seems to be getting worse. In fact, as soon as I hang up the phone, I'm heading back to bed."

"Oh, okay. I'm sorry to hear you're not feeling well, but thanks for letting me know."

When Loretta hung up, she glanced at her watch, debating what to do. It was too late to find someone else, which meant she'd either have to miss the cooking class or take the children with her.

Loretta drummed her fingers on the edge of the counter. *I wonder if Heidi would mind.* She could call and ask, but it wasn't likely Heidi would check messages in the phone shack before Loretta left home.

Guess I'll chance it and take the kids with me. Loretta cupped her hands around her mouth. "Conner! Abby! Grab a book to read. You're coming to the cooking class with me."

Walnut Creek

Heidi moved about in the kitchen, checking her list and

making sure all the ingredients were out for the main dish her students would make today. Lyle had made himself scarce, saying there were some things to do outside and in the barn this morning.

A knock sounded on the door, and Heidi went to answer it. She found Kendra and Charlene on the porch. Charlene, her usual cheerful self, grinned as she entered the house. Kendra, on the other hand, shuffled in with shoulders slumped and lips pressed tightly together. Heidi noticed dark circles beneath the young woman's eyes. Kendra looked like she'd lost her best friend. *Should I say something? Do I ask her what's wrong? No, she might think I'm being pushy and ought to mind my own business. If Kendra wants to talk about what's bothering her, I'm sure she'll speak up.*

"You're the first ones here, so feel free to take a seat until the others arrive." Heidi gestured to the living room.

"What are we making today?" Charlene seated herself on the couch.

"German pizza." Heidi smiled. "It's not a traditional pizza made with a flour crust, but I hope you'll enjoy making it."

"If it's as easy as haystack to make, I'll be pleased." Charlene clasped her hands to her chest. "Oh my, it tasted so good. I'm anxious to fix it for Len and his parents when they come to my place for supper next week." She crossed her legs, bouncing her foot up and down. "Or maybe, if I like what we make today, I'll fix it instead."

"Either would be a simple yet satisfying meal." Heidi glanced at Kendra. She sat in the rocking chair with her head down and hands resting against her stomach. "Have you had a chance to make haystack since our last lesson, Kendra?"

The sullen young woman's only reply was a brief shake of her head.

Heidi was about to ask if Kendra felt all right when the front door opened and Ron poked his head in. "Hope I'm not late. Had trouble sleeping last night, and by the time I did fall asleep, the light of day was streaming through the RV's windows and woke me." He ambled into the room and took a seat on the recliner, where he'd sat the last time.

"How come you didn't sleep well?" Charlene asked.

Curling his fingers, Ron scraped them through the ends of his short beard. "Just didn't, that's all."

Heidi figured she'd better say something to release the tension in the room. She looked over at Ron and smiled. "I was telling the ladies we'll be making German pizza today."

Ron's eyes brightened a bit. "Good to hear. I like most kinds of pizza—especially pepperoni with black olives."

"This isn't a traditional pizza with a regular crust." Heidi went on to share what she'd told Kendra and Charlene before he showed up.

"What? To me, a pizza with no crust doesn't sound like pizza at all." Ron's forehead wrinkles deepened. "How's a person supposed to eat it, anyway?"

"I'll explain how it's made and the best way to eat it once Eli and Loretta get here," Heidi replied.

Ron seemed satisfied with her response, for he flipped the recliner back and closed his eyes. Would he snooze right there on Lyle's chair? Heidi glanced at the grandfather clock across the room. *What's keeping my other students?*

Chapter 21

Ron opened his eyes and glanced around the room. *Still no Eli. What's wrong with that guy?* As far as Ron was concerned, time was wasting, sitting here waiting for Eli to arrive. Ron took a frustrated breath. *If the guy had to make the rest of us wait, he oughta quit the class. Course, Loretta's not here yet either. Wonder what's holding them up?*

"Did you have a good week, Ron?" Charlene asked.

"Okay, I guess. Got the part for my RV, but I've been too busy helping out around here to do anything with it yet." Ron yawned and readjusted the chair's footrest. Sitting here doing nothing, he felt sleepier by the minute.

"If you need to get your vehicle running, don't worry about us. Take care of your motor home first," Heidi interjected. "If the chores don't get done right away, it's okay, they can wait."

"I'll see," he mumbled. "I promised Lyle I'd get certain things done though. Since I don't need to go anywhere right now, what's a few more days going to matter fixing my rig?" Ron grasped the handle on the side of the chair and put it back to its normal position. "How much longer are we gonna wait on Eli? Shouldn't we get started now?"

"We're not waiting just for him," Kendra spoke up.

"Loretta's not here yet either."

Ron folded his arms. "Humph! Maybe they both need to learn how to tell time."

Kendra stopped rocking and rose from her chair. "Ya know what, Mr. Hensley? You're rude and crude!" She walked over to the fireplace, staring up at the mantel.

Ron's face heated. "I'm only being honest, and you oughta mind your own business, young lady." The last thing he needed was some smarty-pants girl giving him a piece of her mind. *What is it with young people today, thinking they can talk to adults any way they choose? Where's the respect?* He shifted on the chair, ready to recline again. If he really thought about it, who was he to complain about disrespect when he'd stolen from the Troyers, right under their noses? It surprised him, but he actually felt a twinge of guilt.

Heidi left her seat too and moved over to the window. "I see Loretta getting out of her minivan now, so as soon as she comes in, we'll go to the kitchen and get started. When Eli arrives he can join us."

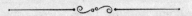

Tension knotted Kendra's neck and shoulders as she stood by the fireplace. *The audacity of that man, Ron. He is so ill mannered.* She focused on the beautiful oil lamp sitting on the mantel. This was certainly more charming than her parents' mantel, always cluttered with candles, fake flowers, statues, and the like. Framed pictures of Kendra and her sisters would have been better than all the junk Mom thought was important to display.

Kendra's clenched fingers dug into her palms. *First Max, then Dad. Why do men treat me so awful?* Of course Kendra knew not all men were bad. The affectionate gestures she'd seen Lyle give Heidi on the few occasions he'd been here had almost brought her to tears. Good men were certainly hard to find though. Now she had to deal with someone like Ron, when the whole purpose of learning to cook from an Amish woman was supposed to be putting some fun in her life.

She scrubbed a hand over her face. *I can't win.*

Eli pedaled as fast as his legs would allow. He didn't want the class to start without him. He'd planned to walk to Heidi's, but cleaning up after the skunk meant he was running late. Riding his bike was quicker than harnessing the horse to the buggy, and besides, a little exercise would probably be good for him.

Coasting down the hill, Eli felt the warm breezes gently brushing his face. Today's weather was beautiful, and everything seemed right with the world. Maybe the fresh air would help mask whatever might be left of his skunky smell. While the birds sang, nature's blooms burst at the seams. Eli breathed deeply, hoping to capture the wind's sweet scent.

Even though he was in a hurry, the ride was peaceful and soothing, until a car came up behind him. The noisy muffler filled the otherwise serene morning with an annoying reverberation.

Eli watched as the car sped up the road. For no reason that he could see, the driver slammed on his brakes. Then the vehicle spun around and came back, whizzing past Eli way too close. In an effort to keep from losing his balance, he gripped the handlebars tightly.

Eli kept pedaling and never looked back, but he sensed what was about to happen. The blaring muffler drew closer, until the older model Mustang pulled up beside him, keeping pace with his bike. Four teenage boys—two in the front seat and two in the back—pointed and jeered at him. Several dents on the front fender of the car, amid scratches and dings throughout the paint, gave evidence of neglect.

"Hey there!" The freckle-faced driver snickered. "Where's your horse and buggy, Mr. Amish Man?"

Eli ignored them, looking straight ahead. *Who needs this type of aggravation, especially this morning? I'm gonna be late for sure.*

"Come on, man." One of the boys in the backseat snickered. "Can't ya pedal any faster than that?"

The teens whooped and hollered. *Do they get a thrill out of harassing me?* This wasn't the first time something like this had occurred. Others in his community had been teased and taunted by boisterous kids out for a good time. *If I ignore them, maybe they'll go away.*

Luckily, no other vehicles passed on either side, as the driver pulled away from Eli, weaving in and out of both lanes. *They must be drunk or high on something.*

When the vehicle slowed up and moved closer to him again, one of the teens leaned out the window and knocked Eli's straw hat off his head. Eli wouldn't give them the satisfaction of watching him peddle away without his hat. He stopped and went back to retrieve it. Eli hoped the boys would drive onward, but to his disappointment, the car stopped. The young driver got out and, like a menacing cat on the prowl, meandered slowly toward him, while the other guys, arms folded, stood by the car and watched.

Eli held his arms stiffly at his sides. *Keep calm. Don't do anything foolish that could rile them further.*

"Hey man, ya know what? You smell like a skunk." Pointing a bony finger at Eli, the lanky adolescent plugged his nose.

Eli's brain told him to stand his ground—*Be polite,*

don't cause a scene. But his body tensed, hands drawing into fists. Giving this boy a piece of his mind would bring much satisfaction. The words formed in his head, but Eli kept quiet. Though it would get him nowhere, a good tongue-lashing would have made him feel better.

The snickering kid came almost face-to-face with Eli. He stood several seconds then, eyes growing wide, whirled around and rushed back to the car. Eli raised his arms to shield his face when stones kicked up from the spinning wheels. He coughed as the dust settled down and the car's motor grew fainter, until it was out of sight.

"You okay?" Lester Hendricks, one of the patrol officers in the county, pulled up alongside Eli.

"Yeah, I'm fine." Eli dusted off his hat. "Just a bunch of kids having fun, I guess. They sure took off when you came along."

"I saw the Mustang and know the teen driving it." Lester frowned. "I've had a little trouble with him before—nothing big that would put him behind bars, but several warnings. If you want to file a report, I wouldn't blame ya."

"Naw, I wanna forget it. Kids will be kids. I'm glad the incident's over."

"Okay, but if you experience any more trouble with that bunch, you'd better contact the sheriff's office."

"Will do." Eli nodded and got back on his bike. "Thanks for stopping."

When Heidi opened the front door, she was taken aback, seeing a young boy and girl standing beside Loretta.

"My babysitter canceled at the last minute, and I didn't want to miss the class, so I brought Abby and Conner along." Loretta glanced down at the children. "I hope you don't mind."

Heidi shook her head, holding the door open for them. "It's fine. I'll find something to occupy them with while we're having our class." She showed Abby and Conner a basket of toys. "I keep these on hand to entertain my nieces and nephews." Heidi turned to Loretta. "The children can either play in the living room or come to the kitchen with us and play on the floor while we cook the meal I have planned for today."

"If you don't think they'll get in the way, I'd feel better if they came with me so I can keep an eye on them," Loretta replied.

"Whatever you prefer is fine with me."

Loretta glanced around the room. "Isn't Eli coming today?"

"I believe so. When my husband checked for messages this morning there were none from Eli. I'm sure he would have called if he couldn't make it."

"Here, let me carry that to the kitchen." Ron took the toy basket from Heidi.

After the adults were seated around the table and the children got settled on the throw rug in front of the basket, Heidi went to the refrigerator and took out the ingredients they would need.

"Today we're making German pizza," Heidi explained to Loretta. "Instead of a regular crust, baked in an oven, we'll use shredded potatoes for the base and cook the meal in a skillet on top of the stove." She handed everyone a three-by-five card with the recipe printed out. The verse she'd included on the back this time was Psalm 71:1. *"In thee, O Lord, do I put my trust: let me never be put to confusion."* Heidi hoped this scripture would be helpful to one or more of her students during the next few weeks.

"It certainly seems different than a regular pizza." Loretta stared at her recipe card.

"It is, but I hope you'll enjoy it." Heidi gestured to the ingredients after placing them on the table. She also gave everyone a small skillet. "The first thing you will do is brown the ground beef with chopped onion, diced green pepper, salt, and pepper. We'll do this two at a time, since it'll be easier to double up at the stove. Charlene and Kendra, after you get your onion and pepper chopped then you can go first."

While everyone got busy, Heidi watched Loretta's children at play. Abby seemed fully engrossed in a book as she sat cross-legged on the braided throw rug, thumbing through the pages. Conner found a wooden horse and buggy belonging to Lyle when he was a child. A smile formed on Heidi's face as she watched the young boy push the horse along, making *clip-clop* noises with his tongue. He was obviously familiar with the sound.

Loretta has children but no husband. A knot formed in Heidi's stomach. *I have a husband but no kinner. Since I haven't suffered the loss of my mate, I should feel thankful. Poor Loretta's heart must be broken, becoming a widow at such a young age. She needs her husband, and these precious children need their father. It's hard to understand why certain things happen. At times, life can be so unfair.*

Hearing a knock on the back door, Heidi jumped. Before she could get to the door, it opened and Eli let himself in. "Sorry I'm late. Ran into a little problem at home this morning, and also on the way here."

"Are you all right?" Loretta's fingers touched her parted lips.

"Yeah, I'm fine. Hope I didn't make you all wait too long." Eli slipped his straw hat over a wall peg near the door.

"It's okay, we've barely gotten started." Heidi pointed to an empty chair at the table. "You can begin by chopping the onion and green pepper set out for you."

As Eli walked past Heidi, her nose twitched. *Is that a skunky odor?*

When Eli took a seat at the table, Ron's nose wrinkled, sliding his chair to the left, which put more distance between the men. When it appeared Ron might say something more, Conner hopped up and darted over to his mother. "What's that yucky smell?" He closed his eyes and plugged his nose.

Loretta put a finger to her lips. "Shh. Conner, don't be impolite."

Then Abby walked over to Eli and sniffed. "Phew! You stink, mister."

"Abby Donnelly!" Loretta shook her finger. "Apologize to Mr. Miller this instant."

Kendra and Charlene sucked in their breath, while Ron sneered at the child. Heidi's sympathy went to Abby when her little chin quivered.

"There's no need to apologize, little lady." Eli's face flamed. "I'm afraid the yucky smell is me. Got my arm sprayed by a skunk hiding in my woodpile this morning."

"What did the skunk do after he sprayed you?" Abby took a step back before asking her question. Conner walked over and stood next to his sister.

Eli rubbed his beard. "Well, the last I saw of Mr. Skunk, he was making a run for it toward the field behind my place."

Abby giggled. "You're funny. You called him 'Mr. Skunk.'"

"Do you think he'll come back?" Conner tilted his head.

"I hope not." Eli lifted his arm. "Skunks are kinda

cute, but they don't smell good when they lift their tail and let loose with a spray."

"Did you use anything to get the smell out?" If he hadn't, there were a few things Heidi could suggest.

"I rubbed half a tomato on my skin, plus lots of soap and water." Eli's mouth stretched downward. "Figured the smell was gone."

"Hardly." Ron rolled his eyes. "It's far from gone, Eli. Can't ya smell it?"

"Not really. But then, I've been havin' a little trouble with my allergies lately, so my sniffer isn't working as well as it should." Eli pushed back his chair. "I'd better head back home so I don't ruin your cooking class. Don't want your house to get all skunked up."

Heidi shook her head. "Nonsense. I want you to stay. The odor isn't so bad, and if I open the kitchen window it'll ventilate the room. After we're finished with our German pizzas we'll take them outside and eat our meal at the picnic table. How's that sound?"

"Oh boy. A picnic!" Abby jumped up and down. Conner joined in.

"Settle down now, you two," Loretta scolded.

Still a bit red in the face, Eli returned to his seat. Heidi hoped no one else would comment about the aroma of skunk. *Eli has been embarrassed enough.*

Chapter 22

While Loretta shredded potatoes, she glanced at Eli. Perspiration covered the poor man's forehead, and he sat as far away from the others as possible. The smell wasn't so horrible—at least from where she sat. Her eyes watered, but the odor from the onions she'd cut up could be the reason.

Since Eli had been the last to arrive, Loretta wanted to be polite and introduce her children to him. She could have made introductions sooner, when the kids made comments about the skunky odor, but it didn't feel appropriate right then. Besides, Loretta had been so embarrassed by what they'd said, she wasn't thinking clearly. Now Abby and Conner were happily playing again, and Eli left the table to brown his ground beef. It might be best to wait until they'd finished making the pizza and were relaxing at the picnic table outdoors to make formal introductions.

Between the pungent odor of ground beef cooking and the telltale stench of skunk coming from Eli, Kendra struggled with nausea. She tried chewing gum and some peppermint candy, but neither helped much. She had forgotten to bring mint tea and saltine crackers again and would be glad when they finished making their pizzas and could go outside to eat it. At least the air would be fresher out there. She even thought of asking Heidi if she had any menthol rub. Smearing the ointment on the end of her nose would surely mask the odors making her stomach queasy. Eli seemed like a nice person, so Kendra wouldn't embarrass him further by asking Heidi for menthol rub. Aside from Heidi's husband, Lyle, Eli was probably one of the nicest men she'd met. Certainly more polite and respectful than Ron.

Kendra glanced at Loretta's children and noticed Heidi staring at them. In fact, she seemed more interested in the kids than teaching her class this morning. Kendra almost pitied their teacher, with that faraway look in her eyes. Even her smile appeared forlorn.

Too bad Heidi doesn't have children of her own. I'll bet she'd make a good mother. Kendra tapped her chin. *I wonder if she and Lyle have considered adoption.*

"Here are some cut-up veggie sticks to go with your pizza." Heidi placed the platter on the picnic table and took a seat on the bench where Loretta sat with her children. She'd already given Conner and Abby cheese sandwiches and potato chips. Lyle joined them for lunch and suggested they all bow their heads for silent prayer. When the prayer ended, everyone began to eat.

"This is yummy," Charlene spoke up. "I never imagined pizza could taste so good without a crust."

"The shredded *grummbier* makes up the crust," Eli interjected.

Abby nudged her mother's arm. "Mommy, what'd that man say? He said a strange word."

"I'm not sure, but first things first. Let's get proper introductions made." Loretta gestured to Eli. "This is the nice man who gave us the whoopie pie cookies the other day. His name is Eli Miller." Loretta placed her hands atop her children's heads. "Eli, I'd like you to meet my daughter, Abby, and my son, Conner."

"Nice to meet you both." Eli shook their hands. "Oh, and the word I said—*grummbier*—is the Pennsylvania Dutch word for potatoes."

"Grummbier," Abby repeated. Then Conner said it too.

"Thank you for the cookies." Abby grinned while rubbing her stomach. "They were yummy."

"I agree with you." Eli bobbed his head. "Would ya like to learn the Pennsylvania Dutch name for cookies?"

Both children, as well as Heidi's other students, nodded.

"The word for cookies is *kichlin*."

"Kichlin." Abby giggled. "That's a funny word."

Loretta tapped her daughter's shoulder. "Now don't be impolite."

"Sorry." The little girl lowered her head.

"It's okay." Eli's brows jiggled up and down playfully. "To most English people, many of our Amish words sound funny."

Lyle chuckled. "I remember once, as a young lad, our English neighbor girl, Yvonne, told us everything my brother and I said in our native language sounded funny to her. She used to laugh and try to figure out what the words meant. Sometimes we'd tell her, and sometimes we didn't. Whenever she was with us, we had fun speaking words only the two of us understood."

"Is anyone hungry for dessert?" Heidi asked. "I made a peach cobbler last night."

"Sounds good to me." Ron thumped his stomach. "I'm always in the mood for dessert."

"Me, too," Charlene added.

Everyone else agreed.

Heidi got up. "I'll clear some of these dishes and get the cobbler when I'm inside."

"Let me help." Kendra grabbed the plates and silverware, piling them on the serving tray.

"I'd be glad to help too," Charlene offered.

"Same here." Loretta rose from the bench.

"No, that's okay." Kendra motioned for them to stay put. "I used to work part-time as a waitress when I was taking some college classes, so I'm pretty good at managing dishes by myself."

After Heidi and Kendra entered the kitchen, Kendra placed everything in the sink then turned to face Heidi. "Mind if I ask you a personal question?"

"Not at all. What would you like to know?"

"I watched how you interacted with Loretta's kids earlier. Made me wonder why you don't have any children of your own."

"Oh, that's right. You were in the bathroom during our first cooking class, when I told the others about my situation." Heidi released a lingering sigh. "My husband and I would like to be parents, but in the eight years we've been married, I've not been able to get pregnant."

"That's too bad. Have you considered adoption?"

"I'd love to adopt, but Lyle. . ." Heidi stopped talking. Why discuss this with Kendra? She probably wouldn't understand Lyle's refusal to adopt. Heidi didn't understand it either.

"If you'd like to take small plates from the cupboard, as well as enough forks for everyone, I'll get the peach cobbler." Heidi moved across the room to the refrigerator.

"One more question." Kendra set the dishes and silverware on a tray.

Heidi placed the cobbler on another tray. "What is it?"

"Would it be all right if I come by here sometime between our classes, to visit and get to know you better? My dishwashing job isn't full-time, and I have Saturdays off."

Kendra's question surprised Heidi, but it pleased her too. She was almost certain Kendra needed someone to talk to. Maybe she would open up and share her struggles.

Heidi gave Kendra's arm a gentle pat. "Feel free to drop by anytime. I'd enjoy getting better acquainted." She picked up the tray and followed Kendra outside.

———————⌘———————

"Eli, I noticed you rode your bicycle today." Heidi pointed to the tree it leaned against.

He nodded. "I wanted to walk, but since I was running late, I chose the bike instead." It still bothered Eli to ride a bike because it stirred emotional feelings concerning Mavis's accident. He had to admit, in light of what happened on the way here with those teens, walking wouldn't have been much better. In hindsight, Eli wished he'd brought the horse and buggy.

"This peach cobbler is excellent," Charlene commented as everyone ate the dessert.

"Yes indeed. . . My wife can cobble with the best of them." Lyle's eyes twinkled as he winked at Heidi.

Eli's shoulders hunched, unable to deal with his envy. His wife used to make good cobblers too. But the dessert wasn't the cause of his jealousy. Lyle's look of adoration, and the sweet smile Heidi gave him in return, tugged at Eli's gut. He longed for such a relationship and continued to miss the special moments he and Mavis had shared. *Well, I can't bring her back, so I need to quit feeling sorry for myself and get on with life.* How many times had he given himself this lecture? How often had he fallen prey to self-pity and longing for something he couldn't have?

"The others are right," Eli told Heidi after taking a bite. "It is good cobbler." Then looking at Lyle, he added, "I'm surprised you're not auctioneering someplace today."

Lyle swatted a bug when it landed on the picnic table. "This is the first Saturday in a long while I haven't been called to an auction."

"I've always been fascinated with auctioneers and their ability to speak so fast." Loretta wiped her fingers on the napkin beside her plate. "How did you get into that line of business, Lyle?"

"I've been wonderin' about that too," Ron put in. "Just kept forgetting to ask."

"Well,"— Lyle scratched behind his left ear—"in my teenage years I became fascinated with auctions and the fast-talking people who conducted the events." He paused and drank some water. "Had to be at least eighteen in order to learn the trade though. So when I was old enough I took classes to learn how to legally run an auction."

Kendra leaned her elbows on the table. "I thought the Amish didn't go to school past the eighth grade."

"It wasn't like high school or college," Lyle explained. "Following the classes, I had to take a test. Afterward, I served a yearlong apprenticeship and then took another test. Once I passed, I got my auctioneer's license."

"Don't it make you nervous to stand in front of a bunch of people and talk so fast?" Ron questioned.

Lyle shook his head. "At first it did, but not anymore."

"I can talk to my kindergarten students easily, but if I was faced with what you do, I'd be a nervous wreck." Charlene gave her ponytail a tug.

"I like my job. Standing in front of a large crowd gives me a rush of adrenaline."

"Hey look! There's a big balloon in the sky."

Eli looked where Abby pointed. Everyone else did the same.

"See how colorful it is." Charlene's eyes widened as she continued to watch the enormous balloon.

"I'd love to be up there right now," Kendra said wistfully.

"Same here." Even Ron seemed intrigued by the colorful sight.

"Could be one of the balloons coming from Charm, or it might be one from Millersburg." Lyle tipped his head back, holding one hand above his brows. "Every now and then we see 'em drifting over our farm."

"From what I've heard, they have several locations around Ohio where you can take a balloon ride," Eli stated.

The children ran farther into the yard, while the rest of them stood and watched the brilliant balloon against the deep blue sky.

Eli chuckled when the kids waved at the people in the balloon. It was almost overhead now, and low enough that he could make out a few people in the basket suspended underneath the giant orb. The children squealed with delight when the riders responded by waving back.

"They're waving at us!" Abby shouted, while Conner jumped up and down.

Everyone watched as the balloon drifted onward, until it could barely be seen.

"Now that was an unexpected surprise," Heidi said when everyone returned to the picnic table to finish eating their cobbler.

Eli couldn't quit watching the children as they giggled and chattered to each other. Obviously seeing the balloon was a magical moment for them, and to be honest, it seemed to put the others into a friendlier, more relaxed state of mind. He grinned as Loretta tried to calm her children when they asked to go for a ride in a balloon.

"Maybe someday, when you're older, we'll see about taking a ride, but for now, I don't believe you'd be tall enough to see over the basket you'd be standing in." Loretta looked at Eli and smiled.

Seconds later, Abby changed the subject. "We have a salamander in our garden."

"His name is Oscar." Wide-eyed, Conner clapped his hands. "He lives under a rock."

While Charlene and Kendra questioned the children about Oscar, Eli glanced at Heidi, gazing at the children with what could only be considered adoration. He could almost read her mind and felt the same sadness he saw in her eyes. Loretta was fortunate to have two great kids. The joy on their faces as they explained about the salamander and their excitement when the balloon floated over were priceless. Ron even commented on the children's pet salamander. *I wonder if he has any children?*

Arf! Arf! The Troyers' Brittany spaniel bounded up to the picnic table, wagging his tail.

Eagerly, Abby and Conner left their seats and began petting the dog. "Can we get a doggy like this?" Abby looked up at her mother.

"Not right now." Loretta tapped her daughter's arm. "Maybe after you and your brother are a little older and can take care of a pet."

Conner's lower lip protruded. "I'm a big boy, Mommy. I wanna dog."

She squatted beside them and stroked Rusty's silky hair. "I know, son, but it will have to wait until I get a job. Feeding a dog and taking care of its needs is an added expense we don't need right now."

Eli imagined how difficult it must be to turn down a request as innocent as Conner's. He finished his cobbler and set his fork down. *It may not be as long as you think, Loretta.*

189

Chapter 23

The following Saturday, Eli hitched his horse to the closed-in buggy. His first stop would be his folks' place, and then on to Loretta's.

He climbed into the buggy and took up the reins. *Sure hope she's home today. I'm eager to see her children's faces when they find out what I brought 'em.*

Heading out onto the road, Eli whistled his favorite tune. Since Mavis's death, mornings were usually the worst for him. Grasping for something to look forward to each day, he felt thankful for a job that kept him busy. Even so, making coffins was work, not fun. But he was good at his craft, and the money Eli earned paid his bills.

Since beginning to take Heidi's cooking classes, Eli's spirits had lifted some, and he no longer dreaded getting out of bed on those days. Of course, it might have more to do with meeting Loretta and her kinner than learning how to cook. Since the time he'd become a widower, Eli hadn't felt as comfortable with any woman until now. It made no sense. Loretta wasn't Amish, and he'd only met her a little over a month ago. He shouldn't even be thinking about her.

"Maybe I'm desperate for female companionship."

Eli's horse twitched its ears.

"Just keep movin', girl; I wasn't talkin' to you." He

leaned back in his seat, enjoying the ride. In his book, traveling by horse and buggy beat any other mode of transportation. Walking was fine if the destination was close. Riding a bike was okay too and provided a good workout. But because Mavis had died while riding her bike, every time Eli got on one, he felt apprehensive. He'd felt even more hesitant to ride his bicycle after last week when he'd been taunted by those teenage boys. Thanks to the deputy showing up, they'd moved on. Hopefully, Eli had seen the last of them.

"Just look at how quickly these weeds have grown." Heidi knelt on a foam pad next to her vegetable garden.

"You talkin' to me?"

Heidi jerked her head, surprised to see Ron standing a few feet from her. "Uh, no. I didn't see you there. I talk to myself now and then."

He chuckled. "I do it sometimes too. I'll only become worried when I start answering my own questions."

Heidi smiled. *So Ron does have a humorous side.* He often seemed so serious and sometimes a bit grumpy. Of course, living all alone, with no home of his own, would be quite depressing.

"Need help pullin' weeds?" he asked.

"No, thanks. Since there's only a few, I can manage. Besides, shouldn't you be working on your RV now that you have the part you need?"

He tugged on his ear. "You're right, I need to get started with it, but I can't seem to get in the mood." He pointed to the blue sky above. "It's nice out today, and I feel like takin' a walk."

"Maybe you should. Fresh air and exercise is always a good thing."

"Yeah." Ron hesitated, as if he might want to say more, but then he mumbled, "See you later, Heidi," and sauntered off.

She watched as he headed down the driveway and out toward the road. Heidi still felt a bit uneasy around Ron, but the longer he stayed here, the more compassion she felt for him.

As Heidi returned to weeding, her thoughts went in another direction. She reflected on her brief conversation with Kendra during last week's cooking class. She'd been surprised when Kendra had asked about coming by sometime to visit and get better acquainted. The poor girl obviously needed a friend. Heidi hoped if Kendra did drop by, she would have an opportunity to talk with her about the best friend anyone could have—Jesus Christ.

Concentrating on the job at hand, Heidi plunged her trowel into the ground to attack a few more weeds. The sun beating down on her scarf-covered head made it feel like summer instead of spring. "Even my dress is sticking to me." She pulled the material away from her skin. The garden gloves she wore felt confining as well, but she'd put up with them until she finished weeding. The warm weather persisted today, as it had all week. *If summer is going to be like this, our grill will get a real workout, because it'll be too hot to heat up the kitchen by using the stove.*

Heidi's hand went to her growling stomach. It was way past lunchtime. Setting her trowel aside, she rose to her feet and headed inside.

"Whew! That feels better." Heidi peeled off her garden gloves, turned on the cold water, and lathered soap over her sweaty hands. Grabbing a towel, she glanced out the kitchen window just as a car pulled into the yard. "Oh good, Kendra did come for a visit." Heidi dried her hands and opened the door to let her young student in.

"I hope you don't mind me dropping by unannounced." Kendra offered Heidi a sheepish-looking grin. "I borrowed my friend's car today to run a few errands, so I decided to stop here on the way back to see if you were home and had time to talk."

"Certainly." Heidi led the way to the kitchen. "I was about to fix myself some lunch. If you haven't eaten, you're welcome to join me."

"I ate a late breakfast, but even so, I am a bit hungry." Kendra smiled. "If it's no trouble, I'd enjoy having lunch with you."

"No trouble at all." Heidi gestured to the table. "Take a seat and I'll fix us a sandwich. Is ham and cheese okay?"

"I love ham and cheese, but let me help you."

Heidi took out the loaf of bread she'd baked yesterday and asked Kendra to get the ham and cheese slices from the refrigerator. "There's a jar of mayonnaise in there too and also some lettuce."

"Do you have any dill pickles?" Kendra snickered. "For some reason I've been craving pickles lately. It's the weirdest thing. The other night when I couldn't sleep, I got up and raided my friend's refrigerator."

"I'm not speaking from experience, but from what other women tell me, craving certain foods is common during pregnancy."

"Yeah, I've heard the same thing."

Heidi cut their sandwiches in half and took out a pitcher of lemonade. "Here we go."

After they took seats at the table, it pleased Heidi to see Kendra bow her head.

Following their silent prayers, Heidi poured lemonade into their glasses. "How's your new job, Kendra?"

"It's okay, but I'm hoping it turns into full-time. I won't

keep sponging off my friend forever." Kendra touched her stomach. "Then there's the expense of having a baby."

"Won't your parents help with the costs?"

Kendra's eyes narrowed as she shook her head. "Since my folks tossed me out when they found out about the pregnancy, I don't expect any help from them at all." Her forehead creased. "My dad paid me a visit the day I got my new job."

"How did it go?"

"Horrible. He chewed me out for talking to my sister Shelly. Worse than that, he warned me not to make any contact with her or my other sister, Chris. Said if I did, he'd show them the door."

Heidi's brows furrowed. "You mean he'd make your sisters move out?"

"You got it." Kendra bit into her sandwich. "He's a mean man, and I hate him. He's not my dad anymore; he's my enemy now."

"Hate's a pretty strong word." Heidi placed her hand on Kendra's shoulder. "The Bible tells us in Luke 6:27 and 28: 'Love your enemies, do good to them which hate you, bless them that curse you, and pray for them which despitefully use you.'"

Kendra's lips curled. "I'm all too familiar with Bible verses and prayer. Grew up attending church with my family. But as far as I can tell, the church is full of hypocrites—the biggest one being my dad."

"If you pray for him, perhaps in time he'll come around."

Kendra picked up her glass and took a drink. "Can we please change the subject? I don't want to talk about Dad anymore."

Heidi said nothing more on the topic. She would remember, however, to pray for Kendra, as well as for her father, asking God to remove the anger and bitterness from both of their hearts.

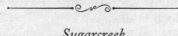

Sugarcreek

Taking a whiff of the air-freshened towels while putting them in the basket, Loretta heard the whinny of a horse. When the buggy pulled closer, she recognized the driver even before he got out. *Eli. I wonder if he came for a visit, or perhaps he brought us more cookies.*

After securing the horse, Eli walked toward her and tipped his hat. "Wasn't sure if I'd find you at home, but I'm glad you're here 'cause I brought your kids a special gift." Looking directly at her, he quickly added, "I hope you'll let 'em keep it. It's in my buggy if you wanna take a look."

Loretta's eyebrows rose, but she followed him to the buggy. When he reached inside and lifted out a small brown-and-white puppy, she gasped. "Oh Eli, I don't think—"

"Please don't say no. I saw the way Conner and Abby loved on Heidi's dog last week. I bet they'd enjoy having a puppy of their own."

"You're right, but puppies are a lot of work, not to mention an additional expense I don't need right now."

"Since I don't live close by, I can't do much to help ya take care of the pup, but I'd be happy to help with the expense."

She shook her head. "Oh no, I couldn't ask you to do that."

"You don't have to ask; I'm volunteering. In fact, I brought a bag of dog food along so you won't have to worry about feeding the puppy for a while." Eli scratched the pup behind its ears. "When the food runs low, let me know, and I'll buy some more."

"You're a nice man, Eli."

His face colored, and he lowered his head. "Tryin' to help out a friend, is all."

Loretta smiled. She'd begun to think of Eli as her friend too.

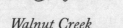

Walnut Creek

When Kendra left the Troyers' house that afternoon, she reflected on the things she and Heidi had discussed. *She doesn't understand my situation. Heidi's never been in a predicament like mine.*

Country scenery went practically unnoticed as Kendra headed back to Mt. Hope. She hit the switch to put the window down farther and rested her elbow there. Even with the warm breezes blowing through her hair, Kendra's thoughts would not elude her. *What did I do to deserve all this? How can some be so lucky in life, and others, like me, seem to attract trouble?*

Kendra noticed something brown by the high weeds along the side of the road. Glancing in the rear-view mirror to be sure no vehicles were close behind, she slammed on the brakes. Kendra raised her eyebrows when she noticed a lone female duck standing like a statue, as if waiting for something. Then, one by one, ten little ducklings surrounded their mama.

Hesitating on her next move, the female quacked and looked in Kendra's direction. Water glistened in the sunlight as Kendra caught a glimpse of a pond on the other side of the road. Watching in the mirror, she gripped the gearshift and put it in REVERSE and then PARK.

After getting out of her car, Kendra slowly

approached the mother duck. "Okay girl, it's safe to cross." She bent low, making a shooing motion with her hands. "But then you probably already knew that, didn't you?" She continued to guide them until the mother and babies waddled safely across and under a fence. Kendra giggled as the tiny ducklings followed like soldiers trailing a drillmaster during boot camp.

Getting back into the car and buckling her seat belt, Kendra gripped the steering wheel with such force her knuckles turned white. "To think what could have happened if I hadn't stopped in time." She put her hand protectively over her stomach. *I have a little one to protect as well.*

Kendra watched the ducks enter the water. At least now they were in a safe place. *If only my parents had half the concern toward me as that duck has for her babies.*

While her father hadn't done anything to despitefully use her, like the verse of scripture Heidi had mentioned, he'd despitefully kicked her out of his house and, worse, now threatened her sisters with the same punishment. *He's not deserving of my prayers. It would serve him right if the church found out about my pregnancy and kicked him off the board. I oughta let someone there know.*

Chapter 24

Sugarcreek

"Come see what Mr. Miller brought," Loretta called through the screen door.

When Loretta glanced back and smiled at him, Eli stood taller. The puppy squirmed and wiggled and licked his nose, as if it knew this was going to be home. The dog was so cute it almost made him regret not keeping one of the litter. If not for Lady, the decision would have been easy. As the pup grew languid and nestled comfortably in his arms, its milky breath reached Eli's nostrils.

A few seconds later, Loretta's children came out. Abby's eyes lit up when she saw the dog. "It's so cute! Whose puppy is it?"

"It's yours and Conner's, if you want it." Eli set the pup on the porch. Instinctively, it went to the children and let out a *yip* while wagging its tail. It ran in circles around them, and woofed several raspy barks, as if it was learning to talk. The puppy seemed to enjoy being the center of attention.

"Yippee! Yippee!" Conner jumped up and down, while Abby's eyes seemed to grow larger by the minute.

Abby knelt beside the dog and stroked its head. "Can we keep it?" She looked up at her mother with pleading eyes.

Loretta nodded. "The question is, what shall we name the little guy?"

Conner, sitting cross-legged on the other side of the dog, shouted, "Donnelly! Cause he belongs to us." The puppy seemed happy getting so much attention from two excited children. It went from Conner to Abby, and back to Conner again, while the kids giggled and took turns petting the dog.

"Donnelly's a pretty big name for such a small dog, but if that's what you want, it sounds good to me." Eli grinned. The boy choosing his last name for the dog was kind of cute.

As if accepting the name, the pup crawled into Conner's lap and licked his chin with a slurpy tongue. Everyone laughed, Eli most of all. What a happy morning it turned out to be. Eli's heart seemed to beat faster to keep pace with all the joy pumping out of it.

"This pup is a Miniature American Shepherd, so he won't get too big. It's from a litter my mother's dog gave birth to eight weeks ago," Eli explained. "Homes were found for all the other puppies except this little fellow."

"We'll take good care of Donnelly, I promise." Enthusiasm shone in Abby's dark eyes.

Eli bent down and patted the top of her head. "I knew I could count on you and your *bruder*."

"What's a 'bruder'?" Abby tilted her head, looking up at him with the curiosity of a child.

"It means 'brother.'"

Abby snickered and pointed at Conner. "You're my little bruder."

"What do you both say to Mr. Miller for giving you such a nice gift?" Loretta prompted.

"Thank you," the children answered in unison.

Conner clambered to his feet and hugged Eli's leg.

"I love our puppy."

"You're most welcome." Eli's throat clogged.

"Is that horse yours?" Conner pointed to the fence post where Blossom stood, swishing her tail.

"She certainly is. Her name is Blossom. She used to belong to my wife before she. . ." Eli's words trailed off.

"Can I pet her?"

"I have no problem with it, if your mother says it's okay." Eli looked at Loretta.

"As long as you're there with him, it's fine with me."

"Absolutely." Eli reached down and scooped the boy into his arms. His heart swelled with pleasure when Conner hugged him tight. *I'd give nearly anything to have a son like this boy.* He glanced at Abby. *A daughter would be nice too.*

"Reach out your hand now and pet her gently," Eli instructed when he stood beside his horse.

The boy complied and laughed when Blossom let out a whinny. "I think she likes me." The horse nickered in response.

"I believe you're right." Eli ruffled Conner's hair. "Say, how'd you like to go for a ride in my buggy? Then you can see how well the horse pulls."

"If Mommy says it's okay."

"Of course. Maybe she and your sister would like to ride with us."

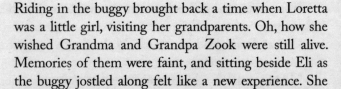

Riding in the buggy brought back a time when Loretta was a little girl, visiting her grandparents. Oh, how she wished Grandma and Grandpa Zook were still alive. Memories of them were faint, and sitting beside Eli as the buggy jostled along felt like a new experience. She considered telling him about her heritage, but would he understand if he found out Loretta's parents never joined the Amish church and left their families soon after they were married? Loretta had always been hesitant to discuss it with anyone—especially when she didn't know the details herself. She'd always been curious about the reason her folks had chosen to be part of the English world rather than join the Amish church, but never asked. Loretta often wished her parents had joined the Amish church, because she'd be Amish now too.

Pushing her musings aside, she glanced over her shoulder and smiled. Wearing huge grins, Conner and Abby sat in the seat behind them, with their hands on Donnelly's head. The pup closed his eyes and let out a whiny yawn.

"It seems they tuckered little Donnelly out." Loretta turned back around.

"Or maybe it's the other way around." Eli grinned. "Don't know who's more tired, the kids or the puppy."

"I see now my kids needed a dog." Loretta paused, briefly touching his arm. "Thank you, Eli, for your kindness."

His smile increased. "My pleasure."

As they rode around Sugarcreek, the kids chattered and giggled. Occasionally, their new puppy let out a small *woof*.

"Sounds like they're having a good time back there," Eli commented.

"They are, and so am I sitting up here. It's nice to ride at a much slower pace."

"Jah." Eli clucked to the horse then began to whistle.

Every muscle in Loretta's body seemed to relax. Was it the buggy ride or spending time with Eli? *Wish I felt this content all the time.*

Abby leaned forward and tapped Eli's shoulder. "Could ya teach me how to whistle, Mr. Eli?"

201

"I'd be happy to." He reached back and patted Abby's hand. "Next time I come to Sugarcreek, I'll stop by your house and give you a lesson. How's that sound, little lady?"

"Sounds good."

Yip! Yip! The puppy barked, wiggling around. Riding past a farm, Eli pulled on the reins so they could watch the activity going on by the edge of the field. Several children and a few adults held on to strings as their kites danced far overhead.

"Look there!" Conner pointed. "See the big smiley face?"

"Yes, and some kites have pretty colors too," Loretta added.

"Remember, Mommy, how Daddy used to fly kites with me?" Abby spoke in a bubbly tone. "It was fun."

"I remember." Loretta had not heard Abby recount many memories about her father since his death. It was good to hear her talking about him now. Conner had only been two when Rick died. No doubt, he remembered very little about his father. Loretta had shared things about Rick with the children and answered questions when they asked.

Eli flicked the reins, and they continued on down the road. "Let's go, Blossom. No reason to dally."

"Can we ride in your buggy again, Mr. Eli?" Abby tapped his shoulder again.

"Most definitely. Next time, I'll take you by to meet my folks."

"That would be nice," Loretta responded. "It'll give me a chance to thank your mother in person for the delicious banana whoopie pies."

"How about next Saturday when our cooking class is over?" Eli suggested. "I'll follow you back to your house after we're done, and we can pick up the children. It'll also give me a chance to see how Donnelly's doing."

"Can we bring our puppy along so he can see his mama?" Abby questioned.

"Great idea. Should've thought of it myself." Eli glanced at Loretta and smiled. "That's a smart daughter you have."

⸺ ⁘ ⸺

Walnut Creek

Ron watched out his side window as Lyle hitched his horse to the buggy and climbed in beside Heidi. They hadn't mentioned going anywhere, but this might be a good opportunity to sneak into their house again and take more money or some other item of value.

Ron waited until the buggy was out of sight then stepped out of his motor home and glanced around. The Troyers' dog lay sleeping in its pen. That was good. He wouldn't have to deal with the mutt barking or pestering him for a treat.

Tromping up the porch steps, Ron tried the front door but found it locked, like it had been the last time they'd gone away and he'd come in uninvited. He hurried around back and discovered that door was also locked.

Drat! Wonder if they discovered the missing money or the oil lamps I took. Do they suspect me? Is that why the doors are both locked?

Ron took a seat in one of the chairs on the porch, resting his chin in the palm of his hand. He couldn't help but notice the clean white wicker. Years ago, he and his wife purchased a wicker rocker for their front porch. It didn't take long for the dirt to show, despite countless cleanings. Eventually they'd gotten rid of the chair and replaced it with something easier to maintain. It was easy to see the Troyers took good care of all their belongings—something Ron didn't choose to do anymore. What was the point?

Ron rose from the chair. *Whelp, I can't sit here all day reminiscing. I need to check the windows and see if any of them are unlocked—or maybe the basement door.*

Since going through the basement to get into the house would be easier than squeezing through a window, he checked there first. Not only was the basement door unlocked, but it was partially open.

"A lot of good it does to lock the front and back door but leave the basement door open," he muttered, stepping into the dark room. "Guess the Troyers slipped up on that one, but it's to my advantage."

He took a few steps and bumped into something. "Should've brought a flashlight." He was about to give up when a thought popped into his head. *There might be something valuable down here. Think I'd better go back to my rig and get a light so I can scope out this basement before I head up to the main part of the house.*

Ron went out the door and was almost to his RV when a van pulled in. A few minutes later, an elderly Amish couple got out with two small suitcases.

"Who are you?" the woman asked, looking strangely at Ron.

"My name's Ron Hensley. And who might you folks be?"

"I'm Emma Miller, and this is my husband, Lamar. Heidi's my niece. Is she at home?"

Ron shook his head. "Heidi and Lyle went somewhere."

"Oh, I see. Do you know when they'll be back?"

"Nope."

She looked at her husband then back at Ron. "I'm

surprised they're not here. I wonder if they forgot we were coming."

Ron shrugged. "Beats me. Neither of 'em mentioned anything to me about expecting company."

"Are you a friend of theirs?" Lamar pulled his fingers through the ends of his long gray beard.

"Guess you could say that." Ron scrubbed a hand down the side of his face. "They let me park my rig here when it needed repairs. I'll be stayin' awhile since I'm taking Heidi's cooking classes."

Eyes widening, Emma's mouth formed an O.

"Don't look so surprised." Lamar elbowed her arm. "Think of all the men who've taken your quilting classes."

"True." She looked at their driver and gave him a wave. "We'll go on in the house and wait till Heidi and Lyle are home."

Ron was on the verge of telling them both doors were locked but changed his mind. They might wonder how he knew and become suspicious if he told them he'd already tried both doors.

"Nice meeting you folks," he mumbled before heading off to his motor home. It seemed odd that Heidi and Lyle would take off if they were expecting company—especially family members. *Oh well, it's none of my business. Just wish Heidi's aunt and uncle hadn't shown up when they did. Now I'll have to wait for a better time to check out the basement, not to mention gain entrance to the house. Just hope when there is a next time that at least one of the doors will be unlocked.*

Parting the curtain an inch, Ron watched the relatives try the front door. When they found it locked, they went to the back of the house. *If they're smart enough to try the basement door they'll be able to get in. If not, they'll just have to wait on the porch. Either way, it ain't my problem.*

Chapter 25

The meal at Der Dutchman tasted good as always," Heidi commented as she and Lyle headed toward home Saturday evening. "I'd considered cutting into the banana loaf I made earlier today when we get home, but I ate so much, I don't believe I have enough room." Patting her stomach, she took a deep breath and sighed.

"I hear ya. I'm so full, I think I might pop." Lyle stuck his finger inside his mouth and made a popping noise. "Whenever we eat from their buffet, I take too much. Guess the ole saying holds true, because my eyes are certainly bigger than my stomach."

Heidi smiled. Lyle could sure poke fun at himself. It was one of the many traits she loved about him. "Now don't get me laughing, or I might end up with the hiccups."

"Laughter's good medicine. The Bible says so, right?"

"True, which is why I included that scripture on the back of one of the recipe cards I gave my students."

He reached across the seat and clasped her hand. "Good thinking."

"Oh, Lyle, before I forget. . . While you were at the auction today, Kendra stopped by for a visit." She squeezed her husband's fingers.

"Isn't she the young, auburn-haired woman who attends your cooking class?"

"Jah, and during our visit she opened up to me about a few things."

"Such as?"

"Kendra is bitter toward her father."

"How come?" Lyle let go of Heidi's hand and snapped the reins, signaling to the horse to pick up speed.

"After Kendra informed her parents she was expecting a baby, her dad told her to leave his house and have nothing to do with her sisters."

"I take it she's not married?"

"No, and the father of her child has moved on with his life and wants nothing to do with helping Kendra raise the child." Heidi had gotten this bit of information during her last visit with Kendra.

Lyle's brows furrowed. "Family is family, regardless of what she did. It's too bad her daed doesn't see it that way."

"Hoping to offer Kendra some support, I shared scripture with her."

"Did it help?"

"From what I could tell, she didn't want to hear it."

"If the Lord laid it on your heart to share a passage from the Bible, then you did the right thing."

"I hope so. I don't want Kendra to feel that I'm forcing my religious beliefs on her."

Lyle shook his head. "To my knowledge, you've never done that with anyone. But we do need to be in tune with the hurts of others. Sometimes the best way to help them is through God's Word."

"True." Heidi sighed. "I only wish I could do more to help her. From what I understand, Kendra's only real friend is the young woman she's staying with in Mt. Hope."

"Don't forget prayer. There's power in our prayers."

"Jah." Heidi felt thankful for her husband's wisdom

and godly counsel. Another trait he was blessed to have. She appreciated being able to talk to him about Kendra.

As Lyle guided the horse and buggy into their yard, Heidi pointed out the front window. "Someone's sitting on our front porch, and it looks like. . ." She stifled a gasp. "For goodness' sake, it's Aunt Emma and her husband, Lamar."

Lyle's forehead wrinkled. "Did you know they were coming?"

She shook her head. "I had no idea whatsoever."

As soon as Lyle brought his horse to the rail, Heidi stepped down to secure the animal then hurried up to the house.

"Aunt Emma, what a surprise!"

"Surprise? Didn't you get my letter about us coming for a visit?" Aunt Emma rose from her chair and gave Heidi a hug. Lamar did the same.

Heidi's face radiated with heat as she shook her head in disbelief. "I haven't received any letters from you, at least not recently."

Peering at Heidi over the top of her metal-framed glasses, Aunt Emma tilted her head. "How strange. I wrote to tell you we'd be arriving today for a short visit before heading to Geauga County to see your folks."

Heidi's eyebrows squished together. "I bet your letter got lost in the mail. If I'd known you were coming, we would have stayed home this evening. Did you try to call?"

"I meant to yesterday, but things got busy and I plumb forgot." Aunt Emma thumped her forehead. "Must be old age setting in. Things come to mind—then they flit right out again."

"You don't have to be old for it to happen either," Lamar interjected with a chuckle. "Just busy."

Heidi laughed. "I can certainly relate to that." She gestured to the porch chairs. "How long have you been sitting out here waiting for us?"

Lamar pulled out his pocket watch. "Oh, a couple of hours."

"I apologize. You should have gone in and made yourselves at home."

"We tried the front and back doors, but they were both locked." Aunt Emma yawned. "So we sat out here and took a little nap."

"Sometimes we leave the basement door unlocked."

"Guess we should have checked there, but it's okay." Lamar stretched his arms over his head. "It's such a warm evening, and it felt relaxing to sit on your porch, listening to the evening sounds. Guess that's the reason we snoozed a little."

"Ach, listen. Isn't that the sound of a whip-poor-will calling?" Aunt Emma pointed to the closest maple tree.

"Jah, I believe so. They arrive every year about this time. Some nights they come in close and 'whip and will' for minutes on end. It almost sounds like those silly birds are singing their name." Heidi giggled. "One evening a whip-poor-will became so annoying Lyle threatened to open our bedroom window and throw his pillow at the winged creature. But I told him, 'You'll do no such thing. How many people get to hear a whip-poor-will serenading them by their window?'"

"So true," Aunt Emma and Lamar said in unison.

It amazed Heidi how alike these two were. Lamar was her aunt's second husband, and the two of them seemed to be soul mates. After Uncle Ivan passed away, Aunt Emma had been lonely. But then ever-cheerful Lamar came into her life and changed all that. It helped too that the couple had quilting in common. Lamar designed beautiful quilt patterns, and Aunt Emma made equally lovely quilts. They worked well together, and Lamar often helped teach his wife's quilting students.

"Well, enough talk about the birds." Heidi moved toward the front door. "I'll bet you two haven't had supper yet."

Heidi's aunt shook her head. "We thought you'd be here, and I figured on helping you make supper."

"I'm so sorry. Lyle and I ate supper at Der Dutchman, but there's leftover chicken from last night's meal in the refrigerator. I'll heat some up for you."

"Don't go to any trouble on our account." Aunt Emma gave a quick shake of her head. "A sandwich would suit us just fine."

"We'll see about that." Heidi clasped her aunt's hand. "How long can you stay?"

"Until tomorrow. We'll go to church with you in the morning, and then our driver will be back in the afternoon to take us up to your folks' place." A wide smile stretched across Aunt Emma's face. "It'll be good to see my sister again. It's been too long since our last visit."

After taking care of the horse and buggy, Lyle stepped onto the porch. "This is certainly a pleasant surprise." He shook Lamar's hand then gave Aunt Emma a hug. "We didn't realize you were coming."

"Aunt Emma sent me a letter, but it must have gotten lost in the mail." Heidi pointed to their suitcases. "We really ought to go inside. After I've fed these dear people some supper, we can spend the rest of the evening catching up with each other's lives."

"I'm anxious to hear about your cooking classes." Aunt Emma slipped her arm around Heidi's waist.

"And I'm eager to hear if you've taught any more quilting classes."

"Heidi, I heard the whip-poor-will when I came out of the barn. Sounded like it was back by the fields along the tree line somewhere," Lyle mentioned.

"We heard one too, only it was out front in the maple tree." Heidi pointed.

"Guess they've returned for the spring and summer months—in time to entertain us in the wee hours of the night."

"Oh Lyle, just admit it." Heidi poked his arm. "You enjoy hearing them as much as I do."

"You got me there." Lyle poked her back before winking at Aunt Emma.

The men picked up the luggage, Heidi linked arms with her aunt, and they all went into the house.

Mt. Hope

Kendra sat at Dorie's kitchen table, staring at the phone book. *Do I call Deacon Tom, and if so, what do I say? Should I blurt out the truth about my pregnancy and then tell him Dad kicked me out? Or would it be better if I make small talk first and lead slowly into the reason I called? Ha! Dad would probably get kicked off the board if this news got out. Well, he deserves whatever's coming to him.*

Kendra reached for her cell phone but hesitated. *If I tell Deacon Tom, he's bound to confront Dad, and then it could explode in my face. Dad might be so mad he'd kick Shelly and Chris out of the house to get even with me.*

Overwhelming anger had gripped Kendra's senses when she'd left Heidi's house this afternoon. Talking about her situation hadn't helped at all. Kendra's heart fluttered and her ears rang just thinking about everything. Maybe it would be best not to contact anyone from church about this mess and wait to see how it all played out. One thing was for certain: She would not pray about her situation, like Heidi had suggested. Nope. She'd done enough praying in the past, and where had it gotten her?

Kendra thought about the verse on the back of the recipe card for German pizza. *"In thee, O Lord, do I put my trust: let me never be put to confusion."* She frowned. *The only person I'm trusting is myself.*

"I may as well face it," Kendra muttered. "I've lost my family, and if I decide to give up my baby, I'll lose him or her too." Truthfully, Kendra saw no hope for her future. Even if she got hired full-time at the restaurant, she wouldn't make enough money to rent her own place and also provide for a child. The only sensible thing to do was relinquish her rights as the baby's mother and put him or her up for adoption.

Kendra wrapped her arms tightly around her middle. *Now I know how that mama duck must have felt, wanting to protect her little ones.* No matter how Kendra looked at it, whatever she chose to do would be difficult. If adoption was the best answer, should her baby go to strangers or someone she knew?

Dover

"Stop fidgeting and try not to appear so nervous." Len rubbed Charlene's back as they stepped onto his parents' porch. "Be nice to my mom, and she'll be nice to you." He lowered his arm and slipped it around Charlene's waist then leaned over and kissed her cheek. "Remember, sweetie, I love you."

"I love you too." She drew in a few deep breaths.

Let's get this over with.

Without knocking, Len opened the door and entered the house. "Mom! Dad! We're here."

Len's mother, Annette, stepped out of the kitchen, wearing a white apron of all things. If Charlene wore a white apron, it'd be dirty within minutes of putting it on.

"You're early. Supper's not quite ready." Annette's pale blue eyes held no sparkle. Not even a hint of a smile on her face either.

"It's okay, Mom." Len gave her a peck on the cheek. "I'd rather we be early than late."

In order to break the ice, Charlene thought to offer Len's mother a friendly hug, but with Annette's cold reception, she changed her mind. Squaring her shoulders and putting on her best smile, she tried something else. "Is there anything you'd like me to help you with?"

"I suppose you could cut more vegetables to put in the tossed salad. I'm not done making it yet."

"I'd be happy to finish the salad." After learning to make Amish haystack, with so many ingredients, Charlene felt sure she could manage a simple tossed salad.

"I'll visit with Dad while you ladies get supper on. Is he in the living room?" Len asked.

"Your father probably didn't hear you arrive." Nodding toward the other room, his mother frowned. "He's watching some documentary on birds of prey, and he'd better turn off the TV and come to the table when I announce supper's ready." She turned and tromped off to the kitchen.

Charlene cringed. Obviously Len's mother wasn't in a good mood this evening. *Sure hope I don't make things worse.*

Chapter 26

Pleased she had done well finishing the tossed salad, Charlene asked Len's mother if she needed help with anything else.

Annette brought a kettle over to the counter and placed it on a pot holder. "You can mash the potatoes while I make some gravy."

"Okay. Do you use a potato masher or portable mixer?"

Annette blinked rapidly, neck bending forward. "A mixer of course. No one uses a potato masher anymore. It went out with the Dark Ages." She opened a drawer and handed Charlene an electric hand mixer.

"The Amish don't use electric mixers," Charlene commented.

Annette quirked an eyebrow. "The Amish? What do you know about them?"

"Well, I. . ." Charlene caught herself in time. She'd been about to say she was taking cooking classes from an Amish woman. Since Charlene hadn't even told Len, she wasn't about to reveal it to his mother. "I've read some things about the Plain People. It's common knowledge they don't have electricity in their homes."

Annette lifted her shoulders and gave an undignified huff. "Sounds ludicrous to me. I can't imagine anyone living in our modern-day age and not making use of electricity." She placed a stick of butter and a carton of milk on the counter, along with salt and pepper. "Make sure the potatoes aren't lumpy. Oh, and Todd likes them nice and creamy, so you'll need to put in enough milk."

Charlene offered no response to Annette's comment about the Amish. She obviously thought they were old fashioned and perhaps even foolish. Charlene thought quite the opposite. Since meeting Heidi and spending time in her home, she viewed the Amish people as hardworking, responsible, and caring. They were dedicated to living a simpler life, without all the fancy things so many English people thought they needed. Charlene felt the Amish people's desire to live life as their ancestors had done was no less than amazing, especially in this day and age. Their focus was on serving God and family, not worldly things.

"I'll do my best with the potatoes," she murmured, hoping they would meet with Annette and her husband's approval. The last thing she needed was to look bad in anyone's eyes tonight. When she and Len went out to dinner last night, they'd set a wedding date. Len planned to tell his folks the news this evening. Charlene hoped they'd be happy about it, but she wasn't holding her breath. She'd figured out almost from the beginning of her and Len's relationship that his mother wasn't fond of her. Perhaps with Len being an only child, Annette wouldn't be happy with any woman he chose. In order to make her marriage to Len peaceful around his family, Charlene would need to win his mother's approval. But how?

———⸎———

"Why are the potatoes so soupy tonight?" Todd's question was directed at Annette. "You ought to know by now the way I like them—creamy, with lots of butter." His nose wrinkled. "I don't enjoy spuds runny enough to eat with a spoon."

Charlene swallowed hard as she watched Len's father hold up his fork, while the potatoes poured through the tines. "Sorry about that. I'm the one who whipped the potatoes. I may have added too much milk."

Annette's eyes narrowed when she took a small bite. "My husband's right; these potatoes are horrible."

"I didn't say they were horrible," Todd corrected. "They're just too runny, is all." Charlene glanced at Len, wondering if he might say something negative about the potatoes or, better yet, come to her defense. Instead he sat silently, eating his salad. *Guess the tossed salad passed the test, at least. So far, no one's complained about that.*

Charlene's thoughts were overridden when Len's mother poked her fork into the salad and pulled out a cucumber chunk. "My goodness, Charlene, didn't anyone ever teach you how to cut vegetables for a salad? They need to be finely cut. This cucumber is so large it won't even fit in my mouth."

Len picked up his knife and waved it in the air. "Come on, Mom, give it a rest. If the cucumber's too big, just cut it to the size you want. Charlene did the best she could."

"Thanks," Charlene murmured. She took pleasure in hearing Len finally stick up for her.

Annette glared at him, giving no response as she pushed the cucumber aside.

Charlene couldn't believe the woman's stubbornness. She behaved like a child. *Is this kind of behavior what I'll have to put up with every time I'm around her?*

Len cleared his throat, while tapping his water glass with a spoon. "Charlene and I have an announcement to make." He reached over and clasped her hand. "We're planning to get married the last Saturday of September."

"What?" Annette's mouth dropped open. "Why, that's not nearly enough time to prepare. It only gives us four months to plan things out for the wedding."

"I'll do most of the planning." On this matter Charlene would not relent. "In fact, I already have my wedding dress picked out."

"Well, haven't you been the busy bee? You know, there's a lot more to prepare for a big wedding than choosing a dress." Annette picked up her napkin and dabbed her lips daintily. "We need to make out a guest list, choose a caterer for the reception, and—"

Len held up his hand. "Whoa, Mom, you're getting carried away. Charlene and I will discuss all those things, and if we need your help, we'll ask."

Once again, Charlene felt pleased by her fiancé's response. Len stood his ground, not letting his mother take over the wedding. Besides, Charlene's parents needed to be included in their plans.

"We can talk about this later." Annette gestured to the platter of chicken. "We need to eat before our food gets cold."

After everyone finished their meal, Charlene got up to clear the table. On her way to the kitchen the silverware slipped off one of the plates she held and bounced on the floor. Wincing, she bent down, picked them up, and made a hasty exit, but not before overhearing Len's mother say, "Your girlfriend is not only a bad cook, but she's clumsy."

Hearing Annette's cutting remark, Charlene struggled with the desire to flee. *Wish I hadn't come here tonight. Seems I can't say or do anything right.* Curious to know if anything more would be said, she paused at the kitchen door and listened.

"Mother, that's enough. Charlene is my fiancée and your future daughter-in-law. Things are awkward enough and will only get worse if you can't find a way to get along with her."

Charlene felt a little better hearing Len speak on her behalf. But it did nothing to alleviate her concerns. What would her relationship with Annette be like once she and Len were married? Would he always take her side, or could there be times when Len stuck up for his mother?

Walnut Creek

"Mind if I ask you a question?" Heidi moved closer to her aunt on the couch and clasped her hand. They'd been visiting since Aunt Emma and Lamar finished supper. The men were in the barn, feeding the horses, so it was nice to have some time alone with her aunt.

"Of course, dear. I'd be happy to answer any question. What would you like to know?"

"Do all the people who come to your house to learn how to quilt have some sort of problem they share with you?"

"Jah, quite often many of them do. Some have come with more serious issues, but many were minor." Aunt Emma held her hands together, as though praying. "With some people, I offered advice and often shared scripture, while others I simply prayed for."

"This is my first group of students, and I've already discovered most of them are facing some sort of problem." Heidi's lips parted slightly. "Some, like the young unwed woman who's expecting a baby, have sought my advice, while others, like Ron, only shared a bit with me and the class."

"Who is Ron?" Aunt Emma asked.

Heidi pointed to the living room window. "He lives in the motor home parked in our yard."

"Oh, so he's the man we met when our driver dropped us off." Aunt Emma's forehead wrinkles deepened. "I asked if he was a friend of yours, and he said you'd allowed him to park his vehicle here. Is that true?"

"Yes. Until a little over a month ago, we'd never met Ron. He showed up one day, saying his motor home wasn't running right and asking if he could stay here a few days until he got it fixed. Then he ended up taking my cooking classes, so we agreed he could stay until the final class, near the end of June."

"It's kind of you to allow him to stay so long. Is he a pleasant person to be around?" Aunt Emma fluffed the throw pillow on the couch and positioned it behind her head.

"Truth is, Ron's hard to figure out. Sometimes he seems nice and polite. Other times, he says rude things and acts kind of jittery, especially around the others during our class." Heidi reached for her cup of tea and took a sip. "He hasn't told us much about his past, but I believe he's dealing with some serious issues."

"He needs prayer then, and perhaps in time you'll have a chance to tell him about God's love."

"I hope so. Even more so, I hope he is willing to listen."

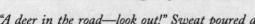

"A deer in the road—look out!" Sweat poured down Ron's face as he slammed on the brakes. He'd passed the place now, but in his side mirror, he could see the deer lying motionless by the side of the road. It was getting dark. Nobody cared about a deer. Ron drove onward. Maybe it wasn't a deer. It

could have been a Vietnamese soldier.

Moaning, he rolled to the other side of his bunk as the scene changed in his head.

Machine-gun fire—grenades going off all around him. The swamp made sucking sounds as he lifted one boot, and then the other. The humidity was hard to bear. His clothes stuck to his skin. Off the bank, he saw an enemy soldier coming toward him with a bayonet. Ron hoisted his gun, as he'd been trained to do, and fired. The soldier collapsed in a heap, sinking slowly below the bog's surface. Ron cupped his mouth with his hand. He's dead. I'm a murderer. The poor fellow never stood a chance.

An owl hooted, and Ron's eyes snapped open. Drenched in sweat, he rose from his bed, relieved to see familiar surroundings. It had only been a dream—a reoccurring nightmare.

Shuffling to the kitchen area, Ron grabbed a glass to fill with water. In need of fresh air, he opened the side door and stepped out, taking a seat on the entrance step. Although well after midnight, the bright moon illuminated the Troyers' yard. Looking at their house, he saw that all was dark.

Ron shivered, running his hands over his arms as he sucked in a gulp of air, hoping to calm himself. *Why can't I get the war out of my head? Will the terrible nightmares ever cease?*

Ron's thoughts turned to his only brother. *Oh Mike, I miss you so much. If not for the war, you'd still be alive, and I never would have enlisted.*

Ron's chin quivered as he held his churning stomach. *It should have been me who died, not you.*

Chapter 27

Sugarcreek

The next Wednesday, Charlene met her friend Kathy for dinner at a restaurant in Sugarcreek. A few minutes after the hostess seated them, a waitress came to take their orders. Kathy ordered fried chicken and mashed potatoes, with a side order of corn. Charlene asked for spaghetti and meatballs, accompanied by a small dinner salad.

"How'd your school week go?" Kathy leaned her elbows on the table.

Charlene shrugged. "Okay, but I dread Friday, since it's the last day of school until fall."

"Aren't you glad to have the summer off? I certainly am."

"The first few weeks are nice, but I soon become bored. Besides, I always miss my students."

"Guess you would." Kathy drank some water. "Try teaching fifth graders, and then see how grateful you are to have the summer off. As much as I enjoy teaching, the kids in my class can sure try my patience sometimes."

"Have you considered teaching a lower grade?"

"Yeah, but with the younger ones comes another set of problems. I'll probably stick with the grade I teach. That way, I'll always have something to complain about." Kathy snickered, tucking her shoulder-length blond hair behind her ears. "So how'd your dinner at Len's parents' go on Saturday?"

Moaning, Charlene slumped in her chair. "What a fiasco it turned out to be."

"Oh no. What happened?" Kathy leaned forward, as though straining to hear above the voices around them.

"For one thing, I made a complete fool of myself."

"How so?"

Charlene explained how she had turned the mashed potatoes into soup. "Oh, and according to Len's mother, I didn't cut the vegetables for the salad small enough either. I also dropped some silverware while clearing dishes from the table." Charlene poked her tongue lightly into the side of her cheek, inhaling a long breath. "Then, while heading to the kitchen, I overheard Annette say to Len and his dad that I'm clumsy."

"Oh boy. Unless you're able to gain his mother's favor, you may be faced with trouble once you and Len are married."

"I know, but the way things are going, I doubt I'll ever find favor with her." Charlene's neck muscles tightened as she shook her head. "Annette goes out of her way to be rude. I'm afraid she'll eventually turn Len against me."

"Perhaps you should reconsider marrying him. Now's the time to bail, not after the wedding."

"I'm not bailing, Kathy. I love Len. If I could talk him into moving away from his parents it might help the situation. At least then, we wouldn't have to see them so often."

Kathy raised her eyebrows. "Good luck with that. Len's job is here, and so are his folks. I'd be willing to bet money he won't leave."

"Well, I won't know till I ask."

"And if he says no?"

Charlene bit the inside of her cheek. "I'm not sure. Guess I'd better wait and see what Len's response is before I make any decision that could affect my future with him."

Walnut Creek

Eli grinned as he stepped out of the phone shack. After checking messages, he'd called Loretta to confirm their plans for Saturday. When class was over, they'd meet at Loretta's house, and Eli would take her and the children to get acquainted with his folks. He looked forward to spending time with Loretta, Abby, and Conner and was eager to find out how things were going with Donnelly. A warm sensation spread throughout Eli's body. *I'm glad I gave them the dog.* He visualized the look of joy on Abby's and Conner's faces. Those kids were so cute and smart. Once again, Eli wished he'd had the good fortune to become a parent. But it must not have been meant to be, or Mavis would have lived and been able to bear children.

Eli's mood shifted, his peppy step gone as he shuffled up the driveway. *I shouldn't let negative thoughts take over like this. Nothin' good comes of it.*

As Eli approached the house, his nose twitched. A foul odor told him something was burning. Remembering the eggs he'd put on the stove to boil, he jerked the door open and rushed inside. Luckily, the kettle hadn't caught on fire, but all the water had boiled out, and the pan was completely dry. Worse yet, all the eggs exploded, and now the mess was stuck to his ceiling. The horrible stench of burnt eggs made his stomach roil.

In addition to cleaning up the mess, the whole house needed a good airing.

Eli sputtered and coughed as he made his way through the house, opening windows and doors for ventilation. "Sure hope this putrid odor doesn't linger or seep into the furniture."

He got out the step stool and scraped off the eggs on the ceiling above the stove. Next, Eli filled the sink with soapy water and cleaned the whole area. Following that, he placed an open box of baking soda on the kitchen counter, hoping to absorb some of the remaining unpleasant aroma. *If I wanted to give the folks in my cooking class a good laugh, all I'd have to do is tell 'em about this.* He smacked the palm of his hand against his forehead and groaned. *What a horrible way to end the day. Guess now I'd better hitch my horse to the buggy and go out to eat supper.*

It had been a busy day for Heidi, with baking, cleaning house, paying bills, and making sure everything was lined up for her class on Saturday. Now for a much-needed break.

Settling into the rocker on the front porch, she closed her eyes, listening to the melodic tinkle of wind chimes. Lyle found the chimes at an auction last week and hung them on the porch eaves close to the kitchen window so Heidi could hear the music when she stood at the sink. As the breeze lessened, the tinkling sound diminished, but a dove's soft cooing took its place.

Smiling, Heidi opened her eyes. Even during tense moments, the sound of a dove's gentle coo offered solace. At a time such as this, when Heidi felt content, her relaxation went deeper. She couldn't sit out here much longer though. Lyle would be home soon, and she'd have to start supper. They'd invited Ron to join them for burgers cooked on the grill. Since it turned out to be such a nice day, they planned to eat outside.

She glanced at Ron's motor home, wondering why he'd kept to himself today. By now he'd usually be out walking around the property or in the barn doing chores for Lyle.

I may have missed him, she thought. *I wasn't watching out the window all day. I hope Ron will be on time for our six o'clock supper.*

Ron leaned forward, rubbing his forehead. He'd sat in his RV most of the day, brooding. Today would have been his brother's sixty-ninth birthday. Ever since Ron was a boy, he'd looked up to Mike. He'd hung on his every word. With only two years between them, they'd always been close and understood one another.

When Mike joined the marines, Ron felt such pride in his brother. He'd worried, though, when Mike was sent to Vietnam.

Ron sucked in a deep breath, remembering the peaceful and quiet afternoon when Ron and his parents had relaxed in the living room after their usual big Sunday meal. Ron heard the crunch of tires as a car pulled in and would never forget what happened when his father opened the door.

Standing somber at the entrance was a casualty notification officer and a chaplain. Ron covered his ears, but not even that could drown out his mother's screams. Dad tried to console her, while struggling not to break down himself.

Nothing was ever the same. It was difficult, but

Ron and his parents moved forward, taking one day at a time. Ron felt like a robot though. Several months later, the sadness in Mom's and Dad's eyes remained. Why wouldn't it? No parents expected to outlive their children.

Ron was lost without his brother and angry at God for allowing it to happen. Even though his parents begged him not to, six months after Mike's funeral, Ron enlisted in the marines. Not long after, he too ended up in the ravages of the Vietnam War. It was exactly where he needed to be. Ron wanted—no, needed—to seek revenge for his brother's death.

Bringing his thoughts back to the present, Ron looked out the RV window and muttered, "Life stinks, but it keeps going on." Reaching for his wallet, he pulled out a folded piece of worn-looking paper. His vision blurred as he stared at Mike's named etched in pencil. Years after finishing his tour of duty, Ron took his parents to Washington, DC, to visit the Wall at the Vietnam Veterans Memorial. While there, he had the chance to etch his brother's name. It was mind boggling to see all those other names and realize, like Ron and his parents, thousands of families mourned the loss of their loved one, while trying to get some semblance of normalcy back into their lives.

But in the years after Mike's death and Ron's time in the marines, as hard as he tried to get back to living a normal life, the nightmares still came. Even getting married and having children didn't make them go away. Ron came to the conclusion this was how it was going to be. His life would never be the same.

Rubbing his finger over his brother's name, Ron whispered, "Happy birthday, Mike. I love you, brother."

Ron's thoughts halted when a knock sounded on his side door. "Just a minute," he called, folding the paper and returning it to his wallet. He went to the sink and splashed cold water on his face then opened the door.

"Supper's ready," Lyle announced. "Heidi made plenty, so I hope you're hungry."

Ron managed a fake smile and nodded. Truthfully, he felt like he couldn't eat a thing. He'd only had one cup of coffee all day, which likely caused some of the jitteriness he felt at the moment. Thinking about Mike had diminished his appetite.

"You okay?" Lyle asked. "I have a hunch you're not feeling so well."

Ron crossed his arms as he gave a slow nod. "Been thinkin' about my older brother, who died in the Vietnam War. Today would have been his birthday." Ron blinked fast. Saying the words out loud made it all too real.

"Loss is hard." Lyle gave Ron's arm a squeeze. "I understand if you'd rather not join us, but maybe a juicy burger and some friendly conversation will offer some cheer."

"Yeah, okay." Ron stepped out of the RV and shut the door. At moments like this, when Lyle was so nice, Ron felt guilty for taking advantage of them. *If Lyle and Heidi knew I'd stolen things from them, they'd probably throw me off their land. And most likely would call the sheriff. Then I'd be sitting in some jail cell, instead of here, where I have it so good. If I still had the stuff I took from their house and barn, I'd put it back. But those items I pawned, and the money I stole from the blue vase is gone.*

Another thought popped into Ron's head. *Maybe I ought to leave now, before I'm tempted to steal anything more.*

Chapter 28

Heidi glanced at the kitchen clock. In thirty minutes class would begin, but everything hadn't been set out. The morning started out a bit hectic. She'd slept longer than planned, and it put her behind.

"I suppose it won't matter if we begin a few minutes late," Heidi murmured, taking a sack of flour from the cupboard and placing it on the table.

"Were you talking to me?" Lyle wrapped his arms around Heidi's waist and nuzzled the back of her neck with his nose.

She snickered. "Talking to myself, silly, and you shouldn't sneak up on me like that. I should have remembered to set the alarm last night so I'd have plenty of time to get ready for my class this morning."

He turned Heidi to face him, rubbing both her arms. "You'll do fine. Some of your students will probably show up late, like they did the last time. So don't fret about starting right on the button."

She smiled and gave his cheek a gentle pinch. "You're right, as usual."

Lyle gave a quick shake of his head. "I don't claim to know everything. Just don't want you to stress out. Remember, these classes are supposed to be fun."

"Oh, they are—at least for me. So far my students

228

seem to have enjoyed themselves." Heidi placed a bowl of red-skinned apples on the table. "Although Ron sometimes acts a bit standoffish. It's hard to read him most of the time."

Lyle's face sobered. "Speaking of Ron, did he say anything to you about leaving?"

"No he didn't. I thought he planned to stay until the end of June, when the cooking classes are over."

"So did I, but when I spoke to him earlier this morning, he said he'd gotten his RV running and figured on heading out today right after class."

Heidi's forehead creased. "It seems strange he'd want to leave now, with only two classes left to take. Did he say why?"

"Nothing clear-cut. Just mumbled something about not wanting to take advantage of our hospitality anymore."

Heidi pursed her lips. "That's silly. He's been here this long. He should stay and finish the classes."

"I told him the same thing. Not sure he'll listen, but at least I tried." Lyle went to the kitchen sink and filled a glass with water. "Ron shared a few things with me the other evening when I went out to his motor home, just before our cookout."

"Oh?"

"The poor fellow was grieving because if his brother hadn't been killed in the Vietnam War, it would have been his birthday." Lyle slowly shook his head. "I feel sorry for Ron. He seems almost lost, and I think he needs a friend."

"You've said before you thought God brought Ron here for a reason. Maybe it's so we can be his friends," Heidi suggested.

"Jah, I believe you're right."

Heidi glanced out the window and spotted Ron sitting on a camp stool outside his motor home with his hands pressed against his head. "I hope by the time my cooking classes are done, that my students, Ron included, will feel as if they've made some new friends. I also hope, due to the scriptures I've shared, that some will have found help for whatever problems they might be going through."

Lyle kissed Heidi's forehead. "Jah, God can minister to them through His Word, as well as things you might say during class, just as He's done to many of your aunt Emma's quilting students."

───────⁕⁓◦⁓⁕───────

Sugarcreek

"There ya go." Loretta gave Abby a hug. "Why don't you take Donnelly outside? Then you can sit on the porch and wait for Sandy to arrive."

"Okay, Mommy." Her daughter skipped out of the room, with the dog frolicking at her side.

Loretta smiled. Abby looked cute in her bright red top. It was a summery shirt her mother-in-law had given Abby at Christmas. Thank goodness, she'd purchased a large enough size. Abby was growing fast, and the cotton shirt, which was too big in December, fit her perfectly now.

"All right, big boy." Loretta scooped Conner up to get him ready as she heard the screen door slam. Glancing out the window, Loretta saw Abby walking the puppy toward the backyard.

Loretta hummed while she changed Conner from his pj's to a pair of jeans and a striped T-shirt. She'd dressed both kids in something comfortable since they'd all be going with Eli later today.

She closed her eyes, breathing deeply. After having the windows closed all winter, it was nice having them open, as the comfortable breeze wafted through the screens. Loretta appreciated the opportunity to allow her children to grow up in this environment. There was plenty of space for them to run, play, and use their imaginations. Abby and Conner enjoyed pretending while they played with their simple toys. She'd decided early on not to own a TV so it wouldn't be a distraction for her or the children.

Loretta also felt grateful for the elderly neighbor next door who'd do about anything for them. It was a comfort being able to call on him if needed. Sam took good care of himself too. Instead of wasting away in front of a TV, he kept moving and doing, many times offering to take care of outside chores for Loretta.

Through the open window, Loretta heard Abby coaxing Donnelly. "Come on, puppy. Do your business now."

Eli had given her children such a wonderful surprise. Even with all the pup's little accidents, once again, Loretta wished she had gotten a dog for them sooner. Although the puppy wasn't consistent yet, the new member of their family was learning quickly. The other night, for the first time, Donnelly scratched on the door to be let out. Afterward, they all praised the dog and gave him a treat for being good.

"Donnelly! Donnelly!" Conner giggled, pointing to the window.

"Yes, I hear him barking." Loretta combed her son's hair. "Okay, let's join your sister now, and we'll wait for Sandy to arrive." Loretta was grateful Sandy was available to watch the kids again while she went to class.

When she got home, Eli would swing by with his horse and buggy, and off to his parents' house they'd go—Donnelly included.

When Loretta went outside to the porch with Conner, she didn't see her daughter in the yard. She'd assumed Abby was with Donnelly, but the barking pup, straining against its leash, sat on the porch by himself. Abby had apparently wrapped the end of the dog's leash around one of the lawn chairs, and Donnelly, even though little, had dragged the chair over and was about to go down the porch steps with it trailing behind him.

"Conner, do Mommy a favor and stay right here with Donnelly, while I go look for your sister." It wasn't like Abby to leave the puppy alone. She'd been watching over Donnelly like a mother hen ever since Eli gave them the dog.

Loretta's heart filled with gratitude when Sandy pulled in. She sprinted to the babysitter's car before the motor was even turned off.

Sandy rolled her window down. "Is everything all right?"

"Oh Sandy, I'm so glad you're here. I have an emergency, but I need you to stay with Conner." Loretta pointed to the porch. "He's waiting there, and I'll explain later."

"Of course." Sandy turned off the ignition and ran toward the porch.

"Abby, where are you?" Loretta hurried toward the garage. She turned the knob, but the door was still locked, so her daughter couldn't be there. *Don't panic. Stay calm.* Her brain sent messages, but her mother's instinct kicked in, ignoring all reason. As she headed toward the back of the property, something red caught her eye.

The property that adjoined the back of her and Sam's lots belonged to a farm over the ridge. Normally the cows didn't graze this far. From Loretta's home, the farm buildings weren't visible, but on rare occasions, the herd would venture farther and wind up at this end. Abby and Conner always wanted to see the pretty black-and-white Holsteins, so Loretta would take them to the fence to watch. Sometimes they'd feed them grass. But what Loretta saw now made her eyes grow wide as her hand went to her mouth. Abby stood in the field, a few feet from a monstrous black bull. Holding a clump of grass, her daughter walked slowly toward the massive animal. Loretta faintly heard Abby coaxing, "Here's somethin' for you to eat."

Loretta took no thought of the beautiful wildflowers blooming along the fence row or the birds tweeting merrily from the trees. Her focus was on the giant beast flicking its ears while staring back at her precious child.

As Loretta ran toward the fence, her breath burst in and out. Abby probably thought this was one of the gentle cows. The bull looked Loretta's way then back at Abby. *Oh, why did I put a red shirt on my little girl this morning?* Maybe it was a myth, but Loretta had heard bulls didn't like the color red.

"Abby." Loretta spoke calmly as she climbed over the fence and walked slowly toward her daughter. "Don't go any closer, honey."

Loretta approached Abby and scooped the child into her arms then stood trembling as she kept an eye on the bull. His neck and shoulders were huge and muscular. Loretta's impulse was to run, but it might set him off. Without breaking contact with the bull's steady gaze, she backed slowly away. Despite her best efforts, the beast began pawing the ground with both his front feet, sending dirt flying in all directions. *What to do now?* Loretta trembled when Abby asked, "Mommy, is the cow mad at us?"

"I'll explain later. Just hold on to me." Loretta turned. The fence was at least sixty yards away, but it might as well have been five miles. If the bull wanted to, he could run the distance in seconds, before she reached the fence.

Loretta's lungs burned as she sprinted toward safety, the whole time praying for help. She looked back once and shuddered when the bull lowered his head, shaking it from side to side. Big puffs of air escaped the animal's nostrils. All Loretta wanted to do was get her precious child to safety. *Please Lord, help us.*

As though God heard her plea at that very moment, there was Sam, running past her, waving his arms and shouting, "Boo-Boo. It's all right now, settle down."

The bull lifted his head and, for the moment, seemed subdued. Was it the name Sam had called him?

"Walk to the fence, Loretta. Don't run," Sam instructed. "I called the Blakes. It's their bull, and as you heard, his name is Boo-Boo."

Abby laughed as she clung to Loretta's neck. "I like his name, Mommy. Don't you?"

All Loretta could think about was how in the world an animal that massive could be called Boo-Boo and how grateful she was that Sam had shown up when he did. God most certainly had answered her prayer.

———— ✦·◦∘◦·✦ ————

Walnut Creek

Charlene glanced at the clock on her dashboard and grimaced. She'd never seen so much traffic on this stretch of road.

Ah, so there's the reason. Everyone seems to be heading for the Walnut Creek Cheese store today. The parking lot was full of cars. Even the hitching rail for Amish horse and buggies looked full to capacity. *The store must be having a sale. Either that or everyone picked this particular Saturday to do their shopping.*

After pausing to let a car turn in front of her, Charlene moved on. Even though she looked forward to attending the fourth cooking class, her nerves were a bit on edge this morning. This time, however, it wasn't for fear of making a fool of herself in front of the class. Today she struggled with her plans to speak with Len about his mother during their dinner date this evening. Charlene had spoken to him only once this week, to make plans for tonight. While she could have told Len what was on her mind then, Charlene preferred not to do it over the phone. It might go over better if she discussed it with him in person.

She held tightly to the steering wheel. *What will I do if Len says no to my request? If he's not willing to move, maybe I should end our relationship before his mother ends it for us.*

Tears pricked Charlene's eyes, and she blinked rapidly to keep them from spilling over. She loved Len and couldn't imagine spending the rest of her life without him. *Is it right to make him choose between me and his mother?*

Charlene sniffed deeply and kept her focus straight ahead. *If I get the chance to speak to Heidi alone today, maybe I'll ask her opinion.*

———————◦✦◦———————

Eli couldn't stop smiling as he guided his horse and buggy in the direction of the Troyers' house. Normally, he wouldn't have bothered to take the buggy such a short distance, but since he'd be heading to Loretta's as soon as the cooking class was over today, it made sense. No point walking or riding his bike then going home and hitching the horse. This way would save time.

He looked forward to seeing Loretta again and taking her and the children to meet his folks. *Bet Mom will enjoy seeing the puppy again too. Wonder what she'll think of the name Abby and Conner gave the* hund. *Personally, I like it. It's a catchy name. Course Loretta's kids are cute, so everything they say and do is liable to impress me.*

Eli shook his head. *They're not angels though. I'm sure Conner and Abby are naughty sometimes. But I'll bet their mother handles it well. Loretta seems kind and patient. Even so, I doubt she'd let her kinner get away with anything.*

With little coaxing, Eli's horse turned up the Troyers' driveway. Of course, since they were in the same church district and Eli was Lyle's friend, he'd been here a good many times. The trusty animal could have probably found the way, even without Eli's guidance.

As he pulled up to the hitching rail, Eli spotted Ron walking toward the house with his head down and shoulders slouched. *Wonder what his problem is. Maybe he's not happy to be here today.*

When Loretta pulled her van into the Troyers' yard, she spotted Eli's horse and buggy. Her pulse raced a bit as she thought about his invitation to take her and the children to visit his parents this afternoon. Abby and Conner looked forward to it, and if Loretta was being honest, so did she.

Her hands still shook from the morning's experience, but thankfully, her daughter had been unscathed. In fact, when they'd walked back to the porch, Abby couldn't wait to relay the story to her brother and Sandy.

Loretta was eager to tell Eli but would wait and let Abby share her adventure. In her childlike eyes, it had been an adventure, and Loretta wanted to keep it that way. She did not wish to instill fear into her children's minds but had calmly explained how most bulls were uncomfortable around people.

Thank goodness Sam heard me calling for Abby and saw the bull when he looked out his kitchen window.

Loretta thought's returned to Eli. *Did I do the right thing agreeing to go with him this afternoon? I hope his parents won't get the wrong idea and think Eli and I are courting.*

Loretta thumped her head. *What am I thinking? We're only friends. I'm sure Eli's informed his parents of that. I do have to admit, though, I enjoy his company, and if he were English. . .*

Loretta turned off her engine and stepped down from the van. She was almost to the house when her shoe caught on an odd-shaped rock. All the contents of Loretta's purse spilled out as she lost her balance and landed flat on her back.

Chapter 29

Straining his ears, Eli hoped it was Loretta's minivan he heard pulling in. She was the only one left to arrive. When he went to the living room window to look out, he was stunned. Loretta lay flat on the ground. Without a second thought, he rushed out the door and dropped to his knees beside her. "Loretta, what happened? Are you hurt?" His heart beat so fast he found it hard to breathe.

"I tripped on a rock, and. . ." Moaning, she turned onto her side and sat up. "My ankle hurts. I. . .I hope I can stand."

Heart still pounding, Eli stood and swept Loretta into his arms as if she weighed no more than a feather.

Heidi was at the door waiting for them when he stepped inside. "What happened? Is she hurt?"

"She tripped on a rock and fell." Eli spoke between ragged breaths. "She injured her ankle. I hope it's not broken."

"Better take her to the couch."

As Eli placed Loretta gently down, everyone gathered around.

"I'm okay. Don't look so worried." Loretta winced when Heidi touched her ankle. "Guess I should have been paying closer attention."

"You might want to go to the hospital and get an

X-ray taken," Kendra suggested.

Loretta shook her head. "I'm sure there's no need for that." She stood and took a few steps then lost her balance and fell back onto the couch.

"Here, let me take a look." Charlene stepped forward, and Eli moved aside. "I'm trained in first aid."

Eli held his breath as Charlene examined Loretta's ankle. "The good news is, I'm almost sure it's not broken—maybe just a sprain. Heidi, do you have an ice pack we can put on Loretta's ankle?"

"Yes. I'll get it right now." Heidi hurried from the room.

Eli felt relief hearing Loretta wasn't seriously hurt. His main concern now was that she might not feel up to visiting his folks this afternoon. *What's wrong with me? I'm being selfish. Above all else, Loretta's comfort is the important thing.*

"How do you feel now?" Heidi asked after Loretta sat for fifteen minutes with her leg propped up and an ice pack on her ankle.

"It feels a little better. Look, it's not even swollen." Loretta twirled her ankle in a circular motion. "Sorry for holding up your lesson, Heidi. We should head to the kitchen now so you can get started."

"Are you sure? If no one's in a hurry, we can wait awhile longer."

"Oh, please don't." Loretta waved her hand and pushed herself to a sitting position. "I'm fine, really."

Heidi led the way to the kitchen, and everyone followed. Glancing over her shoulder, she saw Eli offer his arm to Loretta as she gingerly walked beside him. After observing the look of concern on his face when he carried Loretta into the house, Heidi wondered if Eli had more than a casual interest in Loretta. Although she was a sweet woman, Loretta wasn't Amish. It would be difficult for them to develop a serious relationship without one of them giving up their current way of life.

Pushing her concerns aside, Heidi pointed to the table. "Today we're making apple cream pie, so we'll take turns mixing and then rolling out the crust." She gestured to the finished pie she'd made this morning. "This is what it looks like when it's taken from the oven. Once we're finished, you'll each have your own pie to take home today, along with the recipe for it." The scripture Heidi had written on the back of their cards was Ephesians 4:32: *"And be ye kind one to another, tenderhearted, forgiving one another, even as God for Christ's sake hath forgiven you."* She hoped it might speak to someone this week.

"Is your oven big enough for all the pies to bake at once?" Kendra asked.

"No, but two pies can bake at the same time. If no one's in a hurry to go, there should be plenty of time to get them all done."

"The young woman I hired to watch my children today has somewhere she needs to go later this afternoon, so I'll have to leave by one o'clock," Loretta spoke up.

"Not a problem. We'll make sure yours is one of the first pies to go in the oven." Heidi looked at the others. "What about the rest of you?"

"I can stay awhile longer," Charlene responded. "I have plans with my boyfriend, but not till this evening."

"I'll leave when Loretta does, because. . ." Eli paused and moistened his lips. "Well, I have some plans for this afternoon." He glanced quickly at Loretta then back at Heidi.

"It's fine. Your pie can go in with Loretta's." Heidi looked at Kendra. "How about you?"

"I'll stay longer."

Heidi smiled. "And Ron, since you're staying here on our property, I would assume you won't mind if your pie goes in last?"

Ron hesitated then nodded. He seemed quiet today. Could it have something to do with him telling Lyle he planned to leave? As soon as class finished, she'd speak to him about it.

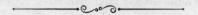

Just what I need, Ron grumbled to himself. *Sure didn't want any delays today.* He'd planned to cut out right after class. He was afraid that with any more holdups, he'd end up changing his mind. The last couple of days, Ron went back and forth with the idea of leaving. But he'd already told Lyle he would go. Otherwise, it wouldn't take much for Ron to relent and stay, at least until the final cooking class was over.

The other evening, while listening to the radio in his RV, Ron had heard an advertisement about the mobile display of the Vietnam Wall coming to the Columbus area. He'd considered heading in that direction today. The Moving Wall was being set up for the upcoming Memorial Day holiday next week, to honor and recognize those who'd served and sacrificed their lives in the Vietnam War. The half-size replica of the original wall had been touring the country for more than thirty years, which made it easier for people who didn't have the opportunity to travel to Washington, DC, to get some idea of what the Wall was all about. Since Columbus was a little over one hundred miles away, the drive would take about two hours. Once there, Ron hoped to find a place on the outskirts of the city, reasonable in cost, where he could set up camp for a few days. It had been years since he'd taken his parents to the original Wall, and now he felt the need to see his brother's name again, especially with the holiday to honor veterans approaching. Ron wanted to retrace Mike's name too since the one in his wallet had become tattered and worn.

Ron almost felt guilty leaving the Troyers like this, especially since they were kind of growing on him. Had Lyle told Heidi about his plans to leave, or should Ron spring the news on her after class?

A knot formed in his belly. This farm felt more like home than any other place he'd stayed. Even Lyle's horse seemed like a friend. Ron had found himself unloading on the animal when he just needed someone to listen to him. The horse's soft nickers offered solace for Ron, even if Bobbins didn't understand.

What's more, Heidi and Lyle's Brittany spaniel had gotten used to seeing Ron around the place. Some mornings, Rusty came to the entrance of Ron's RV and barked until he responded. The dog sat patiently waiting for Ron to open the door and pat him on the head or give him a scrap of food before returning to the porch to lie down.

While Ron listened to Heidi explain more about the pies, he figured anytime he bugged out would work, as long as he didn't lose his nerve. If he could find a place for his RV by nightfall, it was half the battle—at least that's what he kept telling himself. But Ron wasn't sure what would come next after the Memorial Day holiday.

Don't worry till the time comes, he told himself. Ron felt like a lost soul moving from one place to another, without any real goals or purpose. Truth was, his life had no meaning anymore. He had no family, no friends, and no real reason to get up each morning.

When Charlene's turn came around to roll out her pie-crust, she picked up the rolling pin with trembling fingers. Mixing the ingredients for the crust had been easy enough, but she wasn't sure how to roll it correctly. The last thing she wanted was a too-thick piecrust. Or worse yet, one she could see through. *You would think by now my nerves would settle down, especially with Heidi as a teacher. Too bad Len's mother doesn't have Heidi's patience. Otherwise, I wouldn't be faced with the discussion I'll be having with Len this evening.*

"Press firmly and roll from the inside out," Heidi instructed, leaning close to Charlene. "That's it. You're doing fine."

Charlene smiled. It wasn't as difficult as she'd expected. In fact, the whole process ended up being fun. Carefully, as Heidi guided her, she picked up the dough and placed it in the pie pan.

"Here's a tip I'd like to share with all of you about fluting the edges of a piecrust before it's baked. Once the pie shell has been put into the pan, place it on a cake stand. This will make it easier to turn the pie plate, and you won't have to stoop over. Of course you may use your fingers to flute the edges, but it's also fun to try some kitchen utensils to make more decorative edges." Heidi picked up a spoon and made a few scalloped edges. "You can also use a fork for different patterns."

"The spoon looks easy enough. I'll try that." Between the lessons she'd already taken, and the time spent practicing at home, Charlene felt confident she'd be able to cook a decent meal for Len soon. And maybe even surprise his parents.

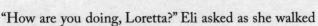

"How are you doing, Loretta?" Eli asked as she walked slowly to the stove to check on her pie.

"My ankle still hurts, but not as bad as it did earlier." She smiled, appreciating his concern.

"Glad to hear it." Eli moved closer and lowered his voice. "If you're not up to going over to my folks' today, we make can it another time."

She shook her head and whispered, "I'll be fine. Abby and Conner would be disappointed if we didn't go, and I'd never hear the end of it." Loretta glanced back and felt relief that no one seemed to be watching them. "Besides, I'm eager to meet your parents."

"Okay then." He peered into the oven and grinned. "Our pies are lookin' pretty good. Maybe I'll take mine along to Mom and Dad's, and we can eat it while we're there."

"I'll take my pie too. That way, if we're all hungry we can have a second piece." How long had it been since Loretta felt this lighthearted? Nothing, not even her sore ankle, could keep her from going with Eli as planned. After what happened earlier today with the neighbor's bull, an afternoon with Eli and her children was just what she needed.

"Yum. I can almost taste the pie already." Eli's smile widened. "I'm looking forward to this afternoon."

Feeling warm and fuzzy inside, Loretta gave a nod. "So am I, Eli." *More than you know.*

Chapter 30

As soon as Ron took his pie from the oven, he set it on the countertop and headed for the door. Kendra's pie cooled next to his, and since she and Heidi were engrossed in conversation, he figured it was a good time to make his escape.

Ron's hand touched the doorknob when Heidi called out to him. "Where are you going, Ron? Don't you want your pie?"

He halted and turned back around. "Uh, it's too hot to carry right now."

"You're right, but here's a box to put it in, like I did for the others before they left."

Ron hesitated. "Sure, okay then. Guess I can take it with me."

Heidi put on a pair of oven mitts and placed the pie inside a cardboard box. Then she handed it to Ron and followed him out the door. "May I ask you something?"

"Yeah, sure." With his back to the porch railing, he turned to face her.

"Lyle mentioned you were planning to leave without finishing the cooking classes."

Ron shifted the box as heat crept up the back of his neck. "Well, yeah, I was. Figured I ought to be moving on before I overstayed my welcome."

She shook her head. "You haven't, Ron. We'd be pleased if you'd stay until the classes are done."

"Okay, I'll stay." What else could he say with her looking at him so kindly? To be honest, Ron didn't really want to leave—at least not until he'd finished the classes. He shuffled his feet. "See, the thing is, there's someplace I want to go for a few days."

"To visit your family?"

"No way! My ex-wife and kids don't want anything to do with me, but I can't really blame 'em." He scratched behind his right ear. "I'll be driving down to Columbus to see the Vietnam Veterans Memorial Wall. Saw the original many years ago in Washington, DC, and figured since it'll be this close for a few days, even though the replica is only half the size, I'd like to take the opportunity to see it again."

"How long will you be gone?"

"A few days. I'll be back before your next cooking class."

"Good to hear. If you know when you plan to leave, I'll make sure you have some snacks to take along."

"It's nice of you, but don't go to any trouble on my account."

Heidi smiled. "It's no bother. I'm always baking and trying out new recipes, which means I usually end up with more food than Lyle and I can eat."

"Okay, I'll let you know before I head out." Ron stepped off the porch and made a beeline for his motor home. *Sure wish the Troyers weren't such nice people. They've been nothing but kind to me. I told Heidi I'd be coming back, but maybe after I leave Columbus, I should head in some other direction. Guess I'll have to wait and see how it goes. Don't know why I can't make up my mind.*

Heidi returned to the kitchen, and Kendra hoped this would be a good time to finish their talk. She'd barely opened her mouth when Lyle came in, saying their horse and buggy waited and they could head to town to do some shopping now.

Kendra picked up the box with her pie in it and started for the door. "I'll see you in two weeks," she called over her shoulder.

"If you're free next Saturday, please drop by," Heidi responded.

"I'll see how it goes. Since next weekend's a holiday, I might do something with Dorie." Without waiting for Heidi's response, Kendra hurried out the door. Before getting into Dorie's car, she glanced at the horse and buggy waiting at the hitching rail. *I wonder what it's like being raised Amish. "The simple life." Isn't that what some call it? Sure hope I get a chance to talk to Heidi before our next cooking class. If she and Lyle would agree to adopt my baby, the child would be a lot better off than living in the English world with me.*

Sugarcreek

When Eli directed his horse and buggy onto Loretta's driveway, he saw Abby and Conner sitting on the porch with their dog between them. As Eli approached, Donnelly's ears perked up and his tail started wagging.

Loretta came out of the house. "I'll get my pie and be right with you," she called.

"Sounds good. I brought my pie along too." Eli got out of the buggy and secured his horse to the fence post. Then he helped the children into the backseat of his buggy.

"Don't forget Donnelly," Conner reminded him.

"No worries." Eli bent down, scooped the pup into his arms, and put him in the buggy between the children. "There's a box on the floor by your feet, Abby. Please don't step on it, and don't allow Donnelly to get near it either."

"I won't, Mr. Eli." Abby shook her head. "We'll hang on to the puppy the whole ride."

Eli smiled. "Good to hear."

When Loretta came out carrying a box, he took it from her and placed it on the floor by the passenger seat. "Here, let me help you." He held his hand out to her. "How's that ankle?"

"About the same, but no worse either." She barely made eye contact with him.

After Loretta got situated, Eli asked her to hold the reins while he untied his horse. A few minutes later, he hopped into the buggy and she handed back the reins.

"I'm glad your horse didn't bolt, because I'm not sure about handling a horse and buggy. I've never driven one before."

"If you're interested, I'd be glad to teach you sometime."

Loretta nodded slowly. "I'll let you know if I can work up the nerve."

I'd enjoy being your teacher. It would give me more opportunity to spend time with you. Eli didn't voice his thoughts. The feelings creeping in toward Loretta were unexpected. *Must be because I miss Mavis and desire female companionship.* He mentally shook his head. *But that's not really true. When I'm with other women, I don't feel like I do when I'm with Loretta. Is it possible that she feels the same way about being with me? Sure wish I had the nerve to ask.*

Loretta felt lighthearted as she glanced over at Eli. He was such a kind, soft-spoken man. The more time they spent together, the more she enjoyed his company. Abby and Conner liked Eli too. They'd mentioned him several times since he'd given them the puppy. *If only he weren't Amish.*

Twisting her watchband around her wrist, Loretta shifted on the buggy seat. As much as she looked forward to meeting Eli's parents, she couldn't help feeling apprehensive. *What if they don't approve of him seeing me? Of course, Eli and I are not courting. We're friends—nothing more—so it shouldn't matter.* The trouble was, Loretta had been thinking about Eli a lot lately. *Too much, maybe.* She'd even fantasized about them becoming romantically involved, which wasn't even possible, since she was not Amish. It was difficult to admit, even to herself, but Loretta hadn't felt this way about anyone since Rick died, and she'd known Eli shy of two months.

Perhaps I'm merely in need of male companionship. Yes, that's all it is. Of course, Loretta visited with her neighbor Sam quite often, so maybe it wasn't a simple need to spend time with a man.

"Mr. Eli, did Mommy tell you about the big cow I tried to feed this morning?" Abby leaned over the seat and touched Eli's shoulder.

"Why no, she didn't."

"The cow was bigger than the other ones we feed. His name is Boo-Boo, and he had a ring in his nose."

"Is that so?"

"Uh-huh. But I don't think he liked me too much, 'cause he looked kinda mad. Then Mommy climbed over the fence. She carried me out of the field while Sam helped Boo-Boo's owner take him back where he belonged."

"Sounds like you had quite an adventure. I'm glad it turned out okay." Eli reached back and patted the child's hand. "Better sit back in your seat now, Abby. Don't want you to get jostled around."

Without question, Abby did as he asked.

Loretta leaned closer to Eli and whispered, "I didn't want to scare her about Boo-Boo, but he's a mean bull. I feared for Abby's life and needed to get her out of there right away."

"It's important for you to stay in your yard, Abby," Eli called over his shoulder. "A cow like Boo-Boo is a lot bigger than you, and you should never leave your yard without your mother's permission."

"Okay, Mr. Eli."

Loretta smiled and mouthed the message, *Thank you, Eli.*

He grinned back at her. "Guess what, kids? My parents have a few cows, and one big bull too. I'll take you out to the barn to see him if he's in there today."

While Abby and Conner clapped their hands, Loretta grew nervous. Eli must have sensed her fear, because he added, "Don't worry. My parents' bull is a big ole baby. His name is Biscuit."

"Biscuit." Conner giggled.

"How'd he get that name?" Loretta questioned.

"Well, when he was about a year old, my mom took some homemade biscuits out of the oven and wrapped them in a cloth to keep warm. She put the biscuits, along with some butter and jelly, in a picnic basket and took them out to the barn where Dad was working."

"Mommy makes good biscuits," Abby said. "She gets 'em at the store and they're in a tube."

Loretta's face heated. *Oh my, Abby. Did you have to*

bring that up?

"They are good, aren't they? I make that kind sometimes too." Eli winked at Loretta. "Anyway, my folks' little bull was in a stall next to where Mom and Dad sat on a bale of straw. They weren't paying attention to the sneaky animal as they talked and enjoyed Mom's home-baked treat. Then, unexpectedly, the young bull stuck his head through the railing and pulled the plate of biscuits into his stall."

Loretta and the children laughed. "What'd they do then?" Loretta asked.

Eli chuckled. "By the time my dad got in the stall and took the plate away, the overzealous critter had eaten every last one of those homemade biscuits."

"That's funny." Abby giggled again.

"Yep. My poor dad only got one biscuit that morning. My siblings and I didn't get any till Mom made another batch. This time she told us the biscuits were not to leave the kitchen. So that's how Biscuit got his name."

Loretta held her hands loosely in her lap, enjoying the interesting conversation. "I can almost picture it, Eli. What a cute memory, and a good name for the bull too."

"My folks have told that story many times when people ask why they gave our bull such an unusual name."

"Is Biscuit friendly?" Loretta still felt a bit concerned—especially after what had happened with Boo-Boo.

"He's quite massive, and definitely not little anymore, but Biscuit still thinks he's a baby." Eli glanced back at the children. "Not all bulls are friendly, but as long as I'm there, you don't have to worry about Biscuit at all."

As they traveled farther, Loretta tried to concentrate on the passing scenery instead of thinking about Eli. Seeing how good he was with her kids, she felt sure he would have been a wonderful father.

Soon, they pulled onto a gravel driveway. "We're

here," Eli announced. "This is where I grew up and where my folks still live." He glanced over his shoulder at the children. "This is where the mother of your puppy lives too."

"Bet Donnelly will be excited to see her," Abby said.

"Bet Donnelly will be excited to see her," Conner repeated.

Eli chuckled. "I'm sure she'll be glad to see her pup again too."

Loretta watched as an Amish couple came out of the house. The man, who appeared to be in his early sixties, walked up to the horse and secured him to the hitching rail, while the woman waited on the porch.

When Eli got out of the buggy, Loretta did the same. After she reached in and took out her pie, Eli came around and helped the children and their puppy down. Loretta assumed they'd feel shy and stick close to her, but with Abby holding Donnelly, they both darted up the porch steps and stood directly in front of the Amish woman.

"My name is Abby, and this is my brother, Conner. We brought our puppy to visit his mama."

Conner bobbed his head. "His name is Donnelly. He used to live here."

The woman leaned down and shook both of their hands. "It's nice to meet you. I'm Eli's mother, Wilma Miller."

Loretta glanced at Mrs. Miller then looked back at Eli, still talking with his father. *Should I go up and introduce myself or wait for Eli?* Repositioning the box that held the pie, Loretta gave herself a pep talk. *Quit being such a scaredy-cat and get on up to that porch.* She drew a deep breath, straightened her shoulders, and headed for the house.

Chapter 31

Mom and Dad, I'd like you to meet Loretta Donnelly and her children, Abby and Conner." Eli motioned to Loretta after he and his dad stepped onto the porch.

His mother smiled. "I've already met Loretta and the children." She leaned over to pet Donnelly's head. "Looks like Sadie's pup has found a good home."

"The children love him," Loretta interjected. "He seems to have adjusted well to his new surroundings."

When his folks' dog started whining from inside the house, Mom opened the screen door. "Come out Sadie and see your pup."

Eli chuckled as Sadie, tail wagging, greeted Donnelly with slurps and yips. "It's almost like a family reunion watching those two get reacquainted."

"I hope your dog won't be upset when we leave with her pup." Loretta looked at Eli's mother.

Mom shook her head. "Sadie might miss her at first, but she'll be fine."

"So, Mom, I promised Abby and Conner I'd take 'em out to see Biscuit." Eli pointed to the barn. "Is he there?"

"Nope. He's in the pasture," Dad responded. "Let's walk out to the fence. Maybe he'll come over to greet us." He gestured to Donnelly. "Better not take the pup along though. Biscuit gets a bit spooky around dogs."

"I'll keep him with me," Mom volunteered. "And our dog too." She held out her arms and the pup went willingly to her, while Sadie stood watchfully by. "I doubt Sadie will let Donnelly out of her sight."

"Before I forget, Loretta and I brought pies." Eli handed a box to his mom. "How 'bout a little later on we all have some?"

"Okay, let me take them inside."

"I'll help." Loretta walked in behind Mrs. Miller with her pie but glanced back at Eli. "Will you please wait till I come back out?"

"Of course." Eli remained on the porch with the children until Loretta joined them again. "Okay, kids, are you ready to meet Biscuit?"

Together, Abby and Conner hollered, "Yes!"

"I'd better go along to keep an eye on the children." Loretta eyed the field with a cautious expression.

"Don't worry. I'll be with them the whole time." Eli took each child's hand. "Loretta, why don't you wait with Mom on the porch so you two can get better acquainted?"

Loretta seemed hesitant at first but finally smiled and said, "Okay." She held a paper sack under one arm and handed it to Eli. "Your mother said to give you this."

Eli tilted his head. "What's inside?"

"Biscuits, and I don't think they came from a tube."

Loretta's cute little grin charmed Eli. He was tempted to stay on the porch and visit with her and Mom but didn't want to disappoint the children. He took hold of Abby's and Conner's hands. "Now don't worry, Loretta. I won't let these two out of my sight."

Abby stood on the fence rail, while Eli's father held Conner. "Watch this." Eli opened the paper sack and held it in front of him. It wasn't long before Biscuit the bull trotted over to the fence, tongue swiping over his big lips.

"Would you like to feed him?" Eli asked the children.

Abby eagerly nodded, while Conner answered, "I'm gonna watch."

"Come down here with me." Eli motioned for Abby as he took a biscuit from the bag and hunkered down on one knee. "Here ya go. Hold this treat in your hand and through the two rails."

Abby squealed when Biscuit's long tongue scooped up the pastry. "He's a nice bull and a pretty color too." Her eyes sparkled with enthusiasm as she watched the tan-colored animal. "The cow I saw this morning was all black."

"Sounds like it could have been an Angus. Ole Biscuit here, he's a Jersey," Eli's dad explained. "Most times he's quite docile."

"What's that word mean?" Abby looked up at him inquisitively.

Eli's dad glanced at him and grinned. "Docile means the same thing as tame. But I never turn my back on Biscuit, because you can't completely trust a bull. Believe me, I learned the hard way."

"Was Biscuit bad?" Conner asked innocently, while his sister fed the bull another biscuit.

"Well, let's just say I gave him an opportunity to be bad." Dad scrubbed a hand down the side of his face. "I bent over the water trough one morning to fill it with fresh water. Ole Biscuit must have thought he was a goat, 'cause the next thing I knew, he butted me into the water." He chuckled. "I ended up with two baths that morning."

Abby and Conner laughed, and Eli joined in. Even though he'd heard the story a good many times, it still made him chuckle.

"Maybe the next time you and Conner come for a visit, you can help me brush Biscuit." Eli snickered. "He likes to have his ears scratched too."

"Can I scratch his ears now?" Conner asked.

"Don't see why not." Dad picked Conner up and held him in a safe position to reach Biscuit's ears. Biscuit leaned closer, and more giggles escaped Conner's lips.

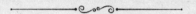

Loretta took a seat in the chair beside Eli's mother. "I want to thank you for the banana whoopie pies Eli shared with my children and me a few weeks ago."

Wilma's eyebrows lifted. "He gave you some?"

Loretta nodded. "They were delicious."

"Well, I shouldn't be surprised. My son's always had a giving nature." She laughed. "Once, when Eli was a boy in school, he gave away his lunch to a girl who'd forgotten hers. What made it even more sacrificial was I'd put several of Eli's favorite cookies in his lunch pail that morning."

Loretta smiled. Although she'd only known Eli a short time, she could picture him doing something so kind. His personality was a lot like her husband's. Rick always did good deeds and helped others.

"Eli seems to enjoy Heidi Troyer's cooking classes," Wilma commented. "Maybe now he can fend for himself without worrying about burning the house down or starving to death from lack of eating proper meals." She looked pointedly at Loretta. "How come you signed up for the classes? Are you lacking in cooking skills too?"

Heat flooded Loretta's face as she shook her head. "I took the class for two reasons. One, to do something fun, and two, because I'm interested in the Amish way of life and their home-style cooking."

"I see." Wilma rocked slowly in her chair. "Eli's wife, Mavis, was an excellent cook. He still misses her a lot."

"I'm sure he does. I miss my husband, Rick, as well."

"Eli took her death hard. I doubt he'll ever recover from it."

Unsure of what to say, Loretta merely nodded. It felt as if Mrs. Miller might be throwing hints about her son not looking for another wife. Did she suspect Loretta was beginning to have feelings for her son?

A short time later, Eli, his father, and the children returned. "Biscuit's big, but he's nice." Abby announced. "Do ya wanna see him, Mommy?"

"Maybe some other time, Abby. I'm visiting with Eli's mother right now."

"Eli said next time we come we can brush Biscuit." Abby's eyes gleamed.

"And scratch his ears," Conner added.

Loretta glanced at Eli and noticed *his* ears had turned red. It pleased her to know he wanted to bring them here again.

"Why don't we have some of the apple cream pie Loretta and I brought along?" Eli looked at his mother and wiggled his brows. "The children and I are *hungerich*."

"That means 'hungry.' " Abby grinned. "Mr. Eli taught us that word while we were talkin' to Biscuit. He said the bull was hungerich."

"Well then, if someone will take the sleeping pup from me, I'll go inside and slice those pies." Mom stood and handed Donnelly to Eli, as Sadie moaned from her comfortable position and got up with a doggy grunt. "Since it is so nice out today, why don't we eat our pie on the porch?" she suggested.

"Good idea. I'll help you, Wilma." Loretta rose from her chair but paused to look at Eli. "Would you please keep an eye on the children?"

"Sure thing. It's a privilege to watch your kinner."

When Loretta held the door open for Wilma, she heard Abby say, "Mr. Eli, are you gonna teach me how to whistle today?"

"You bet. How about a lesson right now?"

Abby bobbed her head.

Once more, Loretta couldn't get over how well Eli responded to her children.

Berlin

"Oh look, there's your sister, Regina," Heidi mentioned when she and Lyle entered the market.

He looked in the direction she'd pointed. "You're right. Guess we'd better say hello before we start shopping, in case she's getting ready to leave the store."

Heidi followed him to the other side of the store, where Regina stood beside her three-year-old daughter, Mary.

"Hey big sister, it's nice to see you today." Lyle gave Regina a hug, and Heidi did the same.

"Nice to see both of you too. It's been awhile." Regina smiled at Heidi. "How are things going with your cooking classes?"

"Quite well," Heidi replied. "It's fun teaching, and I've enjoyed getting acquainted with my students."

"All but one of Heidi's students are English," Lyle added.

Regina tipped her head. "Interesting. Who's the Amish person learning to cook?"

"Our friend Eli Miller." Lyle bent down and gave little Mary a hug. "How's my favorite niece?"

The child's blue eyes sparkled as she looked up at him with a dimpled smile.

Regina poked Lyle's arm. "She may not be your favorite niece much longer. I'm expecting another boppli, and it could be a *maedel*."

Heidi forced a smile and gave her sister-in-law another hug, even though the news cut deeply into her heart. "Congratulations, Regina." *If only it were me announcing a pregnancy.*

"Danki. Irvin's hoping for a boy, but a little sister would be nice for Mary."

"I'm sure." Heidi nodded.

As though he sensed her discomfort, Lyle gently squeezed Heidi's arm. She was certain her husband also wanted children. If only he wasn't so against adoption.

In an effort to take her mind off the situation, Heidi changed the subject. "Did you plant a garden this year, Regina?"

"Oh jah." Regina gestured to her daughter. "Mary even planted some lettuce, carrots, and bean seeds in her own little garden plot."

"She'll enjoy watching the seeds sprout into plants," Lyle commented. "Maybe growing her own vegetables will make her want to eat them when they mature."

"I'm hoping." Regina took her daughter's hand. "We should be moving on now. I have a few more things to get, and then I need to go home and start supper."

"Okay. Hope to see you soon. Tell Irvin I said hello." Lyle bent down and tweaked Mary's nose. "You'll always be my number one niece, little one."

As Heidi and Lyle moved on through the store, she glanced over her shoulder. *Does Regina realize how fortunate she is to have Mary and now another child on the way?*

Dover

"You're kind of quiet this evening," Len commented as Charlene sat across from him at Sammy Sue's Barbeque, fidgeting with her napkin. Coming into their dinner date, she'd been set to ask if he'd be willing to move to some other town. Now she was beginning to lose her nerve. Charlene had hoped to discuss her situation with Heidi last Saturday but never got the chance. Now she wondered if she should bring up the topic at all.

Len reached across the table and took her hand. "Charlene, did you hear my question?"

"Umm. . .yes." She took a drink of water.

"Is something wrong?"

"Not exactly, but I do have a question."

"What is it?"

"Well, I've been wondering about something." Why was this so hard?

"And?" Len flapped his hand, as though encouraging Charlene to speak.

"I was wondering if you would consider moving after we get married."

Deep wrinkles formed across his forehead. "Move? Move where?"

She shrugged. "I. . .I'm not sure. Some other town, where we can start over."

"Why would we want to start over? You have your teaching job here in Dover, and I'm working for my dad. His business is doing quite well." Len looked at her earnestly. "The solar business is growing, and I can't leave now. I'm in a good position—one we'll both benefit from someday."

"Yes, but I'm sure we could find other jobs, and—"

He held up his hand. "Wait. What brought this on all of a sudden? You've never mentioned wanting to move before. I thought you loved teaching the kids here. You're getting to know their families too."

"You're right, Len, and that would be the hard part." Charlene drank more water and set the glass down. "It's your mother. She does not like me, Len. If we stay here in Dover, we'll see your folks more often, and she'll always find fault with everything I say or do, like she already does."

Len shook his head briskly. "First of all, my mother doesn't find fault with everything you say or do."

"Yes, she does. You heard her curt remarks the last time we were at your parents' place for supper."

"I'll admit, sometimes Mom tends to speak when she should be silent, but I'll have a serious talk with her if you want."

Charlene's spine stiffened. "If I want? If you truly love me, Len, then you should have already put your mother in her place and stood up for me."

Len's face flamed. "I have stood up for you, and you're making too much of this. Once we're married, I'm sure Mom's attitude will change and you two will learn to get along."

"Learn to get along?" Charlene's voice rose. "I've tried to get along with her, Len. She doesn't want to get along with me, and I can't believe you're defending her."

Glancing around at the other tables, when the room grew quiet, Len leaned forward, putting his fingers to his lips. "Keep it down, Charlene. Everyone's looking at us."

Charlene drew a frustrated breath. Seconds later, when the restaurant's chatter began again, she took a quick look around. All seemed normal.

"Now listen, Charlene," Len spoke in a low voice. "I'm not defending my mother. I only meant. . ."

"Are you willing to move once we're married or not?" Now that she'd found the courage to bring up this topic, Charlene was determined to make him understand.

"No. My job is here, and if you ask me, you're overreacting to my mom. Anyway, how are you going to get close to her if we move away?"

"First of all, I am not overreacting. As I said before, your mother doesn't like me. If she has her way, she'll turn you against me." Charlene spoke through gritted teeth. Why didn't Len seem to get it? Was he blind where his mother was concerned?

"No, she won't turn me against you." Len looked around again. "And please, can we drop this? People are staring."

"You know what?" Charlene dropped her napkin over her half-eaten plate of food. "I've lost my appetite. Would you please take me home?"

"You're kidding, right?"

"I'm not."

"Come on, Charlene, you're blowing this whole thing out of proportion."

"You think so? Well, I'm beginning to wonder whether you love me or not."

"Of course I love you. I wouldn't have asked you to marry me if I didn't."

"But you don't love me enough to move out of Dover, right?"

Len lowered his gaze. "I don't see any reason to move, and it's unfair of you to expect me to. Especially now, when the business is booming."

Charlene folded her arms. "This discussion is getting us nowhere, and if you won't take me home, I'll call a cab."

"Okay, okay. I'll get the waitress to bring our bill, and then we can leave without finishing our meal. Will that make you happy?"

Charlene gave no reply. Her hands trembled and tears stung her eyes as she reached for her glass of water once more. It was hard to believe Len didn't love her enough to move. Well, if that's how he felt, there would be no marriage. If Len cared more about his job than honoring her request, he wasn't the man for Charlene.

Chapter 32

The next Wednesday afternoon, Charlene sat at the kitchen table, staring at her cell phone. She was off work for the summer, and school would not resume until early September.

"What to do? What to do? What to do?" Charlene drummed her fingers on the table. She'd already vacuumed her condo and washed the breakfast dishes. She had plenty of time now to pursue her photography hobby. Trouble was, she didn't feel like doing anything.

Charlene hadn't heard from Len since their dinner date last Saturday evening. Their conversation went round and round in her mind. He'd been upset when she asked him to move, but she'd hoped by now he would have thought it over and called to discuss things with her.

Should I call him? She shook her head and stubbornly pounded her fist on the table. *No. If Len wants to talk, he ought to call me.*

Charlene got up and poured herself a cup of coffee. She blew on it and took a tentative sip, trying to calm down as she reevaluated things. *Len's right, I enjoy my teaching job here. If we moved, I'd have to find another position at a new school. I wouldn't get to see my former students either.*

Len had also been right in what he'd said about her students' families. Charlene had gotten to know the parents quite well. Whenever she saw one of them at the store, she always made it a point to say hello. Charlene felt a part of the community. She got along well with the other teachers at the school.

Maybe moving to another town isn't the best choice. I might not be happy living someplace else, and Len wouldn't be either. It wasn't fair to ask him to leave his family's business, especially since it's growing and doing so well. What would I do, though, if we stayed in Dover? I'm not sure his mother will ever accept me as part of their family.

Tears welled in Charlene's eyes and dribbled down her cheeks. She either had to make a clean break with Len or improve her relationship with Annette. She reflected on the verse printed on the back of the apple cream pie recipe card Heidi gave her and the other students. Ephesians 4:32: *"And be ye kind one to another, tenderhearted, forgiving one another, even as God for Christ's sake hath forgiven you."*

I need to be kind to Len's mother, and forgive her for the put-downs she's aimed at me. Lord, thank You for Your forgiveness. Please help me show love to Annette.

Walnut Creek

Eli had no more than finished filling the bird feeders than a horse and buggy pulled into his yard. Surprised to see his mother, he stepped up to the hitching rail and secured her horse.

"*Wie geht's?*" Mom asked when she climbed down from the buggy.

"I'm doin' fine." Eli gave her a hug. "Wasn't expecting you to come by today. Are you here for any particular reason?"

She gave his arm a playful pinch. "Can't a mamm drop by to see her *sohn* for no particular reason other than to say hello?"

He grinned. "Course you can, and this son of yours is happy you dropped by. Feel free to do so anytime you like."

"Actually, I do have a reason for coming here." She reached into her buggy and took out a plastic container. "I baked peanut butter kichlin this morning. Thought you might like some."

"Might?" Eli thumped his stomach. "Of course I would. But if you keep bringing me desserts all the time, I'm gonna get fat." He took the offered cookies.

She shook her head. "As hard as you work in your shop and around the place here, I doubt you'll ever struggle with your weight."

"You're probably right. I never gained weight when Mavis was alive. She was an excellent cook."

Mom hugged him. "You still miss her, don't you?"

"Jah, but it's gotten easier since I met Loretta and her kinner. They're a lot of fun to be with."

Her brows furrowed. "Have you taken a personal interest in Loretta?"

"Well, I. . ."

"If you have, you need to nip it in the bud."

"What are you talking about, Mom? We're only friends."

"She's not one of us, Eli."

Eli clenched his teeth. He wasn't prepared to deal with this right now. Moving toward the picnic table, he took a seat on the bench and motioned for his mother to do the same. "You have nothing to worry about. Loretta's a nice person and, like me, she's lonely. I've enjoyed getting acquainted with her and also the children. Spending time with them has given me something to look forward to. In fact, I haven't felt this lighthearted since Mavis died."

Mom touched his arm. "I'm glad you've found someone you can relate to, and it sounds like you've made a good friend, but you need to be cautious. While you may not have serious feelings for Loretta, what if she has them for you?" Her brows lowered. "She could try to talk you into leaving our way of life and turning to the English world."

Eli shook his head vigorously. "I would never choose the English way of life, and I'm sure Loretta wouldn't expect me to either."

Mom's face relaxed a bit as she squeezed his arm tenderly. "I'm thankful your daed and I raised a *schmaert* sohn."

Eli wasn't sure he was all that smart. Truthfully, he hadn't admitted it to himself until now, but if Loretta were Amish, he could easily be interested in her beyond friendship.

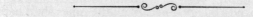

Carefully, Heidi climbed the ladder to the hayloft. One of the barn cats had given birth to a batch of kittens yesterday, and Heidi wanted to check on them.

Following the sound of pathetic mews, she located the black-and-white kittens and their mother, whom Heidi had named Mittens.

Heidi made herself comfortable on a bale of hay and sat quietly, observing the kittens as they nursed. As adorable as they were to watch, a deep sadness came over her. She cupped her mouth, hoping to stifle the urge to cry. *Mittens can have* bopplin. *Why can't I? It isn't fair that I'll never experience motherhood firsthand.*

Giving in to self-pity, Heidi's guard was broken, and the tears flowed. *If only Lyle would agree to adopt. Why is he being so stubborn?* She had asked herself the same question so many times. When she'd convinced herself she could be happy without a baby and feel comfortable living a childless life, something always happened, causing Heidi to focus on her need to be a mother. The other day, hearing Regina was expecting another baby had reopened Heidi's emotional wounds. Avoiding the painful subject seemed to be the best way to deal with it, although the desire to raise a child was never far from her thoughts.

Heidi's contemplations halted when she heard the barn door creak open and click shut. Wiping her nose with the tissue she clutched, and drying the tears on her cheeks, Heidi crawled to the edge to go back down the ladder. Thinking Lyle was home from his errands, she was about to call out to him when she heard a muffled voice. Heidi remained quiet and still, and when she looked down, she was surprised to see it was Ron who'd entered the barn. Was he talking to Bobbins?

Heidi had no trouble recognizing the soft nickers of her husband's buggy horse. In all the times she'd had conversations with the animal, Bobbins always nickered at the right time, as though she understood everything being said. By now the horse was no doubt used to Ron, since he'd often mucked out her stall.

Heidi continued to listen but only caught bits and pieces of what Ron was saying. Being careful not to make any noise, she scooched on her stomach to the far side of the hayloft. When Heidi looked down, she saw Ron stroking Bobbins's neck.

He'd left their place over Memorial Day weekend and returned late last night, but this was the first time she'd seen Ron since he'd come back. Seeing his motor home parked in the usual spot this morning, Heidi had known he was there. Quite often Ron came up to the house in the mornings to have coffee with Lyle and ask what chores he wanted done. This morning, however, Ron remained in his motor home. Heidi assumed he was tired after the drive back from Columbus and had slept in. But why was he here in the barn now, talking to Bobbins?

What Heidi heard next made the tears flow again, only this time, it wasn't for herself. The heart-wrenching sight below caused Heidi to cover her mouth.

Standing beside the stall, Ron continued to rub the horse's neck, and as if she understood, Bobbins lowered her head. With his forehead pressed against the mare's head, Ron spoke again. "Oh Bobbins, right now you're my only true friend."

The horse nickered in response, and Ron started to cry. His shoulders shook as the sobs grew louder and more intense.

Barely breathing, lest she be heard, Heidi kept listening as Ron poured out his grief.

"Dear God, please help me deal with this agony. I miss my brother so much. Seeing that wall again made me realize how much I've messed up in every area of my life." Ron's voice cracked. "Wish it had been me You took, instead of Mike. My brother was a good person and deserved to live. I don't deserve anything except trouble, because I've done nothing but hurt everyone in my life."

Heidi's heart went out to this poor soul. She wished she could offer Ron comfort, if only a listening ear. But he hadn't opened up and shared his pain with her—only a bit to Lyle. She certainly would not let him know she was eavesdropping on his conversation with Lyle's horse.

Sniffing, Ron shuffled over to a bale of hay and sat down, hands cradling his head.

Heidi remained motionless until, several minutes later,

he left the barn. Ron truly was a troubled man. Did he for some reason blame himself for his brother's death? Or maybe it was God he was angry with. If only Ron would talk freely about his situation, perhaps she or Lyle could help. She wondered if Ron had read any of the scriptures she'd put on the back of the recipe cards. If he had, she hoped he might find comfort or direction through God's Word.

Closing her eyes, Heidi lifted a prayer on Ron's behalf. Then, brushing pieces of hay from her dress, she slowly descended the ladder.

Canton

Kendra's hands grew moist as she drove up the driveway to her parents' home. She'd worked the early afternoon shift at the restaurant and borrowed Dorie's car this evening. Coming here wasn't easy, but Kendra felt compelled to speak to her mother. She had chosen this particular evening because she was almost certain Dad would be at church for the monthly board meeting. When Kendra saw Heidi again, she was prepared to ask if she and Lyle would consider adopting her baby. But if there was the slightest chance. . .

She turned off the engine and leaned her forehead against the steering wheel. *If Mom agrees to let me move back home, maybe Dad could be persuaded.*

Kendra stepped out of the car and hurried up the porch steps, glancing around to see if the neighbors were watching. *I wonder if they've heard I was kicked out of my parents' house. Is the word out around the neighborhood that Bridget and Gary Perkins' oldest daughter got pregnant?*

She drew a deep breath and rang the doorbell. Several seconds later, the door opened and her sister Shelly appeared. She blinked rapidly. "I'm surprised to see you here, Kendra. Did you tell Mom and Dad you were coming?"

Kendra shook her head. "Dad's not here, I hope."

"No, he's at church for the board meeting."

"That's good, 'cause I need to talk to Mom." Kendra stepped quickly into the house. "It's important."

Shelly clutched the book in her hand as though holding it as a shield. "I hope you realize what you're doing. I'd be in trouble if Dad knew I'd talked to you, much less let you into the house."

"He won't know who let me in unless you tell him." Kendra glanced around. "Where's Mom?"

"She's in the kitchen with Chris, putting the clean supper dishes away."

"Okay, thanks." Kendra moved speedily in that direction, glancing over her shoulder as Shelly retreated to the living room.

When she entered the kitchen, she cleared her throat a couple of times. Mom turned around, and seeing Kendra, let out a gasp. The dish she held slipped out of her hand and fell on the floor. Luckily, it didn't break. "Kendra! What are you doing here?"

"Came to see you. There's something I need to say. Can I speak to you privately for a few minutes?"

Mom pursed her lips. "Your dad would not approve of you being here, Kendra."

"I'm well aware, but what I have to say is important."

Mom gave a huff then bent down to pick up the plate. She turned to Chris. "Would you please leave us alone?"

Glancing briefly at Kendra with a placid expression, Chris left the room.

Mom placed the plate in the sink then pulled out a chair at the table and sat down, gesturing for Kendra to do the same. "What do you need to talk to me about?"

"The baby." Kendra sat down and placed both hands

on her stomach. "*My* baby."

Mom stared at her blankly, making little circles on the tablecloth with her finger.

Kendra rubbed her damp hands down the side of her jeans. There was no way to say this, except to blurt it right out. "I'm putting my baby up for adoption, unless. . ."

"That's a wise decision. Under the circumstances, I'm sure you're not able to properly care for a child on your own."

"No, I can't, but I hoped maybe. . ."

"What are you hoping for, Kendra? Did you think we would offer to help raise the child?" Mom spoke in a monotone voice.

Does she have no feelings at all? Kendra curled her fingers into the palms of her hands until her nails bit into the skin. *Dad sure did a number on her. Mom and I used to be close. It's as though she can't think for herself. Doesn't she care how much I'm hurting?*

Kendra decided to try a new approach. "Don't you want to be a part of your grandchild's life?"

"I would if it were under different circumstances." Mom blew out a quick breath. "I'm sorry you got yourself into such a predicament, but I will not go against your father's wishes, so there's really nothing I can do." Mom's hands flailed in front of her. "Your child will be better off with adoptive parents."

Kendra's mouth twisted as the muscles in her shoulders and neck tightened. At that moment, it hit her how truly alone she was in this. She had no other choice. Kendra could not be the mother of the baby she so desperately wanted to keep.

Leaping out of her chair, she turned and fled from the house without bothering to say goodbye to Mom or her sisters. Unless they came crawling to her, begging for forgiveness, she would never return to this place or make contact with anyone in her family again.

Chapter 33

Dover

Charlene had gotten up later than planned this morning and rushed around to get ready to leave for Heidi's fifth cooking class. She looked forward to going, because it would give her something meaningful and hopefully fun to do. Other teachers might be enjoying their time off from school, but Charlene had quickly become bored.

I wonder if Heidi will have another class after ours is finished in two weeks. If she does, maybe I should take it. At least learning to cook new things might help take my mind off the situation with Len. He still hadn't called her, and as the week had dragged on, Charlene had debated calling him.

She didn't know why it was so hard to make the first move, but since Len hadn't, Charlene had convinced herself that he no longer loved her.

If I don't hear from him by this evening, I'll make the call. She grabbed her purse, apron, and keys then headed for the door. Charlene's footsteps halted when her cell phone rang. She paused to check the caller ID, hoping it might be Len, but the number on the screen was not familiar. Normally, she would have ignored such a call, but her curiosity was piqued, so she answered. "Hello."

"Is this Charlene Higgins?"

Charlene didn't recognize the woman's voice. "Umm, yes, it is."

"I'm calling about the picture you submitted several weeks ago for a contest in the magazine I represent. I want to congratulate you. The photo you took of the mare and her foal won first place."

Stunned, Charlene could barely form a response. "Oh my. I never expected. . . I'm so surprised." She moved back to the kitchen and sank into a chair.

"Yes, and unless you already have one, we'll be sending you a copy of this month's issue, showing the picture you submitted on the cover."

"No, I don't have the magazine." Charlene hesitated but explained anyway. "I normally look at your magazine when I'm at the store, but I haven't purchased a copy in a while."

"I'm glad I had the opportunity to surprise you with this news. You'll also receive a two-year subscription to our magazine."

"Thank you." Charlene could hardly believe her good fortune. "It means so much that you thought the photograph I entered was good enough for the cover."

"It certainly is, and we thank you for entering. Now don't forget, we have a contest every year, so keep your camera clicking."

After Charlene exchanged a bit more information with the woman, the phone call ended. She sat in stunned silence. This exciting news added a bright spot to her day. She couldn't wait to share it with someone.

Walnut Creek

When Kendra pulled into the Troyers' yard, she spotted

Ron sitting on a camp stool outside his motor home. She'd come early, hoping to talk to Heidi before the others arrived. Since no other cars were here, unless Ron decided to come inside right away, it looked like she'd get the chance.

Kendra got out of the car, hurried up the steps, and knocked on the door. A few seconds later, Heidi greeted her.

"Hope it's okay I came early." Kendra smiled while Heidi held the door open for her.

"No one else is here yet, and I'm still setting things out in the kitchen, but you're welcome to visit while I finish up."

"Okay, thanks." Kendra entered the house and followed Heidi to the kitchen. "Is there anything I can do to help?"

"You can get out the sour cream, bacon, and onions." Heidi gestured to the refrigerator.

"Sure, no problem. What are we making this time?"

"German potato salad." Heidi pointed to the potatoes on the counter. "It's served warm instead of the traditional cold potato salad."

"Sounds good." Kendra went to the refrigerator and took out the ingredients; then she placed them on the table. "I've made a decision about my baby." She moved closer to where Heidi stood at the sink, washing the potatoes.

Heidi turned to look at her. "Oh?"

"My folks want nothing to do with me or the baby, and I'm not in a position to take care of a child by myself." Kendra paused to rub her forehead before she continued. "I've thought about it long and hard and will be putting the child up for adoption." She made direct eye contact with Heidi. "So I was wondering—well, hoping might be a better word. Would you and your husband be interested in adopting my baby?"

Heidi gasped and dropped the potato in the sink before bringing both hands up to her chest. "You. . .you want us to raise your baby?"

"Yeah, that's right. After getting to know you these last several weeks, I believe you would be a good mother, and—"

Heidi lifted her hand. "Wait a minute, Kendra. I don't think you fully understand what that would mean. If Lyle and I agreed to such an arrangement, your child would be raised Amish. When he or she got older, they might join the Amish church, as so many of our young people do."

"I've considered that and have no objections. In fact, the child will most likely be better off raised in a simpler fashion."

Heidi took a deep breath and released it slowly. "I can't give you an answer right now. I'll need to talk it over with Lyle."

"Of course." Kendra placed her hand on Heidi's arm. "I've given this a lot of thought. You and your husband are the parents I want for my baby."

After the other students arrived, it was difficult for Heidi to concentrate on the lesson. How could she think about teaching someone to make potato salad when a short time ago she'd been offered the chance to become a mother? She could hardly wait for Lyle to get home this evening so they could talk about Kendra's offer. Heidi closed her eyes briefly. *Dear Lord, please let my husband say yes.*

"Is something wrong with the way I cut my potatoes?" Charlene's question cut into Heidi's thoughts.

"Uh, no. Why do you ask?"

"You looked at them with a curious expression."

Heidi blinked. "I'm sorry. My thoughts were someplace else." She motioned to the ingredients set out. "Now that your boiled potatoes have been cut and placed in a bowl, you'll need to combine the dry ingredients, vinegar, sour cream, onions, and bacon pieces, making sure to stir them well." She waited for everyone to do as she instructed then said they should toss lightly, until the potatoes were coated well with the dressing.

"Do we eat the potato salad while it's still warm?" Loretta questioned.

Heidi nodded. "It's a bit different from traditional potato salad, but I personally believe it's every bit as good, and hope you'll enjoy it too."

"It's not hard to make either." Eli looked at Loretta and grinned. "Don't you agree?"

Smiling in response, she nodded.

Heidi noticed how Eli had taken a seat beside Loretta this morning. They'd conversed quite a bit, smiling and laughing whenever the other said something. It didn't take a genius to see the attraction between them. *Might there be a future for Eli and Loretta as a couple? If so, one of them would leave behind their way of life.* Heidi hoped Eli would not abandon the faith he'd belonged to for so many years. But if he should choose to leave, she felt sure Eli would adhere to his strong religious beliefs and not stray from his faith in God. It would be difficult for Loretta to become Amish, but not impossible.

It's none of my business. I have my own things to worry about. Redirecting her thoughts, Heidi glanced at Ron, to see if he might comment on the potato salad. However, he sat silently, toying with his wooden spoon. Was he still thinking about his brother who'd been killed in the Vietnam War?

Heidi had told Lyle what she'd overheard Ron saying to Bobbins in the barn, and Lyle had a talk with Ron the following day, but he wouldn't respond.

It wasn't good for a person to hold their feelings inside, but if Ron didn't want to talk about it, at least they'd tried. Their prayers would continue for him, in hopes that he would someday find peace.

Turning her attention to the task at hand, Heidi posed a question to her students. "I have some German sausages, as well as a package of hot dogs we can barbecue on the grill. How would you all like to join me for lunch outside?"

All heads nodded, even Ron's.

Eli chuckled. "And this time we won't be eating outdoors because I smell like a skunk."

"Did you ever solve the problem with the skunks in your yard?" Charlene asked.

"I believe so. At least I haven't seen or smelled any around my place lately." Eli gestured to his bowl of potato salad. "Think mine's as done as it's gonna get."

"It looks fine, Eli." Heidi smiled. "If everyone else is finished, we can move outside and start the grill."

───────── ⌁∘⌁ ─────────

"How are Conner and Abby?" Eli asked as he sat on a picnic bench beside Loretta.

"Doing well. Of course, those two are always full of energy, which keeps me on my toes."

"How about Donnelly? Is he settling in okay?"

She nodded. "The pup can be a handful at times, but the children enjoy him so much. I'm happy about that."

Eli leaned closer to Loretta and was about to whisper something when Charlene stood up and tapped a fork against her glass, making a tinkling sound.

"I have something I'd like to share with all of you." Charlene's dimples deepened when she smiled. "I took your advice, Kendra, and entered a photograph in the contest you told me about."

"To tell you the truth, I'd forgotten all about it. Did you enter the picture you showed us a few weeks ago?" Kendra asked.

"Yes. It was the one of the foal and mare," Charlene continued. "After I entered, I'd forgotten about it too— until a lady from the magazine called me this morning."

"And?" Heidi waited, as did the rest of the group.

"Well. . ." Charlene held back.

"Oh, please," Loretta coaxed. "Don't keep us in suspense."

Even Ron seemed eager to hear, as he leaned slightly forward.

Charlene took a deep breath before announcing her news. "Well, I found out this morning that I won first place."

"Wow, that's great!" Kendra left her seat and gave Charlene a hug.

There were many congratulations, and a few more hugs.

"What did you win for coming in first place?" Ron questioned.

"The photo I submitted is on the front cover of this month's photography magazine." Charlene shook her head, as if still trying to comprehend it. "It's so weird. I usually stop by the stand and browse through the magazine when I'm at the store, but I haven't done it in a while. If I had seen the recent addition, I'd have discovered the picture of the mare and foal I'd taken."

"Is that all you get—just the satisfaction of having

your picture on the cover?" Ron's brows furrowed. "Seems like a lame prize."

"It's an honor for me to have one of my photographs on the cover of a prestigious magazine, not to mention I'll get a free two-year subscription to the magazine."

"Now you won't have to stand in the store and read the magazine." Everyone laughed at Kendra's remark.

"You got that right," Charlene agreed.

"With your interest in photography, maybe this will open the door to other opportunities for you," Heidi commented.

"It might, but if it doesn't, I'm okay with that." Charlene sighed. "Having a photograph I took be good enough for the cover of this magazine is a dream I never expected to see fulfilled. It speaks volumes for me— more than money."

When things settled down, Heidi scurried about, making sure everyone had what they wanted. While everyone else engaged in conversation, Eli took the opportunity once again to ask Loretta a question. "Do you have plans for supper this evening?"

She shook her head.

"Would you and the children like to join me at Der Dutchman here in Walnut Creek? I could come by your place later this afternoon with my horse and open buggy. Then after we visit awhile, we'll head out to eat."

Loretta glanced around, as though worried someone might be listening. "Since Sugarcreek is a ways for you to go, how about I drive my car and meet you at Der Dutchman?"

Eli dropped his gaze to the table. He'd hoped for some extra visiting time with Loretta and the children before they went out for supper. "How would it be if we ate at one of the restaurants in Sugarcreek? It would be closer to your house, and I believe you and the children might enjoy riding in my open buggy."

"It sounds like fun. Once Abby and Conner find out you're coming, they'll be excited. Don't be surprised if they're waiting on the porch, like the last time you came by."

Eli smiled. Despite his mother's warning, his yearning to get better acquainted with Loretta and her children increased. If he had his way, he'd drop by to see them every day this coming week. But with work piling up in his shop, he wouldn't have time for that.

Chapter 34

Sugarcreek

Noticing how quiet her children had become, Loretta glanced over her shoulder. The motion of Eli's buggy must have put them to sleep, for Conner's head leaned against his sister's arm, and both children's eyes were closed. Since neither Abby nor Conner had taken a nap today, it was nice to see them resting. Hopefully, they would both be in good moods when they got to the restaurant.

"Traveling in an open buggy is fun." Loretta looked over at Eli and smiled. "It reminds me of riding in my dad's convertible many years ago."

"My friend Dennis had a convertible when we were going through our *rumschpringe*. We enjoyed running around in it. Of course," Eli added with a snicker, "for me, it wasn't nearly as much fun as taking my horse out with the open buggy."

"It is kind of nice to travel at a more leisurely pace." Loretta motioned to the trees alongside the road. "While driving my minivan, all these lovely trees wouldn't be much more than a blur."

Eli grinned. "Don't believe I've ever met an English woman who sees things the way you do. I find it refreshing."

"Must be my Amish heritage."

"What?" Eli's mouth opened slightly.

"My grandparents were Amish but have since passed away. Unfortunately, I didn't get to be with them much because my parents never joined the Amish church. Mom and Dad moved from Lancaster, Pennsylvania, to Cleveland, Ohio, soon after they were married. They live in Pittsburgh now."

When Eli shook the reins and made a clucking noise, the horse began trotting a little faster. "Well no wonder you're different. The Amish way is in your blood." He cocked his head to one side, looking at her through narrowed eyes. "How come you never mentioned this before?"

She pursed her lips. "I wasn't sure how you'd respond."

"What do you mean?"

"I was worried you might frown on my dad and mom moving away from their Amish families and choosing the English way of life."

Eli shook his head. "It's not my place to cast judgment on others. Your folks must have had their reasons. Besides, not everyone raised Amish decides to join the church and remain part of the Amish culture. We're all given the opportunity to choose. Course," he quickly added, "most Amish parents are disappointed when one of the children doesn't join."

"It's understandable. In all honesty, a part of me has always wondered what my life would have been like if my parents had joined the Amish church. I wish I knew their reasons, but it's never been talked about, and I wasn't sure if my folks would be upset if I asked."

"Did they teach you some of the Pennsylvania Dutch language? Is that how come you know a few words?"

"No, I learned those words from my grandparents

when we went to visit them one summer. Wish I could have known them better though." Loretta fiddled with the straps on her purse, wondering if she should say more. "Umm. . . I've been wondering about something, Eli."

"What's that?"

"How hard would it be for someone like me to join the Amish church?"

His brows shot up. "Are you serious?"

She gave a decisive nod.

"A few English people have made the transition, but it's difficult, due to the language barrier, plus giving up modern conveniences and following the church rules."

"I believe I could give up modern things, and I am interested in raising Abby and Conner in the kind of life where the emphasis is on God and family, rather than gaining material things."

Eli smiled. "If you're serious about this, I'd be happy to help you take the necessary steps to make the transition."

"Yes, yes. I'd appreciate it." Loretta didn't admit it to Eli, of course, but in addition to seeking a simpler way of life, if she joined the Amish church, it would open the door for a possible relationship with him. That is, if he was interested. So far, Eli hadn't given any indication that he cared for her as more than a friend.

Dover

The muscles in Charlene's shoulders felt strained as she stood on the deck at the back of her condo. For the last fifteen minutes, she had been holding her camera in the same position, hoping for a close-up picture of a hummingbird. She'd hung a feeder out the other day after seeing a couple of hummers flitting around an azalea bush behind her place, but so far she hadn't seen any at the feeder. *Oh well, maybe another time. I can't stand here all day.*

Charlene took a seat in one of the deck chairs and leaned against the cushion behind her head. She hadn't called Len yet, and the longer she put it off, the more difficult it became. What if he didn't want to talk to her? Maybe in his mind, their relationship was already over.

But if I don't call, how will I know? Charlene rose from her chair and headed to the kitchen, where she'd left her cell phone. Punching in the first three numbers, she paused when the doorbell rang. Placing her phone on the table, Charlene went to the door and leaned toward the peephole to look out. She gasped, seeing Len standing there. With no hesitation, she opened the door.

"Mind if I come in?" Rubbing the back of his neck, he shuffled his feet and gave her a sheepish grin.

"Of course not. I was punching in your phone number when you rang the doorbell." She opened the door wider, and he stepped inside.

Len handed Charlene her ecru-colored shrug. "You left your sweater in my car the last time we were together, and there's something wrapped inside."

Charlene looked down. "Our date did end abruptly."

Len pointed to her sweater. "Go ahead; open it."

Charlene unfolded the shrug and was surprised to discover a floating frame—the kind used for protecting and displaying magazines. Framed inside was the photography magazine, exhibiting the winning cover. "How did you get this?"

"Saw it on the magazine rack at the drugstore." Len smiled. "Congratulations!"

"Thank you." It touched Charlene that he would go

to the trouble of framing this special edition.

"It was worth getting my car banged up so you could get this great shot and win the competition. I'm proud of you, honey."

Her throat constricted, and she swallowed hard. He'd called her *honey*, and it nearly melted her heart.

Len took a step toward her. "The magazine isn't the only reason I came by though."

"Oh?" Her hand trembled as she placed the frame and sweater on the entry table. Did she dare hope they could work things out? Charlene held her breath as Len clasped her hands.

"I'm sorry for not calling you since our disagreement. Believe me, it was a struggle not to, but I needed time to think things over." Pausing, Len cleared his throat. "I love you, Charlene, and I don't want anything, or anyone, to come between us. Seeing you standing here now, I don't know how I stayed away this long." He squeezed her hands more snugly. "I guess what they say about 'absence makes the heart grow fonder' is fact, not fiction."

"You've always had my heart, Len." Unconsciously, she parted her lips.

"Ditto. I want to tell you something else too. I've come to a decision."

"Oh? What's that?"

"If you really feel relocating is the best thing for you, then I'm willing to move. In fact, I'll start looking for another job right away. You just need to tell me where you'd like to go."

Love swelled in Charlene's heart, and with no hesitancy, she rushed into his arms. "I've been thinking things over too, and it wouldn't be fair to ask you to give up your job in the family business. I don't want to give up my teaching position here either."

"But what about my mother?"

"I need to quit worrying and make the best of the situation with her."

Len pressed his forehead against hers. "I don't want you to make the best of the situation, honey. I'll talk with Mom again and try to make her understand how hurtful she's been toward the woman I love and plan to marry." His lips brushed hers with a tender kiss. "Now, how about going out to dinner with me so we can make up for our last dinner date that ended on a sour note?"

She took several deep breaths, savoring the moment. "I have a better idea. Let's eat here, where we can talk without the distraction of other people and restaurant noise."

"Good idea. Should I make a call to get some pizza delivered?"

Charlene shook her head. "Tonight, I'd like to fix something special for you. It's a simple yet tasty meal the Amish enjoy."

Len's eyebrows squished together. "I'm confused."

"I have been waiting to tell you this, but every other Saturday since the first part of April, I've been attending cooking classes at an Amish home in Walnut Creek. Heidi Troyer, the woman who teaches the classes, is an excellent cook. She's helped me feel more confident in the kitchen." Charlene squeezed Len's arm playfully. "You can be my first guinea pig."

He lifted his gaze toward the ceiling. "So I've gone from being your future husband to a guinea pig now, huh?"

She giggled. "It was only a figure of speech. I am anxious to see what you think of haystack though."

His brows lifted a bit. "Haystack? Will we be eating a meal or harvesting a field?"

Charlene felt lighthearted since the worry had been

lifted off her shoulders. "You're silly." She gave his stomach a gentle poke. "The way to a man's heart is through his belly, you know."

Len placed Charlene's hand against his chest. "You'll always have my heart too, sweetheart."

Charlene didn't resist when he pulled her close for another kiss. When the kiss ended, she linked arms with Len. "Okay now, future husband, come to my kitchen, and I'll show you my newfound culinary skills."

Walnut Creek

Heidi paced the kitchen floor, waiting for Lyle to come home. He'd gone to another all-day auction, and she had been counting the hours until his return.

Ever since Kendra's offer to let them adopt her baby, Heidi had thought of little else. She had no idea how she'd even made it through the cooking class today. Heidi hoped and prayed Lyle would be willing to adopt the baby, because she felt sure this was the answer to her prayers. All they would need to do was find an adoption lawyer to draw up the papers to make it legal. Hopefully, his fee wouldn't be too high, but at this point, she would gladly borrow the money if she had to, so she and Lyle could raise a child together.

"I'll teach more cooking classes to help with the expense," she murmured as she took out a loaf of bread for bacon and tomato sandwiches.

"There you go—talking to yourself again." Lyle stepped up behind Heidi, turned her to face him, and gave her a warm, gentle kiss.

"You startled me. I didn't hear you come in." She spoke breathlessly.

"Had my driver drop me off by the phone shack so I could check for messages. That's probably why you didn't hear his car." Lyle stroked Heidi's arms, sending chills up her spine. "So, what's this about teaching more cooking classes?"

"If we need extra money I'm willing to teach additional classes. Maybe every Saturday, instead of every other week."

"Heidi, there's no reason for that. I'm making a decent living, and there's nothing we need extra money for right now."

She sucked in her lower lip. "There would be, if we had a boppli."

"What are you saying, Heidi?" His eyebrows lifted. "Has God given us a miracle? Are you expecting a boppli?"

"No, but we've been offered the chance to adopt."

"How can it be? We haven't contacted an adoption agency."

Heidi pulled out a chair at the table. "Let's take a seat, and I'll explain the situation."

Lyle hesitated at first but did as she suggested. Heidi took the seat beside him.

"Kendra, the young expectant mother who attends my class, arrived early today so we could talk before the others got here." Heidi reached for Lyle's hand. "She wants us to adopt her baby."

He sat quietly for several seconds then slowly shook his head. "It's out of the question, Heidi."

"How come?"

"We don't know much about this girl, and besides..."

"I know she wants us to raise her child."

"We've discussed adoption before, and I've made myself clear on the topic. I don't feel it's right for us."

His voice was steady and lower pitched than normal.

"But why? You've never really explained your reasons." Heidi could barely speak around the burning thickness in her throat.

"Jah, I have explained, Heidi—many times. Maybe you just weren't listening. If it were God's will for us to have children, you would have gotten pregnant by now."

"Perhaps God sent Kendra to my cooking class for a reason. Maybe this is His will."

Lyle's shoulders pushed back as he shook his head. "No, Heidi. I don't believe this is the way."

"Why not? Kendra must believe we would make good parents to have asked if we'd raise her baby."

"That's just it—*her baby*. Would we ever feel like the child was completely ours?"

"I believe so."

He shook his head once again, more firmly this time. "It's not meant for us to raise someone else's child." Lyle's hands touched his chest. "It hurts to think I'm not enough for you."

"Oh no, Lyle, it's not that at all." Heidi clasped his arm. "You mean the world to me, Lyle. I only want us to have a family." Heidi's throat constricted as tears sprang to her eyes.

"I've always thought we were a family." Lyle placed his hand on hers. "You're all I need."

When he put it that way, it was hard to know how to respond. Heidi wanted to say Lyle was all she needed, but the words seemed to be stuck in her throat. She loved him with all her heart, but so many times— especially during the long hours he was gone— loneliness set in, and her arms ached to hold a baby. Why couldn't he understand her feelings and share in the desire to have a child?

"All right, I understand," she murmured, struggling not to break down. "I won't bring it up again." Heidi pushed her chair back and stood. "I'd best get the sandwiches made so we can eat."

Lyle got up from his chair. "While you're doing that, I'll take a quick shower." He gave her a peck on the cheek. "I love you, Heidi."

"Love you too."

When Lyle left the room, Heidi turned toward the refrigerator to get the bacon and tomatoes. She dreaded seeing Kendra again and having to tell her she'd need to find someone else to adopt her child. Her shoulders drooped as she lowered her head. The disappointment Heidi felt penetrated her soul.

Chapter 35

Sugarcreek

Perspiration beaded on Loretta's forehead as she crouched beside her garden to pull weeds. It had been four days since she'd told Eli she might be interested in joining the Amish church, but she hadn't heard from him since. *Maybe he's changed his mind about helping me. Or perhaps he's been too busy with work.*

Sitting up from her bended position to wipe her forehead, she noticed Sam next door, walking up and down the rows in his raspberry patch. About the same moment, he glanced her way and gave her a neighborly wave.

"How are the berries doing?" Loretta hollered.

"Should be ready to pick in another week or so. I'll see you get some."

"Thanks, Sam. I'm looking forward to it."

Sam was such a good neighbor. Loretta smiled when she saw him come to the edge of the yard as Abby and Conner took their dog over to greet him. Then she noticed Sam take something from his pocket and hand it to each of the kids. Abby and Conner ran over to Loretta, with Donnelly nipping at their heels. Sam gave another wave then headed toward his house.

"Look what Mr. Sam gave us." Abby held out a five-dollar bill, and Conner did the same. "He said we can use the money to buy Donnelly something."

Conner's wide-eyed expression revealed his excitement as he repeated what his sister said.

"Better let me hang on to that for you. Did you both remember to thank him?" Loretta was pleased when they both bobbed their heads before handing her the money and running off to play with the dog again. She slipped the bills into her skirt pocket then went back to weeding her garden, humming a merry tune.

"Only one more row to do, and then I'm done." Loretta spoke out loud. As she looked toward the sky, she added, "Oh Rick, I hope I'm making you proud, raising our children the best way I know." As if on cue, a bluebird landed on a nearby branch, singing in soft, warbling tones. This might have meant nothing to most people, but to Loretta it was special, since bluebirds had been Rick's favorite birds. She felt as though God sent the bird to give her a sense of assurance that she was doing right by her children.

With renewed energy, Loretta set back to weeding and thought about what to have for lunch. Today would be a good day to pack the children's lunch so they could eat under the big tree. Conner and Abby always enjoyed having a picnic, even here in the yard. The fresh air did them good too.

Loretta sat up on her knees to watch Abby and Conner trying to teach Donnelly how to fetch a stick. *Could my children adjust to the Amish way of life? How would they feel about wearing Amish-style clothes?* They were still young, so learning a new language would probably be easier for them than it would Loretta. But with help, she felt sure she could learn. Giving up modern conveniences shouldn't be too difficult for the children or Loretta, although turning in her van for a horse and buggy might prove to be quite a challenge. Perhaps she could ease into the simple life—giving up a few things at a time to see how it went. Taking it slow might be a better adjustment for the children too.

"Mommy, come look at Donnelly!" Abby's excited tone drew Loretta's thoughts aside once more. "See how he goes after the stick?"

Loretta turned her head in the direction Abby pointed. Sure enough, the pup bounded across the yard to fetch the stick. Donnelly's tail wagged, and he let out a *woof* after dropping the stick at Conner's feet. Conner cheered and Abby clapped. Loretta did the same.

"Kids, don't forget to praise Donnelly, so he will know he did well."

"Good boy!" Abby patted the dog's head, while Conner gave Donnelly a hug.

"Now you should teach him how to sit or speak," Loretta coached. "I'll go inside and get the doggy treats. When he does what you ask, you can reward him with one."

Abby and Conner were all smiles. What a joy to see her children so happy. They would be even happier when she surprised them with a picnic lunch.

While the kids continued to work with their pup, Loretta went inside and packed their lunch. She hoped as Conner and Abby grew into adults, they would always find something to be joyous about, especially the little things in life.

Walnut Creek

Heidi clipped a pair of Lyle's trousers to the clothesline and paused to rub her throbbing forehead. She'd woken up with a headache this morning—no doubt from lack of sleep and clenching her teeth. Ever since Lyle had refused Kendra's request to adopt her baby, Heidi felt depressed.

She dreaded telling Kendra Lyle's decision. Surely, the young mother-to-be would look for another adoptive couple as soon as she found out, or contact an adoption agency.

It wasn't right to feel this way, but Heidi could barely look at Lyle without feeling bitter. In her mind, he was being unreasonable and selfish. Didn't he comprehend how much love they had to offer a child? Truth was, Heidi had enough love in her heart for both of them.

Keeping busy helped some this week. In fact, she tore into housework like never before. One day, she'd cleaned out the closets. Another time, Heidi did the kitchen cabinets. The floors were so spotless and shiny she could almost see her reflection. But even with all the work, her thoughts returned to the situation with Kendra.

Several birds chirped in the trees nearby as Heidi forced herself to concentrate on hanging the rest of the laundry. When she finished the chore, she picked up the empty basket and hauled it into the house.

Thirsty after being outside in the heat, Heidi went to the sink and filled a glass with cold water. Popping an aspirin into her mouth, she swallowed it down. *I hope this takes hold quickly.*

Glancing out the kitchen window, she noticed Lyle talking to Eli near the barn. Eli's bike rested against the fence. *When did he arrive?* With her thoughts so internally focused, Eli could have been talking with Lyle for over an hour, and she wouldn't have noticed.

Normally, Heidi would have gone out to say hello and offer the men some refreshments. Not today though. She wasn't in the mood to converse with anyone, much less act as a joyful, gracious hostess.

Sighing, she turned away from the window and wet a paper towel, holding it against her forehead. *Think I'll go to my room and take a nap.*

"Got a question for you. Would ya happen to know anyone who has an easygoing buggy horse they might want to sell or loan?" Eli asked, moving closer to Lyle.

Lyle quirked an eyebrow. "What's wrong with your buggy horse? Is he havin' a problem?"

"Nope. Timmy's good, and so is Mavis's horse, Blossom. The horse is for a friend of mine, and I think she'll eventually need one."

"Anyone I know?"

Eli's ears warmed. "It's, uh, for Loretta Donnelly."

"Isn't she one of Heidi's students?"

"Jah."

Lyle leaned against the barn, near the slightly open door. "Why would she need a buggy horse?"

"Loretta's thinking about joining the Amish church, and I'm gonna teach her how to drive a horse and buggy. If she catches on, she'll probably want her own horse and carriage."

"Wow! Does Heidi know about this?"

Eli shrugged. "Loretta may have told her. I'm not sure, but I've said nothing to anyone else. I found out about her desire to seek a simpler life when we were together last Saturday evening." He removed his straw hat, flapping it at a persistent fly buzzing around his head. "I took Loretta and her kinner out to supper."

"Ah, well, did you tell her how difficult the transition would be?"

"Jah, but it's not impossible. See, Loretta's grandparents were Amish, so she already has a connection."

"What about her parents? Weren't they Amish too?"

Eli shook his head. "They never joined the church. Guess they preferred to go English."

Lyle eyed Eli with a curious expression. "Is there something going on between you and Loretta? Something more than casual friendship?"

"Sure is gettin' warm out." Eli felt sweat trickling down the back of his neck and reached up to swipe it away.

"Umm. . .we weren't discussing the weather." Lyle's shoulders lifted almost up to his ears. "But if you don't want to talk about Loretta, it's fine by me."

"I. . .well. . .maybe I should." Eli licked his parched lips and swallowed hard. He hoped he could express his feelings without stumbling over every word. "Well, actually, there could be more if she became Amish, although I haven't expressed my feelings to Loretta yet. I don't want to rush things and need to be sure she has feelings for me before I blurt anything out."

A slow smile spread across Lyle's face. "Heidi's had an inkling about you two, and I guess she was right." He gave Eli's shoulder a hefty squeeze. "Good for you. I hope things work out."

Eli lowered his head a bit. "This doesn't mean I've forgotten about Mavis. She'll always hold a place in my heart."

"I understand. You two had a special relationship."

Eli nodded. "Same as you and your fraa do."

Lyle looked away then back at Eli. "There is only one thing coming between me and Heidi right now."

"Can't imagine anything getting between the two of you. I hope everything's okay. Or am I bein' too nosy?"

"She wants to adopt a baby, and I do not." Lyle closed his eyes briefly, drawing a deep breath. "I believe if God wanted us to have kinner, Heidi would be able to conceive."

"Hmm. . ." Eli folded his arms, clasping both wrists. "Children are a blessing, and fatherhood is something I've always longed for. If Mavis had lived, we may have considered adoption."

"Really?"

"Jah, only, thanks to that hit-and-run driver, her life was snuffed out before we had a chance to talk about it." Eli's toes curled inside his boots, reliving the instant he'd been notified of his wife's untimely death. No moment could have been worse. His whole world seemed to fall apart. Until he'd met Loretta, Eli had never thought he could even consider falling in love again, much less with an English woman. Now if he just knew how Loretta felt about him.

Grabbing a broom, Ron began knocking down cobwebs in the barn when he heard voices outside. Setting the broom aside, he moved toward the door to see who it was. When he spotted Lyle and Eli outside, Ron stepped back, hoping they hadn't seen him and wouldn't pull him into their conversation. He'd had another nightmare last night about the deer, an old silo, and a soldier holding a bayonet. No way would he be good company today. In fact, Ron wasn't sure he could speak a pleasant word to anyone right now.

After all these years, why was he still tormented by memories of the war that took his brother's life and so many others? He was reminded once again that thousands of families had been affected in the same manner. Ron wondered how they coped and moved forward.

No air stirred in the barn, and a cold drink of water would surely taste good right now. Swatting at an annoying bee, Ron's ears perked up when he heard Eli talking to Lyle about his wife's death.

"Every time I drive past that old silo on County Road 172, I think of how Mavis was killed that evening, a year ago on April 24." Eli paused and cleared his throat. "I can't understand how the person who hit her bike could have left the scene of the accident and never called for help or reported it to the sheriff."

"It's hard to believe anyone could do such a thing." Lyle's voice rose a bit. "It's even harder to understand why the law never found out who was responsible."

Ron froze in place, his heart beating so hard he thought his chest might explode. He'd been driving that road last year, on the evening of April twenty-fourth, and remembered seeing the silo seconds before he'd hit a deer. At least he'd thought it was a deer. The silo had been in his nightmares as well, but until now, he'd never thought much about this detail.

A sudden coldness hit the core of his being. He'd suffered a flashback from the war moments before the impact, but kept going, since he saw no point in stopping to report a dead deer.

Oh no! Ron's hands seemed to rush toward his mouth of their own accord, as he stifled a gasp. *I hit a woman, not a deer. It was me. I killed Eli's wife.*

Sickened by this revelation, Ron dashed to the back of the barn, grabbed a bucket, and threw up. As he leaned against the wall for support, Ron tried to catch his breath. With nothing left in his stomach, dry heaves took over, making him lurch to the point where his throat felt raw. The knowledge of what he had done to poor Eli's wife was far worse than any nightmare he could imagine. The right thing to do would be to turn himself in, but the thought of spending years in jail with hardened criminals was too much to bear. If only the earth would open up and swallow him. It would be a far better punishment than a lifetime in jail. Wishful thinking wouldn't make it happen though. Ron needed to get far away from here and, if it were possible, forget what happened.

Chapter 36

As Heidi cleared the table after eating lunch by herself, she thought about the rest of her afternoon and what she would do to keep busy. Soon after Eli left on his bicycle, Lyle went to a dental appointment. He'd told Heidi he planned to grab a bite for lunch when he got to Mt. Hope, where he had some business to take care of concerning an upcoming auction.

One could probably hear a hairpin drop with the quietness of the house. Heidi found herself at a loss for something to do. At least the nap did her some good, and the headache was gone.

"Wish I could get away for a few days," she murmured. "Maybe go over to Geauga County and visit with Mom and Dad." Since Heidi's next cooking class wasn't for another week and a half, she couldn't come up with a reason not to go, unless Lyle preferred she stay home. When he returned this evening, she would ask if he'd mind if she hired a driver so she could visit her folks.

Some time away might be good for me. She glanced at the calendar on the kitchen wall. *If I share my situation with Mom, she might help me deal with what I'm going through right now.*

Heidi put the dishes in the sink and glanced out the window. It surprised her to see Ron's RV pulling out of the driveway and onto the main road.

I wonder where he's going. Maybe Ron is low on food or supplies and is heading to the store. Since Ron's motor home was running well again, he went in and out of their place, although he usually mentioned to either Lyle or Heidi where he planned to go.

Heidi filled the sink with warm water and added detergent. *I'll bet he told Lyle he'd be going out.*

A short time later, Heidi was surprised when she spotted Kendra getting out of her car. Because of her job, she usually didn't stop by on a weekday—especially at this time of the day.

Heidi dried her hands and went to answer the door. "I'm surprised to see you, Kendra. Did you get off work early today?"

Kendra shook her head, tears gathering in the corners of her eyes. "I lost my job at the restaurant. The person I've been filling in for came back, so now I'm once again out of a job."

"I'm so sorry." Heidi gave her a hug.

Kendra sniffed. "Guess I should have expected it. Nothing ever works out well for me."

Heidi cringed. *When Kendra finds out Lyle and I won't be adopting her baby, she'll be even more disappointed.*

"Would you like to come in and have a glass of iced tea?" Heidi offered. "I made some fresh this morning."

"Sounds good." Kendra followed Heidi to the kitchen and took a seat at the table.

Heidi took the jug of cold tea from the refrigerator, put ice in two glasses, and poured some for both of them. *Should I tell Kendra right out about not adopting her baby, or wait till she asks?*

Heidi didn't have to wait long for Kendra to bring up the subject. "Have you talked to your husband about adopting my baby?"

Heidi sat in the chair across from her, wishing she could vanish into thin air when she saw the hopeful look in Kendra's eyes. "Yes, I have spoken to Lyle, but he feels it's not the right thing for us to do."

"How come?"

Heidi swallowed hard, hoping her swirling emotions wouldn't spiral out of control. "Lyle believes if it were meant for us to be parents, I would be able to get pregnant."

Kendra's brows furrowed as she pinched the bridge of her nose. "If every person who couldn't bear children felt the same way, no baby would ever get adopted."

Heidi couldn't argue with that, but at the same time, she wouldn't say anything negative about her husband. Lyle was the head of their home, and whether Heidi agreed with him or not, she must accept his decision.

Kendra's chin quivered as her eyes filled with fresh tears. "I'm sorry to hear it. I truly thought, and still do, that you would be the best choice for my baby." She placed one hand on her stomach, rubbing in circles. "Guess now I'll have to look for someone else who might want my baby, or contact a lawyer who specializes in adoptions."

"You could also get in touch with an adoption agency. I'm sure there are some listed in the phone book or on the internet." It hurt to make the suggestion, but Heidi wanted to give Kendra some positive feedback.

"Yeah, I'll check on those options." Kendra gulped down her tea then pushed the chair aside and stood. "I'd better get going. My friend let me borrow her car today because I told her I'd be stopping by to see you. But she'll be getting off work soon, and I need to pick her up."

Heidi left her seat and walked Kendra to the door. "This may not be much consolation, but I wish things had worked out differently." She slipped her arm around

Kendra's trembling shoulders, wishing there was more she could say.

"Yeah, me too." Sniffing, Kendra turned and hurried out the door.

Struggling to squelch the sob rising in her throat, Heidi shuffled into the living room and lowered herself to the couch. She sat several seconds, staring at the floor, before grabbing the throw pillow and giving in to her tears. One thing was certain: Her future was clear. She would never become a mother.

Sugarcreek

Eli grinned when he pulled his horse and buggy into Loretta's yard and spotted Abby and Conner frolicking on the front lawn with their puppy. He'd no sooner secured his horse to a post than the children ran up to his buggy. Eli was thankful they'd held back until he had the horse safely tied. Of course, with Loretta sitting on the porch, he felt sure she would have warned them.

"Mr. Eli, come see what our puppy can do," Abby shouted.

Conner clung to Eli's hand. "Donnelly sits. Donnelly speaks. Donnelly—"

"Plays fetch," his sister interrupted.

Eli chuckled. "It sounds like you two have been quite busy teaching your dog some tricks. I'm anxious to see for myself what little Donnelly can do."

Conner ran over and grabbed a stick. He threw it across the yard, and the pup chased after it. Tail wagging, Donnelly dropped the stick at Eli's feet.

"Oh, so you want me to play now, do ya?" Eli bent down and picked it up. Then he gave the thin piece of wood a hefty toss. Eli laughed, and the children jumped up and down when the dog leaped into the air and caught the stick in his mouth.

"All right, you two, settle down now." Loretta called the children to the porch. "Here you go. I packed a surprise lunch, so why don't you go over to the big tree and have a picnic?"

"Oh boy, a picnic just for me and Conner," Abby squealed. "Thank you, Mommy."

"I'm hungry." Conner thumped his stomach.

"While Mr. Eli and I talk, you and your sister can eat what's in the picnic basket." Loretta handed the wicker basket to Abby. It was one they had used many times when Rick was alive. "Conner, you can carry this tablecloth and help Abby spread it over the grass to sit on."

"Okay, Mommy." After Loretta gave him the checkered tablecloth, Abby took her little brother by the hand, and they ran toward the mighty oak, with Donnelly at their heels.

"Have fun!" Eli called.

"We will, Mr. Eli." Conner turned and waved.

Eli joined Loretta on the porch. "Those two are sure well behaved. You've done a good job with them, Loretta."

"Believe me, I try." She smiled. "My husband was a good father. In fact, he set a fine example for all of us."

Eli quickly changed the subject, so he wouldn't end up feeling sorry for himself because he had no children. "I came by to tell you what I found out about the things you'll need to do in order to become Amish."

Her eyes brightened. "Wonderful! I'm anxious to hear, but before you explain, would you like something cold to drink? Oh, and have you had lunch? I made two extra sandwiches."

Not one to pass on an invitation that included food,

he gave an eager nod. "That'd be nice."

Loretta excused herself. When the door closed behind her, Eli sat quietly, listening to the squeals of laughter as Abby and Conner sat on the tablecloth, enjoying their picnic lunch. *If I married Loretta, I could help raise her children.* He removed his straw hat and placed it on his knees. *Now, don't hitch the buggy before the horse. Loretta would have to be Amish before I could consider asking her to marry me. And if she does decide to join the church, I'll need to make sure we truly are compatible.* Eli couldn't deny the definite attraction he felt, but he didn't know Loretta well enough yet to be sure it was love.

Loretta came out of the house and handed him a glass of lemonade and a sandwich. She also had one for herself. "Here you go. Hope you like ham and cheese."

"Danki. I like most any kind of sandwich." Eli bowed his head for silent prayer. It pleased him when she did the same.

When he finished praying and opened his eyes, Loretta smiled and took a sip of lemonade. "I'm eager to hear what you have to tell me."

"One of the things you'll need to do to become Amish is learn the Pennsylvania Dutch language." He shifted in his chair. "That might be the most difficult part."

"I believe you're right. What else, Eli? I want to know everything that will be expected of me." She leaned slightly forward with an eager expression.

"Well, first off, one of the ministers in our church said you should live in an Amish community for at least a year." He winked at her. "Think you've already covered that one, since you live here in Sugarcreek where there are many Amish folks."

Loretta moved her head slowly up and down. "Rick and I came here because the community is slow paced and peaceful. I've always felt comfortable around my Amish neighbors." She paused to take a bite of her sandwich. "What are some other things I'll need to do?"

Eli held up three fingers. "Attend Amish church services every other Sunday. If you'd like to attend church in my district, I'll act as your go-between to introduce you to the church and its members."

"I would like that. At least then I'd know someone and wouldn't feel like a stranger."

"Also, if you decide to seek employment, it would be best if you found a job working among Amish people. It'll help you understand our work principles and get more familiar with Amish customs."

"If my husband's insurance money holds out, I plan to get a job once Abby starts school. I'll either hire a babysitter for Conner, or put him in preschool or daycare. Of course, any of those choices will cost money."

"I'm sure one of the Amish women in this area would be willing to watch the kids for a reasonable price while you're at work." *But if you married me, you wouldn't have to work outside the home.* Eli kept his thoughts to himself. It was too soon to speak of marriage.

Loretta looked out in the yard. "Just listen to those two." Smiling, she shook her head. "Ever since you gave Abby a whistling lesson, she's been trying to teach Conner."

"Your daughter is smart and learns quick." Eli finished his sandwich and brushed the crumbs off his pant legs. "The day I showed her what to do, she began whistling in no time."

"Don't I know it?" Loretta laughed. "I hear Abby nearly every night after I put the little munchkin to bed. I believe she whistles herself to sleep."

Eli clapped his hands. "Now that's cute."

"Is there anything else I'll need to do in order to

become Amish?" Loretta questioned.

"Jah. After a year's gone by, which could be sooner where you're concerned, you'll receive instruction in the ways of the church and its ordinances. Then the church members will take a vote on whether to allow you to join. If they vote yes, you'll become a full member of the Amish church."

"There's a lot more involved than I realized."

"Also, I've been trying to find a well-trained horse you can borrow for a time, as well as a used buggy. As I stated before, I'd be glad to teach you how to handle the horse and get used to using a carriage."

"It would be most helpful." Loretta released a lingering sigh. "It won't be an easy road, but I'm willing to try. In fact, I'll give it my best."

Walnut Creek

"Whelp, guess it's about time we head for bed." Lyle looked at the clock on the fireplace mantel. He yawned and stretched his arms over his head. "It's been a long day, and I'm bushed."

"I'm tired too, but before we go to our room I want to tell you something."

He turned to look at her. "I'm all ears."

"Kendra dropped by early this afternoon. I told her we wouldn't be adopting her baby."

"How she'd take it?"

"Upset, of course, but I suggested she contact an adoption agency, so I'm sure things will work out for her and the baby." Heidi looked away, hoping to hide her disappointment. The decision had been made, so no point in trying to get Lyle to change his mind. Besides, she'd promised not to ask again.

"Before I forget. . ." She moved toward the living room window. "Did you notice that Ron's motor home is gone?"

Lyle's forehead wrinkled. "It is?" He walked over to the window and stood beside Heidi, looking out.

"Jah. I saw him pulling out earlier today, but figured he'd be back by now."

"I hope his RV didn't break down."

"Does he have our phone number? Do you think he would call if he had a problem?"

"I believe so. If he isn't back by morning, I'll check the phone shack for messages."

"Good idea." Heidi walked beside Lyle toward the bedroom. "Say, I have another question. Would you mind if I went up to Geauga County to see my folks for a few days?"

"I don't have a problem with it." Lyle clasped Heidi's hand. "You've been working hard lately. A little getaway might do you some good."

"Okay. I'll call my driver in the morning. If she's available to take me, I'll let Mom and Dad know to expect me sometime tomorrow afternoon."

* ⊶⊷ *

Geauga County, Ohio

When Ron had first pulled out of the Troyers' yard, he had no destination in mind. He'd driven around Holmes County a few hours and then headed toward Geauga County. He'd heard some Amish communities were in the area and hoped he could park his rig at one of their farms.

All afternoon and into the evening hours, the conversation he'd heard earlier today, between Eli and Lyle, came back to haunt him. Even now, the man's words echoed in his head: *"Every time I drive past that old silo on County Road 172, I think of how Mavis was killed that evening, a year ago on April 24. I can't understand how the person who hit her bike could have left the scene of the accident and never called for help or reported it to the sheriff."*

Before, when Ron dreamed about hitting a deer, he'd felt like he was a murderer. Now the proof was there—it was true, only it wasn't a deer. He'd thought the flashbacks were bad. How could he deal with what he now knew was reality?

Chapter 37

Middlefield, Ohio

As Heidi sat in the front seat of her driver's van, she felt herself relax. They were almost to her parents' house, and she was eager to see them. The Geauga County Amish were fewer in number than those in Holmes County, but growing up here had been slower paced. In some ways, Heidi missed it. Fewer tourists came here. Where she and Lyle lived, people often gawking at the Amish and snapping pictures became annoying at times.

But the main reason Heidi wished she still lived in Middlefield was to be closer to her folks. It would be nice to drop in at the spur of the moment and have tea with her mother, or invite Mom and Dad for dinner at her place. As it was, they only saw each other a few times during the year. Heidi missed going shopping, canning, and baking with her mother, as they'd done before she married Lyle.

Guess I should be glad we're only a few hours away. Some of their Amish friends had family living in a different state, which meant costly trips to hire a driver or travel by train or bus for visits.

Heidi reflected on Philippians 4:11: *"I have learned, in whatsoever state I am, therewith to be content."* It was the scripture she'd included on the last recipe card she'd given her students. The message was meant for Heidi as much as for those who attended her class.

Closing her eyes, she sent up a silent prayer. *Thank You, God, for all I have. Help me remember to count my blessings.*

As Heidi's driver, Sally Parker, turned onto the next road, Heidi spotted a motor home. If she wasn't mistaken, it looked identical to Ron's. The RV was pulled into a deserted-looking lane. *But if it is Ron's, what's he doing here? Surely Ron is back in our yard by now. I'll ask Lyle about it when I call to let him know I got here safely.*

"When do you want me to come back for you?" Sally asked when she pulled into the yard of Heidi's parents'.

"How about Monday of next week? It'll give me a chance to go to church with my folks on Sunday, and I'll be home in plenty of time to prepare for my last cooking class next Saturday."

Sally smiled, pushing her short brown hair behind her ears. "Monday works for me. If I leave Walnut Creek around ten in the morning, I should be here shortly after noon. Or would you rather I pick you up a little later in the day?"

"Why don't you try to be here around noon? Then you can join me and Mom for lunch. I'll say goodbye to Dad in the morning, since he'll be at work when I leave. We can head home after we eat. It'll be better to travel on a full stomach, and we won't have to look for a place to stop along the way."

"Good point," Sally agreed. "I'll make sure I'm here as close to noon as possible."

When Heidi got out of the vehicle, she spotted both of her parents heading toward her with happy smiles.

"It's mighty good to see you, daughter." Mom gave Heidi a welcoming hug, and Dad did the same. "We're so glad you came to spend a few days."

Dad bobbed his head. "Your mamm's right. It's been too long since we had a good visit. I'm only sorry Lyle couldn't join us. I'm always interested in hearing about things that go on when he's conducting auctions."

"He has a few of them to preside over this week," Heidi explained, "but we'll both come up some other time when he isn't so busy."

"Sounds good." Dad said a few words to Sally before taking Heidi's small suitcase out of the van. "Have a safe trip back." He waved before turning to Heidi again. "Now let's go up to the house so we can catch up on each other's lives."

Heidi said goodbye to Sally and was getting ready to follow her folks up the sidewalk when she remembered the phone call she needed to make. "I'll meet you two in the house shortly. First, I want to call and leave a message for Lyle so he knows I made it safely."

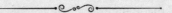

Later in the day, Heidi returned to the phone shack to see if Lyle had left her a message. Sure enough, there was one. She listened to it twice to be sure she heard everything.

"Heidi, thanks for letting me know you made it to Middlefield. I miss you already, but I hope you have a great time with your folks. In response to your question about Ron: No, he has not come back. It would seem as if he's gone for good. Sure seems strange he'd leave so suddenly, without telling either of us where he was going or if he'd be back."

After Lyle's message ended, Heidi remained on the wooden stool, rubbing her chin. *Could the motor home I saw earlier have actually been Ron's? But why would he be parked in such an odd place? Sure wish I'd had the chance to talk to him and find out why he left Walnut Creek so suddenly.* Ron had always kept somewhat to himself, but after returning from Columbus, where he'd spent

Memorial Day weekend, he'd become even more aloof.

Heidi reflected on the day she'd heard Ron talking to their horse in the barn, and how the poor man's gut-wrenching sobs pulled at her heartstrings. *If only we had been able to help him. Now all we can do is continue to pray for Ron and hope he finds the help he needs.*

Dover

In an effort to make peace with Len's mother, Charlene had invited his folks to her place for dinner this evening. She'd made German pizza and a tossed green salad—a simple yet tasty meal. She felt pleased it had turned out well. Of course, it remained to be seen what Annette would say about it.

"Well, everything's ready." Charlene smiled at Len, who sat on the living room couch. "We can eat as soon as your folks arrive."

He glanced at his cell phone and frowned. "They should have been here by now. Sure hope they didn't forget."

"Maybe you ought to give them a call."

"If they don't show up in the next five minutes, I will. Can you hold supper a little longer?"

"Yes. I turned the stove down. It'll be fine." She took a seat beside him and smiled when he clasped her hand. Charlene was glad she and Len hadn't parted ways because of his mother. She doubted she could find another man she loved so much.

They sat quietly together until the doorbell rang. Charlene jumped up. "It must be your folks."

Len went to the door with her, holding his arm around her waist, as if to offer support. Charlene relaxed a bit. *He must sense how nervous I am.* She opened the door and, putting on her best smile, greeted Mr. and Mrs. Campbell.

"Sorry we're a little late." Annette looked at Len's dad. "Todd had a phone call to make before we left, and it took awhile."

Todd shrugged his shoulders. "What can I say? Business is business, and it couldn't wait."

"Well, everything's ready, so if you'll take a seat in the dining room, I'll bring dinner out." Charlene headed for the kitchen, and she was surprised when Annette followed.

"Is there anything I can help you with?" she asked sweetly.

"You can get the tossed salad from the refrigerator if you like."

"Certainly." Annette took out the salad and started toward the dining room with it but then turned back around. "Len showed us the photography magazine with the picture you took on the cover. You did a great job, Charlene. Congratulations."

"Thanks. Photography's only a hobby for me, but I truly enjoy it."

"Have you considered doing it professionally?"

"No, not really."

"Perhaps you should. You have an eye for capturing a good photo." Annette glanced at the stove and sniffed. "And if the delicious aroma in here is any indication of the meal we're about to eat, I'd say we're in for a treat."

Charlene clamped her teeth together to keep her mouth from dropping open. Could this be a sign of things going better between her and Len's mother? It certainly appeared so this evening.

⁕━━━━⟜ e∾o ⟞━━━━⁕

Mt. Hope

Kendra had been lying around Dorie's place most of the

afternoon, bored and depressed over her situation. After spending the morning searching the internet, she still had no job prospects. But one problem would soon be solved. She'd decided to call a lawyer to discuss finding adoptive parents for her baby. Between the loss of her job, plus the uncertainty of her baby's future, worrying had become part of her life.

Sighing, she repositioned herself on the couch. *I can't rely on Dorie indefinitely. Sure wish I could get a place of my own. But without a steady income, there's no way that's gonna happen. Why can't anything be easy? Things seem to go well for other people. I must be jinxed.*

Hearing a vehicle pull into the yard, Kendra got up and looked out the window. When she saw Dorie get out of her car, she sat back down.

A few minutes later, Dorie entered the house. "I'm home," she called from the hallway. "Did you have a nice supper?"

Kendra waited until her friend joined her in the living room before responding. "No, I haven't eaten. Thought I'd wait for you."

Dorie blinked rapidly. "You're kidding, right?"

"What do you mean?"

"I told you before I left this morning I'd be having dinner with Gene after I got off work." Dorie took a seat in the rocker across from Kendra.

Kendra folded her arms across her stomach. "Guess I forgot."

"You seem to be forgetting a lot of things lately," Dorie muttered. "I asked you to take the garbage out yesterday, but there it still sat, under the kitchen sink this morning."

"Sorry." Kendra leaned her head against the back of the couch and groaned. "My brain isn't functioning well these days."

"Kendra, I understand you're dealing with a lot of stress, with a baby coming and no job." Dorie rubbed her fingers across her forehead. "I hate to dump one more thing on you right now, but Gene and I plan to get married next month. So you'll need to find another place to stay as soon as possible." Dorie offered Kendra a too-quick smile. "I'm sure you realize how awkward it would be with you, me, and Gene living here in the same house."

Kendra stiffened. "Yeah, I agree, but this is all kinda sudden, don't ya think?"

"Not really. I told you last month Gene and I were talking marriage. Guess you weren't listening then either."

Kendra had no recollection of Dorie mentioning plans to be married. She wondered how much worse her life could get. If only she could convince her folks to take her back. But it seemed highly doubtful. She may as well try to move a mountain with her pinkie finger. Kendra had no idea where else she could go. Maybe some women's shelter in one of the larger towns in the area would take her in.

"Will you have a big wedding, Dorie?" she asked. "If so, you don't have much time to plan."

"No, Gene and I are going to save the money we'd spend on a wedding and put it in the bank to someday buy a house. We don't want to live in this rental too long. Our folks are all for it and agree with our plans."

"Sounds nice." *So much for learning to be content, like that Bible verse Heidi wrote on the back of the recipe card for German potato salad.*

Kendra swallowed hard, struggling not to break down. "I'll be moved out before the month is over." She clenched her teeth. *Oh man, where do I go from here?*

Chapter 38

Middlefield

W hat a beautiful Saturday it's turned out to be."
Heidi's mother pointed to the cloudless sky. "This
is certainly good gardening weather."

Heidi pulled another handful of weeds then paused
to wipe the perspiration from her forehead. "It certainly
is. I only wish it were a little cooler. This heat is getting
to me, and my clothes are sticking to my skin."

"Let's finish weeding this row of peas, and then we
can stop for a glass of iced tea and some of those delicious ginger kichlin you made yesterday." Mom's voice
sounded light and bubbly. "I appreciate you chipping in
the way you have, but these last few days have not been
restful. You should relax while you're here visiting."

"It's okay, Mom. I didn't come here to rest. I came to
spend quality time with you and Dad. I'm still not one to sit
around, and I am more than happy to help out. Besides, how
could I do nothing while you and Dad are doing chores?"

"You've always been a hard worker. Even as a little
girl, barely able to walk and talk, you were eager to help."
Mom chuckled. "I remember one time when I cleared
the breakfast table, and you pointed to the silverware
and declared, *"Wesch's gschaar."*

Heidi laughed. "Wash dishes, huh? Guess I didn't

see it as a chore, but something fun to do."

"More than likely you simply wanted to help." Mom shook her head. "Never had much luck getting your brothers to do the dishes."

"But Lester and Richard have always helped Dad a lot."

"True, and those young men still do whenever they come over from their homes in Burton."

"How are they both doing?" Heidi grabbed another clump of weeds. "I'd hoped to see them and their families while I'm here."

"They're good, and so is their masonry business. Richard and Lester, as well as their wives and kinner, will join us for church tomorrow, since it's an off Sunday for them in their church district." Mom stood and arched her back. "Whew! I've had enough weeding for now. Let's rest awhile and enjoy some refreshments."

"Sounds good." Heidi stood too and followed her mother into the house.

After they were seated at the table with cookies and iced tea, Heidi felt it was the perfect time to bring up the topic of adoption. "There's something I've been meaning to talk to you about."

Mom tipped her head to one side. "I'm all ears."

"There's a young woman who's been attending my cooking classes, and she's expecting a boppli."

"Oh?" Mom reached for a cookie.

"Kendra Perkins is her name, and she's not married."

"I see."

Heidi took a drink of iced tea before she continued. "Kendra's been coming over to visit me between classes. Recently, she asked if Lyle and I would be willing to adopt her baby when it's born."

Mom's eyebrows lifted. "Is this something you and

Lyle are agreeable with?"

"I would be, but Lyle won't agree to it. He believes if God wanted us to have kinner, I'd be able to conceive. Since my husband is the head of our house, I need to abide by his decision." Heidi sighed deeply, touching her chest. "It hurts right here, and my arms ache more than you can imagine to hold a child of my own."

Mom leaned closer and put her arm around Heidi's shoulders. "Can't say as I fully understand, since I've given birth to three kinner of my own, but as your *mudder*, I feel your pain, dear one."

Heidi was sure her mother probably would have liked to have had even more children, but getting married later in life and having her first baby when she was forty-two didn't give her too many childbearing years.

Tears sprang to Heidi's eyes, blurring her vision. "I'm trying to accept Lyle's decision, but still praying he will change his mind. Is it wrong for me to hold out hope?"

Gently, Mom stroked Heidi's cheek. "It's not wrong, but if he doesn't change his mind, then you should accept it and look for the good things in your marriage."

Heidi sniffed. "I'm trying to remain positive and content. With God's help, I hope to become stronger and able to accept things as they are."

Dover

Charlene pulled into the Campbells' driveway and turned off the ignition. She'd baked an apple cream pie and felt somewhat proud of herself. The pie turned out like the one Heidi taught them to bake last month at one of the classes. "If this tastes as good as it looks, I have half the battle won."

Last Wednesday, when Len's parents came over for dinner, the evening had gone better than Charlene hoped. But the urge to make sure things continued in the right direction with Len's mother had prompted Charlene to pay this unexpected visit.

With one last look in the visor mirror, Charlene was glad she'd taken extra time to fix her hair. She wore it pulled back away from her ears and secured with a pretty ribbon. "Here we go." She glanced at the pie container sitting next to her on the seat.

When Charlene got out of the car, she gripped the dessert carefully and walked slowly toward the house. The last thing she needed was to drop the pie.

"Hello, Charlene." Annette greeted her, coming from the other side of the house, holding a box of flowers. "What brings you by today?"

Charlene smiled. "This morning I was in a baking mood, so I made a pie. Since I can't eat the whole thing by myself, I wanted to share it with you and your husband."

"That's so nice of you. After I'm done, we'll go inside, and I'll put the coffee on. I have one more batch of flowers to transplant and water." Annette walked to the flower bed near the house. "Why don't you put the pie on the kitchen table? Then come back out and join me."

"Okay, I'll return in a jiffy." Charlene stepped inside. The house felt cool and comfortable, since the air conditioner was running, so she saw no point in putting the dessert in the fridge. They'd be cutting into it soon.

When Charlene returned to the yard, Annette finished putting extra dirt around the flowers she had just planted.

"I've been anxious to transplant this clump of mums so they can spread in this area of the flower bed. It'll look nice this fall when they bloom." Annette adjusted the triangle-shaped scarf covering her hair. "Now all I have to do is water them." She pointed toward the hose. "I already unraveled the hose, but could you please turn the water on at the spigot? It's over there on the other side of the porch."

"Sure, I'd be glad to." Charlene walked past the porch and clasped her hands together near her chest. *Thank You, Lord, for things going better between Len's mom and me.* Annette was acting like a totally different person toward Charlene.

When Charlene turned the spigot handle to open the water line, Annette let out an ear-piercing scream. Charlene didn't know what had happened. *Did Len's mother get stung by a bee?*

Charlene ran back around and couldn't believe what she saw. The water came out full force, aimed right at Annette. The poor woman held out her hands as if to shield her face, but it was no use.

"Oh no!" Charlene bolted to get to the end of the hose, which spewed water like a dancing snake. In the process of turning the nozzle off, she also got wet. Afterward, she looked at Annette, now soaked to the bone, and watched as Len's mother flailed her arms in an attempt to get some of the water off. Charlene couldn't speak. What would she say? Why now, when things seemed to be going so well between them? Would this incident ruin it all?

Annette looked at Charlene, while Charlene looked back in disbelief, wishing she could disappear. It did not look good. Just when things couldn't get any worse, Len's mother started laughing hysterically. In fact so hard, she doubled over, holding her stomach. "Look at me! I must look like a drowned cat." She twisted the bottom of her blouse and wrung water out. "Guess I forgot to turn the nozzle off last time I used the hose."

"Oh goodness, should I go get you a towel?"

Nodding, Annette pointed at Charlene. "From the looks of your wet clothes, I think you'll need one too. Come on. Let's go in the house so I can find us both something dry to wear."

When she approached, Len's mother draped her cold, wet arm around Charlene's shoulders. "Too bad you didn't have your camera with you. What a great picture I would make."

As they giggled and stepped onto the porch, Charlene said, "I think it's time for some of that pie." *Who knew a mistake with the hose could end on a positive note?*

———————⌘◦⌘◦⌘———————

Walnut Creek

As Kendra headed down the road in Dorie's car to visit Heidi, she struggled to keep from breaking down. She'd promised her friend she would move out by the end of the month but had no idea where to start looking.

"I thought our friendship meant more to Dorie," she mumbled. "How could she do this to me? Doesn't she care that I have no place to go? I won't even have a car to drive once I move out."

Kendra closed the car windows and switched on the AC. All that blew out was hot air, worse than what was outside. After a few minutes, hoping it would eventually cool the car inside, she opened the windows again. "Oh, come on! What else is gonna go wrong? Dorie didn't tell me the air-conditioning broke in her car. Or did she?" Kendra hit the steering wheel and accidently blew the horn. The driver in front of her flung his arm out the window and made a fist. She could see him yelling something in the rearview mirror.

"Sorry, mister," Kendra mumbled. "It was a slipup, for goodness' sake." *Seems like my whole life lately is one big mistake.*

Kendra hoped Heidi might be able to help or at least offer some advice. She might know of someone in the area who needed a live-in housekeeper or babysitter. Kendra felt desperate.

When she arrived at the Troyers' a short time later, Kendra spotted Heidi's husband in the yard, filling one of the bird feeders. She parked the car near the barn, got out, and headed across the yard. "Is Heidi here, Mr. Troyer?" Since Lyle hadn't agreed to her adoption request, she could barely make eye contact with him.

He shook his head.

"When will she be back?"

"Not till Monday. She's up in Geauga County right now, visiting her folks."

"Oh, I see." Kendra turned to go but stopped in her tracks when Lyle called out to her.

"Wait, Kendra! If you have a few minutes, I'd like to talk to you."

She walked back to him, a bit uncertain. "Sure. What'd you wanna say?" Kendra picked nervously at her chipping nail polish.

"I wanted to explain my reasons for not wanting to adopt."

She shrugged her shoulders. "I'm aware. Heidi told me."

"Okay, but there's something you don't know. After praying about it since Heidi's been gone, and talking to a good friend who's had adoptive parents since he was an infant, I've changed my mind. If you're still willing to let us adopt your baby, I'll contact a lawyer to get the paperwork started."

Barely able to believe her ears, Kendra teared up. "I'm willing." *Maybe things will work out after all. Now if I could only find a job and a place to live.*

Middlefield

Not wishing to ask favors of anyone, Ron had parked his RV in a secluded spot off the main road. He'd barely been able to eat or sleep since he left the Troyers' place. When he managed to fall asleep, recurring dreams tormented him about hitting the deer.

"Only it wasn't a deer." Ron pounded the table where he sat drinking a bottle of beer to help numb the pain and shame of what he'd done. "It was Eli's wife I hit. If he found out what I did, he'd probably hate me for the rest of his life."

As the day wore on, it turned warmer and more humid. Ron felt like everything had closed in around him. At the Troyers', where his RV had been parked, shady trees kept it cooler, not to mention their neat little farm was more scenic to look at than this dreary place.

Here it was secluded but hardly picturesque. From what Ron could tell, this was an old tractor path he'd pulled onto, no longer used by anyone. Somewhere farther down the path, Ron imagined there'd be a wide-open field once used for farming, although he didn't care to find out.

Overgrown shrubs and out-of-control weeds made up the landscape Ron saw out his motor home windows. Even the worn-out gate off to the side of the path was held in place by invading weeds.

Not only did Ron's nightmares keep him from getting a good night's sleep, but the sounds and smells outside kept him tossing and turning as well.

One night, two animals were out there fighting. Shortly thereafter, the disgusting odor of a skunk permeated his RV. Now he knew how Eli must have felt when he'd shown up at class with skunk smell on his arm.

Another time, Ron heard something snorting. Later, headlights from a vehicle pulling in behind him lit up the inside of his living quarters. Ron heard someone yell about finding another place to go, and then a second person giggled. He figured this old path might be a parking spot young people frequented for partying. Ron remembered those days well, when he and his brother hung out with friends.

Not only did these new surroundings make him feel suffocated, but the knowledge of what'd he done to Eli's poor wife seemed to choke the life out of him.

Ron shook his head, wondering where things had gone wrong. He hadn't been aware of it then, but for a little while, he'd gotten used to a routine at the Troyers', making him feel like he belonged somewhere. In an unplanned sort of way, Ron felt he had somewhat of a family. How long had it been since he'd believed someone actually cared?

He finished drinking the remainder of the beer and tossed the bottle into the garbage can under his sink. At first Ron thought he could run away from all this, but the guilt weighed so heavily, he felt as if he were drowning in his sins.

A plaque he'd seen on the wall in Heidi and Lyle's kitchen came to mind. Burned into the wood were the word of Proverbs 10:9: *"He that walketh uprightly walketh surely."* It had been a long time since Ron had done anything uprightly.

I need to go back and admit what I did. No matter what punishment awaits, it'll be better than living with the agony of this. Eli deserves the truth, and I deserve to be punished.

Ron rubbed his pounding temples. He didn't know where Eli lived, but Eli would be at Heidi's last cooking class a week from today. *Should I wait and go there to tell him, or would it be better if I bite the bullet and turn myself into the sheriff, and then let the law do the telling?*

Chapter 39

Walnut Creek

Heidi stepped out of her driver's van and smiled when her dog ran up to her. "Hey Rusty. Did you miss me, boy?"

The dog wagged his tail and licked Heidi's hand when she leaned down to pet him. Rusty had the softest wavy coat, and an almost fawn-like color mixed in with mostly white fur.

She glanced around the yard, wondering where Lyle could be and why he hadn't come out to greet her. Figuring he might be busy in the barn, Heidi paid her driver and hauled her suitcase up to the house, with Rusty following close behind.

Once on the porch, she turned, waving to Sally as she drove out toward the road. She'd had a nice visit with her folks, but like always, it felt good to get home.

Heidi paused to look at the bird feeders, active with many types of birds. A quick glance around the farm told her all but one thing looked normal. Ron had not returned. It looked odd to see the empty spot where his motor home had been parked. She'd become used to seeing it there. A dry patch of grass where the RV once sat was the only evidence Ron had ever been there. *Guess I'd better water that spot and hope it turns green again.*

When Heidi entered the kitchen, she found a note from Lyle on the table, saying he'd gone out to run an errand and would be home in time for supper. In the center of the table, a vase filled with stems of honeysuckle sent a sweet fragrance throughout the room. Honeysuckle bloomed along the fence row on the far side of their farm, and depending on which way the wind blew, sometimes the pleasing scent drifted all the way to the house.

Heidi remembered when she was little her mother had taught her to get the droplet of nectar from the honeysuckle by pulling the stamen out of the flower. No wonder the hummingbirds enjoyed it too.

A few daisies intermixed with the sweet-smelling blossoms made a pretty bouquet. Heidi loved when her husband made these simple, yet thoughtful, gestures. It was a pleasant reminder of what they had together.

Rusty seemed content to have Heidi home, as he made himself comfortable by the door. Round and round he went, until he plopped down with a grunt. Heidi giggled when the dog groaned and stretched his legs out to the side. "If only my life could be as easygoing as yours."

The dog raised his head as his stubby tail wiggled back and forth.

Clicking her tongue against the roof of her mouth, Heidi shook her head. *What a life.*

After inhaling more of the flowers' sweet fragrance, she put away the banana bread Mom had given her before she left and then picked up her suitcase. By now, Rusty slept deeply, so he didn't budge when Heidi left the room.

After she unpacked, she would find something to do until Lyle got home. No doubt there'd be plenty, because the house hadn't been cleaned since she left for Geauga County.

Sugarcreek

Loretta paused in front of the full-length mirror in her bedroom to get a better look at the Amish-style dress she'd put on. She had bought it, as well as a few other plain dresses, at a local thrift store the other day. Loretta hoped wearing the simple dresses might help prepare her for becoming Amish.

Eli would be coming over later today to give her a driving lesson with his horse and buggy, and she felt satisfied with her choice of clothing. Hopefully he'd approve and understand her reason for wearing it. Loretta wasn't rushing things or trying to make a statement, and she certainly didn't want Eli to get the wrong impression.

Since she didn't own an Amish bonnet yet, Loretta had found a black scarf to wear over her bun and secured it to the back of her head. She'd seen several Amish women in her neighborhood wearing scarves when they worked in their yards and felt it would be appropriate.

Loretta's stomach tightened as she tried to imagine how it would feel to drive a horse and buggy. Controlling a full-sized horse with a mind of its own would be a lot different than driving a car. She wouldn't let her fears get the best of her though. "I'll have to learn many new things if I want to be part of the Amish community." She spoke out loud. More and more, the reality of this change grew stronger, but Loretta felt ready for the work and new challenge.

Sam had offered to keep an eye on Abby and Conner while she was having her first lesson from Eli.

Anxious to help Sam pick raspberries, the children had asked to go to his place as soon as they finished eating lunch. Loretta walked them over and, after returning to the house, went to her room to check her attire in readiness of Eli's arrival. She tried not to feel too eager, but her emotions won out. Each time she and Eli were together Loretta found herself eagerly looking forward to the next time she would see him.

The affection Loretta had developed so quickly for Eli frightened her. She'd heard of people falling in love soon after meeting someone, but it had never happened to her. Even with Rick, it took several months of them dating before she acknowledged he was the one for her.

"Maybe my feelings for Eli stem from loneliness and missing Rick," Loretta murmured. "Sure wish I knew how he feels about me."

In an effort to keep her mind on other things, Loretta rose from her seat and went to the kitchen to make a jug of iced tea. Eli would likely be thirsty when he got here, so she'd offer the cold drink before they headed out for her driving lesson.

Walnut Creek

Eli stepped into the phone shack to check for messages and jumped with surprise when the telephone rang. Quickly, he picked up the receiver. "Hello."

"Am I speaking to Mr. Eli Miller?" a man's voice asked.

"Yes, I'm Eli."

"This is the sheriff calling. Can you come to our office as soon as possible?"

Eli's heart hammered. "What is it about?" He hoped

no harm had come to his folks or anyone he knew in the area.

"Are you sitting down?"

"Umm. . .yes." Eli lowered himself to the wooden stool.

"The person responsible for your wife's death came forward and confessed. I'd like to give you all the details and would prefer to do it in person."

A rush of adrenaline coursed through Eli's body as he gripped the edge of the wooden shelf where the phone sat. "What did you say?"

The sheriff repeated himself. "I hate to spring it on you like this but figured you'd want to hear. We need to know if you want to press charges."

Eli tilted his head from side to side, weighing his choices. "Umm. . .no, it's not the Amish way. But I do wonder what type of person could have done this, and why they didn't stop or report the accident when it happened."

"I'll explain it all when you get here. Oh, and since you're not willing to take this person to court, the state will no doubt press charges."

"I'll be there as soon as I can. I'm glad you called, Sheriff." Eli's hands shook as he hung up the phone. After more than a year of wondering who was responsible for Mavis's death, the guessing would finally be over.

He stepped out of the phone shack and was about to shut the door when he remembered something. *The driving lesson. I'd better call Loretta.* He lifted a shaky hand to rub the perspiration from his forehead. He couldn't teach her today. In addition to making a trip to see the sheriff, he felt so shook up he wouldn't be able to think clearly enough to teach anyone anything. And why risk putting Loretta in danger? After receiving such startling news, it could be some time before he felt up to doing much of anything. Already, his body felt drained from the anticipation of what would take place at the sheriff's office.

Eli stepped back inside to call his driver for a ride and notify Loretta their plans would need to be canceled. Surely, she'd understand.

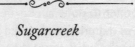

Sugarcreek

When Loretta hung up the phone, she sat at the kitchen table, pondering the things Eli had told her. She couldn't imagine how he must feel right now. Most likely, there were mixed emotions. While it would be good to finally learn who was responsible for his wife's death, he'd no doubt feel like someone opened an old wound and poured hot water on it. Now the agony of what happened to his wife would cause him to grieve all over again. Loretta could almost feel his pain.

She shifted in her chair. *If I were in Eli's place I could barely function right now. I wonder how he will handle all this.* Closing her eyes, she sent up a prayer on his behalf. *Please, Lord, be with Eli and send healing balm for his emotional wounds. He needs You now more than ever.*

Sighing, Loretta opened her eyes. *Guess I'd better go check for the mail. Better yet, think I'll give my mother a call.* She'd been meaning to talk to her folks about her idea of becoming Amish but had put it off, unsure of their reaction. *With the children over at Sam's place, guess now's as good a time as any.*

She reached for the phone and punched in her parents' number. Her mother answered on the second ring. "Hi, Mom, it's me."

"What a coincidence, Loretta, I was just going to

call you. How are you and the children?"

"We're all fine. Uh, there's something I wanted to tell you though." Loretta drew a deep breath.

"I have something to tell you as well."

"Oh. Should I go first, or do you want to?"

"You go ahead."

Loretta sucked in another breath then blurted, "I'm thinking of becoming Amish."

Silence on the other end.

"Did you hear what I said, Mom?"

"Yes, I heard. You took me by surprise, is all. When did all this come about?"

Loretta twisted a strand of hair around her finger, wondering how much she should share or where to begin. "Well, as you know, when Rick and I moved here to Sugarcreek, we wanted Abby and Conner to grow up in a quiet, simple community."

"Yes, I'm aware."

"For some time now I've yearned for a simpler way of life, without the distraction of modern things."

"You don't have to be Amish to simplify your life." Mom's tone seemed more like a caution, rather than one of disapproval, but Loretta figured she should explain a little more. "Before I go any farther, I need to ask you a question."

"Sure, go ahead."

"What was the reason behind you and Dad not joining the Amish church and choosing to become part of the English world?"

Mom cleared her throat. "I was wondering when you'd get around to asking me that. I'm actually surprised you didn't ask sooner."

"Is it a deep, dark secret?"

"No, not at all. We just saw no reason to talk about it."

"So what was the reason?"

"During your dad's running-around years, he bought a car, as many young people do when they want to try out the English way." Mom paused a few seconds. "The truth is, when we decided to get married and were trying to decide if joining the Amish church was right for us, your dad's desire to own and drive a car won out."

"I see." Loretta toyed with the saltshaker in the middle of the table. "So instead of appreciating the simple life, he wanted modern, worldly things?"

"I wouldn't say that exactly. Your dad and I have never gone overboard when it comes to buying, or even wanting, worldly things."

Loretta couldn't argue with that. She remembered, growing up, her parents never had to have the best of everything. They didn't, however, shun modern things like electric appliances, Dad's truck, Mom's car, and a home where decorative items were displayed. If not for the few visits they'd made to visit her grandparents, Loretta would never have known her parents had once lived the Plain life with their parents and siblings.

I wished I'd had this talk with Mom sooner. Loretta set the saltshaker aside. "Would you have any objections if I did join the Amish church?"

"None at all. The choice is yours, Loretta. Have you made friends with any Amish? You'll need someone to mentor you."

Loretta pursed her lips. *Do I tell her about Eli? Would it make a difference?* "Actually, I do have an Amish friend who is willing to help me with the necessary steps." Loretta wasn't ready to share her feelings about Eli yet, especially when she wasn't sure how he felt about her. If things got serious at some point, she would then inform her parents.

"That's good. How do the children feel about all this?" Mom asked.

"They don't know yet. I'm waiting to explain it to Abby and Conner until I'm certain it's the right thing for all of us."

"Makes sense. Please keep me informed, Loretta."

"I will." A slight breeze had picked up and filtered through the open window, giving Loretta some much-needed fresh air. In preparation for becoming Amish, she'd only been using electricity for necessary things like cooking, hot water for baths, and lights turned on as needed. The air conditioner had been staying off, with windows opened for ventilation. "So, what was the reason you were going to call me?"

"From years of going up and down ladders in his painting business, your dad's knees have gotten pretty bad."

"I'm sorry to hear it."

"The doctor has finally talked him into getting knee replacements, and he's agreed to have the left knee done next month. I was hoping you and the children could come here to visit for a few weeks during his recovery. It'll help cheer him up, and you can assist me in keeping him from doing things he's not supposed to do."

"Of course, Mom, I'll be happy to come, and I know the children will be eager to see you and Dad too. I'd like to be there the day he has surgery."

"Thank you, Loretta. I'd better go now, but I'll talk to you again soon. Oh, and I'll be praying that God shows you what to do in regard to becoming Amish."

When Loretta hung up the phone, she sat several minutes, mulling things over. All this time she'd wondered why her parents left their Amish families to start over and had never asked why. She felt as if a weight had been lifted from her shoulders. From now on, if anyone asked, she wouldn't be afraid or ashamed to tell them her parents had grown up Amish, or why they'd chosen not to stay. She appreciated Mom's understanding about her desire to live the Plain life.

Loretta rose from her chair. It was time to head outside and get the mail. She'd just stepped out the door when she heard Abby scream. Looking out across the yard, she saw the child running toward her, frantically waving her hands.

"Honey, what's wrong?" Loretta broke out in a cold sweat. "Where's Conner?"

Abby pointed to her little brother, trailing along behind her. "He's bleedin' real bad!"

Loretta raced toward them, but as the children drew closer, and she saw blotches of red on her son's face, hands, and clothes, her apprehension faded. Smiling with relief, she bent down, enveloping both children in her arms. "Conner's not bleeding, Abby. He's splattered with berry juice."

Conner smacked his lips and held out his hands. Opening his closed fingers, he grinned at Loretta. "Want some, Mommy?"

She stared at the smashed berries and laughed. *Oh, the sweet innocence of a child.* Loretta thanked God for giving her these two beautiful children and for blessing her with wonderful parents. Whether she joined the Amish church or not—and even if nothing serious developed between her and Eli—she would enjoy every moment with her precious son and daughter and always try to be honest with them.

Chapter 40

Walnut Creek

Today was Heidi's final cooking class—at least for this group of students. She'd gotten up early this morning to make sure everything was ready. She planned to teach her students how to make a special meat loaf her mother had taught her many years ago. Heidi also made a delicious broccoli salad. After the lesson, they would share a final meal together before everyone went home.

Today will be bittersweet. Heidi's mouth twisted grimly. She'd miss seeing her students and felt bad Ron wouldn't be here to join them and take the final class. They still hadn't heard a word from him, and she couldn't help wondering where he'd gotten to, and whether it had actually been his motor home she'd seen in Geauga County. Perhaps she'd never find out, but whenever she thought of Ron, she would say a prayer on his behalf.

"You're up awful early this morning."

Heidi turned at the sound of her husband's voice. "Today's my final cooking class. I wanted to make sure everything is ready before everyone arrives."

Lyle stepped up to Heidi and placed his hands on her shoulders. "Speaking of your students. . .there's something I've wanted to tell you, but things have been so busy this week, we haven't had much chance to talk."

"What is it?" Heidi reached up and curled her fingers through his full beard. After eight years of marriage, it had gotten quite long. She'd almost forgotten what Lyle looked like without it.

"Kendra stopped by here last Saturday to see you."

"Oh? Did you tell her where I was?"

"Jah." Lyle motioned to the table. "Let's sit down, and I'll tell you what else Kendra and I talked about."

Curious, Heidi pulled out a chair and sat. Her husband looked so serious, she worried. She hoped he hadn't said anything hurtful to Kendra about the request she'd made for them to adopt her child. The poor girl had gone through enough without receiving a lecture from Lyle.

He took the seat beside Heidi and clasped her hand. "I told Kendra we would adopt her baby."

Heidi's eyes widened. "What?"

"It's not easy to admit, but I've been selfish and was wrong not to consider your feelings about wanting to adopt."

"Oh Lyle." Heidi touched her chest, acutely aware of her heart's rhythmic beating beneath her fingers. "Are you positive about this? Please don't do it just for me."

"I'm certain." Lyle looked at her tenderly then pulled her into his arms.

Tears coursed down Heidi's cheeks as she leaned her head on his shoulder. "Danki, Lyle. Thank you so much." Heidi feared her heart might burst with the joy overflowing. Sometime in October, she would finally become a mother.

When Kendra arrived at Heidi's, her heartbeat quickened. Had anything changed since last Saturday, when Lyle agreed to adopt her child? She hoped he felt the same and was still willing. Despite the worry, Kendra had a good feeling. The day's weather couldn't be better, with clear skies so blue it almost hurt her eyes. A slight breeze blew in the fresh, comfortable air. Kendra breathed deeply, and with outstretched arms, she shouted, "It's good to be alive!"

No sooner had Kendra stepped onto the porch than Heidi came out and greeted her with a hug. "Lyle told me he spoke to you last week and agreed we should raise your baby."

"I'm so relieved." Kendra smiled through her tears as they walked inside together. "I still haven't found another job, and since my friend Dorie will be getting married soon, I'll have to move out of her place by the end of June." She sniffed. "But at least I don't have to worry about what will happen to my baby."

Lyle, who had been sitting on the sofa in the living room, got up and came over to them. "Maybe you can stay here with us until you're able to make it on your own." He looked at Heidi. "Would this arrangement be all right with you?"

With no hesitation, Heidi nodded, tears glistening in her eyes. "We have an extra guest room, so it shouldn't be a problem at all."

"Would you really do that for me?" Kendra could barely speak around the lump in her throat.

"Yes, we would," Lyle responded. "Having you here will give us a chance to get better acquainted and make plans for the baby's future."

For the first time in a long while, Kendra sent up a silent prayer. *Thank You, Lord, for these special people. I'm even more sure now that they'll make the best parents for my little girl or boy.*

A short time later, as Heidi gave instructions to her four students on how to make sweet-and-sour meat loaf, she noticed the smile that never left Charlene's face. It was in sharp contrast to her sullen expression during the previous cooking class.

"How are things with you, Charlene?" Heidi handed her a small baking dish.

"Absolutely wonderful." Charlene's smile widened. "Len and I had a disagreement, but things are better now, and it's been working out between me and his mother." She clasped her hand to her chest. "Guess what else? Remember the colt I took a picture of?"

Heidi nodded.

"Well, I got a call from the owner, and they decided to name the colt after me—Charlie."

"Aw, that's so cute." Kendra grinned. "Bet you feel flattered."

"I do. And get this," Charlene added. "They want me to have little Charlie."

Heidi sucked in her breath. "Are you going to take the little fella?"

"Well, I don't have a place to keep him right now, since I live in a condo, but Len's parents volunteered to keep him at their place until Len and I are married and are able to buy a home of our own—which, of course, would need to have enough property for a horse." Charlene stopped talking long enough to take a breath. "Kitty and her husband also said they'd keep the colt until we're ready, so I'm not sure what we'll end up doing."

"Goodness, a lot has happened since our last class." Loretta patted Charlene's arm. "I'm happy for you."

"I'm sure we all are." Heidi nodded at Charlene then looked over at Loretta, noticing for the first time that she wore a plain, Amish-style dress and a dark colored scarf on her head. "How have you been, Loretta?"

"Really good." Loretta glanced at Eli then back at

Heidi. "I'm taking steps to become Amish, and Eli's helping me make the transition."

"Now that's a surprise. I had no idea you were considering becoming part of the Amish community." Heidi set the ingredients for the meat loaf topping on the table.

"The Amish way feels right to me, and it's actually part of my heritage, which I'd like to share with you sometime." Loretta's eyes sparkled. "I believe it will be good for my children as well."

"You may face some challenges," Heidi commented, "but if it's what you truly desire, then I wish you the best."

Eli opened his mouth, as if he might want to say something, when a knock sounded on the back door.

Heidi excused herself to see who it was. She felt surprise when she opened the door and found Ron on the porch. "Can I come in?" he asked, looking down at his shoes.

"Of course. It's good to see you, Ron." She stepped aside. "The others are in the kitchen, preparing to make a special meat loaf, and then we'll share a meal together one last time before everyone goes their separate ways." Heidi wanted so badly to ask where Ron had been all this time, but if he wanted to tell her, it should be of his own choosing. Silently, she led the way to the kitchen.

Ron stood inside the kitchen door a few seconds then walked over to the table. "I wasn't planning to be here today, and I won't be stayin' for a meal," he murmured to no one in particular. "But I had to come back because I've done something terrible and couldn't face the consequences. My conscience got the best of me, though, so I'm here to confess."

He drew a deep breath and turned to face Eli, heart thumping hard in his chest. Telling this nice man the truth would be the hardest thing he'd ever done, but he had to do it. "I owe you a heartfelt apology, but I don't expect forgiveness, because what I did is. . ." He paused and tried to swallow, wishing he had something to drink because his mouth felt dry as the desert. "Well, it's inexcusable."

Eli tipped his head. "What are you referring to?"

"I'm talkin' about your wife. I heard a conversation you and Lyle had awhile back, and you mentioned the date and place where your wife had been hit." Ron paused and wiped the sweat tricking down his face. "This is hard for me to admit, but I was driving on that same road the very same evening last year. Something triggered a flashback from the war in my mind during the drive, and about that time I thought I hit a deer." One more quick pause, and another deep breath. "But I realized after what you said that it must have been your wife, on her bicycle, I hit, not a deer."

Eli sat several seconds, looking at Ron through squinted eyes. Then, slowly, he shook his head. "You may have hit a deer, Ron, but it was someone else who killed my wife."

The women gasped, and a shiver ran up Ron's spine. "Wh–what?"

"The sheriff got in touch with me a few days ago, and when he gave me the details, I learned that the young man who did it turned himself in and confessed to the hit-and-run." Eli's voice quavered. "When he gave me a description of the teenager, I realized it was the same kid who tried to run my bike off the road last month." Eli paused to wipe a tear that had fallen onto his cheek. "The evening I was first informed of the accident, the sheriff mentioned they'd found a dead deer at the scene. Said he thought the person responsible for the tragedy may have hit Mavis in an effort to avoid hitting the deer. I didn't give it much thought until now." Eli leaped to his feet and clasped Ron's shoulder. "I'm glad you weren't the one responsible for my wife's death. You're a good person for coming here to speak with me about it."

The room got deathly quiet as everyone seemed to digest this information.

------⚬∞⚬------

Heidi stood quietly beside Ron, until he expelled a deep breath and sank into an empty chair. "It's a relief to know I'm not the one responsible, but I am not a good person. I've done many things I'm not proud of, including. . ." He looked at her and winced. "I'm ashamed to admit this, but I took money from a vase in your house, as well as some old oil lamps and a few other things of value. I can't get any of the items back because I pawned them, but here's the money I took, plus some extra." He reached into his pocket and handed her a wad of bills. "I'm so sorry. What I did was wrong— especially after the kindness you and Lyle showed me."

Heidi stared at him, and then with no hesitation she placed her hand on his arm. "I'm glad you came back to tell the truth, and I forgive you, Ron. I'm certain when Lyle joins us for lunch and hears your confession, he will also forgive."

Ron dropped his gaze to the floor. "Thanks, but I don't deserve your forgiveness."

"God commands us to forgive others, just as He forgives us," Eli spoke up. "I've been reminded of that myself recently. Plus, the verse on the back of a recipe card Heidi gave us during one of our classes mentions forgiveness."

Ron nodded. "I've made a decision to see a counselor for help with my postwar issues, and I plan to return to my hometown and try to make amends with my grown children, as well as my ex-wife." He smiled at Heidi, pointing to the plaque on the kitchen wall. "When I thought about that verse of scripture, I realized it was time for a change."

"Good for you, Ron." Smiling, Kendra looked at him. "I'm right there with you and am all about change."

"None of us is perfect, and we all need to be forgiven," Charlene put in. "Coming here to this class has opened my eyes to a few things." She stepped up to Heidi and gave her a hug. "Thank you for all you've taught us."

"You're welcome, and I thank all of you for being such good students." Heidi went to her desk and took out five notebooks then handed one to each person. "This is a small recipe book I put together so you can make some other traditional Amish dishes on your own. There's also a list of helpful kitchen tips at the back." She pointed to the recipe card she'd given everyone today. "I also want to leave you with one final verse to reflect upon. It's Matthew 6:33, and this is how it reads: 'But seek ye first the kingdom of God, and his righteousness; and all these things shall be added unto you.'"

"Thank you, Heidi." Charlene grinned, her face fairly glowing. "The recipes will be helpful when I get married, and all the scriptures you have shared with us will guide me along the way."

The others were unanimous in thanking Heidi too.

As she stood watching her students finish making their meat loaves, Heidi felt rewarded in so many ways. She was glad she'd acted on her idea to teach cooking classes, and appreciated the opportunity to become acquainted with each of her students, as well as becoming instrumental in their lives. Perhaps sometime in the future she'd have the opportunity to teach more seekers—not only how to cook but how to strengthen their faith in God as well.

Heidi's Cooking Class Recipes

━━━━━━━ ⟡ ━━━━━━━

Amish Country Breakfast

INGREDIENTS:

- 14 slices whole wheat bread
- 2½ cups ham, cubed
- 1 pound mozzarella cheese, shredded
- 1 pound cheddar cheese, shredded
- 6 eggs
- 3 cups milk

TOPPING:

- ½ cup butter, melted
- 3 cups cornflakes (do not crush)

Grease 9x13 baking pan and layer half the bread, ham, and cheeses. Repeat layers. Beat eggs in a mixing bowl, add milk, and pour over layers in pan. Refrigerate overnight. Next morning, preheat oven to 375 degrees. Mix butter and cornflakes. Spread mixture over other ingredients in pan. Cover loosely with foil and bake for 45 minutes.

Amish Haystack

INGREDIENTS:

- ½ pound saltine crackers or one bag corn chips, crushed
- 2 cups cooked white or brown rice
- 2 heads lettuce, chopped
- 6 to 8 tomatoes, chopped
- 1 (6 ounce) can black olives, sliced
- 2 cups tomatoes, diced
- 2 cups onions, diced
- 2 cups green pepper, diced
- 2 cups celery, diced (optional)
- 1 quart cooked navy or pinto beans
- 2 eggs, hard-boiled and chopped (optional)
- 2 cups nuts, chopped (optional)
- 1 (14 ounce) can condensed milk
- 2 cans cream of cheddar soup
- 1 (16 ounce) jar Ragu spaghetti sauce or salsa
- 3 pounds ground beef, browned

Put each of first 12 ingredients into separate containers. Mix soup and milk together in a saucepan and heat. Add the Ragu sauce or salsa to browned ground beef and heat.

Each person creates their own haystack by layering items in order given on their plate. Pour cheese sauce and favorite salad dressing on top and enjoy! Serves 12 to 14 people.

German Pizza

INGREDIENTS:

1 pound ground beef,
  browned
½ medium onion,
  chopped
½ green pepper, diced
1½ teaspoons salt,
  divided
½ teaspoon pepper

2 tablespoons butter
6 raw potatoes, shredded
3 eggs, beaten
⅓ cup milk
2 cups cheddar or
  mozzarella cheese,
  shredded

In 12-inch skillet, brown beef with onion, green pepper,
½ teaspoon salt, and pepper. Remove beef mixture from
skillet. Drain skillet; then melt butter in it. Spread potatoes over butter and sprinkle with remaining 1 teaspoon
salt. Top with beef mixture. Combine eggs and milk
and pour over all. Cook, covered, on medium heat until
potatoes are tender, about 30 minutes. Top with cheese;
cover and heat until cheese melts, about 5 minutes. Cut
into wedges or squares to serve.

Apple Cream Pie

INGREDIENTS:

3 cups apples, finely chopped

1 cup brown sugar

¼ teaspoon salt

1 rounded tablespoon flour

1 cup cream

1 (9 inch) unbaked pastry shell

Preheat oven to 450 degrees. Mix apples, brown sugar, salt, flour, and cream. Put in unbaked pastry shell. Bake 15 minutes. Reduce heat to 325 degrees for an additional 30 to 40 minutes. When pie is about halfway done, take a knife and push top apples down to soften. After pie cools, store in refrigerator.

German Potato Salad

INGREDIENTS:

4 boiled potatoes, cut into chunks

1 teaspoon sugar

½ teaspoon salt

¼ teaspoon dry mustard

Dash pepper

2 tablespoons apple cider vinegar

1 cup sour cream

½ cup onions, thinly sliced

2 to 3 slices bacon, fried and cut into small pieces

Paprika

Place potato chunks in large bowl. Combine sugar, salt, dry mustard, pepper, vinegar, sour cream, onion, and bacon pieces. Pour over warm potatoes and toss lightly until coated with dressing. Serve warm with a dash of paprika.

Heidi's Sweet-and-Sour Meat Loaf

INGREDIENTS:

1½ pounds ground beef

1 medium onion, chopped

1 cup saltine cracker crumbs

1 teaspoon pepper

1½ teaspoons salt

1 egg, beaten

Preheat oven to 350 degrees. In mixing bowl, combine ground beef and onion. Add cracker crumbs, pepper, salt, and egg. Mix well. Shape into loaf and place in a 9x5 pan.

TOPPING:

½ cup tomato sauce

1 cup water

2 tablespoons apple cider vinegar

2 tablespoons prepared mustard

2 tablespoons brown sugar

In a mixing bowl, combine tomato sauce, water, vinegar, mustard, and brown sugar. Spread over meat. Bake for 1½ hours.

Discussion Questions

1. Heidi wanted desperately to have a baby, but her husband wasn't willing to adopt. Was it right for her to keep asking, or should she have accepted his decision from the beginning?

2. Heidi's husband, Lyle, thought it must not be God's will for them to have children, so he closed his mind to adoption. Do you feel everything that happens to us is for a reason? If you were unable to have a child, would you see it as God's will, or would you seek to adopt?

3. Was it right for Lyle to think only of himself when it came to adopting a child, or should he have considered his wife's need to become a mother?

4. When Kendra's parents, who professed to be Christians, forced her out of their house after she told them she was expecting a baby, she became bitter against them and their religion. Is there ever a time when a parent should turn their back on a grown child?

5. Because of Kendra's father, her mother didn't stick by her either. Would you be able to choose sides between your husband or child, knowing one of them would be hurt? Was Kendra right in trying to get her mother to take her side against her father's orders?

6. Loretta wanted a simpler life for her children. Could she have found it without joining the Amish church? What are some ways you can simplify your life and still remain English?

7. After the death of his wife, Eli convinced himself he would never fall in love again. Is it possible for one who's lost one's mate to feel the same kind of love the second time around? Why would some widows or widowers feel disloyal to their deceased spouse if they were offered the opportunity for love again?

8. Charlene struggled with feelings of inferiority because she wasn't a good cook. How did attending Heidi's cooking classes help Charlene rise above her insecurities and self-doubt?

9. Should Charlene have made the first move to call her boyfriend after their disagreement, since it was because of her request to move out of the area that she didn't hear from him? Should she have even made such a request, knowing his job, which he enjoyed, was in Dover?

10. Ron had flashbacks and nightmares from the things he'd encountered during the Vietnam War. The things Ron said and did seemed to be related to the emotional scars left from the war. Do you know someone who is suffering from physical or mental postwar trauma? How can you help that person deal with the pain?

11. Ron's children were now adults. Even though his life was messed up due to traumatic things that happened to him during the war, should he have tried to locate his children and attempt to be part of their lives? Have you or someone you know been abandoned by a parent? If so, how did you cope?

12. Eli waited over a year until the law caught the hit-and-run driver who killed his wife. Could you find the strength to move forward and have the patience Eli did in waiting to find out who and why? Would you be able to forgive the person responsible, as Eli did? What does the Bible say about forgiving others?

13. Kendra was devastated when she lost her job and the same day found out the Troyers would not adopt her baby. If something similar happened to you, would you find it difficult to keep a positive attitude and not give up?

14. What are some things you learned about the Amish from reading this book?

15. Could you relate to any of the characters in the story? Were there any scriptures Heidi shared with her students that you found helpful? What is your favorite Bible verse, and how has it helped you during a difficult time?

About the Author

New York Times bestselling, award-winning author, Wanda E. Brunstetter, is one of the founders of the Amish fiction genre. Wanda's ancestors were part of the Anabaptist faith, and her novels are based on personal research intended to accurately portray the Amish way of life. Her books are well-read and trusted by many Amish, who credit her for giving readers a deeper understanding of the people and their customs. When Wanda visits her Amish friends, she finds herself drawn to their peaceful lifestyle, sincerity, and close family ties.

Wanda enjoys photography, ventriloquism, gardening, bird-watching, beachcombing, and spending time with her family. She and her husband, Richard, have been blessed with two grown children, six grandchildren, and two great-grandchildren.

To learn more about Wanda, visit her website at www.wandabrunstetter.com.